ROAR!

*Odyssey of Battles, Betrayals
and Building a Nation*

M. MARQUIS

Ver Venu Publishing

Dedicated to diplomats, peacemakers and warriors.

FOREWORD

Even as we speak, read, go about our business in everyday life, there are others; some just across the city, valley, country, oceans, living their everyday reality, as oblivious to our existence as we are of theirs. We and they, when made aware of "the other" often default to primitive inclinations, wariness and suspicions, failing to accept at face value any redeeming similarities. The farther away people are, the more we become wary of motivations. This is not only geographical distance, but also socio-economic distance. Add to this racial, ethnic, religious overlays and we find ourselves taking to our corners, ready to fight and defend our turf. We become wary of newcomers, or at least skeptical. Little has changed over the millennia. In this book, two parallel stories, their similarities and clashes, eventually merge.

PERSPECTIVE

One of my favorite childhood stories was about the blind men describing an elephant ... it was elegant in its simplicity and certainly adequate for my young mind to help me understand how others might see and understand the same things, only differently. But over the years, we develop a more nuanced perspective, influenced by; culture, experiences, such as love, war, work, travel, awareness of physical world and so much more. Not only do these help shape us, they also direct and guide us. We are similar, yet unique because of the infinite ways we are "put together" by our experiences. But is this not also delightful? Is it not exciting?

History abounds with broken promises, broken treaties, broken hearts, and broken bodies. There are the justifiers of betrayal; changing perspectives; love, hate, heroism, cowardice, greed and generosity, acceptance and violence, all human behaviors that could arise from anyone of us given our personal history and the right situation. The world exploded with a bang and persisted with the roar of oceans, of thunder, of cannon and the roar of humanity. Tell me when this was not always so.

No one person or event shaped history, rather a collection of events, circumstances and people are required to do so. Then, of course, history is mostly written by the victors, from their perspective. The following highlight only a few events that shaped the cultural and political environment of the characters in this fictional piece; ROAR! Odyssey of Battles, Betrayals and Building a Nation.

The Age of Reason or "The Enlightenment," was an intellectual movement in Europe during the late 18th into the early 19th Century. Politics, philosophy, science and communications radically shifted into prominence. Traditionalism was resisted and the Enlightenments proponents believed they could create better societies and better people. The rise of deism was also a hallmark, acknowledging that God does exist, but does not interact with the Universe in a supernatural manner. The Enlightenment evolved partly due to harsh criticisms by German writers in response to the Thirty Years' War (1618-1648), which started as a religious civil war, but was bolstered by extremes in nationalism, advances in war craft and struggle for European balance of power. Enlightened thinkers started demanding equality, fraternity and freedoms such they had not before.

Wars, epidemics, natural disasters and political movements: Throughout history, wars were waged for access to land, trade routes, resources and religion; the other "Silk Roads." For example, multiple battles ensued for port access on the Black Sea for trade purposes by the Russians against the Ottomans (Kinburn Russian-Turkish War, 1787-1792), Siege of Kars (1828-1829) and others.

In Africa, the Zulus in South Africa repeatedly raided their rivals, the Pondo off and on in 1828 for land. The victorious Zulus granted Port Natal to the British to establish a trading post to their mutual benefit. Gradually, the Dutch and British established churches (1825) in the region, issued newspapers, built roads, and at length, claimed sovereignty in South Africa.

After the War of 1812, between the United States and Great Britain, the number of black slaves in both nations started to increase, as did the number of free blacks, although they had limited freedom. The idea of creating a colony for them took shape. British and American clergy and abolitionists raised funds to transport several thousand blacks to Sierra Leone where they would be given citizenship. The reasons were both altruistic and not, wanting to tamp down black rebellion and limit social mixing. In 1820 the British shipped free blacks to British colony Sierra Leone and to Liberia.

In South (Latin) America building tensions to colonial rule by Spain and Portugal developed due to reforms imposed by the Spanish Bourbons in the 18th Century. Economic and political instability occurred. South Americans felt it unfair to attack their wealth, political power and social status. They wanted, then demanded less restrictive trade agreements. Spain aligned itself with France to push back on the colonists. But this alliance, in turn, pitted the two nations against England which was the dominant sea power. England forcefully cut communication between Spain and her Latin colonies giving the colonies more autonomy and paving the way to fully fledged revolutions. South America, which had endured three centuries of colonial rule, gained independence for the entire continent between 1808-1826. This excluded the islands of Cuba and Puerto Rico.

Victorious British battles in India 1757 resulted in local leaders ceding a foothold and revenues to the British East India Company. Overtime, the Company was awarded the right to collect revenue in an expanded Indian sphere of influence. The British appointed a Governor General and commenced more battles, annexing more and more territory. By 1818, British supremacy was complete in India. British colonization spread through many parts of Asia and Africa in similar manner.

The Napoleonic Wars 1803-1815; major conflicts of the French Empire against other European Powers and Russia resulted in alliances against her. France initiated war in an attempt to stabilize her government and economy and defend against would-be invaders. Her failure, among other events, set the ground work for revolutions within her borders.

The Industrial Revolution, 1760 to between 1820 and 1840 permitted the transitioning to new manufacturing processes in Europe and the United States. Urbanization ensued as did the rise of working class families, economic growth and income, but also child labor, dangerous work places and a wider role for women working out of the home.

As part of the Industrial Revolution, the liberalization of trade laws and the growth of factories increased the gulf among master tradesman, journeymen and apprentices whose numbers increased disproportionally by 93% from 1815 to 1848 particularly in Germany.

Advances in cosmology, biochemistry and engineering abounded as did the discovery of photographic methods, telegraphy and electricity.

THE 1830S

The world saw a rapid rise of imperialism and colonialism particularly in Asia and Africa. Conquests took place world-wide particularly under the flag of the British Empire and saw the expansion of the Ottoman Empire in the "middle east" which included northern Africa. New outposts and settlements developed in Oceania; Australia and New Zealand.

Another major influencer of the 19th Century was cholera. Epidemics in the 1830s. 1840s and 1860s caused, besides death, popular unrest highlighting social disparity and resulting in greater conflict among the classes. Much cholera occurred in the lower classes due to hallmarks of poverty; crowding, lack of sanitary conditions, medical care, insufficient food. This was the period which developed the concept of Public Health. Intermittent droughts, famine, high food prices under these new social constructs again led to uprising and revolts.

During the period of this novel (1830-1849) came the "romantic revolutions" of the 1830s, many of which led to constitutional monarchies. In France, Louis Philippe became "King of the French" and Leopold I became "King of the Belgians." As ideas of freedom and equality spread, other nations entered in revolution; Italy, Poland, Portugal and Switzerland among others.

In Africa, France invaded Algiers, at that time part of the Ottoman Empire. France had imported much food under the previous monarchies mostly on credit from Algiers. The Bourbon Restoration started limiting trade. Algiers in return, increased taxes on its peasants, and demanded debt payment from France. These moves and others resulted in unrest by the peasantry in both countries, naval blockades on the Algerian coast and subsequent incursions.

China had been experiencing constant population growth and consequent migrations to expand grazing and farmland. Eventually the land could not absorb so many migrants. Many cultivated cash crops such as cotton, tea, peanuts, later tobacco and "New World" crops such as corn, sweet and white potatoes, in exchange for rice grown in other regions. As farm lands started to erode, fewer crops could be grown and a labor surplus developed. Rice prices fluctuated widely adding to market instability. The Qing Dynasty had already significantly cut taxes such that relief to those in need became inadequate during disasters. With tax reserves dwindling, (which sometimes were in silver, sometimes in food which was redistributed to non-farm people like artisans, government officials or soldiers), critical shortages in the cities and towns occurred. Intermittent droughts, periods of extreme cold coincided with peasant revolts and other uprisings.

THE 1840s

In China, response to devastating flooding of the Yellow River in 1841 was implemented locally rather than centrally and plagued by lack of coordination, corruption and conflict by officers which worsened and expanded the disaster's impact. Migrations of fleeing citizens occurred. In contrast, the earlier 1801 Yongding River flood which was managed centrally and effectively by addressing production, housing, price stabilization and water conservancy had a more stabilizing effect.

1848 was the year of revolutions, known in some countries as the Springtime of the Peoples or the Spring of Nations which brought a series of political upheavals throughout Europe. It remains the most wide spread revolutionary wave in European history; a series of revolts against monarchies beginning in Sicily and spreading to France, Germany, Italy and the Austrian Empire. Some were failures, others resulted in abolishing the monarchy. However, they did not always end repression, and were followed by widespread disillusionment among liberals, making America looking more and more as the promised land.

This writing is a work of fiction, alternative history, and a love story. While many persons, places and events are real, outcomes and utterances are often fiction. The notes at the end of the book are meant to clarify and be helpful. I wish you good reading!

M. Marquis

Contents

ROAR! List of Characters

LIST OF MAIN CHARACTERS IN ALPHABETICAL ORDER

***The Benoît family,** French Canadian ship builders/business people who settled in Mattapoisett, Massachusetts. U.S.A. **Renee** and **Madeleine** are the parents to three daughters Suzanne, Marie-Therese and Bijou.

***Bijou Benoît,** the youngest daughter, Jack Marshall's childhood friend.

***Marie-Therese Benoît**, physician.

***Suzanne Benoît,** oldest of Benoît sisters, businesswoman.

***Karmo Bockarie,** student at College of Fourah Bay in Sierra Leon in West Africa. Son of **Saidu** and one of **Musa's** younger brothers.

***Brima,** Karmo's fiancé.

***Jonny Henson,** philanthropist in Alta California

***Ansa Kabbah,** student philosopher and Karmo's best friend.

***Peter Kroupa,** assistant shipbuilder to Renee Benoît, carpenter and machinist in Alta California

***Lt. Dan,** outlaw, Christian Mullen's right hand man and fixer.

***Lokni of Linwanelowa,** Coastal Miwok Native American in Alta California, husband to Marie-Therese, carpenter and machinist.

*The Marshall family; Leah, housekeeper and caretaker to the Benoît family, Jack, her son.

*Jack Marshall, volunteer soldier, sharpshooter, gunsmith.

*Juan Pablo Martinez (JP), son of Jesse Martinez of San Antonio, Tejas.

*Christian Mullen, outlaw, gambler, sometimes good Samaritan in Alta California

*The Narrator, voice who intermittently comments directly to the reader.

*Pompokum (Pompo), of the Nisenan, Native American in Alta California, Jack's love.

*Santa Anna, at various times either General of the Military or President of Mexico.

*Schwartz, outlaw and Christian Mullen's major competitor.

*Allen White, wild life contractor hired by Alta California governor.

*Carlota Zimi, Native American leader, community organizer, administrator.

ROAR!

Odyssey of Battles, Betrayals
and Building a Nation

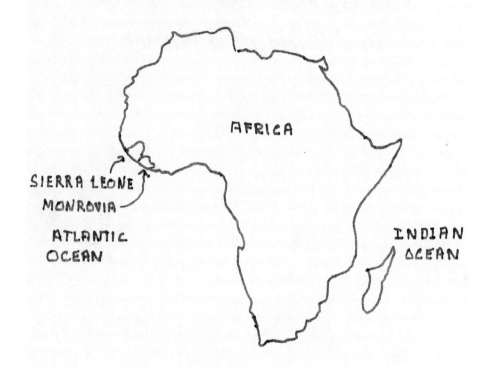

1

Sierra Leone 1830

He is not a lover who does not love forever. –Euripides.

WEDNESDAY

At first, it was the dank, musky smell of dirt and sweat penetrating his nostrils and permeating the stagnant air. Next came the sounds; the awful moans, wails and tears of men in acute pain, intense distress. His own wounds became slowly apparent to him—tracings of fire coursed and roared through his mind, and he experienced a persistent throbbing in his limbs. Barely opening his eyes, he could see only dim shafts of light coming through wooden slats of whatever construct was confining him. *What happened? Who are these other poor devils around me?* he thought. Slowly, his consciousness, which was not completely dormant, revealed uncovered shreds of memory. *An act of perfidy, most ignoble,* thought Karmo. Darkness again overcame him.

～

TUESDAY, THE DAY PRIOR

"One evil act does not make an evil man, Karmo," Brima murmured to him, her eyes looking towards the goings-on in the street. The Mount Aureol neighborhood of Freetown in Sierra Leone was a bustling warren of cobblestone streets connecting dozens of family-owned mercantile shops, bookstores and street vendors. Shade trees surrounded the town square, and warm coastal breezes ushered in herbaceous fragrances from the west. Animal protests and vendors hawking their wares mingled with the animated chattering of villagers. The square also provided entertainment for the local College's diverse student population.

"I do not trust him, Brima. He looks always to make quick advantage of another's foolishness." Karmo replied, "He and the player are both naïve and greedy, thinking it is an easy way to make money, as if they have money to lose!"

The student they were watching, Sahr, was charismatic, mostly harmless and often fun to be with, although he was forever looking for opportunities for easy money and to establish business connections, even when they were morally questionable.

At an outside table in front of the leather-ware shop sat a pair of visitors, also observing the interactions with interest.

"Such foolishness!" muttered Karmo.

The young couple watched Sahr as he laughed and cajoled with other students from the College. He was showing them card tricks; the students, who were drawn in with wonder as to how he so often correctly predicted the outcome, bet their meager funds nevertheless.

"Oooh! He did it again, the dog!" said one of the students, laughing loudly at his companion's loss.

With this, Brima and Karmo walked away down the dusty, busy street to the Farmer's Market. Their friend Ansa would be waiting for them. They stopped to pet one of the many local street dogs. "Look who they are calling a dog," said Karmo gently. "Come here, little one," he said as he took some bread from his pocket and gave it to the scruffy, four-legged beast. "Ha!" he said, "I should be so lucky, should I become homeless in the street!"

Brima gave a quizzical look and shook her head before spying their mutual friend. "Look! There is Ansa, across the way!"

Ansa moved quickly towards the pair, with his wide-open smile, and arms to match. They greeted each other with animation and delight. Karmo and Ansa walked Brima to her father's produce market, where she would work for several hours. "I so look forward to our picnic this afternoon, my love," whispered Karmo, while Ansa made a deep bow with a grand sweep of his arm outward. Brima smiled at them both, curtseyed playfully and nodded.

Ansa turned to Karmo, "I will be back in just a moment. I need to see someone."

~

Ansa Kabbah and Karmo Bockarie had become good friends since they met at Fourah Bay College in Freetown, a newly established college, soon to be known as the Athens of Africa.[1] There they would continue to learn English and French, and be educated as teachers.

~

Karmo Bockarie was from the nearby village of Kissy. He was the second of four sons of Saidu Bockarie. His mother had died of fever two years before. He would have liked for her to benefit from his being the one selected by the village leaders to receive an advanced education. Their support was an honor, which neither he nor his family took for granted, and his mother would have carried that pride humbly and quietly. In this way, he was his mother's son.

His oldest brother, Musa, retained the responsibility of the eldest son and would take over family and community responsibilities upon their father's retirement. Karmo's village was small, nestled at the base of rolling hills where families brought their cows and goats for grazing. Yet, there was a small health clinic and an even smaller library among the shops in the village center, where people met regularly to play board games, and chat about news or the latest gossip.

Karmo was a tall man for the times, with broad shoulders, a high forehead, a strong jaw and a wide, brilliant smile. But his intense gaze sometimes made people feel as if he was trying to read their minds, and that made many people uncomfortable. From a young age, he had an intuitive grasp as to how and why things went awry, and how to get them back on track. He could quickly see the bigger picture and its complexities.

Even at such a young age, he possessed a serious demeanor, the fluid walk and disciplined bearing resembling that of a military man. Indeed, military history was one of his passions. He had studied texts of strategy and tactics and loved maps, as well as the impact geography had on history, boundaries and warfare. He listened to the men of the village quietly speak of their wartime engagements; he was of a generation that knew of no adult untouched by war. Sometimes they would joke or speak of superficial things. They all stopped short of discussing the real pain, the real misery, however, for they knew that such things, when shared, would always multiply. Each came back a different man, part of them left back in field, perhaps the best part. For there, one knew the man next to you would give his life for you. It was simple, but also a simple hell. It seemed as if war was never-ending, yet few lessons had been learned. He had no intention of becoming a warrior, ever. No, his mission was to learn how to defend others and help them live without violence.

Karmo was a young man of few words who preferred to listen carefully to what was said, imagine what was unsaid, and contemplate what he heard or what was, perhaps, withheld. He tended to be so quiet, that there was even a time in his childhood when neighbors thought him simple-minded—that is, until his test scores came back with stunning results. He ranked quite high in critical thinking and, by extension, problem-solving. Indeed, his forte was problem solving; a little fine tuning and it was done ... all in his head. His quietness and stillness let him appear as out of nowhere as he observed people and their patterns.

"You think too much, Karmo!" his mates would sometimes say. "Make a decision, take action! We are too young to sit about like tired and disappointed old men munching about ancient ideas and the old days!" they jeered.

Nevertheless, through his cautious behavior, he anticipated friends or foes, good character or danger. This was a developing trait, one upon which he would later need to rely.

Karmo's good friend was Ansa Kabbah, from Cape Mount, in the south near the Liberian border. Ansa was foretold to be "the lucky one," although no one could tell him why. He, too, was selected to attend college. Broad-shouldered, the same height as Karmo, he had twinkly eyes, the gift of gab, and was exceedingly spiritual, though not in the customary Christian manner.

Ansa found signs of a higher power wherever he looked, from the small insects making their way through life, in groups or alone, to the very trees and vegetation around him, growing in symbiotic cooperation. He felt spirituality in the breezes that enveloped him and that sometimes made him weep for happiness. But most of all, he was awestruck and impassioned by the night skies, the source of all life, he believed, the refuge of the dead and the hope of the living.

As he sat in a gathering speaking to friends and strangers alike, Ansa would carve small wooden trinkets while spinning yarns of fantasy and fables of nature with intriguing characters, some impish, others romantic, or even noble. He told fables of the Greeks, the Romans, and about Christianity. People came to him to feel better, to heal their souls. And while Ansa enjoyed helping others, he had to confess that he was no healer, no religious man, and by no means holy. His wooden tokens were meant to help ground, comfort and remind others of the vast world beyond what one could see. No matter the story, the talisman, customized for the listener, always included an image of the sun or an overlay of a crescent moon and stars on the back. For these were constants in the sky and were free to everyone. By the time his story was finished, so was the talisman, which he then gave to the listener. While some of his stories got him into trouble for his mild blasphemy, Ansa was, nevertheless, well-liked among his peers and elders.

His father thought highly of Ansa and had the means to send him to England at age 17 for a year, to train to become an assistant to a Pastor. Having converted some years before, Ansa's father thought this would give his son a better understanding of, and perspective on, the Anglican Church. When Ansa returned from England, he had a more refined English-speaking voice, but had witnessed much brutality among the classes, even of whites towards whites. Even those Christians who preached peace often wanted it only for their own kind and even over the peace of others. He noted that many people could not conceive that others could hold values of similar merit to their own.

～

The two very different young men, with very different temperaments, became friends through their shared idealism, thirst for knowledge and adventure. They regularly spent time together after their studies sitting at one of the square's cafés drinking tea.

They spoke, as many ideological young men did, of how they might influence the future, fantasizing about how all peoples could be included in a shared community, knowing that would require extraordinary struggle, patience and blood. Perhaps this was going against nature, for don't we all want to protect our own people against the strange ways of others? Acceptance of the different is such a risk and a contrast to what is sure and known and comfortable. They would speculate and argue and otherwise solve the problems of the world as they talked at the little café on the square.

～

Karmo and Ansa made the acquaintance of Sahr at the College. At first they appreciated his vivaciousness and quick-wittedness, but, as they saw how his loyalty shifted to accommodate his self-interest, they mostly avoided him. Sahr amused himself by playing games of chance with other students, always with an eye to making money.

On this day, as Sahr packed up his trick cards, Ansa had circled back to confront him, shaking his head slowly. "One day someone will see through your folly, Sahr," said Ansa with concern.

Sahr just smirked. "Let them try. By then I will be far away, and they will not be able to find me!"

"Sahr, this may be a city, not a village, but people can find you still," said Ansa eyeing Sahr with intense curiosity.

"I have a plan, Ansa, and soon enough you will know about it," he said. Sahr's look turned dark and became less mischievous. But then he smiled broadly again, "Do not worry about me now, my brother," he smiled and walked away.

Karmo had followed Ansa, stepping up to him. As they both watched Sahr saunter off, Karmo remarked, "I have a bad feeling about him, my brother."

Ansa observed attentively with an almost imperceptible smile and mused aloud to no one in particular, "His gait is that of a bushbuck." He turned around and clapped Karmo on the back, answering his previous comment. "Yes, perhaps, but the day is beautiful and Brima is coming to join us this afternoon with a couple of her companions." His eyebrows working up and down with delight as he smiled broadly.

～

Brima was the daughter of a shopkeeper in Freetown. She was bright, loyal to her family, strong in both mind and body and possessed a lyrical laugh and a friendly smile. Karmo admired her modesty and intellect. She was much more patient than he and was inclined towards him. And today, there she stood with the morning sunlight behind her, wearing a dress in yellow, the color she favored. The surrounding light both comforted and mesmerized him, like the home fires. He wanted nothing to interfere with this beautiful, sun-drenched day. Just months before, they had been promised to each other by their families' agreement.

When Karmo first came to Freetown, he saw Brima immediately. He watched her for almost two months as she worked at her fruit stand in front of her father's city center shop. He would walk back and forth in front of the stand, not daring to approach her, eyeing her surreptitiously while seeming to look straight ahead. She would make quick glances at him from under her broad-brimmed sun hat but never allowed herself to smile at him.

At length Karmo got her attention by throwing tiny green plums at her. When she finally had had enough of his nonsense, she threw a melon at his head, narrowly missing him. A good thing he was agile! That's when he knew she was a force to be reckoned with. Even so, he caught the escape of a tiny smile on her lips. He was in love and believed Brima would accept him into her heart.

The very next day, he traveled home and pleaded with his father to accompany him to her parents' house so that he could ask for her hand in marriage. "It is as if she can see inside me, Father. Her eyes flash, but she has a warmness and a fondness towards me."

～

ROAR!

After the engagement ceremony, they met, far away from the noise and bustling activity of the city. Their hands had never touched before, but now they quietly and patiently exchanged glances. Because news of their engagement had been published, they could now appear together in public unaccompanied.

In that quiet space between the sandy beach and the main road to town, alone they paused in their walk. Karmo held Brima by the shoulders and immediately felt a shock of stinging heat such as he had never before experienced. He dropped his hands as if he were touching fire. Brima took note and gazed directly into Karmo's eyes.

"You are my heart, Karmo. You are my breath. I am afraid to exhale, fearing to lose you. Do whatever you feel," she murmured shyly.

Karmo's erstwhile silence abated as he regained his composure. "You are my pride, my hope, my honor. You will always be in my heart as long as there are stars in the sky. My heart cannot even beat without you, Brima. We will marry soon and be free of others' old-fashioned constraints." He kissed her forehead, then took her right hand and held it to his lips looking directly into her eyes as he kissed her fingertips one by one. "Always. Always." Their sincere and gentle words swirled about melding their souls in life's commitment.

2

The Mentors 1830

Advice is like snow; the softer it falls, the longer it dwells upon, and the deeper it sinks into the mind. –Samuel Taylor Coleridge

Karmo's father, Saidu Bockarie, was wise and successful, though not formally educated. He had great hopes for his son getting a college education. *Perhaps he will be a regional administrator*, thought Saidu, reflecting on his son's disposition to help others. In the evening, the men of the village would gather to speak of things big and small. On one of these evenings, when Karmo was back in his village on a break from college, Saidu was in a reflective mood and set aside his Christian beliefs for the moment to tell a folk tale of his people, the Mende.

"Ngewo, the sky god and supreme deity, created all things," he said in a quiet and solemn voice. "He intended his humans to be immortal, but decided first to test them. He sent two land creatures with different messages to the humans. With a toad, he sent the message, 'Death has come!', meaning that humans would be mortal. With a dog, he sent the message, 'Life has come!', meaning that humans would be immortal. In the end, it was the toad who got his message to the people first, because along the way, the dog stopped to eat with other dogs and commenced to fight over food."

Karmo blinked at his father quizzically, then squinted his eyes, deep in thought.

The older man continued, "The toad was resolute in his mission, and though smaller and slower than the dog, his patience and endurance took him to his goal. The dog is a gregarious beast, both friendly and yet

13

ready to fight for whatever he thinks should be his, even when in reality, he has enough. This is why humankind fights for survival, for they have come to believe they must overcome others, not just to share with or accompany each other," Saidu concluded.

Karmo sat quietly, taking all this in. He wondered at the wisdom of his ancestors. The message was simple yet profound.

"Humans will be in a perpetual fight amongst themselves until they can accept all of their kind," Saidu continued.

Karmo, considered the many times he had discounted his father's stories, now realized his thoughtlessness. He stared at his father, this wise man whom he sometimes had taken for granted. He bowed to Saidu and left the group to ponder and reflect on human nature. Shame slowly crept into his being. How could he so easily dismiss the time, the story, *this* man? How could he so easily overlook the history, culture and beliefs of his *own* people? And how fast! Was this what happens when one puts distance between oneself and home? Was not traveling and meeting other people supposed to broaden the mind and perspective? *There must be a balance*, he thought to himself, *a mindful balance.*

～

Karmo had a facility for picking up the languages and history being offered at the College. He used these talents to read stories about the art of war, which he had to study on his own because it was not part of the acceptable curriculum. History always fascinated him. He was intrigued by the variations of the same telling by peoples from different lands and wondered, *"Does anyone know the real truth? Do people believe in only one history and accept that at face value?"*—as many from his village did? There was no sure way to know; even if they were present for an epic event, everyone has their own perspective because of different upbringings in different geographic environments, and different governing.

Before and during his college days, Karmo made a weekly trek northeast of town to meet with his mentor. Although the treks were not secret, he kept the details to himself, so as not to upset the College administrators. His mentor was known as "that lion from the east," wise and experienced in conflict and war. No one knew his real name, nor would he say. They simply called him Efendi.

Efendi was a Krio Muslim, released by the British after having fought for them.[2] Tales were that he was descended from the Mane invaders, whose warriors were more interested in booty and in acquiring people to enslave than taking land. Efendi did not speak of this and maintained his affinity to the far northeast of the continent and the wadi [valley] of his birth.[3] His demeanor was fierce although his voice was quiet and sonorous. Dark, muscular and sleek, he was like a tree that would bend but not break.

"*Alkebulan*, the mother of mankind, was the indigenous name for the northern part of this continent. It was the Romans who named it Africa, Karmo," said Efendi in one of his didactic moods, "and trade has been the consistent and enduring reason for violence throughout much of its history, whether for protection of trade routes, resources, as a source of taxes, or land, or any and all combinations."

"So naturally, people went to war, entering into battles over geography to gain dominance and settle differences. Is that not right, Efendi?" returned Karmo.

"Yes. Too often, that is what happened. But war was often cloaked in something else. Know this, war is not always the answer to differences, my son, but if you must fight, let it be for justice, not for revenge or for someone's greed," he lectured.

Efendi was an avid reader of Sun Tzu's "The Art of War," which had been translated into French before Karmo's birth. Karmo had read it as well, but without Efendi to help him better understand the concepts and share his actual battle experience, it was all very theoretical.[4]

～

Karmo asked about perspective, and how one might view history and war through one's own lens.

"Yes, perspective, Karmo. It is not hard to get men to go to war," said Efendi in a quiet, serious tone, "and that is the tragedy. Deception comes in many cloaks. All that needs to be done is to repeat a lie, a lie for which people are only too ready to embrace. Man will follow the person with the strongest sense of purpose, whether he is right or wrong. Tell them their way of life is being threatened, blame others for their deficiencies, invent examples, undertake violence performed in the guise of outsiders—those who are different—play on fears or hatred. If that does not work, then threaten them, or bribe them with promises that can be broken later.

"Then call on the youngest, most isolated and discouraged men among us to fight for honor and glory and righteousness, and they will follow—if not of their own inclination, then as a result of the pressures their populace will place upon them. It is when they face their first battle that they may learn the savage truth: that waging war is not about righteousness, but victory. And how this is accomplished may be atrocious and brutal."

"Yes, but what of honor, Efendi? Is it not honorable to fight for one's family and country when threatened," asked Karmo, "or for revenge?"

"Go to war for defense, to protect your land and family when they are truly threatened. Be mindful of protecting your honor with right-headedness. Do not confuse rebuffs or pettiness with an assault to honor, lest you pervert the meaning and make excuses to offend and assault in return. As for revenge or justice? They are not the same. No matter the reason, be aware that someone is profiting, and someone is losing, including perhaps, losing their life. Watch who controls the flow of information, who is being kept ignorant, who plants the seed of rumor, favorable or not—for it is rumor that will fill the vacuum of ignorance. Rumors are just tools. Watch who is promising the fighters rewards after battle.

"There has been much fraud in history. And worst of all are the leaders who are delusional and make up reasons for going to war as this goes beyond greed and becomes terrorizing for both sides. These are just a few of the deceptions of war. Revenge is another matter altogether, Karmo, and is often emotional, not rational. Especially *then* should one keep a cool head, to be sure his actions are justified, lest innocents be pulled into the fray."

～

Karmo and Efendi sometimes went on treks, discussing human nature, strategies, tactics, geography and its resources. On one foray, they traveled two days farther than usual in order to observe and learn how to manage in a different terrain. The dry Harmattan winds from the north Sahel contained fine grains of sand and dust that aggravated Karmo's eyes and throat.

"Why did you bring me this far, Efendi?" asked Karmo. "… to show me different weather and terrain? It is so hot and gritty, just unpleasant. I do not recall the men of the village speaking of this."

Efendi was at first amused, then looked at Karmo sternly. "War survival goes beyond staying alive or avoiding getting wounded, my son. The elements and environment can be as harsh as any enemy. There will be times of extreme temperature, hunger, biting insects, deafening noise and deafening quiet. Your limbs could become red with rashes or sore with weariness. Your bowels will revolt in burning and explosive distress, yet you will need to persevere, or you will perish. *This,* he waved his arm towards the land, is a minor discomfort. For now, *here* right now, we have peace."

At long last, Karmo sighed. "I wonder if I could ever be a good soldier if I had to be, Efendi. Yes, while battlefield art intrigues me, I do prefer comfort, surely. Most of all, though, I am not a brave man. I am not sure I could kill anyone—even if he was the enemy."

Efendi studied Karmo's face. "I have known you since your birth, Karmo. You have the most important of qualities; that of being calm and level-headed in a crisis. You have demonstrated bravery many times, perhaps without realizing it. You have defended people against wild animals, and rescued others from drowning in streams; when necessary, you stand up and speak your mind in council. If ever a time comes when you must kill to defend, you will do it; we all have the capacity to kill one another when necessary. It is both a sad and redeeming quality of mankind. The difficulty comes when you are ordered to kill, but do not feel it is justified. This is why deception is often used by the powerful, to get a man to do something he is not naturally inclined to do. But, having

17

said all this, the level of brutality is most often in direct proportion to the leader's inclination."

Karmo listened carefully, taking in what he was hearing, and determining a framework of beliefs he could reconcile. He nodded before speaking. "I am beginning to understand, Efendi. Yes, sometimes it is necessary to kill. However, I do not want to be so rageful as to kill indiscriminately."

Efendi continued, "There is so much more to know and take in. Sometimes the only way to learn it is to live it. Remember, too, that killing is different from execution. Interrogation is different from torture. More falsehoods than truths have been wrung out of a man through torture. Engagement and destroying the enemy is the least valuable tool, Karmo. Demoralization of the enemy can be more fruitful. Take away their sense of hope by out-strategizing them and be ready to attack at the least expected site or time. If you take away their sense of purpose, the high risk of fighting and dying for some vague or immoral reasons such as greed will not encourage a soldier to lay down his life. Release some prisoners, if necessary, and tell them misinformation that will favor your side or disadvantage their side so they can share these falsehoods when they get back to their people. Release some prisoners when prudent, so as not to have to feed and house them, and turn them over to your own cause. There are many ways to win a battle other than by an armed fight."

"It seems so contradictory—kill, do not kill, deceive, do not deceive," said Karmo.

"Remember the intent, Karmo," said Efendi. "Fighting is not easy, nor should it be. Be alert to treachery by one's own leaders, the great pretenders, who will crow at the failure of diplomacy, urge on devolution, and have us resort to primitive and barbaric actions—including the slaughter of innocents."

"No, Efendi, the slaughter of innocents is never justified!" said Karmo, frightened. "Certainly, in the name of humanity, innocents will be spared slaughter."

Efendi again paused. His face took on a haunted expression. Placing his hand on Karmo's arm he continued. "My dear boy, your thinking is sentimental. This is war of which we are speaking. Choose your opportunity to show your humanity carefully, particularly with the vanquished. Your fighters may be frenzied and lust for spoils and revenge. You must balance humanity with the goals of your people, in order to keep them fighting the next battle.

"Slaughter of innocents is a tactic used to demoralize and send a message to others who are inclined to resist. News of atrocities will be broadcast throughout the land, but the results are not predictable. It will either force the enemy into submission, or will strengthen their resolve to fight all the more fiercely. Children, for example, have always suffered in war, be it invisibly such as by starvation or poisoning, or overtly, such as bombing, hanging or being run through by the sword. Some have been impressed to do battle at the forward line, to take the brunt of fire or forced to become spies." He paused and eyed, Karmo before commencing. "Rape as a tactic is just as ancient and prevalent. Its brutality not only demoralizes the other side, it eliminates their future. Do not underestimate the enemy or its resources."

Karmo was at first silent as all this information sunk in, and then said, "Rape, never! Nor would I ever kill a child, Efendi. What honor is in that atrocity?" he murmured.

"Honor, Karmo? No, not honor, but perhaps necessity. There will be fighters on both sides reflecting on these same thoughts, while others only want to sate their anger, whether real or imagined, with blood. But consider your definition of *atrocity*. If a child is armed and trains his weapon towards one of your men, will you let him fire, or will you kill the child? I am not telling you what you should do. I am telling you that what has happened before will continue to happen."

Karmo's face became rigid; his breathing quickened as his chest tightened.

Efendi leaned forward and looked directly into Karmo's eyes, "You do what you must. Atrocity is when your action or its degree is unnecessary. Know that while we cannot imagine committing these acts ourselves, we can imagine others committing them. The hard part is facing your people back in the village afterward, for they will judge you without understanding, and without even having been present."

"You have seen much war, Efendi. How can you speak so calmly about it? Do the memories ever fade?" asked Karmo.

Efendi looked at the young man quietly before he answered. "Each of us carries their memories in a different manner. Even with my eyes open, I have nightmares still. I tell you what I can, but for much of my memory, there are no words." Karmo was again silent, then said, "How will one know what to do on any given day, Efendi? Will the training we receive in the combat skills of war transfer to most any situation?"

"Yes, but only *on the ground* can one determine which skills to use, and the best action for the time and place. That decision comes with experience. Your leadership must be outwardly solid. Your fighters must be competent with using their weapons. This, in turn, gives them confidence. Know your people as well as your enemy, know their customs, strengths, weaknesses and know your terrain. None of this knowledge can be underestimated."

"If people fight for their land, then who are the good and who are the enemy?" asked Karmo.

Efendi gazed upward, then directly into Karmo's eyes, "Sometimes they are one and the same," was his thoughtful remark.

The next day, Efendi took Karmo up the Rokel River into the forest, to teach him tracking, reading terrain, listening to the birds as they called to each other, and observing plant habitat for food, shelter and camouflage. The air was no longer so humid as it had been downstream. Travel was less challenging on the cool, shaded paths—at least for the time being. Karmo's sweat evaporated, and his clothes no longer clung to his body.

"The infidel is obsessed with wealth and material possessions. He believes all men are as well, obsessed with their own comfort. This is the infidel's major mistake about us. The true warrior is not motivated by possessions or comfort. Know your enemy, Karmo, know his weaknesses and his strengths," repeated Efendi.

And so, these discussions went on for months under the shade of acacia trees. Efendi recited tales of Alexander the Great and his swarming tactics, Hannibal's element of surprise, Pyrrhic victories, Sun Tzu's responses to enemy behavior, when to feign disorder, when to evade the enemy, the five dangerous faults of generals, and more.[5] Karmo became more contemplative, listening carefully, asking more thoughtful questions. Efendi continued to answer him, drawing strategizing maps in the dirt and discussing possible tactics.

It was the autumnal equinox. The moon shone brightly upon the two men, who were sleeping outdoors under the trees; a fire had been lit to keep away the beasts. Efendi slept with his eyes half-open, darkness, restless in his mind. Karmo slept fitfully, at length fatigue overcame him, but his mind raced, telling him a story through dreams.

There was an underground tomb for a local chieftain who had just passed on to another world. The village people were superstitious and took good care to supply their leader all he would need for his journey to the afterlife, lest he returned to take revenge on them. He was laid out on a wooden bier in the tomb, looking rigid and fierce. Ampules of wine and grain stood around the walls, as did numerous weapons of war, clothing, and Karmo, who was thrown into the pit alive, at the last moment, to serve the chieftain.

As tall as Karmo was, the pit was too deep for him to gain purchase of the heavy timbers that covered it. Karmo struggled to breathe slowly, trying not to use up all the air before he could figure a way out of the pit. He walked the entire perimeter, looking up. Damp, musky odors emanated from the earthen floor. The walls were stone, cold and shear. He could see thin rays of moonlight through two of the covering timbers; darkness had arrived.

He heard a faint groan and sensed movement from the bier. Karmo's heart nearly stopped. The corpse arose and stiffly moved towards Karmo. In the pitch blackness, he saw a faint green glow around the eyes.

He could hear its breath grunting through its nostrils. Karmo grabbed a lance and held it horizontally towards the walking corpse monster whose searching arms grabbed the lance and tried to wrest it away. Karmo persisted in jabbing at the corpse, who in turn became enraged, roared an ear-shattering scream, and thrashed casks of oil and wine with his bare hands, smashing boulders, scattering them about.

All this was happening as Karmo danced about the pit with the monster, moving away from the sound of its wheezing grunts. The monster was mindless and indefatigable, and would not stop attacking. Karmo realized that, despite that green aura, it could not see him, and he started to reconsider. The thrashing by the monster upended more tools that Karmo could use to trip and subdue the beast. His heart in his throat, Karmo fought and fought, feeling the monster's hot breath in his face, on his back, everywhere—as they stumbled about the pit. Suddenly, the monster stopped thrashing and lay back down on his bier.

Karmo was exhausted, terrified and shaking, but he sat down. He put his fist on the cold stone wall, banging it in desperation before falling asleep. As the moon rose the next night, the monster again awakened and roared, thrashing his arms about. Karmo kept himself ahead of the beast as the two again negotiated the perimeter, now slippery with oil and wine.

Just as suddenly as the monster had awakened, he stopped and laid down on his bier once more. In the melee, a larger pile of rubble formed. Karmo scrambled up quickly, using a spear and his bare hands to pry off the timber cover and dug his way out of the pit, as dirt and gravel rained upon him and into his face. He ignored this latest challenge, as well as the shredding of his fingers and the splinters tearing into his arms. He needed to get out before the beast awoke again. Karmo struggled and labored. Finally, a shaft of light and fresh air came in and welcomed him.

His whole body jerked awake and yet he was wrecked with fatigue. He held his head in his hands and struggled to calm his breathing. *What was that?!* he thought. The roaring monster was dead, yet seemed ever-living.

～

Still shaken from his experiences and dreams, Karmo traveled back to town. There, he met up with some of his schoolmates, who are all young, proud and boisterous.

"Hey! Hey! Look who's back from his crusade!" laughed one friend as he clapped Karmo on the back.

"Karmo!" exclaimed another. "Why do you study so much the fables of unknown worlds? What pushes you to want to know the ways of war?"

Still exhausted, Karmo wondered how he could explain what he had learned and dreamed to his friends. "It is not just war, but history. I study because so many peoples have these warrior beliefs, which perpetuate conflict. Something within me wants to understand their minds, why they should behave like this," Karmo tried to explain weakly.

"What is the point?" asked an exasperated student "The old men spout noble phrases, but in the physical world, they are making up their own morality. We all have seen it, my brother. Who is better? The person who refuses to defend his land by staying true to his beliefs and is kind, or the person who nobly goes into service for his country, but beats his wife in his own home?"

"Leave him alone," said another. "He lives in his head so much, he does not even hear your words."

It was not as simple as this, thought Karmo. But he was disconcerted, for there was some truth to this, and yet he was offended. "It is not my intent to judge anyone, rather my intent is to learn and acknowledge that many have beliefs that lead them to take unjust actions and sometimes provide excuses for them. How does the difference come to be? Who will we be to each other because of these differences? Will we be divided, or come together? This is what I wish to understand. I long to know many people—not just the extremes, like war, but in our everyday humanness. Perhaps I could even help more of us learn to live in that middle space. The difficulty of it all makes me so tired at times," replied Karmo as he raised his hands chest-high before dropping them to his sides.

3

Mattapoisett, Massachusetts 1830

A pearl is a pearl because of the sand's patience. –unknown

With her gaze level and her voice steady, "You will return to the dock and offload that barge today, or I will find someone who will."

"Yes, Ma'am, today, for sure." The dock boss turned and left the room with a twisted sneer she could not see, but probably felt. He had really wanted a day of rest, both for himself and his crew. But that was not to be, he knew. Madeleine Benoît held her gaze for a moment, then slowly let out a long breath. She walked over to the sun-washed windows overlooking the harbor, dust motes floating serenely along a route according to their own mystery, and at all the morning activity on this beautiful fall day. So many men from far flung places were busy at work at the harbor; they hailed from England, France, Canada, Native American lands, Africa, and of course, America. This was now their country, after all—this land where her own family was prospering.

But presently, she had no time to listen to the workers' pretenses and exhortations of who was the better man (beyond their allegiance to their own ship's work crew). She was the wife of Jean Benoît, once a sea captain from the northern British provinces, which the French called Canada. Now he was a ship builder, of whalers mostly, but occasionally frigates for transport. They lived in Mattapoisett, Massachusetts, and had offices overlooking Buzzards Bay. Jean was away north with his lead carpenter to negotiate with a Penobscot, Jim Sockalexis, for timber. The Native peoples had parlayed their lands into a sustainable business by making contracts with a large number of builders. Jean appreciated the Penobscots valuing the land. They replaced their timbering with seedlings on behalf of future generations. He hoped they would prevail in their endeavors. He also enjoyed kicking back by a cozy fire to talk about tribal updates. And of course, there was Jim's delicious pine beer.

Back home, Jean left Madeleine in charge of operations without any trepidation. His wife was also his partner and could pull her own weight. She knew as much of the business as he did.

～

Madeleine shifted her gaze outward beyond the bay toward the horizon, scanning for incoming ships. She was good at meeting new challenges every day, since she was responsible for maintaining their home and the upbringing of their three daughters, and paying all the bills and taxes. Madeleine faced various levels of discrimination—primarily for being a woman. Some discrimination was blatant, some condescending, some dismissive. Plus, there were always attempts to take financial advantage of her.

She let her mind wander as she recalled back when she and her daughters left Montréal to join Jean the year before, just after the dedication ceremony of the Basilique Notre-Dame de Montréal. Prior, he had established his ship building business and could only visit his family sporadically until their arrival in Mattapoisett. Her family had been fur traders, settled in Montréal and did a substantial business. There she met Jean, an amiable man of great energy and heart. But his dream was ship building and that meant relocating to America. The venture only took a few years before he would send for them. Madame Benoît had looked forward to settling in with Jean in their new hometown.

We are a long way from home, she thought to herself. "Henri!" she called to her assistant. "I need the American financial reports. It is time to place supply orders."

A sandy-haired, lanky young man, Henri, quickly brought in a sheaf of reports and newspapers as Madeleine settled in behind the huge oak desk to start her review process.

"You are going to be much missed. How is the family doing, Henri?" she asked.

"They are excited, Madame. We all are looking forward to going home to France. I have already been promised a shipping position in Marseilles, thanks to your recommendation."

"They will be fortunate to have you, Henri. Times are hard now in France. I hope you will be safe," commented Madeleine, with one eyebrow raised.

"Oui, Madame. But France has a new constitution, and Louis Philippe is a promising leader—now that Charles has been forced out.[6] The vigilantes who murdered the enslaved soldiers in the south are being dealt with. Most of the troubles now are small, particularly in the north, but yes, the people are having hard times. We will be safe in Marseilles, be assured Madame," he replied.

Madeleine smiled and looked at him warmly. Henri Le Murier was a hard-working family man and loyal to both her and Jean. She was appreciative that he helped train her oldest daughter Suzanne in his work tasks. Just like her mother, Suzanne had a knack for keeping a finger on the pulse of national finances, and adjusting the company's buying-and-selling operations accordingly.

It had not been easy. Madeleine had learned the running of her husband's shipbuilding company first to assist him, and then to fill in while he was away on business. However, he had been gone longer than expected this time, and the first ship carrying building supplies and goods was already here at the dock for off-loading.

Running a shipyard required a great deal of judgment and business acumen, to which Madeleine took quickly. Not only did she need the complete knowledge of ship construction and the subtleties of different types of timber, she was in charge of 60-70 men, all of whom had to be good at their jobs. She had to be able to calculate up into the tens of thousands of dollars for a job involving all sorts of material: timber, iron, oakum, lead, paint, spars, canvas, cordage and varnish. National finances influenced shipbuilding needs, and shipping was often the first industry brought to a standstill during a recession. There were all sorts of new appliances to size up, as to their true worth in durability and function, and also, on short notice. Above all, she needed to be shrewd at finances and keeping costs down, yet pay her workers with the fairness they were due. It took a true depth of knowledge—and a hundred small miracles—to keep the business afloat. *I am exhausted,* she thought as she allowed herself yet another moment to reflect.

"One more thing, Henri, please send for Suzanne. I need her."

"Oui, Madame." Henri turned and quickly left the office.

Moments later, "Oui, Maman? You wanted to see me?" Suzanne entered the room, smiling. She had been working dockside, checking inventory. Only 18, she was wise beyond her years, in part thanks to the opportunities of being born into a business family, and also being encouraged to partake in the shared responsibilities of running the business. Lithe and well-proportioned, she had dark hair like both her parents, with the piercing hazel eyes like her mother.

"Chérie, we need to talk." Her mother guided Suzanne's elbow, and they sat down on the settee by the window. "What do you see for your future? What do you want it to look like?"

"Maman! Why must we discuss this again? I like what I am doing now, working with you and Papa. I know I cannot always live with you, but I can still work here!" Suzanne exclaimed with only an edge of frustration. Yes, she knew she was eventually expected to marry, but she had been brought up to be self-sufficient in her own right.

"But dear one, I only do not want you to be alone. A good husband can be a friend, a comfort and a support, a partner, just like the teams we have working on the docks. They rely on each other and make the work better and lighter." Madeleine knew she could appeal to Suzanne's sense of practicality, if not to her sentimentality.

"Oui, Maman, only give me enough time to learn more, so I will be able to support a family on my own, if need be," she said with a wry smile. Suzanne well understood the social reality, especially in this industry, that men sometimes could make contacts that women could not—attend shipbuilders' meetings and such. Others sustained serious injury or sometimes just disappeared, leaving their families in financial jeopardy; such a scenario had happened to their own housekeeper, Mrs. Marshall. But Suzanne also was stubborn and determined to prepare herself for independence, whether it was necessary or not.

Madeleine sighed. She could not disagree with the logic, and after all, Suzanne would be of marriageable age for some years to come. She just did not want her daughter to wait too long to recognize the potential suitors who were starting to come around. "Alright for now, Chèrie," said Madeleine. "Tell me, how is the inventory going?"

"It looks good from what I can see, but it is taking longer than usual to unload. The dock boss, Mr. Anderson, is distracted and so he's yelling more than usual. Something is up."

"I have spoken with him already this morning," Madeleine sighed. They reviewed some of the financial reports together and wrote out a number of plans, listing their priorities. At length, Madeleine determined that Suzanne should go back to her work. "I will see you tonight, Chérie."

Suzanne gave her mother a kiss on the cheek and turned to the job at hand, pausing to steady herself on the desk. "Ha! I turned around too fast. Everything will be fine, Maman. I will see you at supper."

～

Alwyn Baker, a compact, loose-jawed man, strutted up and down the dock, screaming at team leaders and attempting to manage details over which he had no authority or knowledge. He trusted few people and needed to be seen as a boss at all times—even when he was plainly interfering.

"What the hell is taking you assholes so damn long?" he bellowed at the ship's crew, who had just docked at the south end of the bay. They had been at sea for a month, bringing in supplies from Georgia for his mercantile company and other businesses, including the Benoîts' business. Although he had no direct jurisdiction over the crew, that didn't stop him from verbally assaulting them.

"Baker, shove off! My men just got in, and they're moving as fast as they can!" The dock boss was well-acquainted with Baker. "Your goods will be delivered as promised. We're even a few days earlier than expected, so leave us to do our work!"

"I don't give a rat's ass if your men's guts are hanging out," he sneered. "Those are my goods, so you work for me! The goods are work you're doing for me!"

The dock boss just shook his head and turned back to his task, irritated that he had both the ship owner and also this ass on his case.

Inside, the Captain was making entries in his log as the first mate approached. "Capitaine, the special delivery?" The Captain stared at him, and took a deep breath. "Yes, bring it to my quarters for now. I'll send a message to Mademoiselle Benoît."

"Mademoiselle Suzanne?"

"Yes," answered the Captain, "quickly, now."

4

The Benoîts and the Marshalls, Mattapoisett 1830

Hope will never be silent. –In honor of Harvey Milk

Their home was one of those rambling, three story affairs set back on a bluff in Mattapoisett, Massachusetts that overlooks the bay. It was shaped like a long, large box with a steeply pitched roof, typical of the day. Only the window shutters and small covering over the front door gave any sign of style. Painted a muted red and trimmed in black on the exterior, it was in good condition when Jean purchased it. The living room was large, by the day's standards. There were carved stair railings, finials and finely milled wood trim throughout. It was much larger than the family needed, but, as it turned out, they had many guests who stayed from weeks to months at a time, and so the accommodations were fortuitous. Jean's travels north to negotiate for more timber was an annual event. He was generally gone for four to five weeks, depending mostly on the weather, but also on his inclinations.

Before the family left Montreal to join Jean, Madeleine spent years alone, with the twin responsibilities of the household and raising her bright and inquisitive girls; Suzanne, Marie-Therese and Bijou. All were voracious readers who spent evenings sharing what they had learned and discussing the ways and ideas of peoples from other lands.

~

Madeleine's two younger daughters were at home with the housekeeper, Mrs. Marshall.

"Oh, its wing is broken!" murmured Marie-Therese as she gently took the bird out of the box and placed it on the table. "Let me see if I can set it."

"Please help, Tessa, the bird is suffering!" cried Bijou.

Little five-year-old Bijou took after her father, with dark eyes, round cheeks, and that dark, wavy hair, kept in braids. She was ever awed and intrigued by the differences in all living things and possessed a generous heart for all those in need. Bijou was forever bringing home stray and wounded animals. She loved the woods, woodland creatures, the sense of peace there. She sensed being a part of something greater than herself, although she could not articulate it. She talked to her family about the kind spirits there in the woods, and said that when she just sat quietly and closed her eyes, she could hear the mysteries of the world unwind. She had no fear of nature; rather, it spoke to her.

While Marie-Therese loved the woods as well, her passion and affinity were for treating people and animals. She hoped to become a physician someday, which was no easy feat for a woman of that time. She was a willing helper to the town's Doctor, Galen Smith, a gruff acting curmudgeon with an exterior that belied his kindness. He tutored her in the sciences, anatomy, and the healing arts. She accompanied him to home visits to check on and treat the sick. On occasion, he brought her along to help him manage traumatic injuries, most often horse kicks, and farm or dock mishaps.

Marie-Therese snapped a small piece of kindling to make a splint for the bird's wing after manipulating it into a neutral position, then tied the splint on with a scrap of cotton. "That is the best I know to do, Bijou," she said as she lowered the bird back into the box. "We will keep the bird here in the kitchen where it can stay warm."

"Now, we need to help Mrs. Marshall get supper ready before Maman and Suzanne come home from work. Let's wash our hands," said Marie-Therese.

Bijou looked at her hands, held them up to Marie-Therese for inspection, with an impish grin, while stating confidently, "Look, they're clean!"

Marie-Therese gave her little sister a sideways glance.

Bijou let out a sigh, "Yes, sister, let's go," for she knew she could never win this game with Marie-Therese.

The discussion around the table was amiable, loud at times because of the young people's exuberance. Madame Benoît, her three daughters, Mrs. Leah Marshall and her nine-year-old son Jack were all engaged in the conversation.

"Mama!" said Bijou excitedly, "Guess what Marie-Therese told me? Guess!"

"I have no idea what, ma Chérie, tell me," answered Madeleine patiently.

Bijou was almost breathless as she exclaimed, "In 1777, a girl named Sybie, Syb, Syla ...."

"Sybil," coached Marie-Therese quietly.

"Oui, a girl named Sybil ... aaaa," Bijou stuttered.

"Ludington," whispered Marie-Therese.

Bijou started again, "A girl named Sybil Ludington rode her horse into the night-time to warn her papa's men—ah, he was a Colonel—that the British were sacking Danbury in Connecticut! And, and, and she rode 40 miles![7] That was more than twice Mr. Paul Revere's ride!!"

"Silly Bijou," teased Jack, "Girls don't ride horses!"

"They do too, do too, dumb-head Jackie!" cried Bijou.

"That's enough, you two," interrupted Madeleine as Leah nodded to her.

"They're a couple stubborn donkeys if I ever saw one," added Mrs. Marshall quietly.

Madeleine tried to stifle a laugh. "That is quite a story, Bijou," she said, sending a glance to Marie-Therese, who only looked up to the ceiling.

"It is so, ma petite," said Marie-Therese to Bijou. "Little is said of it, though. And girls *do* ride horses. But you are a little correct, too, Jack. Not many girls in Mattapoisett ride horses."

"When I get bigger, I'm going to ride a horse, too! I will ride it fast and long, and I will help people, and I will ride into the stars! Mama, when is Papa coming back home? I hope he gets a horse for me!" interjected Bijou.

"End of November or early December, dear, like every season," answered Madeleine. "Until then, we are on our own, but we will be just fine," she proclaimed with all the reassurance she could muster. She knew things would be tight and challenging for them, as there are issues even today that craftsmen, retailers and bankers still don't want to deal with a woman about, however capable she is. Those times when her husband was away meant incessant haggling, questioning and persuading by Madeleine to simply accomplish needed repairs, maintenance and just everyday living.

～

The Marshalls lived in a separate part of the house, a small but comfortable living quarters. Leah Marshall was essentially alone. Her husband had always been a restless man who found family life unexciting. He was a sailor and disappeared from his ship somewhere in the Caribbean three years earlier. The ship and the rest of the crew returned without incident. It had not been a particularly remarkable trip, she was told, and she knew they were all holding something back.

So Leah was grateful to find employment with the Benoîts. The mutuality of the arrangement was both supportive and practical. However, her son Jack was nine years old now and in sore need of a male role model. Leah worried about this and felt both demoralized and angry about her abandonment by her husband. She would sometimes rail to the walls about her husband's shortcomings and ultimate betrayal. Careful never to compare Jack openly with his father, she worried nonetheless that the young boy couldn't help but take his mother's admonishments to heart.

Jack was a good-natured boy who hid his disappointment regarding his father. When, at times, as his mother's resentment rubbed off on him, he became conflicted about family. He appreciated the Benoîts but would not let himself love them, except perhaps Bijou, whom he treated as a sister, and sometimes a pet.

Do not dismiss the earnest and guileless emotions of children, for their passions are every bit as genuine and meaningful to them as they are to adults. Children only lack the perspective that time and experience will bring them.

～

Mrs. Marshall sometimes turned to Jean Benoît for guidance and assistance in handling Jack. She sat at the table, reflecting on a conversation with Monsieur Benoît before he departed for the north.

"It has been said before, "We cannot pick our fathers; the tragedy is when they do not pick us," Jean said to her.

Mrs. Marshall could only nod quietly, holding back tears of shame that she did not deserve. Monsieur Benoît took Jack under his wing and let him accompany him on errands about town and had him do clean-up work around the dock offices when he wasn't in school. He and Mrs. Marshall spoke about more formal training for the boy, perhaps as an apprentice to a tradesman of some kind the coming year.

"The boy has a good mind, Leah," mused Monsieur Benoît.

"Yes. And he really likes to tear apart machines," stated Mrs. Marshall. "That boy will pull apart anything mechanical just to see how it works. Then he can put it all back together again! I don't know how he does it," she added proudly.

"He recognizes the elegance in nature. How it works, how it adapts. He puts two and two together, Leah. He does not have to relearn anything; a fine skill, when something interests him," responded Monsieur Benoît. "When I get back before Christmas, I will find him a fitting place where he can start for a few hours a week. Perhaps with Peter."

"I'd be most grateful, Sir," said Mrs. Marshall. "He'll do us both proud. I know it."

～

One of Jack's responsibilities was walking Bijou home after school. He didn't mind much, even though Bijou was four years younger than he. She was fun to be around, didn't mind mud, and liked playing with bugs and sticks. On their way home, they often spent their time playing around Eel Pond, looking for whatever large and small creatures they could find. One day, they came across a dead baby squirrel. Flies and hide beetles were already roaming upon the poor creature, who likely fell out of its nest. "The cleaners," said Jack thoughtfully.

"What do you mean, Jackie?" asked Bijou who looked away from the carnage.

"All the bugs and worms that come to clean away dead things, even us when we're in the ground," he answered.

"Oh, Jackie, I don't like to think of that!" exclaimed Bijou.

"But it's true! We need them. Otherwise, the world would be an awful foul and smelly place. We come from the earth, we go back to the earth," Jack explained.

"We come from the sky, then we become earth, then we become people … oh! I'm so confused, Jackie," said Bijou. "Anyway, I don't want to see that," she said as she turned away from the dead squirrel and walked on.

Jack took her arm to stop her, then held out his open palm towards Bijou.

"What are those beads?" she asked.

"They're called roly poly's, and … wait a few moments, watch!" he said.[8]

Slowly, the dark gray beads opened up to show themselves as quarter-inch ovals with many, many legs, crawling around Jack's hand.

"Oh, they're so cute! How do they do that!" exclaimed Bijou. "Where did you get them?"

"Easy," said Jack. "They live in the ground or under dead leaves, and mostly come out at night with their whole family to look for food. They'll eat anything, especially dead stuff, leaves, bugs, worms …" He paused and looked sideways at her, "us." Marie-Therese told me they're not unlike lobsters 'cuz they will shed their whole shell for a new one from time to time. And look how they curl themselves up for protection! They're really magnificent, don't you think?"

Bijou took some into her hands and they curled up once again. She giggled. "They truly are, Jackie!"

The children continued their exploration, following the dirt path through outcroppings in the woods and into a marshy area fringing the pond, past the ice barns, then to a canal opening to the bay, before turning home. They kicked rocks up the dirt path and chased birds as they ambled along. It was one of their favorite times of the day.

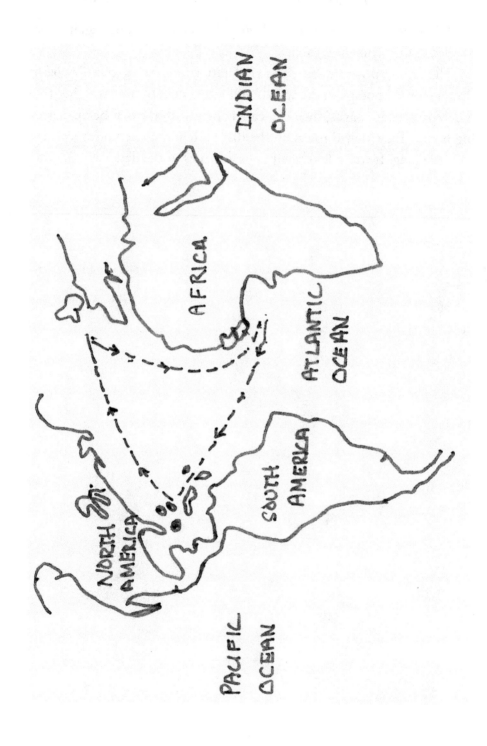

38

5

Sierra Leone 1830

When you betray somebody else, you also betray yourself.
–Isaac Bashevis Singer

Days later, Karmo and Ansa went to the beach at the far end of the bay where the oxalis and dragon spear flowers grew down to the shoreline; Brima's favorite spot near the estuary. They had arranged a picnic with her and some school mates and while waiting, enjoyed the sun and the ocean waves.

"Another ship has come into the bay I see," remarked Ansa. "I wonder why they are not moored at the docks?"

Karmo studied the ship passively. "Perhaps they are waiting their turn. I do not know the ways of shipping, but it appears a difficult life for the crew."

"We are the privileged ones, my brother," exhaled Ansa. "I sometimes wonder about our luck, and feel ashamed that others are suffering."

"Yes," said Karmo, "but instead of feeling shame, can we not find ways to help and support our brothers?" Karmo and Ansa, possessed of the altruism of their youth and privilege, often had such discussions and were again reflecting when Sahr came running out of the forest onto the beach.

"Karmo, Ansa! Come with me! Brima has been hit and run over by a cart in the market square! She may be dying! I will take you to where she is being treated, follow me!" he shouted with a hoarse voice.

Immediately, the two went running after Sahr into the woods, when he abruptly stopped, turned and smiled at them.

"Sahr!" Shouted Karmo, why do you stop? "Take us to Brima!"

Suddenly, there was a rustling in the forest undergrowth and men, sailors with rifles and swords, surrounded them. The two looked at Sahr, perplexed, but it took only a moment for recognition and fear to enter their consciousness.

"Sahr, what have you done?" shouted Ansa, as Karmo, silent, only leveled his eyes at Sahr with a searing contempt.

Sahr grinned arrogantly. "I take care of myself," he said, arms crossed and watching the sailors.

Karmo swung wildly at one of the intruders, knocking one man's tooth out and ripping the skin on his own knuckles. He did not notice the punch to the side, then another and another. Incensed and roaring oaths, still flailing his arms to fend them off, he could not fight so many men. Ansa already lay wasted on the ground. Finally, he was punched hard in the ear, dizzying him into a staggering gait whereupon the men pounced together and tied his hands.

Breathing hard, the sailors slowly approached Sahr. "You're coming too, you black gip!"

Sahr, startled, screamed out, "No! That was not our deal!" He turned and ran into the forest undergrowth followed by the sailors. Karmo and Ansa trembled. Sahr had betrayed them, yet they watched in horror as the drama unfolded. They all heard it. A shot rang out and the sounds, shrieks like a wounded animal emanated from the darkness, followed by a second shot, and silence. The sailors returned from the woods, angry, muddy and wanting nothing more but to get on with their mission. It was clear that Karmo's uneasiness around Sahr was well founded, for Sahr had used his quick wit and cunning to his advantage. He made deals with slave privateers, but this time they turned on him. It was his last deal, one gone so very badly.

"Even Sahr did not deserve that," whispered Ansa.

"It was just!" whispered Karmo, as his world and thoughts turned towards something more inward and isolated.

"Damn you to hell, you worthless dogs! You just lost me money!" yelled a well-dressed man to the sailors as he waded his way from a rowboat, feet from the shore. Mr. Drumple was a financier overseeing this major operation for his investors.

"We couldn't let him get away and reveal our position. He was too close to the road, Mr. Drumple" the Captain offered.

Drumple eyed them angrily, and spat on the ground. "Get on with it then, and bring those two for now," he snarled at the Captain.

Drumple, owl-eyed, and sallow-faced, the owner of the ship and other businesses, did not deign to get his hands dirty, nor would he take passage with this crew. The consortium of businessmen in Western Europe he represented would be loath to give him another chance if they lost most of their investments. Annoyed, but satisfied for now, he left the crossing to the Captain and headed into town to board a finer passenger ship heading for South America.

Karmo and Ansa, already bound and thrown to the ground, regained their bearings. They were still wearing their College uniforms; white cotton suits, blue cravats—their straw hats lost in the melee. Streams of captured men were now gathered and pushed towards smaller boats by sailors armed to the teeth. There was mass confusion, terror and loud, and oh so loud noises of woe. Some few captives tried to jump but were run through by the skewering of swords. Swords were quieter than guns, and they had made enough ruckus on the beach already.

"What do you want with us? We are only students!" Ansa pleaded.

One of the invaders flipped his long rifle upside down and hit him on the side of the head with the butt of his rifle. "Shut your mouth, no talking!" Blood dripped from Ansa's ears, down his chin onto his shirt. He opened his mouth, but remained silent. Nothing like this had ever happened to him before. It was inconceivable.

Karmo tried to move towards Ansa, but a man shouldered him back. He too stayed quiet, trying to size up the situation that made no sense to him at all.

They were rowed alongside the large ship. Once on board, they were shoved face down upon the deck. Karmo dared not look up. All he could see of the sailors were tattoos of pigs and chickens on their feet and ankles before he heard a crack and a searing jolt on the back of his head.[9]

ROAR!

At first it was the dank musky smell; dirt and sweat permeated his nostrils. Then the sounds; moans, wails and tears of men in acute pain, intense distress. His own wounds became slowly apparent to him, tracings of fire coursed and roared through his head, a persistent throbbing in his limbs. Barely opening his eyes, he saw only dim shafts of light coming through wooden slats of whatever confined him. *What happened? Who are these other poor devils around me?* Slowly, his consciousness, which had not completely abandoned him, revealed shreds of memory. *An act of perfidy, most ignoble,* thought Karmo. Darkness again overcame him.

The trip was the very definition of misery. Like the sailors themselves, they were forever wet, clothes drenched with sea water through and through. The best they could do was to wring them out and put them back on. The roll and pitch of the ship was constant. The endless troughs of white water and foam from the sides of the ship looked like graves and delivered a leaden weight of terror into their very bowels. Darkness dropped upon them like a smothering blanket over a bird cage.

Alas however, there would be no rest. Import of enslaved people was outlawed in the United States in 1808. But the market in both North and South America was still strong, too strong to not risk the blockades, pirates and seafaring in general. Privateers found ways to get through British and American patrol ships as it was well worth their trouble. These were not the slave ships of the past, but were brutal in their own right. The captives were under guard as a working crew doing the menial and backbreaking tasks around decks; collecting and throwing out buckets of excrement daily, mopping and scrubbing, scraping and polishing and more. They were beaten because they could be, though not so much as to disable them as they must still be presented as marketable goods at the end of the voyage. Because sundry goods also were being shipped and took up precious space, the Captain opted to store the Africans in a loose packing method of housing to reduce disease and death, offering a better product.[10] It was cold on deck at night and yet could be blazing hot during the day. The constant listing and rocking wrought havoc on the mind and body of those not used to such movement. Below decks the ship was hot and sticky from lack of fresh air, inadequate buckets for excrement and the ever present vomiting. Fetid smells were a curse. The odors stung the nostrils, flowed into the nasal passages, assaulted the soft palate and coated it with a greasy film, followed by an almost immediate churning in the stomach and finally a most relentless wave of cold sweat and vomit of hot, bitter bile. Nausea was almost as debilitating as a beating.

A silent roar brewed within Karmo's being. He could feel it pounding in his head and his heart. He tasted it on his lips, but dared not let it be exposed. He worked to calm his anger and let its energy channel thoughts to a better world, and to summon Brima's spirit.

"How is your wound, my brother? Is it healing?" asked Karmo of Ansa.

"Better, better, but it throbs. I fear this is the least of our troubles, Karmo," answered the philosopher.

Karmo and Ansa were not acquainted with most of the captives, but recognized some of the men from town; Sando, Jahn and Old Okeke. The latter was only about twelve years older than the others, but had the countenance and demeanor of a much older soul. He was having a particularly difficult time with manhandling. The voyage had amazed and changed them all. It was hell but could have been worse as they were part of the working crew instead of being confined below decks for the entire crossing. There were several suicides as men jumped off the ship rather than continue. Others fell and clung desperately to the rails in the midst of storms, others let the rain wash down over them wishing the waves would overcome them. Ansa thought often of jumping overboard for a quicker death but managed to cling to hope that better times and people would prevail. But others did so, taking a last swim with their ancestors, allowing the waters to flow into their mouths and nose to smell and taste the death that would kill them.

Gruel was meager and infested with insects, larvae and rat feces. When a man became too ill to treat, the privateers beheaded him and tossed him overboard. This was intended to terrorize and control the remaining captives as many of the captives believed their dead spirit would never return home without its head.

ROAR!

~

As they approached the Caribbean, a *spouter*, as the crew called the whale man, made a signal to heave to. Captain Job Terry's boat came alongside.[11] Terry climbed up and sprang onto the deck. He and the Captain went to quarters and spoke for hours. Terry was no fan of smugglers and not attenuated to piracy, but on the open sea, he abided by the sailor's code to give information regarding politics, monitoring governments, weather and ascertaining their accurate location. As to location, they may not always agree owing to the limits of their instruments and/or skill in navigating by the stars, but it was always reassuring if their reckonings were close. Fully possessed with the notion that their own mission was the righteous one, they departed on agreeable if not entirely amiable terms.

6

Brima 1830-1831

Though lovers be lost, love shall not. –Dylan Thomas

"But how did this happen?!!" Brima was struggling to speak, tears flowing back into her throat making each breath a choking agony.

"The City Guard believes they were abducted to ships to enslave them. They found Sahr's body shot in the back in the woods. It looked like he had a better chance to escape," said Marai, Brima's childhood friend. "They were probably ambushed as they were waiting for us."

"I do not believe it!"sobbed Brima. "This cannot have happened to Karmo! He is too fast, too strong for them to overcome him."

"Brima, stop! He did not have a chance, they had weapons! If he had tried to fight, he might have been killed like Sahr. We, *we* Brima, might have died because we would have been there had it happened just a few moments later. We heard the gunshots, remember?" said Marai consolingly.

Brima turned to Marai, her voice catching, grabbed her arm and shuddered, "Oh, you are right, Marai!"

Marai added, "Not that it will help Karmo and Ansa, but the authorities said they will put on more patrols to prevent this in the future. They already have a ship off the coast to check for boats without permits."

∼

FOUR MONTHS LATER

"I see that Musa is looking out for you, Brima," said Marai tentatively.

Brima sighed deeply, "Yes. It is the custom. Father Saidu has commended his eldest son to my well-being. He means to take me as his second wife. The engagement ceremony is next week."

"And what do you say?"

"He is a kind man, but I have no inclination towards him. I cannot, but I do not know how to avoid this marriage," she answered with a shaky voice. "I will hold off as long as I can, but unless there is a sign or news of Karmo, my family will comply with expectations. People are gossiping about my condition and single status as if I should be mortified and ashamed at the prospect, Marai."

Entering the town square, the two young women passed through a gauntlet of townspeople, curious and saddened for her sake.

"They turn their eyes from us, Marai," murmured Brima as the two enter the main street in town.

"That is because they do not know what to say, and they know you still suffer," whispered Marai, looking straight ahead. "Say hello, speak to them. If they ask how you are, be truthful. Tell them that you are not well, but thank them for their concern. You will be less isolated with your thoughts, sister."

They paused as Brima cocked her head sideways. "You too, are in a difficult position, Marai. I know your feelings for Musa. Please believe me, I have no part in this pairing, just as he has no inclination towards me. It is a duty for him, an expectation."

Marai felt a cold stone in her throat, emitting only a croaky murmur, "I know. I know. Fate."

Brima continued, "It is like a void in me growing even larger. This void has completely engulfed me. I am lost. I fear I have nothing to hang onto but hope, Marai," said Brima. "Time is so heartless. There is a storm in my heart. It roars with despair, with the cruelty of fate and with fear! I fear ominous clouds are descending upon him. I can barely grasp it still. Will I ever see Karmo again?"

"I think not Brima, but only you can decide when hope has evaporated for you. Your tears have not. We must keep busy. Had not Lord Byron said "the busy have no time for tears?" We still can keep Karmo and Ansa in our hearts, while continuing to live … to the fullest. They certainly would want that for us. They are not likely to return, Brima, but we do not know what fate has waiting for us."

Brima, looking at her friend, exhaling said, "Lord Byron? Please Marai! My eyes turn to no other as my heart stays with Karmo. No, there can be no other, and certainly not his own brother. I cannot just wait here helpless and pitiful."

"It was not my intention to be trite, my sister. I only mean to help and divert your thoughts for a while."

Turning her eyes to the ground, nodding, Brima took gentle hold of Marai's wrist and said hoarsely, "But you are right. It is just that some days, I want to go into the woods and scream … to roar my wounds away! O fate, do not try to do this to me. I will fight you!"

"Then do it, Brima! Do it!" urged Marai. "Send your thoughts, your love, your roars to Karmo! As long as he remains in your heart, you can send him messages through the sky. Love without courage has no future. Fight fate!"

Brima looked at her trembling hands. Was it from fear or rage? Was there a difference?

The women continued their walk through town, trying to look natural so as not invite pity. *My home, my heart, my breath; It is worth living to love you. You are my sky, my heaven. I miss you so much,* she thought to herself. She felt so far away from her past, that it seemed more a story she had read, but she knew it was not and had her bruised soul as a reminder. And yet, she felt disconnected from her present life as well. *"Where do I fit in anymore?"* she wondered.

Returning to her parent's house, a stained, wrinkled letter from far away rested on a side table. Brima shared the contents with her mother. That evening, her mother sold her own gold bracelets to change the course of her daughter's future.

ATLANTIC
OCEAN

←FLORIDA

CARIBBEAN
SEA

MEXICO
CITY

ST. THOMAS

7

The Caribbean 1830

Make the best use of what is in your power
and take the rest as it happens. –Epictetus

Ansa estimated the crossing took about eight weeks until they first saw land, that faint and thin line of earth on the horizon was as if it were dust in his eyes.

The Spaniard, none other than Pedro Blanco, was the ship's captain on this voyage from West Africa to Cuba, one leg of the so-called Middle Passage.[12][13] Some captives were to be offloaded in the Caribbean, some to Brazil, some to America. Captain Blanco hazarded a brief stop in Cuba for supplies and information then continued on to St. Thomas and a cove not far from where the mountains came down to the sea overlooked by the dormant volcano known as Quill. The island of St. Thomas had been a trade port ever since the Europeans made their way there in succession; the Spanish, Dutch, English, then the Danish West India Company. Half the population consisted of African peoples brought here against their will. Pirates from all nations had camped in these coves, and while new slavery had been outlawed by the Danish King in 1754, surreptitious slave trading continued even as the practice was becoming more and more costly. Bribes had to be paid to officials on both sides of the route. Holding times were long as they had to wait for favorable weather and until the port's government cruisers departed to move into deeper waters. This increased costs even more in wages, food and water.

St. Thomas also was where Captain Blanco's favorite wife lived near a garden amongst the caves and jacaranda trees. She was content and at peace there, not having to think of how her life was supported. On clear days she could see Goat Island and Water Island where livestock ran free on pasture land. Lemony morning light streamed through her bedroom windows and the few still existing wild parrots with their vivid reds, greens, and blue plumage called from the trees. Other sailor's wives visited her; theirs, a unique sisterhood, and a world apart from the suffering of others.

~

"Get up Darkies!" the crewman yelled, waving his club. "March!"

There were about 140 Africans left after the ocean voyage. But now they were on land, the dawn breezes were sweet and fresh, and smelled of green.

"Move it!" another shout from their captors, and they commenced a forced march barefoot through a narrow trail, through damp overgrowth with chattering birds, buzzing with mosquitoes and other flying insects. Their school uniforms were long ago shredded and shoes stolen by the crew. Their feet and hands chained-bound in metal cuffs, chafed and scabbed over too many times to remember, and started bleeding again.

"Karmo, my brother, do you think we will live?" asked Ansa.

With that he was knocked to the ground with the butt of a gun, once again. "No talking!" said a captor.

Karmo took this in and watched. Resistance was futile … for now. They would have to bide their time, but he also had grave doubts about escaping anytime soon. *I must stay strong and keep my eyes open,* he thought to himself.

Again, they were on a beach and lined up facing a number of ships anchored out in the bay. Captains were pacing the sands looking over captured Africans who arrived just before them. It was chaotic. The men were being selected by some unclear criteria and were led to different ships. Watching the process, Ansa believed a separation from Karmo was likely because they were captured together and the captors seemed to fear the two could communicate in a language not understood by them. Karmo never let on that he could speak and understand English, let alone French. He allowed them to believe he was simple minded and often played mute. His now rangy body belied his strength and stamina. He prayed quietly to himself that all would be well and thought about what Efendi had taught him.

"Ha! This specimen speaks French and English," shoving Ansa forward. "He'll fetch a good price as a houseman," laughed the privateer Captain.

Now that he was ashore, the Captain was anxious to get to his wife and sloppy about the task at hand even though it was the payoff time for the whole risky undertaking. It was beyond arrogance. It was narcissism. After the most valuable captives' prices were negotiated and settled, he left the haggling to his Second in command and took off down the beach to the east.

"Yeah, I'll take that smart britches," shouted a wild haired lieutenant as he pointed to Ansa. I know a real genteel plantationer in Georgia who is looking just for his type.

Ansa tried to be as stoic as his philosophical nature would allow. He whispered quickly to Karmo, "We will reunite, my brother," before he was jerked away and led to an awaiting ship.

Karmo had no time to answer but nodded to Ansa who looked back at him.

∽

A band of horsemen came riding suddenly out of the eastern sunrise, whooping and hollering, shooting their rifles into the air. It was clear they were celebrating. The Second and crew watched them approach. Karmo took advantage of this distraction; slowly and quietly made backward steps towards the woods. *How was it possible that there were no guards watching the rear line?* he wondered. Slowly, slowly, he moved backwards, crouched below a low canopy of leaves, then buried himself in the wet, sandy soil under ferns and shrubs, leaving only his face above as he continued to watch. These men were too busy getting on with their celebration. They did not see their mission through. *More foolishness,* he thought.

In a matter of two hours they were all gone. Karmo remained hidden until nightfall. He didn't know the peoples of this land; who were friends or who were foes. Hunger was starting to gnaw at him, for as bad and meager the food on ship, it had been almost two days since he had eaten even that. It started to rain, and the warm fresh water was a relief. He thought of Ansa; the artist, the spiritualist, the philosopher. Ansa, who was strong in spirit and expected the good in people. *I hope he does not become too trusting,* thought Karmo.

When he woke, bright orange light and black spidery veins danced on his closed eyelids as he lay back in the morning sun listening to the birds singing their hearts out. The foliage was lush and fragrant with bougainvillea and frangipani flowers, but attracted great swarms of gnats, buzzing and biting insects. He felt stiff and gritty, his stomach gnawing with roars of protest. For two more days Karmo stayed hidden, eating what small insects and lizards that had the misfortune to come near him. It was not pleasant. *Live!* he said repeatedly to himself. Karmo stared at the foliage and the shadowy patterns of light flickering between their leaves. He watched insects moving about their business, traveling from place to place, flying in and out of the lush plantings. He watched hermit and ghost crabs scurry along the beach. "Come to me," he whispered hungrily.

He dreamily observed creatures attending to their lives as nature had intended. *And what of us human beings? What has nature intended for us beyond eating, sleeping and replacing ourselves?* With that thought, in all his misery, he smiled and let his mind wander to Brima, the woman he loved. She, who was strong willed, kind hearted with dancing eyes and flashing teeth. She, who often met him at the bay in a setting similar to this and spent their free time together with food she brought from the local market. They spoke of their days, their futures, their families and how these would be entwined. She was his betrothed, and he loved her achingly. His time progressed with these cherished moments. It was a school mate, Sahr, who ran towards him, brought him the news at their beachy meeting place. *Was she dead? This could not be!* Here, at this new beach he became inconsolable, paralyzed and distraught. He would not, could not leave their beach. Rain started to fall again. No man could be more soaked than he as he looked down a path imagining Brima coming towards him. It was not possible that she was gone. *Just not possible!* His mind was a confused tangle of past and present. Her spirit would always be with him, even as he moved on with this life. He believed the brightness of her eyes, which drove him mad, would light the way through the darkest night. He felt as if her spirit was watching him and that he would be the best man he could be, doing deeds not for her judgment, but for her spirit. She would become his conscience. But the memory, an intrusion, the purity of his dream was defiled, becoming a dark mire as Sahr's betrayal invaded his thoughts. No longer wanting to dwell on Sahr, Karmo closed his eyes, took a deep breath.

The biting sand flies awakened him suddenly from his daydreaming on this foreign beach, and a soft tapping on his face as warm rain dripped again from leaves which concealed him. He allowed himself a deep, grateful breath, and opened his mouth to take in the sweet liquid. Slowly he pulled himself out of the sloppy sand and vegetation, and carefully walked to the beach to bathe himself. In the surf, his stiff limbs groaned with thanks as the warm buoyancy surrounded him. He trudged back under the foliage to consider his situation and next moves.

The sound of voices coming closer broke his reflections. Karmo saw a group of five men approach and wade into the waters to pull out reed baskets in which fish had been trapped. They were laughing and at times kicking playfully at one another. He watched for the half hour the men took to collect fish of all kinds. They spoke a strange mix of Creole with West African phrases. Slowly, he again pulled himself out of the sand and vegetation, stretched his screaming stiff limbs and hunched down to watch and listen more. He judged them to be men of just demeanor, and after a while, he summoned all his courage and stood upright to become visible to the fishermen, a risk which proved fortuitous.

They saw him immediately, one of them pointing to him alerting the others. They approached cautiously, poked at him and circled him. Karmo stood motionless, moving only his eyes as they examined this stranger with his scars and ligature marks on his hands, cuffs on his ankles. They seemed to understand from where he had come as they had often surreptitiously watched the human transactions on the beach. Karmo wondered how it was they were not captured and themselves sold.

Presently, one of them spoke. Karmo recognized some Spanish words as well as West African. He spoke back, trying to make them realize he was no threat and spoke his name.

At first the fisherman just stared hard at him, then the speaker nodded and smiled. Through gestures, words, some familiar, some not, Karmo determined they would help him. They built a fire and cooked fish which they shared with Karmo. The sensation of good food in this belly made him at first thankful, then ecstatic, then he vomited.

"Too much!" they hooted and laughed.

Later that evening, the fishermen took him to their village where a smith hammered off his cuffs. They took him into a small shack where he was alone with a straw mattress and a warm blanket. For the first time in weeks, Karmo rested without having to wonder if he would be alive or dead in the morning. He was not sure he cared. He was sick, wounded and perhaps dying anyway. He thought of his family whom he desperately missed; his brothers, his widowed father, and of course Brima.

The next morning, Karmo slowly opened his eyes, feeling weak, he struggled to reconcile his surroundings. *I get another day,* he thought to himself. The fishermen brought a healer to him. He was given tea made from silk tree leaves. A tamarind tree poultice was spread over his body to relieve the fever and pain of insect bites and deep scrapes of needles, thorns and branches that plagued him when he was in hiding. They bandaged his wounds and gave him fish soup and dark bread.

Over the next few weeks he ascertained the villagers maintained their freedom more due to the relative isolation of their island and their vigilance towards the slave traders. The traders needed a place to get fresh water and a few provisions, so a relationship was developed in exchange for that peace. But still, they remained alert and they were well armed.

They shared with Karmo survival skills, how they did reconnaissance, where the best places for lookouts were and the best places for ambushes if need be. There was a waterfall nearby, good for swimming and which led to a marshy area where herons were abundant. They showed him ways to be concealed in the marsh, to catch tiny fish and spend the night safely covered with mud to avoid insect bites.

He was taken into town by way of the harbor. On the way, the fishermen explained that there had been a terrible hurricane weeks before and many buildings were still in bad shape. Ships were lodged high in the hills, tossed by winds and rising tides. Dead animals still were strewn about, their twisted corpses wrapped around trees, bloated, stinking and attacked by buzzing flies. Flies! Annoying, buzzy things! Why does nature tolerate them? His mind drifted; flies landed on anything looking for food to exist for the short life gifted them. They lay their eggs in food, carcasses, whatever can sustain their maggot off-spring who, in turn, digest away the waste. They always managed to survive disasters! *I suppose we need these scrubbers,* thought Karmo as he slapped a biting mosquito from his arm. "But why do we need YOU!"

The village, however, surprised him. This was a place not unlike his home. Churches, bookshops, meeting halls, a place to post mail and a town square for purchasing food and goods were all here! But he was warned to avoid the omnipresent underbelly of criminality, for while there was generally peace and civil equality, it was not consistently observed.

"Maybe in another hundred years," his companion stated, shrugging. "Maybe then no one need worry about safety in their own land."

∽

After several months Karmo had recovered and felt the need to move on. He felt lost as to his future, but also driven to venture beyond the island. He felt an obligation to find Ansa, the man he looked upon as a brother. The villagers helped him build a small boat, and a couple of them joined him to take him to the land the Spanish named "Florida" before ceding it to the Americans. A beautiful and treacherous land they told him, filled with horrific water beasts and snakes, oppressive steamy heat and more biting insects. The Florida Native peoples continued to defend their land against invaders from the north as they did against the Spanish before them. They may or may not accept him, the fishermen warned.

But Karmo was undeterred and dark thoughts intruded to whisper, *What does it matter where I die. I will move on until I find my resting place. Brima would want me to do so.* He smiled to himself slightly and thought Ansa would likely expound that this is human nature; to socialize and become a community for mutual benefit. "Ansa," he said aloud and smiled. He had to keep his promise to find Ansa.

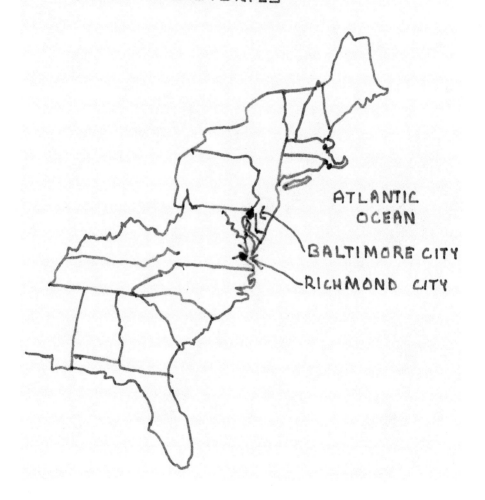

1830's U.S.A. EASTERN STATES
AND TERRITORIES

ATLANTIC
OCEAN

BALTIMORE CITY

RICHMOND CITY

8

Ansa in Virginia 1830

You cannot change someone who doesn't see an issue in their actions.
–Unknown

Ansa, Sando, Jahn and Old Okeke were taken together to a small ship anchored in the bay. They were thrown unceremoniously into the hold, damp and dark from the start. There were fewer captives now, chained amongst crates and barrels of goods which Sando had heard on the beach were bound for Georgia.

"They are not taking us to the Georgia land," Old Okeke whispered to the others as he peered through a hole in the hatch door to the upper deck where crewmen were gathering. "They speak now of a land called "Ginny."

Sando and Jahn looked at each other, dulled by beatings and the consequent sense of futility. "What does it matter?" offered Sando. "I only want to escape first chance I get. Certainly there must be men of honor who will help right this atrocity!"

"Careful, Sando, we do not know what type of peoples we will meet here," said Ansa. "It seems the inhabitants think nothing of us and that this is ordinary business. I witnessed similar business in the south of our own homeland. Perhaps we should be more like Karmo and keep our mouths shut and eyes open until we better know our surroundings."

Sando took a deep breath and cast his eyes downward. "I cannot lose hope. To do so will be death."

"Amen, my brother," said Jahn.

Another week the men endured the rocking, humid and dark hold. They were not allowed above decks to work as before. The poor food they got was riddled with moving insects and larvae, but it warded off the pang of hunger and thirst.

"Wake up blackie! Ansa was kicked in the side by a captor. The white man had a scraggly beard, missing teeth and was soaked in his own sweat, as were all the crew. He was a miserable soul, poor in birth and spirit and so very young.

"Wake up, you scum and get moving!" he bellowed again.

The wharf was bustling with people of all kinds, men in their finery, women selling vegetables, gloves, hats and scarves, livery men and sailors abounded. The smell of tobacco leaves in bulk and spices from across the oceans wafted through the air. He saw two men pour a line of gunpowder on the dock, throw a bit of rum on to it and watch it light in a blaze. The men shook hands at the proofing. It was noisy, humid and oppressive. The sky was bright, blinding their eyes. Buildings were red brick with some wooden decoration and porches, but unwelcoming.

Ansa and the others were led in chains through the streets to the main Virginia market in Richmond. There they stood, heads hung low in humiliation, while white men inspected their whipped, bruised and naked bodies in full public view, and made money bids on them. Before the bidding, Ansa was held back. An earlier deal had been struck for him through contacts with Virginia planter gentry. Ansa was to be sold to a plantationer as a houseman and secret tutor in French and history to the master's children. The new master did not want other whites knowing about Ansa's knowledge as it was not legal to teach an enslaved person to read, but mostly to avoid embarrassment should Ansa's education be superior to his own.

The bidding ordeal took quite a while, and Ansa let his mind wander as he was wont to do. *What is it that makes a man think he is better than someone he does not even know? Surely he is not born that way, surely only through continuous indoctrination is it possible to change a man's nature,* Ansa's disposition was to expect the best of people, but he was not naïve and knew there was evil about. His experience in England and presence in this place confirmed it. It confounded his very nature of thought as he firmly believed it need not be this way. *What to do? This young man who kicked me; he appeared to be of a miserable lot, himself deprived and abused, but instead of showing mercy or compassion, he turned his pain on to others.* His musings were interrupted suddenly as he was pulled up onto the auction block. Surprised, as he had overheard the side deal for his person, he took a moment to survey the crowd before being pulled back down from the block. As he was led away the crowd clawed at him from both sides, hooted, hissed and cursed. He became dizzy at the vehemence with which these people screamed at him. He saw contempt in their eyes, their faces. He stunk, was unkempt after the voyage, but what had he done to deserve this?

"Sold!" screamed the slave master, causing Ansa to look back at the block. Sando and Jahn both were going to one of the local farms for field work. Old Okeke was sold "down the river" which meant he was first going west, then down the Mississippi to work in cotton or rice. Each made a furtive glance at the others, and Ansa closed his eyes, whispering, "stay strong my brothers."

~

RICHMOND, VIRGINIA 1830

Ansa would stay in Richmond. His master's name was Jacobson, and while perhaps a bit more careful with his human possessions, possessions they were. Slavery was not just a business to him, it was economics, pure and simple. He and his family lived a comfortable life outside of Richmond where he was to take Ansa. A businessman by trade, he inherited his land from his father. He owned the main plantation and several smaller farms. With free labor, keeping the land as a working plantation was practical and profitable, though he loathed dealing with foremen and others upon whom he depended to actually run the day to day operations. He saw them as uneducated brutes, bumpkins and louts who would just as soon lie and steal from him if he did not have paid spies … and they all knew of the spies, but not who they were. Suspicion ran rampant and trust was almost unknown. Still, they got the work done through their own brutality and manipulation. Jacobson thought this was shrewd, and many owners followed the model, but it sucked the soul from all involved.

Upon arrival, Mrs. Jacobson took appraisal of Ansa, looking him up and down. Henrietta, her black servant was by her side.

"Henrietta, get this wretch some presentable clothes! Take some of Master Jacobson's castoffs from the sewing room. And make sure he gets a bath! He smells ghastly!" she said with her nose pinched and pointed to the ceiling. "I can't believe Master Jacobson bought this putrid bag of bones to come within an inch of our children!"

Henrietta was a large woman with high cheekbones and wide hips. She was as dark as tar and had eyes that flashed when not in the presence of the family. Her voice was hauntingly resonant and her calmness belied her station in life. She had learned to adapt and temper her impulses in the service of survival.

"Yes'm," murmured Henrietta. She was used to the Jacobson's aversions of dealing with the unclean as the mistress of the house believed it equated with poor moral character. Never mind that they were allotted little water for bathing, no soap and only two changes of clothes annually; one for work and one for inspections by visitors.

Henrietta took Ansa to the barn to bathe. Inside, the only light was from the large double doors at both ends of the building. Seeing that he would be a houseman, he got special amenities. She pointed to a vacant stall with a wash bowl and threw some clean rags to him. "Yo know what soap is, nappy?" she said abruptly.

"Indeed I do Ma'am, and I thank you for your ministrations," Ansa replied purposely in his most crisp and correct British accent.

Henrietta's eyes popped, "Law haf mercy! You'n edgy-cated blackie? You bes not let anyone else know. They'd beat yo hide and knock yo teef out!"

"The Master is well aware, Miz Henrietta," Ansa replied looking her straight in the eye. "It is how I came to be sent here. I am to tutor his children."

"Well don' yo let any o'da field hands or house slaves know neither, dey report yo ta overseer or da law, and Massuh Jacobson won't be of any help cuz they'd be savin they own selves," she whispered. "Yo already spillt nuff beans wif me. And yo bes not look any white man or woman in da eye neitha, or dey's slap yo 'long side odda haid or worse!" Henrietta warned.

She took him to a small room in the basement. "Dis here's yo room an consider yo'self lucky," she said.

"Indeed, I do," Ansa stated as he looked at her nodding. The room had a rough bed frame, sack mattress and a worn blanket, a stool and wash basin, some hooks on the wall.

"We use-aly stuff grasses or whatever we can find into dis heer sack sleeve," she said. Jist shake out de bugs from time ta time. Water is from de small pump in back. Don' yo goin' use de big'un, dat belongs ta Massuh an fambly."

"Thank you Miz Henrietta."

She looked back at him and tilted her head sideways, then turned with a "Hummpf" mumbling to herself.

After a thorough scrubbing, Ansa made his way to the kitchen, hesitated and peered in. He saw Henrietta at the table, entered the kitchen casting his eyes about.

"Well bless mah soul, wot's wrong wif me! Yo stomach's a rumbling, come sit wif me!" she said in a melodious voice. She had softened her demeanor somewhat and offered him some food for which he was grateful.

"You talk mighty purty Mr. Ansa. Do dey all talk like you do where yo come from?" asked Henrietta.

"Indeed, Madam," he answered. "There are many languages spoken from where I come. Most of us speak several of them. I must say yours is quite unique and has a most charming quality. Your voice is quite unusual, if I may be so bold."

A velvety film of perspiration formed on her cheeks and her lips reddened, Henrietta was blushing as she pulled down her high collar ever so slightly revealing a horizontal scar mid-way across her throat. "Got dis heer scar when my throat was cut years ago when I was just a young'un. Frens of massuh broke in my mama and papa's house an commenced ta grabbing at my mama and me. My papa jumped up on 'em an dey clubbed him daid," she said, her eyes tearing even after so many decades. "But deys not gonna get me down! No suh, my parens, my gran-parens are all buried somewheres on dis land! I was born heer an I reckon I'll be buried heer too! This heer is my land!"

Ansa was appalled with Henrietta's story and found her resolve re-markable.

～

At the plantation, Ansa acquired a small whittling knife. He spent whatever downtime he had carving talismans of hope and belonging. The small round discs fit in the palm of a child's hand. He burnished them with another piece of wood and gave them to the enslaved as he tried to share a message of hope and compassion.

It wasn't long before he and Henrietta entered into a survival rela-tionship, one of mutual trust and respect. For as educated as Ansa was, he was ignorant of the ways of this new land. He would tell her stories about faraway lands and peoples and a place where black people were not enslaved, but just as respected as anyone else. Ansa offered, but Henri-etta was afraid to learn to read and write. The gentry had a gut fear of blacks learning to read and write lest they start to think for themselves and mount an insurrection. Indeed, many whites lived in constant fear of being murdered in the night by their slaves and often retaliated in some of the most heinous ways for the smallest infractions. Keeping them ignorant was how the white man could enslave others, they even kept them ignorant of their age. Oh, but the poor were just as deviant as the rich, and learned to use those even more disadvantaged for their own furtherance. Likewise, it was in the best interest of the elite whites to keep poor whites ignorant so they could be manipulated to go to war and work the menial jobs from which the rich continued to profit. Poor men who didn't own land could not vote and so had no say into the laws that the rich passed in their own favor. Many poor were enthralled with the elites' education and cleverness, and accepted that riches were their due. Poverty was for the uneducated and therefore deserved.

～

Several nights later, the Jacobson's hosted a dinner party. The guests were the Whitcombs and Honeycutts, well to do planters from neighboring plantations. They all took turns hosting one another at least monthly to exchange news, pleasantries, and management updates.

The topic came around to England and their tariffs.

"Oh yes!" exclaimed Mrs. Whitcomb. "I remember my grandfather speaking of his ancestors here in Virginia. They fought so bravely for their freedom from that tyrant. Imagine, being enslaved to the King! No one should be forced to live like that!" she admonished, oblivious to her servants.

"Yes, yes, dear. We all know our history. But in these times there are some few who think we are hypocrites and so do these darkies here!" he laughed. "As if they were even men! Those creatures!" snorted Mr. Whitcomb, his big belly bouncing up and down as he almost snorted his wine.

"They have us outnumbered, and some are starting to grumble. I heard of uprisings where they killed their masters and families! We'll catch them, of course, and there will be no mercy, but it is worrisome," said Mr. Honeycutt.

Mrs. Whitcomb held her hand up to her bosom, clutching her pearls and announced, "Well! I just don't know what more those creatures could even want. We give them food and shelter. They get new clothes twice a year. Of course they must work for it all!" Her small mind was so limited by the absolute certainty that there was nothing worth knowing beyond her own experience. "Can't we just send some of those trashy whites to put down the rebellions?"

Mrs. Honeycutt was an observant woman; nevertheless, her experience went little afar plantation life as well. "I saw our milk cow Bessy bawl after her yearling went gone for slaughter. Wonder if when those negroes carry on about their babies being sold off, if it isn't something like that?" she opined looking to her husband.

Mr. Honeycutt rolled his eyes and whispered to her, "Dear, you should not pay any mind to my business and instead look to the running of the household."

~

Jake Jacobson, Henrieta's husband was a rare trusted slave to the family, and as such, was an errand runner from the plantation to the outer farms. He carried a pass signed by the Master whenever he went off the plantation proper to protect him should he be stopped by any traveling white man.

"The further from the plantation's farms, the more brutal the treatment of errant slaves," he shared with Henrietta. He also would share stories with Ansa about the goings on outside the Big House and the farms beyond. In turn, Ansa taught Jake the alphabet, how to write his name and later, two or three letter words. But neither told Henrietta, as the fewer people who knew about it, the safer for all concerned. There were spies everywhere, both enslaved and white. One dared not ever say anything but the most positive things about one's master, for the report of a loose, negative word could result in a flesh-slicing whipping or being sold away, family or none.

Ansa learned the plantation was like a small village back home. But the jobs were all done by the enslaved people's labor, each to their best fit. There were shoe cobblers, menders, weavers, a blacksmith, cartwrights and general workers who took grain to the mill for grinding flour. A head gardener with his crew tended the vegetable and flower gardens and fruit trees. Even young children had their jobs in the kitchen, or pulling weeds, or running to fetch birds killed by the overseer's men who just shot above their little heads. By age 10, they were as likely to go off to the tobacco or hemp fields.

In the dirt yard behind the kitchen were several tall posts, not the usual height for hitching horses or mules. Upon closer inspection though, Ansa noticed umber clots of matter stuck to the posts.

"Dem da whippin' posts," whispered Henrietta as she approached him from her spot under the trees where she had been scaling fish for dinner. "Don' linger around dere, boss man might get some idea to show yo how dey work."

Ansa jerked his head up when he heard her voice and backed away. He had heard of the whipping, but thankfully had not yet witnessed them. Indeed, his first day he saw fingers get sliced off of one man for what infraction he knew not. This atrocity was followed by clubbing the man to death. It made him shudder and wonder what type of land this was that one man could do this to another. He became wary and appreciated Henrietta and Jake's friendship even more.

Ansa was ashamed that his worrying was self-indulgent after seeing the lot cast upon others. He did his best to help Jake and wondered how he might enlighten the master. He believed he had the inner strength to know when to bend, yield and give way to accommodate.

~

NOVEMBER 1831

"Ansa! Get ta Massuh's study, he wants yo now!" called Henrietta.

"On my way Hennie," he smiled at her. They had become quite comfortable with each other.

"And don' you be cawlin me Hennie!" but she blushed and smiled.

As he entered Master Jacobson's study, Ansa thought how fortunate he was to be allowed to keep his own name. Identity was another thing often stripped away from the enslaved. He noted, slave babies were named by the Master and given their surname to connote property. Ansa, stopped and stood in front of the large carved hickory desk piled with journals, ledgers and newspapers. "Sir" he said with a short bow of the head.

"Good, you're here. I need to travel to Baltimore to conduct business and you will accompany me. You will be in your own quarters to review documents during the day. We'll discuss them in the evening. We leave in two days. Pack your best for a week, you need to be presentable. I'll be calling you my manservant."

"Yes, Master," replied Ansa. Ansa was stunned, frightened and elated at the same time. He went back to his small room and sat down placing his head in his hands, breathing hard. The room swirled as he tried to take this in. The enslaved do not leave the plantations. The enslaved do not see people from other regions let alone another state. Ansa was not sure of the geography but knew from Jacobson's cast off newspapers that Baltimore was north and closer to free states. He wondered if there was overlap. He had to learn more about those lands.

The carriage trip was long and wearying. The narrow, dusty roads were lined with dormant tobacco fields and an occasional outcropping of trees such as red bud and chestnut oaks. They spent one night in a small town where Ansa slept in the stall with the horses. *At least it is indoors,* he thought. Calmed by the gentle sound of rain outside, his mind started wandering again, before he spied a small knife near a wood pile and started carving.

A black man, soaked to the skin, ran into the barn and was at first startled to see Ansa, but regained himself somewhat. His face ashen, hands shaking. He looked beyond hopeless as he fell to his knees, head to the ground, his whole body started to quiver.

"What is it, my brother?" asked Ansa as he moved closer and placed his arm around the distraught man's shoulder.

"Dey's go'in ta hang im! Dey's go'in ta hang im! I heerd it jest now in da garten. Da o'r-seer tod da gart-ner."

"Who are they going to hang?" asked Ansa, also shaken. "Not one of the gardeners, it could not be?"

"Naw suh," said the man. It's Nat Turner, da preacher![14] Dey's don' caught im, already kilt mos all his men, but he 'scaped so den dey took it out on slaves whot had nut'un to do wit da fight'n; started lynchin'em jesta flush 'im out. Wimmin and chillin, too!"

"The fighting, my brother?" asked Ansa, shakened.

"Da revolt," The man whispered. "Nat preached dat negroes ain't meant ta be slaves an' treated so bad. He said we oughtta rise up an' take whot is rightly ours so dat we can be free, an' dat de massuhs should die for it. He an' his gang killt bout 30 white folks, I heerd; hacked em ta death! He got away, but den dey got im, dey got im!" and the distraught personage heaved and heaved with burning tears streaming, his face on the ground.

Ansa held on to the hapless man, reflecting on this. Was it true that blacks would think about revolting, to fight the wrongs done to them? How could they win? He thought of the discussions he had with Karmo. Karmo, who studied war and insurrection. Yes, Karmo would fight, and fight to the death if need be, but he would have a plan for after the fight. Ansa slept fitfully that night. When morning broke, a bit of sun showed through the roof slats of the horse barn. Birds sang to each other even this time of year as if nothing had changed, for in their lives, nothing had. Ansa did not know of Nat Turner, and wondered about his strategy. *Did he have a plan for after the massacres? Did he think the whites would just let them all go free? Did he think he could kill them all?* He did not know, perhaps there was a plan, but reflected that ideas conceived in error are just as real as things conceived by reason and necessity, and this idea proved fatal.

This incitement to violence, was there any profit from it? Perhaps this justified even harsher treatment. For the upper classes of people in this land seemed to carefully and systematically urge on disaffection by telling certain classes, blacks and lower class whites, that their life would be better if only certain of their kind behaved, and blamed the outliers for the harsh treatment the rest of their class received, such that they, the lower classes would turn on each other as it is easier to look down than to look up. The result then was for the upper classes to lament and plead innocent when the lower classes eventually did turn on them.

9

Baltimore, Fall 1831

A slaveholder's profession of Christianity is a palpable imposture ....
I look upon it as the climax of all misnomers, the boldest of all frauds,
and the grossest of all libels. –Frederick Douglass.

The plan was to stay for a week. Master Jacobson wrote a pass for Ansa so that he could run errands freely about town without fear of being detained. The city was large by any standard with which Ansa was familiar. It was said to have 81,000 inhabitants, and had architecture new to Ansa. He saw a number of black folk dressed as variedly as white; as workmen, businessmen, shopkeepers. It was all quite intriguing. They were called Freemen, he learned.

The city of Baltimore dominated the flour trade. Its milling depended on steam power which allowed for fierce competition with New York. Cash and short credits were the norm in business relations. This was an industrial town of railroads and commerce. *So noisy!* thought Ansa.

Business had mostly stabilized after President Adams placed a tariff on imported goods a few years earlier. The British had been flooding manufacturing markets with goods with artificially low prices. This antagonized the Southerners who could not abide price hikes for raw materials. It put a crimp in American industry at all levels. Even with the peculiar business of slavery, free labor in the south, it contributed to a rift between the northern and southern states.

Master Jacobson and Ansa drove out to the Smith Dock to meet up with a businessman and discuss materials he was sending by ship to Bowley's Wharf, not far from there. The business man greeted him and showed him into an office in one of the dock buildings. Both men had stock in the Bank of Maryland and generally benefited, but there had been rumblings about the First Bank of the U.S. trying to take over. This was to be a major part of the discussions.

The docksides were just as bustling, loud and dirty as in Richmond, but Ansa saw no selling platforms for slaves, even though this was a slave state. *Perhaps that business occurred on other days of the week,* he thought. Large warehouses made of brick lined the docks, and small wooden stands for general goods were relegated off to the side and back of the buildings. The main streets were cobbled with stone, but there were plenty of dirt side streets for carriages to splash mud upon pedestrians if they weren't careful. This was a city of much civil unrest, downtown fights, torching homes of prominent people. He couldn't quite deduce the exact cause of such goings on, but clearly there was growing upheaval.

Master Jacobson came out of the office with a sour look on his face and had a nearby slave hail a carriage cab in which he and Ansa went to the hotel. Ansa was assigned a storage room in the attic which was the hotelier's favor to Master Jacobson. Ansa was allowed to wait around in the front lobby that evening while Master Jacobson was at a dinner meeting. He gathered from the first few documents he had read in the afternoon that the meeting was about the raw goods being shipped to Baltimore, prices falling and still some banking problems.

Through cautious listening and overhearing discussions in the lobby, a resident named Henley had designated in his will that all his enslaved people would be freed upon his death. This was called manumission. No one was saying why this would happen, and some men in the lobby were clearly against it. It struck Ansa that this country was not as simple and ruthless as he first experienced, nevertheless, he had witnessed some of the most heinous of behaviors when he has first dragged upon this land.

The next day, after breakfast, Ansa was in front of the hotel at the ready to hail a carriage cab for Master Jacobson and himself when directed. There was one additional, more formal meeting to attend, but this time he was to stay outside and wait until summoned. It was cold and raining, generally miserable, but at least there was an awning under which he could wait as the rain dripped around him. While waiting, a young mulatto boy about 13 years of age, cleanly and neatly dressed, ran up and jumped onto the hotel's stoop. He peered into the hotel lobby and let out a deep breath. "I made it in time!" he said.

Ansa looked at him, then into the lobby. "You are waiting for your master, young man?"

"Yes, no, I mean yes, Sir. Master Auld is my master but they treat me well, not like they treat other slaves.

Ansa nodded. They stood there quietly under the awning watching the goings on in the street. Ansa spied a small book peeking out of the young man's coat pocket. "You read, son?"

"Yes, Sir. The Missus taught me my ABCs and small words until the Master told her to stop because it would ruin me" he said politely. "But I kept at it on my own."

"Is that so?" said Ansa curiously. "Have you always lived here in Baltimore City?"

"No, Sir. I'm from Tuckahoe, some ways from here, but I was sent to Baltimore about five years ago. I don't know why, but it surely is a better place. I work for the Master and Missus Auld in their house, far and away better than any field work, though I dare not speak any further on that topic," the young man said.

"Yes, I understand. What's your name son?" asked Ansa.

"Frederick, Sir. Frederick Douglass," the young man stated.[15]

"Nice to meet you, Mr. Douglass. I am Ansa Kabbah," and Ansa tilted and bowed his head to the young Frederick.

The young man smiled shyly and bowed his head to the elder gentleman.

"So tell me, Frederick, why so much disaffection around these parts?"

"Well Sir, there are many white people here who are against slavery and want it abolished. Some others want it done away with, but slowly, and of course, others not at all. There are other arguments about business matters, mostly banking things, but I don't rightly know about all that."

"Hmm, I see. Thank you, son. Also, I have heard the word manumission? Can you enlighten me as to the meaning?" asked Ansa

"Manumission, Sir?"

"Yes, that's what it's called when a holder of enslaved people sets them free, is it not? But tell me more if you can. I am new to these parts," asked Ansa.

"Yes, Sir. Sometimes that works, but sometimes it doesn't because the slaves aren't always listed by name, and so other family members can argue who was to be free and who was not. But there are a lot of free black persons here by this, what you called, manumission or they managed to buy their freedom. Some went back to Africa, to a place called Liberia," the young man stated. "Some are working in the mills or the railroads. They live in their own quarters at the edge of town mostly. I wonder if we might not all become free and live life as anyone else, someday. It seems only right, don't you think, Sir? I would very much want to be part of that," stated the young Frederick quietly and thoughtfully.

"Yes, son, but I think it will be a difficult endeavor, for men who are isolated from outside thought, will fight tooth and nail not to be dissuaded from their own beliefs despite facts or morality. Tread carefully, but keep to your convictions. It seems you are not alone in them," answered Ansa.

"The Aulds allow me some contentment, but it only makes me want more freedom. No, I will not settle for contentment," whispered Frederick, eyes closed and looking upwards towards the sky.

Ansa closed his eyes and looked up as well.

～

In a moment, Master Hugh Auld stepped out of the hotel with a large cigar in his mouth. "Fred, fetch us a carriage" he mumbled. He spit slimy brown juice onto the wooden stoop, glanced towards Ansa with a curious look, but said nothing.

"Yes Sir, Master Auld" said Frederick with a nod to Ansa as he ran off down the street to hail a carriage. Slave and Master departed subsequently.

Ansa remained standing in front of the hotel reflecting; *what a remarkable young man.* He looked up into the skies as it had stopped raining. "Keep him safe" he whispered as he fingered a wooden talisman in his pocket.

"Come Ansa!" It was Master Jacobson, scowling and sour as he had been all day.

"Shall I hail a carriage, Sir?"

"No need, I just want some fresh air! Damn bankers, and even more damned lobbyists!" he swore.

Ansa followed Master Jacobson discreetly behind as the older man stomped down the cobble stone streets muttering to himself. He was at such a disadvantage at the moment, having only a little idea as to what was troubling Jacobson, but he waited patiently. The Master would let him in on whatever was going on in due time during their briefing sessions.

The state of Maryland was less dependent on agriculture than Virginia and points south due to industrial advances. Baltimore was a cosmopolitan city for the times. It had a Jewish population early on from its backwater port days. Classic Swedish architecture was notable. There were craftsmen of all types including silversmiths, blacksmiths, cabinet makers, coopers, bricklayers and on and on. Here there were even Trader and Ordinary licenses to obtain and be listed. *Yet another world within the same country,* thought Ansa. He had the luxury to walk about the city, though he was always on alert lest he cross some imaginary line of behavior or being. An advertisement pasted on a corner building got his attention. He walked towards it to get a better read. Minstrel was a new word for him, a new concept. A man named T. D. Rice, a singer, dancer had blacked his face with charcoal to entertain others under the name of "Jim Crow." Ansa was puzzled, *Why would someone pretend to be black, and why was this entertainment?* This indeed was another world.[16]

Later that evening Jacobsen was reviewing newspapers and shoved some towards Ansa. "What the hell do you make of *this*! The world is falling apart!"

Ansa took a look. "The news is old Sir, almost a year."

"Yes, yes, I know, but see here!" He slapped the pages on the desk. "What happens in Europe can spread to over here! There's revolution in Russia *and* in France. The only good thing is that Russia is so busy fighting the Polish and their own people that they can't control their trade rights out west on the Pacific coast. Can't you feel it! The pulse? History is still happening over there. Here, it's still quiet. We can at least take advantage for now. It's all about advantage! We can tell others it's our God given right, but it's an *advantage*!!"

Ansa was a bit perplexed. Was Master Jacobson angry or proud or both? The advantage was not his, but for people of his own kind. Perhaps that was enough to soothe the worry.

"Never mind about this, I have more immediate concerns. The tariffs on goods from England are hurting my business. Jackson is so damn busy moving Indians around, he's not paying attention to the banks![17] Mine is failing and I am losing shares. I'm going to have to sell a few assets, which includes you Ansa," he said, eyeing Ansa for a reaction. "Nothing personal, just that you will fetch a better price than any of the other darkies," he added. "You are an extravagance to me, and of quite some value to certain others. I was discrete in peddling you and your attributes to find the right buyer, and found a good one."

Ansa only bowed his head to Master Jacobson. "As you wish," he stated.

"We'll discuss it in the morning after I've met with the potential buyer I have in mind. Be ready by 7 am."

"Sir." Ansa bowed and left the room.

Late evening, in his own room, Ansa thought hard about his lot. Master Jacobson had been good to him compared to other masters he heard about. He obviously had the man's trust, and now needs to be given up and sold to help stave off financial difficulty. *What do I owe this man who essentially saved me from being sold down the river to be used up, tortured and left for dead in the cotton fields? What is the requirement for loyalty, and what will happen to Henrietta and the others should his business suffer?* he wondered. His choices were limited, he felt betrayed and a choking feeling came over him. *What is my responsibility?* He thought of

Karmo and their talks in happier days, then he packed his small bag and quietly left the hotel.

There was a meeting house on Lovely Lane, behind which was a small out building, a light burning within. Coming closer, Ansa looked about, and seeing no one, stepped out of the shadow and up to the door, heavy for such a small abode. He knocked three times and waited, terrified. The rain had started again, and he felt cold and miserable. The door slowly opened only a crack and a voice from within whispered, "What will you?"

"Liberty," Ansa whispered back.

A hand grabbed him by the arm and pulled him inside quickly. A large man dressed as in simple woolens with a watch cap covering his head stood before him. Walked to the stove and offered Ansa a steaming cup of tea. "Forgive the manhandling, son, we must be careful not to be discovered."

Several days later, Ansa was again on a ship on rolling seas, his nausea overtaking him from time to time, the trip tense and surreptitious, but his limbs were not bound. And he had been given edible sustenance. Lying on his mattress he watched as the moonlight crept stealthily over his body, and he let himself relax a fraction. The address was memorized as well as the code words. He was going north to a place called Mattapoisett.

U.S.A. GULF STATES, FLORIDA, AND ISLANDS

ATLANTIC OCEAN

FLORIDA

GULF OF MEXICO

ST. THOMAS ISLAND

CARIBBEAN SEA

10

Karmo in Florida 1831-32

Associate yourself with men of good quality if you esteem your own reputation, for 'tis better to be alone than in bad company.
—George Washington

The sea journey from the island was long but uneventful, even peaceful as the camaraderie of others working as one made the tasks easier and meaningful. The men skillfully made their way from island to island before sighting the massive land known as Florida. Karmo's state of mind began to shift perceptively. He experienced an esprit de corps and felt it overtake him. And while he had studied warrior culture with Efendi, the time had had its limits being only with one, however wise, person.

The men pulled up their paddles and let the pole man direct their small boat into a tree lined cove, before sliding onto the sandy beach. They stepped out into the warm, clear water, dragging the boat onto land. "We will gather up some food and water and stay the night with you, Karmo," said one of the men. "We will show you the path, but we must go back tomorrow."

Karmo was grateful and not a little anxious. "You have been good to me. I do not know how to repay you."

"Live a just life, Karmo," the man answered.

～

From the Florida coast, Karmo wound his way to one of the few black men's forts not destroyed during the First Seminole War.[18] There he found former enslaved peoples, escapees, Natives and even a few

Freemen; black peoples freed by the Spanish. They survived by aligning themselves with the Seminole and Creek Natives both for protection and community to manage a thriving trade system and farms. Most of the Creeks had already been forced out of Florida by the state of Georgia and the U.S. government through false treaties and promises, and when that didn't work, by murder. Life was uncertain as the invaders from the north persisted in expanding their territory for business and profit. Karmo stayed at the fort for several months finding work as a laborer at a gristmill on a small farm owned by one of the black Seminoles. He became contemplative about his life's journey and thought about how things might have been different with Brima. Alas, he was no dreamer, but a realist and endeavored to make peace with himself and his new life. But there was to be no peace as there were continued skirmishes and raids from the northern invaders and from the U.S. Forts on Florida's western border, particularly in his area along the Withlacoochee River.

The American forts often served dual purposes; one to house soldiers, the other as a trading post. Karmo visited the white fort for trade. He carefully approached the wide, wooden gates; sentries posted on either side. They searched him and his goods for weapons, eyed him up and down and let him enter. Inside he went straight to the trade area. It was an open air concern with tables filled with all varieties of everyday needs, harnesses, rope, pots, pans, farm implements and food staples. It was covered by a strong looking shed roof. Nearby, women were rendering tallow for making soap and candles. Farther to the east side of the fort, oxen were driven around a mill stone where grain was ground into flour. It reminded him a bit of home. Underneath the shed roof were ten or twelve men and women of all stripes looking over the offerings for the day. He listened carefully to conversations and found them to be quiet, thoughtful, non-provocative.

"What can I do for you young fella?" asked the proprietor, a northerner.

"I brought these pelts and would like a metal pot and a shovel if you have any."

"You bet. Right here," the proprietor showed Karmo his wares. There were pots of different sizes, but the shovels were all alike.

Karmo looked over the pots while the man flipped through the pelts. "I'll take one of these pots and that shovel," he pointed.

"Fine and dandy. These are nice pelts. We can trade for four of them. That should do it, you think?"

Karmo looked at the man a bit surprised. He expected an unpleasant exchange, but got only respect and a fair bargain. This is not what he had been led to believe by those on the farm. His business concluded, he turned to depart. Walking towards the gate, he sensed being watched. Soldiers were indeed observing him but did not move. Passing through the gate, one of them spit tobacco juice on Karmo's boots and grinned at him. *Say nothing and keep walking,* he thought to himself. *So, this is the rest of the story ....*

~

An 1832 treaty signed by runaway Seminoles made both African and Creek-Seminoles residents of the same nation. The Treaty of Payne's Landing forced Seminoles to move to Arkansas territory. The United States President, Jackson, had already signed the Indian Removal Act, forcefully moving Native peoples west of the Mississippi to make room for Americans. Natives were promised suitable farmland and hunting grounds, however, by direction of the U.S. government, two American administrators, Peacock and Symes, penned a secret agreement dividing the lands between Georgia, Florida territory and the so called western Indian territory.[19] Instead of suitable farmland, which was to be saved for Americans, Natives would be allocated smaller, poorer tracts than promised. Native trust would be forever lost.

~

"They attacked the Samsun farm!" cried a Native as he raced into a small neighboring township. The Native was breathless, rivulets of dirt and sweat streamed from this body. He fell to the ground, gasping for air as people gathered around him with a general sense of alarm and oaths. They sat him up, and someone brought water. Still gasping, he told of a vicious attack eight miles away, across the river. "They are all dead! Hacked and shot, even the children!" A collective scream arose from the crowd and some commenced crying. Men's jaws dropped as they looked at one another. Others showed their anger.

"Gather your weapons! We need to stop them now!" said one of the town's leaders. "We must decide who will go to fight and who will defend, quickly!"

I am an academic and do not know how to fight, Karmo thought in a panic. *But I cannot stand back from this.* He joined the fighters immediately, and thus was thrown into skirmishes, he had only before imagined and pondered. Over the course of two months, he saw valiant defense of towns and villages, brave attacks on invaders and heinous atrocities. His mind spinning, it threatened his soul. He could see that these people needed a more ready and trained fighting force.

With the unrelenting turmoil surrounding him, Karmo departed the group to look for John Horse, a black Seminole who was one of the hold-outs along with other Seminole leaders Osceola and Sam Jones, against pressure to relocate to Indian Territory.[20] He did not know what would become of his efforts, but he felt a deep need to be part of an organized resistance.

11

Mattapoisett, Late Fall 1831

I don't know, and you don't either. —Unknown

"Another special delivery in the office Mademoiselle Suzanne," whispered the dock boss.

Suzanne nodded, "Merci. I will take care of it now."

In the dock office, Suzanne met face to face with an African from Virginia by way of Baltimore. She had been abetting this smuggling of beings for a year now, and although the trip was dangerous with betrayal at any time, thus far she had been successful, and the cargo willing. But this dapper black man in front of her was a surprise, a departure from the usual furtive, ragged looking passengers she had helped in the past. Tired but standing erect, respectful and yet questioning, he was every bit of a gentleman that one who had endured such travels could be. She knew peoples of all walks were kidnapped and brought to the states for slavery nevertheless, this was not the norm.

"You are safe here Sir," she said, "but still we must be careful for a while. I am Suzanne Benoît, the daughter of the ship builder here. What is your name, Sir?"

Ansa looked about the room and then directly at the hazel-eyed young woman in front of him, nodded and bowed slowly. "Ansa, Miss, my name is Ansa Kabbah."

"Mr. Kabbah," she said, "you are coming home with me now. Please, put on this cloak. It is very cold outside."

∼

He entered the large house with Mademoiselle Suzanne. Another visitor, another soul saved from the terrors of that "peculiar institution."[21] Mrs. Marshall looked up from her housekeeping chores and blinked at the well comported black man. *Another one,* she thought to herself. *This family is going to get us all in trouble with the law sooner or later.*

Ansa was introduced to the family. Marie-Therese, Bijou, and Jack took turns at asking questions and were intrigued. Mrs. Marshall held back and listened, her eyes darting from one to the other as they spoke.

"Mr. Ansa will stay here and join us for supper, Mrs. Marshall, please set a place for him in the dining room. I am sure Maman will want to engage him in conversation this evening.

Mrs. Marshall, turned her head towards Suzanne, and only nodded.

Bijou was beyond curious. She had met many a stranger in her house, but this man spoke funny. "Where did you come from, Mr. Ansa?"

"What would you like to know, Mademoiselle?" answered Ansa. "Where did I get on the ship which brought me here? Where was I born? Where was I before that?" he smiled playfully.

Bijou was perplexed and excited. "I only wondered why you speak so funny, but now I want to know where you were before you were born!!! I mean, uh, before here!"

Suzanne looked at the two of them and shook her head before saying, "There will be plenty of time for more questions, Bijou. Let us show Mr. Ansa his room where he can rest before Maman gets here. Mr. Ansa, this way please."

～

Quickly Ansa became part of Benoît's extended family. He tutored the children, and became somewhat of a spiritual guide to them. As the townspeople had become used to seeing free black people around and especially near the docks, so did Ansa's presence rarely stir any particular interest. Ansa naturally was somewhat tentative at first over the disparity between Richmond and Mattapoisett, but became at ease quickly. In the small room of his own, Ansa thought of Karmo, and tears came to his eyes.

"Here I am, comfortable, safe, with people who want to befriend me. Where is my brother? Where is Karmo?" Ansa looked out the window into the starry night. "Karmo, my brother, are you safe?"

~

Fall 1833

Ansa assimilated well into the community and became a trusted and even beloved friend of Madeleine's family. He spent part of his evenings, welcomed at a favored pub, La Figue Dansante, where he entertained patrons discussing philosophy, spiritualism or with yarns of fantasy while carving his specialized talisman for various patrons. He also carved for the Benoît daughters. He told them they could whisper their worries and secrets to the token, and the token spirit would keep their secrets. Each token had the girl's initials carved on the back. Ansa explained to Bijou, the youngest, that the sun and moon make us look up at a world bigger than we are, so we can hope and dream.

One cool night, Bijou and Ansa were sitting outdoors with others taking in the fresh, crisp air and the clear sky.

Looking upwards, Bijou said, "Before you came, when I was little, there was a rain of stars, so many that no one could count them. My Mama said it was a star shower!"[22]

"Indeed?" said Ansa. "That must have been marvelous! Or were you afraid?"

"I wasn't afraid! My Mama wasn't afraid, so I wasn't afraid!" asserted Bijou. "But why did they fall?"

"The stars and the planets are travelers, Mademoiselle, and they just changed their path. Such as our earth travels around the sun. I do not know why they changed routes. Perhaps they are telling us something. The stars are all of us, you, me, those not yet born and the dead; the fierce and the fading. Whenever we see the stars, we are never alone; they are as varied and infinite beyond your imagination and mine, and so, with infinite possibilities."

Bijou looked puzzled, but liked the words so asked, "Do the stars tell us stories about people, Mr. Ansa?"

"Oh yes, Mademoiselle. There are many stories, told especially well by the Greek people. Look to the east over there, do you see the stars patterning out a W?" said Ansa.

Bijou cocked her head and scanned the evening sky. "Oh, over there?" she said as she pointed, her little index finger slightly cocked.

"Yes, that is it," replied Ansa. "That is a constellation, a group of stars telling a story. That one is called Cassiopeia."

"Cass-o, Casspeea ..." stumbled Bijou.

"Cass-i-o-pe-i-a," corrected Ansa patiently.

"Cassiopeia!" exclaimed Bijou.

Ansa smiled and continued, "Cassiopeia was the Queen of Ethiopia, a land far away on the eastern coast of Africa and the wife of King Cepheus. She was renowned for her beauty and boasted that she was more beautiful than even the sea nymphs. The nymphs in turn, complained to the God of the seas, Poseidon, and asked that Cassiopeia be banished to the sky. It is a long and complex story. Suffice it to say Poseidon sent a sea monster, Cetus, to ravage the Ethiopian sea coast, but the supreme God Zeus interceded by telling the King and Queen that they and their country could be saved if they sacrificed their daughter Andromeda by chaining her to the sea rocks as an offering to Cetus. And they did!" Ansa exclaimed with mock anxiety.

"Oh no!" cried Bijou. "Why did they do that, Mr. Ansa!"

Ansa continued, "They did not want to send Andromeda, of course, but they needed to save their land and people, so they believed they had no choice, Bijou. Fortunately, the hero Perseus, who had just slain Medusa came flying by on this winged horse Pegasus, and ..."

"Wait, wait, who is Medusa?" interrupted Bijou.

"A moment, Mademoiselle," said Ansa, "Medusa was a monster called a Gorgon, and she had hundreds of snakes sprouting like hair coming out of her head! And anyone who gazed at her instantly turned to stone."[23]

"But how could Perseus kill her without turning into stone?" asked Bijou, her chin jutting out and eyes squinting in disbelief. "Are you storying me? And a flying horse!?"

"Of course this is the story, Mademoiselle; it is a very old one, but it is a good one. Let me continue" says Ansa with a smile. "So, Perseus is clever and when he sneaks up on Medusa, she turns towards him, but he holds up his shiny silver shield in front of his face. She sees her own reflection and instantly turns to stone herself!!!"

"Ha!" exclaimed Bijou.

"And then, quickly, Perseus cuts off her head with his mighty sword and puts it in a leather bag to take home to Ethiopia. Well, when he got home, that is, when he saw Cetus about to devour poor Andromeda, he quickly pulled out Medusa's head and flashed it at the sea monster who instantly turned to stone! Naturally, Perseus and Andromeda were married and when they died, they all took their place as star constellations in the night sky. Now look over there," Ansa stated as he pointed north, "See the up and down row of stars with two arms? That is Perseus. Now, do you see that hazy patch of stars? That is Andromeda."

Bijou continued to stare into the clear November night, then said, "The good won! The good always win, right Mr. Ansa?!"

He looked into her guileless eyes of innocence. "Sometimes yes, sometimes no, child. Sometimes only the sword and wits of the brave can save the day. We must try to do good, expect good in others until they show us otherwise."

She blinked and nodded before looking back into the sky, "The world is truly big, Mr. Ansa."

"Yes dear one. It is the Universe; bigger than we can see, with stars and planets and all kinds of bits and pieces following their way, maybe their life. We are fortunate when we can see into the night, for a life without looking at the stars is no life at all. You should always look at them like it was your first time."

Just then Bijou sighted a shooting star and made a wish quietly to herself. "I will be that star over there," she pointed. "Papa will be the sun and Mama will be the shooting star."

Bijou looked up to the sky. "I'm so small."

Ansa smiled at her. "You are part of something greater than the imagination. We are all bits of that sky formed into ourselves. Do not feel small, dear one, you are of the Universe, and you are mighty!"

I need to tell my Jackie. Bijou thought to herself.

~

A week later, both Bijou and Jack joined Ansa on the back stoop after supper. The fall sky was dark, but clear, and the stars were plentiful and brilliant. Ansa showed the children the Milky Way. He told them the Earth was really a part of it and that they were inside looking out this glorious body of stars and planets. The children were puzzled and awed.

Ansa was more reflective than usual that night. He said aloud as much to himself as to the children, "When the time comes, we will rise up to these stars. We will rise back to the sky and watch the earth from there. Then we will understand. We will see from there that a dust speck flying in the night, an ant or a person is no different. Life is life, be it in a human, a dog or a turtle. Take away our shell and our essence is the same."

He looked at the moon, shining bright and enticing, he whispered, "Where are you my brother?"

~

Two days later. "I carved this for you, Mademoiselle Bijou." Ansa handed her a round wooden disc, a second one, this with the sun carved carefully on one side, a crescent moon and a shooting star on the reverse.

"Oh, it's so pretty!" exclaimed Bijou as only a child of eight could. She turned it over and over in her hands, held it up and stared at the burnished disc. "What is it?"

"You could call it a good luck piece, a talisman, or you could keep it in your pocket holding it to give you strength, to keep you from feeling scared. For whatever you need it, it is for you. You can believe it if you dare," explained Ansa.

Bijou looked at Ansa with a tinge of anxiety, "But is this a basf, a basfmey?"

"Blasphemy?" Ansa looked down at Bijou's innocent face and said, "Should it not be allowable to believe as one sees fit? There is no contradiction to your religion, dear. Human beings consist primarily of the brain, heart and soul. The heart gives us passion and compassion. The soul allows us to believe. The brain helps us determine right from wrong. What does it matter how we name our god or that we even have one? Our behavior towards each other weighs most heavily on our actions. You can decide. Little Bijou can decide."

Bijou pondered. "You talk funny, but I like it Mr. Ansa" she responded. My Mama told me God made everything in the whole world, and we should talk to Him, but I can't hear Him when I talk to Him."

"If all things great and small were created by God, would not speaking to birds, trees and even insects be like talking to God? And because we do not understand what the birds sing or the trees rustle, does that mean your God does not speak to you?"

Bijou considered these words from Ansa. *He doesn't believe in God, but he talks about God,* she mused.

~

Some days later, Bijou took a solitary walk, yet did not feel alone. She was surrounded by life, and with a light heart, she started to run. Flowers like petaled stars and grassy comets streaked the green universe as she raced from the copse into the meadow. Slowing down to take in her surroundings, she made her way home into town. She stopped to look at the hard pan foot trail and let her imagination drift as she imagined feeling the sensation of those who preceded her in life, their lingering indent in dark matter still in the air. Stepping on the very path and foot-bridge as they did, she thought of them and wondered of those coming after her. *Will this tree be here still, will that boulder or stream, as they were for the people before me? Will birds still sing and children stare in awe of an owl swooping towards the ground, quiet like a ghost?* It made her head spin. It was all like magic. *Mr. Ansa is magic!* she thought to herself.

12

Maine Fall 1833

Goodbyes are only for those who love with their eyes. Because for those who love with their heart and soul there is no such thing as separation.
–Rumi

Jean Benoît and Peter Kroupa, Jean's master carpenter, departed for Maine as usual in late fall of the year. They booked quarters on a packet ship out of Boston, and arranged to transport their lumber back to Mattapoisett in like style. They would be gone a month to six weeks depending on how long it took to conduct business, get the materials to the ship for a full cargo load and sail back to Boston, then home to Mattapoisett.

Peter had made many a half-model in his time, samples of ship design and construction.[24] He had worked with Monsieur Benoît for several years now and each understood the other's strengths and needs. They got the heaviest and strongest timber for the keel, but needed a variety of wood, both soft and hard to complete the build. This year would be the last building year as the financial risks were ever increasing due to economics, foul weather and pirates. Shipping merchandise and raw materials was much more safe and profitable in the long term as these were less expensive to insure. In fact, Benoît was already transitioning the business to shipping goods, and business was doing well.

Setting out on the crisp fall morning, breezy yet with a bit of sea smoke on the water, the ship belched and bellowed out its own clouds of steam. *A far cry from my sailing days*, thought Jean. He and Peter were on deck taking in the sea air, when Jean became nostalgic.

"You know Pete, sometimes I miss sailing on the open seas. Yes, yes, I know it is not for me anymore, and Madame Benoît would have my hide if I even suggested trying it again. But, there is nothing like being alone with your thoughts looking into what seems like forever, where the sea meets the sky; the vastness, the enormous, the bottomless, the infinite … far beyond any control," Jean mused. "The sea changes a man, Petey. He becomes a philosopher, in awe of the beauty and fury".

Peter nodded reverently, "Yes sir, I would imagine so."

Jean looked at him thoughtfully, then clapped Peter on the shoulder. "So tell me about what is going on between you and my Suzanne."

Peter jerked his head towards Jean and blushed, "Sir, there is nothing to tell. Nothing is going on. If anything, she ignores me. I mean, there is nothing between us, Sir"

Jean stared intently at the young man. "Give it time, Pete, there will be a time for you. I know she has an affinity towards you, but she has an independent streak. She will come around. Let us go in and get something warm to drink. Sometimes I just get a bit loopy out here," he chuckled.

Peter found himself lost in thoughts and remembrances, how Suzanne would sometimes welcome him warmly and other times treat him as a stranger. She invited him to sit with her and discuss happenings in the world, musings and the stars. He was in love with her, but was not sure how she felt towards him. She perplexed him.

∽

Later that evening, the men arrived at their destination and obtained a room above a saloon, the only boarding establishment in town. The room was comfortable enough, although the night air was filled with the loud sounds of men having a good time into the wee hours.

The next morning they headed to the lumber site to meet the owner, Jim Sockalexis who took them out to the river to see his new steam powered barge.

"My oh my, Jim, what a fine piece of machinery you have there!" admired Jean.

Peter nodded in appreciation, eyeing carefully the workings of the contraption, and wondering how or what might break it down and then how to fix it. He couldn't help it. This was his way of looking at things, seeing beyond the external.

"Yes, thank you, Sir. It sure has changed things around here. It is safer and faster than the men going out on the river with peaveys," returned Jim. "Although they still do that further up river."

Jean nodded and asked, "Things settled down any with the British?"

"Not quite. There is still fighting about the border line and their lumbermen keep cutting timber around Bangor. There is huge land speculation even down into the Penobscot River valley and beyond. But so far, I have been lucky with my sources," responds Jim. "I do not know how it will end."

"You would think there could be a reasonable agreement. Let us hope it does not end up with blood shed. What an awful shame that would be. Sad and wasteful!"

"One can only hope," answered Jim.

Jean turned to Peter. "Pete, Jim here is a Penobscot, one of the Wabanaki Confederacy from up north.[25] Now *there* is a group who knows about generosity and sharing! Always keep that in mind, son. People of good intent can always work things out!" said Jean.

Leaning over a balustrade from the upper floor of the shop, the three men were silent for a while as they took in the surrounding woods and then below where the great saws were cutting boards, inhaling that glorious, fresh smell of newly cut wood mingled with evergreen limbs. The deciduous trees already let their leaves drop. And as far as one could see, there were more and more wonderful, ever replenished trees.

Turning back to Jim, "Well, Jim, it has been great doing business with you all these years. Between you and Pete here, I know I have just what I need for building. I am much obliged for your hospitality. Give my best to your wife," said Jean.

"The pleasure is ours, Mr. Benoît. Good meeting you, Pete. You two have a safe trip back," said Jim, his pleasant eyes reflecting a sincerity reserved for brothers.

ROAR!

~

The morning was one of those wonderfully translucent and mystical days along the Maine coast. At the dock, Jean and Peter monitored their lumber as it was hoisted onto the ship, a rigorous and tedious venture. There were huge cranes with ropes through pulleys looped and secured around pallets of lumber. One by one, the stevedores directed the pallets into the ship's cargo hold through a large opening on the center deck. It would take only the morning to get completely loaded as they were an efficient lot. The noise was loud and boisterous.

"Well, they will be done in a bit over an hour at this rate, Pete my boy. Let us go get some dinner before boarding time," hollered Jean over the worker's voices.

"Sounds good, Sir," said Peter. "But we should walk over here by the offices out of the way, there is a carriage coming."

"What was that, Pete? Oh, the carriage, yes. I see."

Jean moved quickly towards the ship side to avoid the on-coming carriage. Creaking sounds emitted into the air as a gust of wind swayed the pallet and a fraying rope gave up its twisted strands one by one until it snapped enough to slip part of its load.

"Sir!" screamed Peter.

The thunderous rumble and quaking of the dock below obscured any other sounds of the hapless men working the platform, including Jean Benoît. His death was mercifully, instantaneous. But the screams and moans of the injured ripped Peter to the core of his being. He stood frozen with horror for a terrible moment, then ran into the chaos of jumbled lumber with the dock men, stevedores and others who witnessed the terror.

The rescue itself was dangerous as the load was unstable and could shift again to injure others. Stevedores ordered onlookers to stay back as they stabilized the load so the rescue and recovery could commence. In the chaos, a din of noises and scraping timber mixed with screams and pleas for help sliced through the hot and dirty air. Blacks, whites and Natives worked side by side to render aid.

One of the gravely injured begged, "Please! Don't let me die alone!" Pete could only hold the victim's hand as the man passed from this life. A makeshift infirmary for the injured was set up in front of one of the emporiums. Another temporary shelter was formed off to the side for the deceased.

Peter and a passerby carried Jean's extricated body and covered it with a blanket. He looked down a moment, taking off his cap, before running back to help. Rescue and recovery was gruesome and arduous, but punctuated with small victories as one by one, a survivor was found and recovered for treatment, taking an hour more before all souls were recovered; eight altogether, three deaths. Peter worked with the local undertaker to prepare Jean for his final voyage. He wondered how he could ever tell Madame Benoît. It was a devastating waste of a good heart.

13

Karmo in Florida 1833-34

One man doesn't believe in god at all, while the other believes
in him so thoroughly that he prays as he murders men.
–The Idiot, Fyodor Dostoevsky

Others had joined Karmo to fight in Native militias. They board-ed small boats which made their way up the coast and into the marshland where the banks swelled with tide water. Sea oats, palmettos and reeds formed their own barrier between the open sea and land. The moon rose from the waters, plump and silver that first night. Karmo just stared at it until he turned in.

With the help of local Native groups, Karmo met up with Billy Bowlegs and other Seminoles who refused to leave their land.[26] They were fighting invaders coming to remove and slaughter their people. He learned their fighting tactics including how to best hide in the sur-rounding woods. Some would show themselves to the invaders and re-treat, enticing the enemy to follow. Once the invaders were "in their pocket," the others would swarm like bees, trapped them and annihilat-ed them. The Seminoles taught their fighters to fight as one team and to be unrelenting. Their small battles were successful, but they lacked the superior weapons and numbers of the invaders.

Karmo was still looking for John Horse to join with him. Billy Bow-legs, sensing a good use of talent, sent Karmo to help Horse with tactical advice. He gave him directions, a talisman and a warning to be on the watch for small bands of northern volunteers. "They have little training and next to no restraint."

Karmo's machete slashed the thick, green undergrowth to find an old foot path to a Seminole out post. Birds stopped singing. He paused and looked about, when suddenly he was tackled by a shadow of awesome weight that must have been the size of a bear. The contact knocked the wind out of him, followed by a strike in the face with a fist hard as a rock, almost rendering him unconscious. Seeing shooting white bursts tracing through the darkness in his skull as he gained his awareness, an angry, growly voice demanded of him, "Whose dog are you! Who sent you here!"

Karmo answered slowly and weakly, "Billy Bowlegs sent me," he whispered.

The bear man got off of him and hunched down to Karmo's side. He put his large, grizzly face close to Karmo's and said, "Billy Bowlegs, heh? Prove it!"

With that, Karmo sat up slowly on one arm and motioned to his bag with his head. "Over there, look inside."

The bear man rummaged around and pulled out a cypress talisman. "Humpf," he said. "You come with me."

Karmo followed, limping, struggling to be patient. They came upon a well-defended clearing with a few tents and make-shift lean-to's where he was introduced to John Horse. Like Karmo, the leader was six feet tall and powerfully built. He was turbaned, wearing a hunting shirt cinched at the waist with a sash. He made quite an impression. Horse stared hard into Karmo's eyes before he motioned to him to sit. "Tell me about Billy Bowlegs. What is happening with his teams?" demanded Horse.

The two spoke long into the night about the current state of battles, teams in the field, strategy and tactics. Horse was adamant the Seminoles would stand their ground to keep their Florida lands, and not be forced to the so-called Indian Territory west of the Mississippi.

"Some actions do not build character as much as they reveal it. The northern invaders do not countenance shame of coveting that of others.

If they want it and can take it, it is theirs for all time," explained Horse to Karmo. "Only their interest is what pricks them on."

Karmo listened and nodded, for this was the ever recurring cycle of war, prosperity and nation building he had heard and studied.

～

Dosar, a Seminole, was in charge of training. He spoke to Karmo, "You can not change the past, but the future is in your hands. Look, everything can be a weapon; a handful of dirt, sticks, rocks. The trick is to move like lightning and not to stop until your opponent is subdued." They trained in hand to hand fighting. "Use your body to roll him over your hip. Here's how you block, hit back in one motion ..."

Karmo fought with John Horse and the Seminoles for almost three years against the northern invaders. Many Native villages were well established, some had their own gristmills, sawmills, tan yards. Individuals operated ferries and raised cattle, horses and swine. Mostly they just wanted to tend their farms and livestock, but more and more they needed to protect their lands. They were far outgunned, but had knowledge of the land on their side and knew how to take advantage of geography. They continued to hold out despite their lack of overall strength. It was a behavior which impressed Karmo who recognized the pattern from his time with Efendi.

It was to be a skirmish like so many before. Against what he thought was his nature and inclination, Karmo evolved into a killer. While he remained intrigued and dedicated to planning actions, in battle he relished hand to hand combat, movements became automatic and focused without thought, for now that was the only way. At dawn, he was part of the advance team to take out the sentries quietly with knives and their hands only. As they quietly approached the drowsing enemy, he channeled his rage into his fists, took hold of the enemy's head in both hands and with a quick twist, snapped the man's neck. There was no time for reflection. He moved to the next victim and then the next and the battle was on.

～

The U.S. military was stretched thin along the western shore, but there were a good many bands of American volunteers and militias. These were more often composed of the poor; young men and even youths, who listened to the repeated stories of how their plight was due to savages and black men who wanted to take their god given rights to a livelihood from them. They knew no differently and were willing to suffer and die to do their part for the businessmen of their country who would support them in order to improve their commerce. The farmers relied on these educated men to know what was right for them. For was it not their superior knowledge as to what was right that allowed them to become so successful? The young eventually became more and more brutal as the horrors of war unfolded and they felt more justified in their own brutality. It became what fed their acts of atrocity. They listened to the preaching that they were doing right; that they could kill and maim without conscience, that nothing could stop them from killing, as right and God was on their side.

～

Karmo saw genuine affection develop between the men with whom he fought, those brothers who were striving to do what was best for the team. It was as if mystical bonds forged a synergistic force. *Teams, brotherhood, another strategy which worked well,* reflected Karmo. He thought of the posted sentries as well. "Ah, the sentries' guard duty; one's honor and one's pride; most noble and yet most dismissed," said Karmo aloud. "In the most extremes of weather, or gloom of a long night, they may never let their minds wander, never doze off, for doing so puts them and their brothers at risk. They must fight the boredom which itself is wrapped in fear and danger as constant alertness creates its own fatigue. They wait and pray for a peaceful sunrise while ever straining their ears and eyes."

Still another tracking and planning for ambush ensued. Horse's team watched as a small enemy band appeared through the thickets. They were mostly volunteers, but with several child soldiers, who carried rifles as long as they were tall … sent in front to be slaughtered. Karmo bit his lip. It broke his heart and felt as if his very soul was being ripped from him. Tears ran down his cheek as he calmly and purposely fired into them. *Oh Brima, what has become of me!* Was remorse a weakness? A moment unfocused and a bullet whizzed striking Karmo in the upper chest, then another in his left shoulder, knocking him backwards into tall biting grasses. Time stood still; he measured his time left on earth in seconds. He felt the pulsing of blood vessels in his ears, a pounding in his heart, the searing pain of the bullets and generalized weakness. He could not move. *I am dying,* thought Karmo to himself. With that realization, every cloud above, every leaf, every twig, every whisper of wind spoke to him. Life and time is precious and nothing else was important at that point.

Suddenly, he was grabbed up by a comrade, Haco, and dragged back to camp to be patched up. Well or not, a week later he would fight again.

~

The invaders continued their raids into villages, wreaking havoc everywhere. An injured villager, having lost his weapon, hid from the soldier under a mass of leaves. He stilled his breathing as an indigo snake slithered across his face. Watching as a soldier neared him, he flinched when the man stepped on his hidden, injured leg. The villager then pulled up his body and bit viciously the invader's calf muscle down to the bone, blood squirting into the air and onto his face. The soldier screamed, kneed the villager in the face and sliced him behind the ear twice with his machete. "Savage bastard!" yelled the invader as he repeatedly kicked the writhing dying man. The commotion alerted the team and the invader was subsequently dispatched.

~

The men around Karmo were getting fired up. "Above and beyond, we will fight!"

"Above and beyond? There is no such thing!" growled Horse. "We do what we must, here and now!"

"We are ready, Sir. We die on your command!"

"This is not the time to die! This is the time to kill!" exhorted Horse.

Karmo alternated being lead and follower depending on his assignment and seniority. He held no inclination towards any more than to fight for the cause. More skirmishes were fought, more died on both sides; sons, brothers, husbands, fathers, whole families, gone. In the end, little was gained but the spirit of the fight.

14

Mattapoisett, March 1834

There is no footprint too small to leave an imprint on this world.
—Unknown

La Figue Dansante was one of those roomy neighborhood public houses frequented by families and dock men alike. There were several rooms, and even private rooms to meet various needs, business or pleasure. Tidy rooms for rent were kept upstairs, but only for legitimate visitors as the owners had a reputation to maintain. There were four fireplaces to keep the pub cozy and comfortable during the chilly seasons. The keepers were the Malenfants from the Quebec province as were a number of long-time residents.

"See what the boys in the back room will have, Yvette!" called out Patrice Malenfant, wife and partner of Pierre Malenfant. They prided themselves on providing a place for everyone, and believed in providing good food and service. Madame Malenfant was sometimes bawdy, sometimes motherly. It all depended on who was "in the house" as she would say. Her customers loved her as she was their surrogate for all they lacked elsewhere without even knowing it. "They are fine, Madame," Yvette reported back. "They are philosophying again," she chuckled. "Monsieur Kabbah is having a good time with Monsieur Edington."

Madame Malenfant nodded, smiled and turned away to other business.

In a darkened corner, a couple of local businessmen were close by eyeing the back room, hearing the boisterous conversation. They had been joined by an out-of-towner of their acquaintance, visiting to conclude some trade at the docks.

"What do you think of that, Jonesy?" asked Baker, one of the table mates.

"Not much, and I don't much care either. Those birds of a feather ain't hurtin no one so long as they keep to themselves," he said and shrugged.

Baker looked at him with disgust and said, "Isn't that Benoît's guy? It jist ain't natural. He needs to be taught a lesson."

"Why are you always looking for trouble, Baker?" returned Jonesy. It isn't any of our business what they do. It doesn't concern us, so just leave things be."

"A lesson is to be taught. Taught, taught, taught a lesson. I say, should a rope not be taut? I taut I saw a rope. A rope is not a snake. A snake is not a rope. A rat's ass is not a snake. Rats at the dock, rats at the dock! Poison!" exploded Baker as he threw his dinner plate on the floor.

Jones looked at Baker, then his companion. Slowly shaking his head, he offered, "Don't mind him. He goes off like that sometimes."

As a servant came over to clean up the mess, Baker kicked her. "Serves you right!"

Meanwhile, in the backroom:

"Says who?!" jibed Ansa.

"Say's the Bible!" rejoined William Edington, fist pounding on the table, his voice louder and higher pitch than normal.

"Exactly! says who?!" teased Ansa, his voice getting quieter.

"I said, says the Bible!"

"Bible? Which Bible?!"

"The only Bible!"

"Whose Bible?!"

"My Bible!"

"Says who?!"

"Say's me! Damn you all to hell, Kabbah!"

"Exactly!" Ha, ha, ha, ha, ha, ha!

"What's wrong with your head, Kabbah?! Don't you know in the Bible Leviticus 25, says you may purchase a male or female to enslave them and treat them as your property, even pass them to your children as a permanent inheritance?"

Ansa took a deep breath, placing his hand over his heart, "Why Sir, that is mighty Christian of you! You cite your scriptures and turn a blind eye to injustice. Have you no sense?" With that Ansa stared at Edington and commenced to smile ever so slightly.

Edington, an avowed abolitionist, hesitated, then did the same as he had come to enjoy these little tête-à-têtes with Ansa.

"You bastard you!" he laughed big and loud at Ansa.

"Why Sir!" feigned Ansa, hand to heart again and bowing his head. "You give me no choice than to demand satisfaction at dawn down by the river."

"Ha! Good one my dear Sir! But one day someone may not be as gallant as I, and just get his drunken buddies to string you up for their amusement ... down by the river," intoned Edington.

Ansa raised his eyebrows at this turn of conversation. "Alas, Edi, we live in such times when some of us are guilty for the way we are born." He looked at his partner and said solemnly, "Your book does have some very good instruction, but it lacks fluidity. It does not stand up for all times."

"Sir, permit me with all deference to hint that some of your remarks are injudiciously worded," jabbed Edington.

And so the evening continued with not just a little sherry to make it all go down.

~

Earlier the same day

The road was on the western edge of town past open fields, dotted with a copse of trees here and there. While the ground was still mostly frozen, buds pushed forth their swelling in the ever returning search for rebirth. Chilling cold when the sun went down, the day was bright with only a few clouds about in this early spring. School had resumed a few weeks back, having been suspended during the holidays and for excessive snow. The small, two roomed building was only four miles from home, out from one of the main routes to the dock, along a slowly thawing creek.

Bijou was happy to return to school and see her friends. She had spent much of her birthday month in isolation. Now, the days were glorious if short still. She waited in the school yard with other children for Jack to come to accompany her home as always. She wanted to show him the talisman Ansa whittled for her; a shooting star passing in behind a crescent moon.

These were the heady days of youth, when one is fearless, reckless and invincible. They were the days when life still valued innocence. Jack appeared smiling from around the school house and spotted Bijou.

"Bijou, I'm here!" he called out.

Just then three boys Jack's age came riding by on horseback, two on one horse. He knew them, of course, and often spent time with them by the creek fishing or looking for small animals, polished rocks or whatever would entice boys of their age. There they were, Tomas LaRoque, his cousin Guy and Ben Jefferson. Today, though, their demeanor changed when they saw him with Bijou.

"Haha, ha Hah, haa! Haha, ha Hah, haa!" they jeered. "Hey, hey Jackie! Spending time with your little Frenchie sweetheart? Ben sang out.

Guy gave Ben a quick punch in the arm, "Hey you! Shut up!"

Ben turned quickly towards Guy and said "Oh, ho!" Then turned back to Jack, smiling wryly, "Hey, what's with your girlfriend, Jackie!"

"What's wrong with you guys?! Get lost, I'll catch up with you later!" Jack rebuffed.

But Ben persisted. "Are you turning *girlie* on us, Jackie-boy?"

With this, Jack turned red and shouted angrily, "She's just my job to do. I have to see her home! I'll meet up with you later, I said!"

With this they all just laughed and took off sauntering slowly and singing, "Haha, ha Haah, ha! Jackie and Bijou sitting in a tree ...."

Bijou was hurt and mortified that Jack, whom she thought of as her big brother, would treat her this way. "I'm not your job, Jackie! If you don't want to walk home with me, then you can go with your dumb head friends!" she cried, stomping her foot.

Embarrassed now, Jack lashed out at Bijou. "It's getting dark! If you're so smart, why don't you just go home alone!"

"I prefer it! Go, Jackie, go! Go be with your dumb head friends!" she shouted, involuntarily biting her lower lip. "And you're a dumb head too!"

They both stared at each other, stubborn and neither giving an inch.

"Fine, you'll be sorry to walk all alone in the dark!" he shouted. With that, he spun around and hollered after the boys who turned and waited for him as he ran up and pulled himself on the horse behind Ben. They turned and sauntered off towards the main part of town.

Bijou stood a few moments watching as they disappeared down the hilly road. She blinked and looked to the sky which was clear. *There will be moonlight*, she thought. She decided to take the shortcut that would get her home faster. It was a narrow wagon path used to haul lumber passing Eel Pond. "Dumb head, Jackie," she muttered as she turned and kicked stones along the route home.

The road cutting through the woods was rutted and rocky. Slender tree branches waved gently in the breeze, mesmerizing to the young mind. The sky tinged orange and pink as the sun was setting. Bijou saw a man on horseback coming towards her, not unusual for this time of day. People were leaving businesses and pubs to get home for supper. The two exchanged customary nods and passed one another. Bijou started daydreaming again, enjoying the hint of seasonal change in the air, fingering the charming spirit talisman in her apron pocket. She heard the thick clomps of muddy horse hoofs behind her, turned to, just as her head was suddenly slammed against the rocky earth. She could barely breathe from the stunning hit. Her mind was in an uncontrollable riot with thoughts and sensations. Something large and heavy upon her was squeezing away her breath, but she could not see because of the mud and hair in her face. She was being pummeled repeatedly and she was aware of her flailing her arms, but her efforts were of no avail. Then came a sharp, stinging, hot sensation down the sides of her body. He was cutting her clothes with a knife and taking little care of the flesh underneath. Bijou struggled as a cry strangled in her throat. She remained aware of his breath, foul with whiskey and decaying meat. How odd, the things which go through one's mind in such a short, horrible time! An excruciating pain forced her to catch her breath as he entered from behind. He was a vicious brute, but his hands were soft. Soft! He riddled her over and over into the mud, her face shoved farther into it, choking her. At last, came a final sickening crack as her head was slammed into a large stone, followed by a warm trickle down one side of her face. Black, white, red colors filtered through her consciousness, then just dark and quiet.

Night fell. Bijou aroused slowly and was aware only of cold mud and pain. Her heart fluttered like butterfly wings. She could not slow it down. Her body felt light and delicate. Her breaths became sharp and shallow. With much effort, she turned her head to the side and looked up into the darkness. A shooting star jettisoned across the sky, eliciting some small comfort. She smiled weakly, as tiny pearls of tears fell from her eyes. "Mama?"

Nearby roly poly's uncurled and started their march.

∾

"Bijou!! Bijou!! Where are you, Bijou!!!" called out the search party. Family and community members walked the paths and surroundings in methodical formation holding torches and lanterns as they searched for the little girl, their girl, in the dark night.

At length, the Malenfant men and men from the pub came across Bijou, disheveled in the mud, clutching her talisman.

"She's here!!" someone yelled. More searchers came running and gasped as they saw the small body riven and muddy. Some were stunned into silence. Another placed his coat over her still body.

"We cannot let Madame Benoît see her like this!" said Pierre Malenfant to the search party around him. "You there!" he pointed to one of the men. "Go! Tell Mademoiselle Suzanne that Bijou is dead and to get her mother home. Tell her we will bring Bijou to her," his voice shuddered.

～

A week later, Suzanne and Marie-Therese knelt on either side of their mother who was sitting in Jean's armchair as she stared out the window at the bay waters. She hadn't spoken in days after Bijou's death. She slowly moved her lips, but only unintelligible whispers emerged. Marie-Therese gave her a glass of water from which she sipped.

"Maman, we are here for you, will you not speak to us?" whispered Suzanne.

Finally, the fog lifted and Madeleine took a deep breath, turned her head slowly to look into Suzanne's face, then into Marie-Therese. "I have neglected you, my darlings. I am sorry," she said.

They started to protest, but when Madeleine shifted her body, they stopped. Another day later, she whispered, "A mother carries her child in her body for months, gives birth. The child is a part of her forever. She watches as that child grows and learns to walk, to talk, to laugh. A mother wants to live long enough to see that child grow up, fall in love and have her own family. She never wants to leave her until she knows the child will be safe in the world. But there is always a little place in the heart where fear hides; fear that the mother will not live long enough to help her child on her way. Nowhere is there a place for the thought that the child will die before her, because that's unthinkable, unbearable, unnatural."

Mrs. Marshall, who had been standing quietly near the doorway murmured, "A winter's sun is glorious, but short-lived. Perhaps we must keep breaking our heart until it opens.

～

From sadness to outrage, townsfolk started looking for the murderer; someone to blame for this heinous act, this assault not only on Bijou and the Benoîts, but on the whole town.

15

Mattapoisett 1834-1835

Every man is guilty of all the good they did not do. --Voltaire.

Jack, too, was devastated, his innards in a turmoil and head constantly pounding, he felt responsible, guilty. It was his fault, he believed, even though no one said so. Madame Benoît would not look him in the face. No one asked why he wasn't with Bijou. It no longer mattered. But Suzanne inquired, "Did you see anyone around, Jack? Do you know why she took that path instead of the usual one?"

Jack, choking back tears, only wagged his head back and forth, and looked down at the floor. Eventually, he said, "There was no one else around. I didn't see anyone else but me and my friends."

The house became somber. The family members went through the motions of getting by with the barest attention to needs. Marie-Therese became the primary caregiver to her mother with the help of Mrs. Marshall. The loss after the accidental death of Jean had already taken its toll, but Bijou's death shattered her. Madeleine became mute again. She had to be cared for like an infant, being fed and bathed for she would not, could not move.

A week later, Jack could watch this no longer. *It's like living with ghosts*, he thought to himself. He packed his few belongings that night and left quietly, secretly without a word to anyone, not even a note.

Do not think for a minute that a child's heart cannot break as much as an adult's.

Acquainted with the ships and their routes, Jack managed to stow away on one bound for Richmond. There, he wandered the docks for days before he joined the world of restless men; men who knew not their goals, only that they were angry, and believed treated unfairly. These were fighting men who roared and fought to relieve their misery, to feel better through the screams of others.

∾

MATTAPOISETT

"That darkie larkie did it," bellowed Alwyn Baker. "He's always hanging around, hanging round, hanging in town, hanging down, hanging upside down. Let's hang him! Hang him, that Ansle, Ansa, Anlee!"

The Benoît's knew Ansa was innocent, as they knew and loved Ansa as family. Patrice and a number of people saw him with Edington at the time of the murder. Nevertheless, there were always those who looked for any excuse to express their most base beliefs through despicable actions. Facts were at times an inconvenience. Baker's incitement was just the catalyst they needed. A few men gathered outside La Figue Dansante one evening and grabbed the unsuspecting Ansa. Dragged into the street, they commenced beating him with their fists and clubs to nearly unconscious. Baker, watching as he leaned against the side of the tavern laughed maniacally before other patrons intervened.

"You bastards!" screamed Patrice. "You know he is innocent, you scum, you, you …! She was so angry and repulsed, she could not find her words as she hurried to the downed Ansa, his body bloody and bruising. Patrons carried him into the pub and placed him gently on a sofa.

Get me some warm water and cloths!" demanded Patrice to her staff. "You! She pointed to one of the men, go get Mademoiselle Marie-Therese, now!" She did the best she could for Ansa until Marie-Therese arrived to help. Ansa's eye was swollen shut, already puffed and hideously red. It would be forever frozen in a drooped position. His leg, broken in two places would cause a slight limp. Marie-Therese reduced the break, splinted and bandaged it. "Stay off of it until I tell you, Mr. Ansa," she said gently. "Let him stay here tonight and we will take him home for his recovery tomorrow," she said to Patrice.

Patrice nodded, "Of course Marie-Therese, I will see to him myself."

Alwyn Baker's son had been summoned. Having had enough of his father's maladaptiveness, he took the elder Baker to an asylum for idiots and lunatics up in Worcester.[27] There, some years later, through his bitterness and sense of entitlement, the elder Baker descended into a quieter madness of his own making, his own circle of hell, never to leave the hospital again.

~

ONE YEAR LATER 1835

In six months' time both her husband and youngest daughter died, both horribly, the latter inexplicably. A year later, the killer was still at large. Madeleine was grateful for Suzanne's shouldering the bulk of business responsibilities as the older woman had secluded herself to gather her thoughts and ascertain as to how and if there was a willingness to continue.

In early June, Madeleine made her first public outing at the family side of La Fique Dansante. She and Patrice had a nice dinner and were about to order coffee. It was relatively quiet, save for a table of businessmen in the far corner.

"How are you doing, Madeleine?" coaxed Patrice gently.

Madeleine smiled absently and said, "I am doing all right, Patrice, really. I live every day with the pain of her absence, only more calmly. I remember the day of her birth, the smallness, the perfect fingers grasping mine, the sweet smell and tiny voice. I cried when she cried. She was my blood, my life, my sin, my good deed; everything I wanted to be, but could not. After all, a child is the greatest responsibility entrusted to you by nature. That is why a parent is willing to lose everything in this world, but a child? Never!"

Patrice covered Madeleine's hand with hers and squeezed. "Death is only painful for the living. You can die with the dead, my dear, but please stay strong for your family."

Madeleine gave her a wan smile. "Oh, Patrice my dear friend, the greatest grace is to be buried by our children, not the other way around.

Bijou's murder still haunts us all. An illness, an accident; we would still mourn, but heinous acts upon a child does not rise to any level of humanity." Madeleine paused, "But yes, I am blessed to have two healthy and intelligent daughters and of course, dear friends like you. Yes, Patrice, I am fine. I have to be."

"Yes, my dear. We all grieve. This sin was against all of us, but for a mother …." Just then, she was called to the kitchen to check on a delivery. "I'll have our coffees sent over and be back in just a moment," she said.

"Merci, Patrice," said Madeleine and mused about how she and Patrice were so much alike in behaviors, but with very different personalities. *I suppose that is why we get along so well,* she thought to herself. She did not look around, but stared straight ahead engulfed in her own inner thoughts.

He approached her straight and assured, smiled wryly and shamelessly, "You were watching me. I noticed. Allow me to introduce myself. Red Jefferson Beauregard at your service, Madam. I am in town conducting business with Messrs. Bennett and Jones over there, he gestured with a sweeping arm."

He wasn't a particularly tall man. He had broad enough shoulders, a round head and an accent from the southern states. But his obnoxious and boorish demeanor was so very off putting. *He is so full of himself and speaks with not a small hint of condescension,* thought Madeleine. She managed to allow herself a mix of startled and annoyed expression when he spoke to her, and was either too polite or too taken aback to counter his assertion. She gave him a lukewarm "how do you do sir?" and a nod to be civil.

"I do just well and I'm of good fortune, madam. Business is quite good," tipping his chin to his partners at the far table with a flourish. They nodded to Madeleine and then smiled and laughed quietly to each other. He spoke waving his cigar, dropping feathered ashes onto her table.

"Beg pardon," he laughed as he made a haphazard attempt to flick them off with his other hand.

Madeleine held her handkerchief to her face and looked down at the table for a moment, before saying, "I'm here with a friend, thank you," she answered. "Please do rejoin and enjoy yours." And with that she turned her head away from his leering gaze towards the window pretending to be interested in the goings-on outside.

A waiter came to her table with coffee service and honeyed palmiers, followed close behind by Patrice glancing at the retreating Mr. Beauregard.

"What did *he* want?" she whispered as she sat down.

"I do not understand it, Patrice. I am barely a year and a half a widow, and he has the nerve to approach me in such a manner, I do not even want to describe it," whispered Madeleine her face red from embarrassment and not a little bit of anger.

Patrice took Madeleine's hand and in a lowered voice said, "Ah yes, do not be so naïve my friend. Pardon, but now you are the widow Benoît and sole owner of a successful shipping business. There are bound to be many men looking for easy prey in the guise of coming to the aid of a lonely widow, a mere woman. And a fine looking one, I might add."

Madeleine looked at Patrice in shock, but noticed her crinkly eyes, her twitchy, almost smiling mouth, and they both burst out laughing.

"Oh Patrice, what would I do without you!" exclaimed Madeleine holding back tears of laughter.

"Things will be alright, Madeleine," said Patrice as she wrapped her arm around her friend's shoulders and squeezed gently.

"Yes they will! I have every confidence," stated Madeleine adamantly. "I too, am of good fortune, after all! Ha!" she mocked.

∾

A few days later, Madeleine and Suzanne were together in the office. There were many offers for the business although Madeleine had expressed no intent of selling. People just assumed her intent. Two men from Boston called upon her to ascertain her disposition of sale and asking price.

"Madam, said one in a condescending voice, "This is a rough business and very complex for delicate sensibilities. There will be shrewd men about, at times even evil, and who will make it their mission to take advantage of you. One needs to be tough to deal with such snakes and the cruelty they can inflict."

It was a not too veiled insult, but Madeleine returned with words of civility as was her custom. "Will you please enjoy a cup of tea, Sirs?"

As she listened to their proposals, she looked at the two men trying to size them up, wondering if they genuinely were trying to just warn her in their inept manner or obscuring their own malicious intentions. She settled on the latter.

At length, putting her cup down she looked them in the eyes, first one then the other. "You think because I am a woman that I am kind and soft. Let me tell you, gentlemen, we women have forgotten more cruelty than you will ever know!" scowled Madeleine as she stood up. "You may leave now, good day!"

The two men bowed and left the office grumbling, as Suzanne entered watching their departure and looked quizzically at her mother.

"Suzanne?" said Madeleine quietly while looking out the windows into the harbor.

"Oui Maman? What do you need?"

"Condescending ignoramuses!" she fumed before calming herself. "Chérie, do you remember the discussions we had with Papa about moving the business to Mexico? To Alta California?" she said turning around to face Suzanne.

"Mais oui, Maman. He thought it was a growing country and that supplying dry goods businesses should do well there. What are you thinking?"

Madeleine was pensive and stating as much to herself as to Suzanne, "I am thinking perhaps we should sell our business after all and move to San Francisco."

Suzanne squealed with excitement, so uncharacteristically, "Oh Maman! Are you serious? Are you just thinking out loud?"

"Oui, Suzanne, both. I am serious and thinking out loud. But having said it, I think we can do it! I think we should do it!"

"Oh I cannot wait to start packing!" exclaimed Suzanne, then she stopped suddenly. "I am sure Marie-Therese will be excited, but I do not look forward to telling Mrs. Marshall and Monsieur Kabbah. They are like family."

"Oh Suzanne, they are of honorable stock, they surely will understand," said Madeleine, then paused, closing her eyes in thought. "Suzanne, why not ask them to come with us? I am thinking more for us, I know, but perhaps it is time for them as well. At any rate, do let us extend them the invitation."

"We can do it together after we talk to Marie-Therese. She will be so excited!"

"Now let me think," said Madeleine. "I need to start writing a plan for selling and buying. Please bring those newspapers and financial reports. We will look at them together. We will need a contact for San Francisco and more research. Oh, and please place an order with Henri in Marseille …"

"Henri Le Murier? Our Henri, in Marseilles?" interrupted Suzanne.

"Oui, Suzanne. It will take a good deal of time to ship goods to the west. Order enough silks for twelve dresses, five bolts of madapolam for a start. Please do the calculations for 150 pantaloons and have him ship fifteen bolts of tissu de Nîmes to us in San Francisco as soon as possible, said Madeleine.

"Tissu de Nîmes, Maman?"questioned Suzanne.

"Ah!" exclaims Madeleine. "I am thinking too fast. Oui, cloth from the city of Nîmes.[28] They weave cotton in a new manner that is tight and extremely suited for rough work such as on farms or docks.

"Henri, he knows of this cloth?" asked Suzanne.

"Mais oui, Suzanne. Nîmes is not that far from Marseille. The workmen, especially the sailors and dock workers have been making use of this blue cloth for some time now," explained Madeleine. "We will sell it in San Francisco."

~

Two months later, in the west salon of the Mattapoisett home Madeleine and Ansa sat in high-backed stuffed chairs near the fire. They were to depart by ship the next day.

"Oh, Monsieur Ansa, I am so glad you agreed to come with us to Alta California. You have become such a support to us, you are family," said Madeleine.

"Madame, I am the one honored by your invitation. It is most generous and I look forward to being of assistance however possible," Ansa said with a serious nod.

"There is a part of me that mourns leaving this place, my daughter, my husband. It is as if I died as well," murmured Madeleine.

"We cannot change the past, Madame, but the future is always in our hands, or at least our attitude towards it. They will be safe in your heart, and you will keep living until you are alive again," answered Ansa thoughtfully.

Madeleine reached her hand out to Ansa, "It will be an adventure, a new life for all of us," she said.

～

Suzanne sat on the stoop of the back porch feeling a bit light-headed, as she watched the stars slowly unveiling themselves, the light of ages, of the past. She smiled and took a deep breath before tears and tightening chest caused her to make a tiny, painful gasp. She heard the footsteps and tried hard to pull herself together, wiping her face and sitting up straight. It was Peter.

"Oh, it is you," she said as he approached quietly. She could feign surprise, but could she feign indifference?

"It's me," he said as he sat down next to her. "When were you going to tell me?"

"Tell you? Is it for me to tell you? You purchased our business. You would have known from the outset. Why would I need to repeat what is already happening?" she answered disjointedly.

Peter noted a strangeness in her demeanor, an edginess not like her. "Would you not bid me good-bye?"

Suzanne looked at him impassively, "Good-bye now."

"What is it, Suzanne? How can you be so cold?" asked Peter.

"Cold? How should I be, Sir? You are an acquaintance of the family. You bought the business. Do I owe you any more than a polite adieu?"

Peter looked at her intently, his heart pounding as every fiber in his being struggled to remain calm in light of her outrageous behavior.

"You are so wrong, Suzanne, so wrong. Good Luck to you, then." With that, he departed.

It is better this way, Suzanne thought to herself, still sitting on her stoop.

1830'S U.S.A EASTERN & SOUTHERN STATES AND TERRITORIES

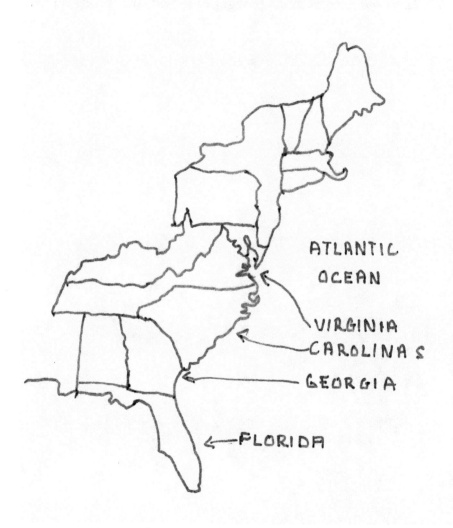

ATLANTIC
OCEAN

VIRGINIA
CAROLINAS

GEORGIA

← FLORIDA

16

Jack in Florida 1836

Ever tried. Ever failed. No matter. Try again. Fail again. Fail better.
–Samuel Beckett

Jack Marshall made his way to Carolina and joined a group of militia volunteers traveling south through Georgia to Florida territory. Many of the older men from Georgia had fought in the war of 1812 with the militia, where some picked up smooth bore .72 caliber guns from fighting the Creek and Choctaw. While not as accurate as a rifled gun, it would kill all the same. But most had their own pistols and rifles or used muzzleloaders with Greener balls.[29] Fighting without uniforms, they relied on their white skin to identify union and their mission. At first they performed honorably, secure in their belief they were saving their country's and people's interests. But changes which were once imperceptible, became blatant, urged on by their President, Andrew Jackson, to wreak havoc and mayhem amongst the Natives.

The Carolinians and Georgians fought with the Army regulars, but often sensed being looked down upon for their modest training and country bearing. Their leaders roared a permanent and persistent clamor of freedom, glory and righteousness. Before long, none fought without looting; what was the point otherwise? Those in charge encouraged them to do so, and sometimes that included taking anything and anybody for whatever they wanted right then.

Most had no dog in the fight other than the elusive push for honor, duty and often an imagined threat to their way of life. Sometimes there were promises of land and community; promises often broken. They rationalized their actions by calling themselves freedom fighters. But just because one gives something a name, doesn't make it real. They would defend what they believed were their rights by taking away those of others. In Georgia, federal troops, farmers and ranch hands joined the march. Poisonous words dripped into their ears by the leaders back home. They became frenzied and ready to destroy all in their wake. Each group had their preferred method of maiming. Annihilation was the end game; clearing out the Natives who had refused to leave for Indian Country west of the Mississippi, and doing away with the refuge for runaway slaves. Eventually they made their way into central Florida, having joined yet another band of volunteers who moved southerly, sometimes splitting off and joining government troops. There seemed to be no pattern other than to obliterate villages.

Life changed for Jack. Now only 15, he felt used up. The Native villagers were mostly farmers growing corn, beans, squash and melons. They gathered berries, hunted and fished. They lived in log cabins with thatched roofs that even had openings for ventilation. *How were they so different from the small farmers he met during his march from Virginia?* he wondered.

He started to see a developing brotherhood of sorts among his group. Most of the men became fiercely loyal to one another. They watched out for the other, listened to their stories of home, some shared their disdain for the dirty missions. *How could they fight together any other way?* Jack became so confused.

In time they met up with A. J. Steele, a U.S. Army commander. Steele was a large man, tall with a dark beard and eyebrows sprouting wildly like brambles. He was of harsh demeanor, ineluctable, and spoke with a voice of chthonic resonance as to make one's flesh crawl. No one knew his story other than his boasts of being in league with General Andrew Jackson, that gambler, that bringer of darkness. He bragged that the two had met at a social gathering where he was introduced to Jackson's good friend, Eaton and his lady, Miss Peggy. Jackson would work the crowd with his foul mouthed parrot on his left shoulder and mistress at his right side. In this circle, they were free to express their inclinations. Neither Jackson nor Steele had anything but contempt for the Natives. Steele spoke as if he sprung up from the roaring depths below, ready to fight. Indeed, his battle cry was "Fight or back to Hell with us!" screaming with blood curdling gusto.

Steele eyed the new band of raggedy volunteers. "Ah, ha! Even the *North* Carolina boys are here!"

Jack's volunteer leader looked at Steele flummoxed but stated, "Yes, Sir! We're here to join up with you, but what made you think we're from *North* Carolina?"

Steele narrowed his dark eyes at the man, then looked up and rolled them. "Your boots, asshole, your boots! They're still caked with Carolina tar sands! You tar heels best be more sharp-eyed in the field. This ain't no picnic we're on! Now fall in at the back behind the Georgia boys!"

~

As yet, Jack did not know if he had killed anyone as he always fired the rifle given him with his eyes closed. This was not what he intended when he left home. But now, he depended on these men for his life and mostly ran errands for them such as fetching water, gathering firewood, and occasionally hunting small game. He felt tethered to his own hell.

Steele was especially brutal to the younger boys like Jack. One night the older man sat down next to him at the campfire.

"Hey now, Jackie boy, want to see smoke come out of my eye?"

Jack, scared and cautious, didn't want to incur the wrath of this man. "Yes Sir," he said hesitantly.

"Now then, watch my eyes closely," said Steele, "Don't look away."

Jack warily focused on the man's reddened, fierce eyes. Slowly, Steele put his lit cigar to Jack's bare arm burning him.

"Yeow!" screamed Jack, rubbing his arm and trying hard to hold back tears as much for the betrayal as for the pain.

"Ha! You missed it! I told you to watch for the smoke, ya sissy! Ha! Did you see that boys? That will teach him to pay better attention! Ha, ha, ha!" laughed Steele, clearly enjoying his little trick.

As crude as this behavior was, it paled to the times he pushed Jack or other boys into the woods for his own prurient amusement.

Some of the men were getting restless. It had been a week since their last raid. "We need a battle! Villages to burn and plunder! My sword is getting rusty, heh, heh, heh!" bellowed the red bearded Sergeant Richard Dick. He stood out from the group in his stiff sergeant's tunic.

"No one here cares about your sword, Dick!" jabbed another sergeant.

Dick laughed, "But I need fresh meat my friend! Heh, heh, heh! Heh, heh, heh! Heh!" he roared.

"Two more days, Dick!" yelled the sergeant. "Two more days! We all need to take a break and catch our breath." The sergeant turned to another grinning, "Then he can finally give his hand a break."

It was hot, humid and in general, miserable, as the invading troops slashed their way through swamp-land clearing the way of Natives to gain land and position for further expansion. The waist high fan palms and sawgrass ripped into their bodies. "What do we want with this forsaken hell hole for?" muttered one of the men. Others agreed, but continued nevertheless.

Some U.S. landowners had offered up their enslaved people to fight along with the white militias. Joey was one of these. He was Jack's age, but smaller. That and his club foot made him easy to be offered up for the fighting. Joey had seen enough cruelty on his master's plantation to look for opportunities to run away. Being sent to fight seemed just that for this gentle boy, schooled in the ten commandments and a smattering of proverbs. The white troops resented him and consistently shoved him to the front of danger, armed only with an ax to hack foliage as they didn't trust him with a gun.

It was twilight, they came upon a small Creek compound and set fire to the homes. As the occupants ran out, the group shot or slashed with large knives or axes. They rounded up young women and girls and stripped them bare. Those who weren't dragged towards the river were forced to stand still as they were used for target practice. Clouds of gunsmoke appeared and disappeared one after another in a rhythmic fashion. Shaking, the screams were thundering through his head when the commander ordered Jack to ax a young girl. She was the age of Bijou when he last saw her and had the same round dark eyes. He was transfixed. Hesitantly, he looked at his commander.

Joey spoke up, "Does not the Bible state thou shalt not kill?!"

With that, a shot rang out and hit directly into the girl's face. Her body blew backward like so many duck feathers.

"Didja see that?! Didja see that boys?! It blew to hell! Ha, ha, ha, ha," Sergeant Dick's belly shook up and down under his tunic as he took in his amusement.

Jack horrified, vomited. His chest felt as if crushed by malevolent claws and his head spun dizzily. He became aware of a terrible dreamlike state when he saw troops grab up Joey and tie him to tent poles formed into a crucifix.

"God detests the hands that shed innocent blood!" Joey screamed before someone stuffed a rag in his mouth

"We've had enough of your lip, preacher boy!" they howled. Nourished by their own rage, someone threw kerosene on Joey and lit him up. Joey's muffled screams were that horrible, sustained sound of panic, agony and dying. His disbelief and torture were unbearable. It continued for six minutes until the inhalation of searing smoke burned his throat and lungs and he could utter no more. Only his writhing and the torture of the flames continued. The air smelled of burnt hair, like singed bird feathers mixed with searing flesh, sweet and nauseating. Joey's lips were gone, showing only discolored, crooked teeth protruding from his jawbone. His skin scorched and drew tight over his limbs folding into themselves grotesquely followed by the knotting up of cartilage and tendons in his joints.

"He dishonored us!" yelled the Steele. "These people are beyond saving. There is no hope for them. Look! He burns and still he lies!"

"He was yella, and a traitor!" offered another, "Serves him right!" They wanted to be done with Joey and they found their justification. He was an American until he was no longer useful.

Jack was traumatized and speechless. Shaking, he could only look at the troops, then the dead girl. He could not look at Joey. Jack guardedly glanced at Steele, struggling not to show his rage. The muscles in his shoulders and neck tightened. He balled his hands into fists behind him, fingernails digging into the palms. This was a pain he could understand. The other was beyond comprehension. A grimacing smile choked on his face in defense of fear of a wanton violence to his own person.

When the flames died down, the troops left Joey as he was, charred and unidentifiable. Georgia volunteer, Jeff Bradford, was so haunted by the atrocities he wrote of the event in a letter home to a friend. "Those grandees sit comfortably, safe at home and list our faults. They know nothing about what happens here." He found the action not only unconscionable but soul killing. Nevertheless, he judged that he best acquiesce to the leadership lest he be its next victim.

Some of the men whispered about it later. "I hope this campaign ends quickly," one said.

"Hope?" said another, "with those men in charge? Hope is a poor man's food. Sure, we have bread. We have water, but my soul is starving! Starving I tell you! When will hope save us from *them*?"

Some of the militia men nodded in unison. One answered, "Yes, but one can not go forward without it.

～

Small American enclaves and trading posts dotted Florida's interior. An uneasy truce prevailed for the purpose of trade. At one such trading post, some of the poorer members of the invading army were talking among themselves. "We were promised land if we fought. We could set up our own farm," said one weary fighter.

"You mean take their farms?" asked another.

"Well, they're just heathens, right? Besides, we didn't know they even had farms or wore clothes. We were always told they were wild savages running about the wilderness with no sense," the fighter returned.

"We'll get ours in due time. Don't let's worry. I hear whispers of another raid coming soon."

～

Four days later, the troops surrounded yet another village in the early morning hours before dawn. It was quiet and should have been easy pickin's they thought, but for the alert by a big brown and black dog, a home dog; brave, loyal and protective of the family within.

Dogg was outside the cabin door, his usually floppy ears were perked and his muzzle was up. He let out a low, slow growl, followed by quick, menacing barks.

"Dogg! Dogg! Quiet!" yelled someone from inside a cabin. "Must have seen a raccoon," muttered the man inside.

"Dogg does not bark for no reason, Beno," replied his wife.

The man looked at her as an urgency came over his face. He got up quickly and quietly grabbed his rifle, which stood at the ready. He listened. "You are right. Stay back," he whispered as he peered out the window. His eyes slowly adjusted to the dim light as he made out figures moving slowly about in the foggy gray light. Dogg started barking fiercely, his tail straight out and teeth bared as he charged one of Steele's men and knocked him down, biting him in the throat. Blood gushed from the ripped opening, spraying Doggs face as well as that of his quarry.

By then, other villagers came out of their cabins, their weapons aimed into the woods where Dogg was in frenzy, charging after yet another intruder.

His weapon aimed at Beno, the shot was diverted by the huge canine springing upon him. Sergeant Dick knocked Doggs skull with a rifle butt. Dogg screamed loud as only an animal can and lay panting hard on his side in a thicket.

"I'll take care of you later, you mangy mutt. You just wait!" muttered Dick. A bullet whizzed by his head and he instinctively ducked. The snap of a dry stick alerted him to movements amid some underbrush where he found two women huddled. One covered the mouth of the other who, squatting, was finishing giving birth. The infant was on a raggedy blanket on the ground and the placenta was being expelled. The assistant had tied off the cord. She looked up at Sergeant Dick forlornly, hoping for mercy before asking him to cut the umbilical cord with his bayonet as she had nothing to do so.

Dick had long dissociated from his humanity, rendered callous and craven from his own brutal upbringing. He nodded, then smiled before stabbing the infant in the heart. Both women choked in horror at the wriggling being which quickly succumbed. They were next.

Dogg's alert gave many villagers time to disseminate into the woods. Again, a village burned out of existence, but this time Steele's men sustained casualties. The volunteers were getting antsy; their buddies' deaths killed the thrill of war. Steele himself was badly wounded on his side. He ordered Sergeant Dick to take the men and move on out, that he would meet up with them later.

The Sergeant spied a young Native woman frantically making her way through the trees away from the village. "Boys, you go on. I've some sword work to attend to," laughed Dick with a menacing smile. He followed the woman into a sun drenched clearing where she stopped, turned around and smiled at him.

Sergeant Dick grunted in delight as he approached her when suddenly he heard rustling sounds. Natives closed in around him.

Jack had been ordered to stay back to tend to Steele and hide themselves. He watched the men march off and as they passed a small live oak tree, he noticed something had been nailed onto the trunk. He walked up slowly to the back of the tree, but when he saw floppy brown ears, he turned quickly away. He dragged Steele back into trees, gave him water and then stared hard at him.

"What the hell you looking at, you little bastard!?" he growled at Jack.

"Don't rightly know," murmured Jack, his head cocked to one side as he took in the situation. Jack calmly picked up a rope and commenced binding Steele's arms and legs.

"What the hell!!" yelled Steele. Just then a shovel slammed across the Commander's face. The thwack of metal biting against a skull was distinct. Steele was out cold.

He gained his senses while surrounded in darkness but could make out the surrounding pit, not quite five feet deep. The dirt walls were damp and the earthiness was pronounced. Hands and feet still bound, he was in a sitting position, his head throbbed.

"Jack, Jack, you little shit! Get me the hell out of here! Swear to God I will kill you with my bare hands!" Already he was getting his hands loose.

Jack slowly walked up to the side of the pit, bending down really low so Steele could see him. The torch he shoved into the ground by his feet illuminated the pit and Jack's face like a ghostly presence. Then he lifted his rifle.

"What the hell?! No Jack, no! I didn't mean it! I'll let you go if you just get me out of here! Please Jack help me out of here!" screamed Steele.

Jack opened the choke of the shotgun and fired a wide spray of pellets into Steele's right shoulder. Steele screamed, "Please Jack, stop!" Some of the shot hit Steele in the face and neck. Droplets of blood oozed blackened from gunpowder. Steele screamed and writhed, turning his body to protect his shredded shoulder.

"*That's* for the girl!" screamed Jack. He closed the choke and shot Steele in the left hip. "*That's* for Joey!"

Steele screamed like an enraged wild animal. "You can't do this! You're not a murderer!"

Jack paused, looked at him hard before screaming back. "You don't know Jack! ... But don't worry, Commander. You won't die of your wounds. You are, however, going back to Hell!" He raised the rifle again and shot Steele in his right leg. "And *that's* for all the boys and the damn dog!"

"Help me Jack, help me! Have mercy, Jack," his pleas barely audible.

Jack picked up a shovel and started throwing dirt into the pit.

"No Jack, no!" Steele's scream was guttural and desperate as Jack slowly continued to cover up his handiwork. When he was almost finished, Jack saw a hand just above the mounded earth, loosened from the bonds, still and lifeless. He slammed it into the mound with the shovel as one last gesture. "And *this* is for me! I'm *done!*"

Jack mounded over the pit some more, looked up at the stars contemplatively. His was a pain so raw he could only scream it. Into the sky, he roared his tearful rage with a strength not his own. "Yaa-aaah! Ye-aaah, yaaaaaah!" Breathing heavily, he turned and disappeared into the forest.

~

The U.S. fighters never found Steele, but some days later, in a small clearing at the edge of shadows cast by bald cypresses, they thought they saw a goat head in the field. As they tracked closer, they became horrified to discover that it had been a man buried up to his neck. They fired off a shot to scare away the panther who was playing with the head; the fleshy parts gone, yellow teeth grimaced at them, the last bit of tendon held it to the buried torso. In the brush, were scraps of reddish fuzz and shreds of a sergeant's tunic.

"Dick!" said one of the fighters.

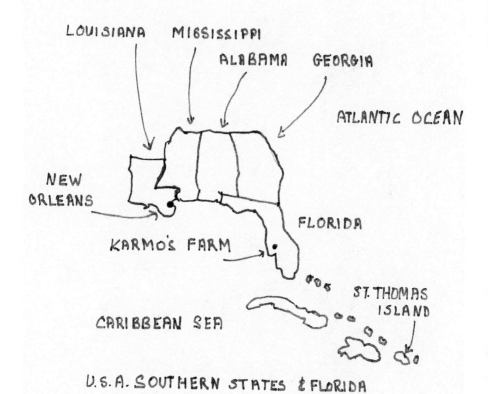

LOUISIANA   MISSISSIPPI

ALABAMA   GEORGIA

ATLANTIC OCEAN

NEW
ORLEANS

KARMO'S FARM

FLORIDA

ST. THOMAS
ISLAND

CARIBBEAN SEA

U.S.A. SOUTHERN STATES & FLORIDA

17

Karmo goes to New Orleans 1835

Whoever you are, I've always depended on the kindness of strangers.
–A Street Car Named Desire, Tennessee Williams

Karmo's team was on a mission. For five days, they shadowed the invading troops, most of whom were volunteers. They came upon a small village of burned-out homes still steaming with smoke and powder, the carcass of a dog nailed to a tree with the grimace on his face testament to his torture, families shot and hacked to pieces.

When one of the Seminoles recognized his kin among the tortured, he collapsed beside him. "Cousin!" he screamed as cradled the mangled body, shaking the corpse. "I will tear out their lungs and feed them to the dogs. I will rip out their hearts before your blood dries!" he screamed.

Justice is not revenge, Efendi's words swam back to surface again in Karmo's mind. Nevertheless, it was clear that the Seminoles needed to find this group of killers and stop them. These invaders were no ordinary soldiers; no, they were not even soldiers, in fact. There was no honor, no restraint, no rules in their non-existent code of behavior.

They followed the tracks. Karmo watched as Dosar sent small bands out ahead of the invading troops, allowing themselves to be seen so as to entice the invaders to follow. The greater number of Seminoles lingered behind and then slowly enveloped the invaders on two flanks as the troops approached the river. Karmo's team joined the others, took its advantage, and advanced on the troops. The invaders could only smash through the water grass towards the river infested with alligators and snakes. Eventually they were trapped by two things: their arrogance and their ignorance of the terrain. Karmo and his men fought fiercely, as if possessed. All but three of the enemy were killed, and those three escaped. None of Karmo's men fell. His reputation was confirmed that day. The survivors reported the defeat of the others, their escape and their shame. Now, imminent death followed Karmo around like a shadow. Like some of the others, his name was known and his head was definitely at risk.

The next day at dusk, luminous beetles, symbolic of the heart's inner light, flew upward into the sky amongst the trees. Karmo gazed at these flying jewels with admiration; they were points of light in the midst of unimaginable savagery.

Dosar and Haco built a campfire and reflected silently on the past months. Sentries were posted in double rings around their camp to watch each other's backs and to foil any attempts at penetration by the enemy, who would be surrounded if even the first circle was breached.

"Those men directly reflected the beliefs of their country," muttered Karmo. Inside his heart, there was fire and storm, but his outer bearing was cool and deliberate.

"Perhaps," said Dosar. "The individual soldiers do not always know for what they are fighting. They are told stories that enrage them, embolden them, make them hate the enemy without even knowing him. The individual often has so much taken away from him by their leaders, he loses hope. There are others who prick him on, perhaps betrayed themselves. The man who gets a raw deal is not only angry; he is ashamed, that all these wrongs happened to him. He skewers others' hope because he himself is hopeless. That is the biggest crime: killing hope."

"I do not understand," Karmo remarked. "What does hope have to do with killing?"

"Hope is something that has to be fed. In turn, hope feeds success, action and life, the feeling of righteousness despite heinous behaviors. But these behaviors start to wear on soldiers, tears at their souls without their realizing it. The fighter does not know that some of his own kind are the cause of his losing hope. They get him to fight for the lies they have fed him," explained Dosar. "That is when fate turns its head and looks the other way …"

"If you are fighting, it means your fears have come true," added Haco. "The fears your own leaders have beaten into your conscience."

Karmo was puzzled. "But we *are* fighting. Have fears been beaten into our consciences as well?"

"Yes, of course," said Haco. "The difference between us and the invaders is that they invade our lands, which they believe to be rightly theirs, and what makes them kill is the fear that they and their families will be slaughtered if they do not seize what should be theirs. It matters not that we, the Seminoles, Choctaw, Cherokee, Creek and the Chickasaw were here for generations."

"They name us savages, intent on believing that what names we are called matters more than who we are or what we have done," offered Dosar.

Karmo considered all this, struggling to reconcile these messages with the teachings of Efendi.

∾

A few captives, four or five, from previous skirmishes, were brought to the camp. Karmo dragged a Georgian named Bradford, over, and sat down across from him on a stump. His eyes drilled into the man. It was the first time he had ever spoken to the enemy directly. Food was placed before the prisoner. Bradford ate ravenously as Karmo watched, contemplating how hunger exposed the essence of the man before him. Intrigued, Karmo asked curiously, "You have been fighting a long time. Tell me why you came here. What made you participate in these horrific atrocities?"

Bradford, battered and bruised, looked down as more bread was put before him. He grabbed it like an only son used to getting what he wanted, before looking up directly into Karmo's eyes, then away, before speaking. "This land was ceded to the United States, Mr. Karmo. It belongs to us." He paused before continuing. "We are mostly good people, although we did things we'd never, ever conceived of. Even some of our team leaders were dragged onto this path, following orders, striving to do the right thing. But do we ever know the whole story, get the whole picture? We do not. Only with time does the curtain lift.

"I do not condone the tactics; the annihilation, the torture and the atrocities. Real strength means being compassionate. But that by itself will get you killed in battle. I make no excuses; only understand that we are a desperate people, many of us noble and brave, but some of us with sore grievances, and others with deep fear of the unknown. Fear leads you to compromise your values. We fought hard. We fought through our fear and fatigue. But we are the lottery losers. This war, this fighting, is like running back and forth between defeat and hope. We believe we are fighting for our very lives!"[30] Staring into the flames, Bradford collapsed back into silence.

Karmo listened, remembering his own question from the past; and recognized sentiments that had materialized in Bradford's explanation, *Who are the good, and who are the enemy?* Efendi's conclusion could be heard: "Sometimes they are one and the same." Considering this, Karmo asked himself, *How does a warrior carry on, but for loyalty to his country and his brothers? What stories do they tell themselves, and what stories have they been fed to put certain death into their future? Was everything false? Was it evil? Was there not at least a bite of truth?*

No. Loyalty is about keeping secrets, staying quiet until Judgment Day. One cannot bargain with loyalty. One either is loyal or is disloyal. Whereas, evil is forever by your side. One day evil will come and ask for all your loyalty, completely and forever.

Our enemy is evil itself, not just evil people, just as tyranny itself is our enemy, not just tyrants, mused Karmo. The two men spoke a few minutes more before Bradford was taken back where the other prisoners were secured.

Karmo sat alone, staring at the campfire, when Haco joined him. "You are deep in thought, my friend. But if ever there was a time to do so, this is it."

"What will become of the prisoners, Haco? What will you do with them?"

"What do you think we should do with such men? Men who invaded our lands, tortured, maimed and killed innocent people? Huh? What do you think?"

Karmo remained quiet a few moments. "If you release them, many will regroup and fight again."

"Yes, they will, Karmo," replied Haco. Then after a very long silence, he said, "Perhaps some will return home."

Karmo turned to Haco. "I think that man Bradford will go home and tell a truthful story of what happened here. Do you not think so?" he added cautiously.

Haco looked straight out into the darkness at the luminous flying beetles. "Yes, I think he would."

~

Another three weeks went by, and many Native bands converged to determine their further strategy. Over the region, they were so outnumbered. They were being destroyed or scattered, one by one. Karmo was distraught; *how would these people fare?*

"Each defeat is a knife in the heart of our illusions," said Haco quietly. "But we will fight for our land, for its soul and for the hearts of our families. The enemy will try to force us down, but we will go on. One does not fail, one only stops trying."

~

The fighting took its toll on both sides. While the U.S. would clearly win, small bands of their fighters were left alone, isolated for long durations to fare on their own. Karmo spoke to more prisoners, noting they no longer thought about right or wrong. Such distinctions did not register in their minds. They had gone so long without having to make decisions for themselves, and simply followed the will of their leader, either without question or out of fear. That instinct for saving humanity, that tightening in the gut that said *something is not right*, was gone, all gone.

"Leave, Karmo! One man more or less will make no difference here. Leave while you can, and tell our story. Reveal the lies!" said the Chief.

But Karmo did not want to leave. He saw how the lands were being overrun, then slowly he started to agree with the Chief. He thought of Bradford. The truth must come out.

As the evening sky darkened, and the stars started to shine upon the huddled group below. *I will tell their stories*, Karmo thought to himself.

~

Humankind has always tried to fight against destiny. And perhaps it is right to do so. Life would be meaningless otherwise. Oftentimes it is the fight itself that keeps one alive. But now and again, there comes a time when we have to accept what we are going through. At that point, resistance only hurts you and others around you. Our world is mortal. There will be both births and deaths.

~

First Karmo traveled through Florida, Alabama and Mississippi. He traveled by land, by freight and by small boats, and now, after miles and miles of humid, still air, a light breeze greeted him as he entered a maze of waterways. He was with a small group of men traveling on flat-bottom boats going west, keeping away from larger settlements in order to avoid confrontation.

These routes were known to the Natives for portage long before they were discovered by the French. As the water became less salty, the marsh with its tall reeds gave way to the fresher water of the swamps, and hardwoods. The men slowly poled their way past the 200-foot tall cypress trees whose branches stretched out and met each other across the water. The long, ragged scarves of moss that were draped from their boughs lent both an ephemeral and a serene countenance to the swamps and bayous. These same trees became bald during the winter. There were stands of other hardwoods; oak, maple. Slow-moving water pooled into the sawgrass and pickerel plants, then into larger rivers and lakes along the way. Long-beaked birds seemed to explode from the water as they approached. The red-winged blackbirds screeched loudly to their compatriots as a communal warning. Stealth was not straightforward in this area that was teeming with symbiotic life.

This coastal land was just as swampy as Florida and Georgia. Large cypresses held on by their knees, rising from the root base in the silty black water, and provided cover for alligators and wild boar alike. In this haven, this maze, his companions eventually split off from the group, one by one, to make their own way. He did not blame them, for this, he hoped, was their point of last scatter; their last time hurtling between the transparency of the past and opaqueness of their future. Karmo mused, *We knew not what awaited us, only what we wanted. We wanted the freedom to make our living peacefully, and to make our own mistakes. Was that even possible, living with others?*

Those who lived here in the swampland built houses on stilts and boated through the maze of waters under canopies of trees and vines to hunt, to fish and to trade. For days, Karmo watched them from afar as they went about their daily routines. He managed to subsist on fish caught in a makeshift basket, as he had seen done in the Caribbean. Bass, trout, and gar were plentiful and he ate well enough; even turtles would do, though they tasted of mud. He had not the strength, nor weapons, to kill the deer, raccoons or boar that roamed about.

One sunny day, a sudden and strange musty smell emanated from the opposite end of the log upon which he was sitting. He looked and held his breath as a large, dark snake with a triangular head exposed its fangs and revealed an open mouth as white as snow. Stretched out fat and seemingly annoyed, it stared at him menacingly. Karmo jumped straight into the air and took steps backward, nearly falling into the water. Steadying himself, he thought about killing and eating the snake, but it slithered down the trunk and dipped back into the water, even as he searched for a weapon. He watched it swim away on the surface of the water. His heart drummed in his chest, a primal reaction, for he had learned about these venomous snakes in Florida.

Off and on he heard voices in the distance, but remained quiet and untrusting of strangers until he could observe them closer. This caution had served him well before. Their French was different from that to which he was acclimated. Their patois had a languid and lyrical quality, but with effort and context, it was understandable to him.

For several days more, Karmo continued to thrash about in the swamps, running, hiding from people whose intent was unknown. He was always on the look-out for alligators, their motionless bodies gathering warming energy into their horny plates, those chitinous scutes, and for other menacing living creatures. Slow-flying insects, their wings heavy in the humidity, could barely produce an audible buzz. This was Honey Island, buzzing with the business of bees, he later learned. "Bees. Yes." Although weary, he fondly remembered Ansa telling him a metaphor for life in general. "If you want honey, you must tolerate the bees. Sooner or later, you will be stung," he would say. "Ansa, my brother. Where are you?" Karmo asked aloud.

One evening as the sun was setting, he covered himself in mud to protect himself from insect bites, as he always did in Florida, curled up tight under a large tree and listened to the river water lapping towards him. He closed his eyes and thought he might die. As the rising moon shone upon him, thoughts of Brima circled in his mind as he looked up into the starry night. "See me, my love," he whispered, before passing out from exhaustion.

∾

"Shh!" said a voice quietly.

Karmo felt the heat of a fire and the weight of a blanket covering his body. He remained still, listening to the lyrical voices of the men around him. *If they were going to kill me, they would have done so already,* he thought to himself. A contagion of whispering was upon him as he came to. *Am I to be saved again?* Slowly he opened his eyes.

"*Il est réveillé!*" whispered a nearby voice.

"Hey, hey, *mon ami!*" came another voice as an arm shook his shoulder gently.

Karmo, still in a haze, looked around at the shack that sheltered him and the three bearded men who encircled him. They were dressed in homespun, with vests of pelts, pants with ribbons down the sides and high, heavy leather boots. Close-fitting, pointed caps on their heads held shaggy hair out of their faces; the cap points drooped to one side.

He had been found delirious, wracked with fever, when one of the men pulled him from the tree site. He passed out again, and for two days more he was unconscious. His powerful frame belied his condition. They treated him with poultices from the tamarind tree to relieve fever and pain of insect bites, and the deep scrapes of needles, thorns and branches that plagued him when he was hiding; they cleaned and dressed his chafed ankles, knees and shoulders, bleeding sores and lacerations—and a large, gaping wound in his right thigh.

Now, as he became able to do so, they forced him to drink tea from the black willow leaves, and another tea made from mahogany tree bark with salt, both to relieve fever, for they were well-versed in the ways of medicine needed in these parts. When he was a bit stronger, they gave him bean soup and a boiled mush of arrowroot tubers. During his recovery, he sat out-doors on a small, covered porch. He observed blankets of Spanish moss, pulled by pickers and dried for sale in the markets, which were not far away. Alligator meat in strips and wild boar parts hung in smoking sheds. Crocks of honey, herbs and barks were lined up at the ready on shelves nailed to the sides of the shack.

These people had learned a subsistence way of living, and seemed no worse for it. They were friendly, generous and, seemingly, satisfied. They shared what they had for the sake of humanity, but also out of necessity. He got to know them, their weaknesses, and their strengths. They were descendants of the exiled Acadians from Nova Scotia during Le Grand Dérangement. Here, in this Bayou region, they had developed their own culture, which, over time, became known as Cajun. They shared the land and waters with Creoles, as both were peaceful peoples.

Pierre was one of the men who found and tended to him. He had an extraordinarily good ear to discern so many sounds in nature; animal calls, subtle moves in leaves and grasses, whether human or otherwise. The two men spoke much about this gift.

"A gift, perhaps," answered Pierre. "But I grew up here. I know the sounds that belong and those that do not. One needs only time, and to pay attention."

ROAR!

The Native peoples know their land best, thought Karmo to himself.

One evening, a Creole sang a tabanca, describing the bittersweet emotion of being left by a lover. Karmo listened, not entirely understanding the words, but certainly the emotion. *Our differences are so superficial,* he thought.

Pierre observed him. "You cannot wait for your life to be perfect in order to laugh, Karmo. Our souls need to be nourished by the good around us, to feel the awe of nature and the warmth of kinship. It is for our very survival."

He looked around at his benefactors, smiled in appreciation and nodded to Pierre. They had little, but it was enough and they were safe. For weeks, Karmo was at peace. He wrote a letter to his father and to Brima, hoping against all odds it would get to the other side of the ocean.

The nearby city was a shipping center, where people and goods came and went. He ventured out carefully from time to time, but did not feel entirely at ease. As long as he stayed close to this small community, he was safe from the world of strife. Or, so he thought. Once again, his peace was shattered by news of slave hunters venturing deeper into the bayous. He knew his time here in this city was limited. He needed to leave again.

꙲

A few days later, Karmo heard excited voices. Someone was approaching the shack. He strained his eyes to see what could only be described as a willowy, wild man; black, bald, with his beard midway at his chest and streaked in gray. His followers ran up to him, hugged him, kissed his hand and helped him with his sacks. The men repeatedly bowed to this wizened creature, who looked upon them with gentleness and murmured some type of blessing to each of them. The venerable personage looked up at Karmo, and cocked his head, his eyes penetrating Karmo's very being.

"Karmo?" the old man pronounced hoarsely. His sunburnt and furrowed face was so contracted that his eyes almost disappeared.

"You know me, grandfather?" questioned Karmo, utterly perplexed.

The old man remained still, with a large gap-toothed smile, but said nothing.

Karmo stared and stared. Then, slowly, tears welled up in his eyes and the most trembling of smiles came over his face. As if the wind had been knocked out of him, he took a step, felt his knees weaken so much that they might give way, and staggered towards the old man. Looking up, he whispered, "Okeke."

Old Okeke had survived his trip downriver and the brutality of the Louisiana cotton fields long enough to escape to New Orleans City. There, he had the good fortune to come under the protection of the Widow Paris, whose second husband, Monsieur Christophe Glapion, had just passed from this world, in June.[31] Over the years, Old Okeke was initiated in the art of voodoo, and became a minor, but revered, practitioner in the bayous. He commingled his new knowledge with the practices and stories from Sierra Leone. But one of his most important practices was not magical at all.

"I survived through my wits and my accomplices. Keep spies everywhere, Karmo, and take good care of them; protect them," he said. "You would be surprised what gets discussed freely in the presence of servants and the invisible children of the street."

Karmo nodded thoughtfully in understanding. "And what news of Sando and Jahn?" he added.

"Perished, my son. They died on their feet, picking cotton," replied Old Okeke sadly. "I heard of it through our web of messengers. The brutality of one man upon another is incomprehensible! And oh, what they do to the women, even their own! These are the mothers of the world! To beat them, denigrate them and disregard them is the greatest injustice. Someday, female grief will rise up and overcome humanity like a cloud of darkness. Surely this is not what nature intended."

The two talked of home, their families, their loves. Old Okeke had given himself over to his new life, but encouraged Karmo. "One who walks without love carries a corpse as a body, Karmo. Keep your love with you, if only in your heart."

Ah no, this place would not be where Karmo could find peace. He had to leave. Old Okeke gave him a small gray bag on a lanyard to hang around his neck. "Keep this with you always. It will protect you from harm, and give you the gift of foresight and perspective. At the very least, it will give you comfort, Karmo."

Karmo took the gris-gris bag reluctantly, for he did not believe in such things, but he was more averse to insulting Okeke in any way. The bag gift reminded him of Ansa and the talisman carvings. He kissed the old man's hand and departed.

He could not go back, so he would push westward. He thanked his benefactors, who instructed him where to find a freighter that would take him to a small harbor at the mouth of the San Antonio River in the land called Tejas. He left them two letters to post, but had little hope the letters would ever be received.

Dockside, Karmo was alone with his passion and a desperate heart. His only witness was the shimmering moon, its light sparkling on the dark water. He could feel the shadow of death, its coldness slowly, teasingly wrapping around him and squeezing him with its heavy silence. He did not avoid or fear death, but he would not accept it, either, for he had hope, and promises to keep. He shook off the feeling and looked into the sidereal solitude of the night sky, watching for movement. Speaking to the stars, he said, "We all have our journeys, our paths to travel. I will not concede defeat. I will not succumb until I cross paths with you."

Turning his head to gaze out onto the waters, he held out his hands with the palms upward. *Was that a dream that happened, on a night like this so many years ago?* He again scanned the sky, then with eyes closed, sent thoughts, like ripples moving at the speed of light, across the waves—and prayed while he patted his heart. When he finished praying, he asked out loud, "Brima, do you hear me? Do you feel me?" Karmo squeezed his eyes closed and waited for the moment to pass before quietly stealing onto the boat.

Thousands of miles away across the seas to the east, a shiver ran down her back and around her shoulders, followed by a warming sensation. Brima's eyes were closed, with tears welling up, "Karmo," she whispered tenderly.

PACIFIC
OCEAN

MEXICO

U.S.A.

ATLANTIC
OCEAN

ALBA
SAN ANTONIO
SAN JACINTO
GOLIAD

MEXICO CITY

CITIES IN MEXICO & MEXICAN TERRITORY

18

Santa Anna in Tejas, Fall 1835

If your enemy takes ease, give him no rest.
If his forces unite, separate them.
–The Art of War, Sun Tzu

He left New Orleans by freighter, as a stowaway in the hold. Karmo made his way to the eastern edge of Mexican territory, snaking through coastal outer banks where he thought he would be free, since slavery had been abolished in Mexican lands. Nevertheless, these lingering practices remained, as at this small outpost town near the mouth of the San Antonio River where he had arrived in the dark of night. He managed to keep the grey voodoo bag given to him by Old Okeke. Karmo's fighting experience and ability to hide served him well. For, here again, his dark skin clearly marked him as a foreigner.

Brima's voice suddenly entered his conscience. It was September, and the days were still searing hot. In the midst of this blistering suffering, he imagined her cool, gentle hand on his cheek. In battle, he heard her soft voice, "Live, and come home to me." In quiet moments, his mind searched for and reached out to her. *We are looking at the same sky,* he thought to himself.

～

Ever on the alert, he didn't know who they were, but he felt he was being followed. Karmo saw a figure in the shadows, moving off to his right. It was a Mexican villager, crouching, silently motioning him to come over to him. He sensed safety by the man's demeanor, and so instinctively followed him. There was a well-hidden cave with a tunnel in the back, about fifty feet long. Both men entered the cool, dark cave; the Mexican signaled Karmo, his index finger to his lips, to be quiet.

From this place of seclusion, they saw outside, the swaying light of lanterns and heard people's footsteps brushing through the shrubs and turf grass. Karmo looked quizzically at the Mexican, who whispered, "Invasores."

Karmo looked at the man with both fear and gratitude because he was being protected, for this man took him in, he, a stranger who could just as well have been a thief or a murderer.

～

For now, Karmo was safe, as long as he could be discreet and keep his forays outside the cave to a minimum. So he made the cave his home for months. He learned that the Mexican man's name was Jesse. With Jesse's and his trusted friends' help, Karmo found enough work in the small village nearby to buy food and goods. He also became acquainted with friendly Native tribes and learned the local Spanish dialect. News of fighting on all fronts was reported by travelers who came into the town square. Both the Mexicans and the invaders from the east were fighting Natives, often making no distinction as to which tribes they were, whether they were friend or foe. Karmo did not understand this, and thought it short-sighted.

～

Until 1830, Mexico relaxed the immigration laws in the territories of Coahuila and Tejas, as they were sparsely populated, and the government needed people to populate the region quickly so as to better protect and govern it.[32] The Apache and Comanche tribes fiercely defended their ancestral lands.

Additionally, Mexico had abolished slavery. All enslaved people brought in from other lands would be freed within six months of arrival. All children born to slaves in these regions were to be free at birth. Immigrants and invaders often simply converted their slaves to indentured servants with a 99-year term. This practice, too, was outlawed by

Mexico in 1832. But it was hard to enforce in this land so far from the central government; the American empresarios persisted.

An American, Sam Houston, saw an opportunity and went for it.[33] He was a part-time agent for the Indians, as the Americans called the Natives, but he had bigger aspirations. He was a former U.S. House representative from Tennessee; at one time, he was tried and convicted of beating another House member who had disparaged him. He had already defrauded hundreds of farmers in land deals, and had abandoned his wife when the heat of conviction was upon him. He escaped to Tejas, where he complied with the laws of Mexico long enough to get his land grant. Laws in Mexico granted land to settlers in the Coahuila and Tejas territories, contingent on the fact that they would become Mexican citizens and convert to Catholicism.

Houston did so, and got word to other Americans to come to Tejas for easy land and good business ventures. Once he got his land, he renounced his religion and citizenship, dishonoring the contract. This was not uncommon among the invaders from the east, as they maintained that this land was simply owed to them. Other Americans merely came illegally and squatted on land. Many men came and—as Sam Houston had done and sometimes married local women to strengthen ties to their land holdings.

Many had disdain for the Mexican people, who had mixed blood. This became the prevailing sentiment of subsequent invaders, not much different from the sentiment in many parts of the U. S at the time. It became an excuse for further incursions and denigration. Houston knew the U.S. wouldn't accept Tejas as a state, because he and his partners wanted to bring slavery there, and that would cause an imbalance between the slave and non-slave states in Congress. No, Tejas would indeed become a country unto itself, and Houston had aspirations to be its president.

~

Among those fleeing to Tejas was a man named Travis, a lawyer escaping from Alabama to avoid arrest for debts. He too saw an opportunity to expand his business.[34] He abandoned his wife and children, after first killing his wife's alleged lover. Tennessee legislator D. Crockett told his colleagues to go to Hell rather than abide by the wishes of his constituency.[35] He also left his family. The banker and slave runner J. Bowie disemboweled a man with a large knife in an all-out brawl, then escaped to Tejas.[36] Such men and others like these made their way over the border to Tejas, which had easy land for the taking, and many opportunities for business.

～

The empresario boomed to his cronies, "Gather every scumbag you can. They will be our team of provocateurs. We will use them to incite the populace to take part in anti-Mexico rioting with lies and killing raids, in order to instigate a war. We will use bombs. We will even dress as Mexican soldiers. The more chaos, the bigger the profits!"

Cut-throats fresh from American jails, adventurers and corrupt tradesmen—all took up arms for Tejas. Honest farmers and city dwellers, Native, Mexican and American alike, got caught up in the drama, but found little mercy shown them from either side.

Once incited, in order to beef up forces, pleas were sent out to the Louisiana territory for fighters, often men of good faith and integrity, to do their patriotic duty and protect fellow invaders from the east, who were endangered in Tejas.

Volunteers left their homes and families with mixed emotions. Others abandoned their families more willingly, for either real or feigned reasons. Some just wanted to start over, unencumbered by family, for the sake of adventure. Some were self-centered, arrogant men who wrapped themselves in smokescreens of enterprise and the glory of country, leaving their families to suffer and become homeless. Although some abandoned families could move in with relatives, others were without resources, fell ill and died on the streets. Mothers and wives with few or no options turned to prostitution; children ran away or became indentured servants.

～

After the latest battle at Tampico, Mexico, and the Federalists' loss in November 1835, General Antonio López de Santa Anna planned a major assault on the dissidents in Tejas. He easily put down insurrections, such as those at the small city of Gonzalez. Only a small battle, it was nonetheless a beginning, a declaration from a community taking up arms to separate itself from Mexico.

Thousands of men were mobilized into the Mexican army. The army was a mixed bag of conscripts, untrained peasants, and well-drilled professional officers. At the time, they actually had the best cavalry in the world. The field generals ran the gamut, as in many armies, from skilled, to incompetent, to opportunists. Middle-rank officers were first-class, while foot soldiers were cannon fodder. They traveled over snowy mountain trails, coastal plains and into the interior of Tejas with provisions, powder and many, many cannons.

～

The Texicans established a protection group called the Rangers, to keep new settlements safe by ridding the area of threats, primarily from the Comanches.[37] Plain and simple, the gang received bounty for scalps, ostensibly from warring Natives. But who would actually know whether the scalp was from friend or foe, male or female? They paid out all the same.

Out tracking a band of Natives for bounty one day, the gang came upon an old Pawnee man named Kuruc, who had just fired up a communal bread-baking oven outside his village. Dusty, tired, and frustrated, the gang approached Kuruc menacingly. They got off their horses, encircled him, and commenced to shove him from one to another. "Which direction, old man?" demanded one of the Rangers.

Kuruc just shook his head repeatedly, and in fear; he didn't understand their language. They beat him, pulled his finger joints apart and broke his knees with cuts of firewood. They were trying to get him to tell them the direction the band of Natives had ridden. One man punched him in the head, knocking him down. As the Pawnee man righted himself, another kicked him in the belly and sent him flying backwards onto the hard-pan dirt. Tiring of the game, one of the Rangers whispered to the others, who all started laughing. A man on either side of him grabbed Kuruc by the arms and began walking towards the oven. Kuruc's eyes widened in terror, and his mouth twisted as he was stuffed into the oven, which was roaring with fire. The door was slammed shut. The muffled screams subsided almost immediately, and then a loud sizzling and white smoke emanated from the chimney. The men wanted to take off on their journey, but the leader said, "Wait!" Presently there was a cracking sound and a loud "pop."

"What the Hell?!" yelled a Ranger.

The leader smiled broadly. "Now we can go. The bastard's skull exploded!" he announced, laughing.

"No shit! No bounty for that scalp!" They all whooped and hollered, mounted their horses, and took off after new quarry. The world went silent, save for the wind and hoof-beats fading into the distance.

∾

Karmo, like everyone else in the village, heard about Kuruc, and was dizzy with both rage and terror. He felt the very fiber of his being stretched, and shuddered. His chest tightened and his head felt as if it would explode. He was no longer a young, naïve man, but still at least hoped to hang onto his humanity.

Such brutality in the world! For what end! He thought. After this latest atrocity, Karmo decided to join the Mexican side, recalling Efendi's words to avoid going to war unless it is to protect your land and family—and also to be aware as to who will profit. He would fight the invasores.

He traveled with the local Mexican-Native militia and contributed to both their battle strategies and tactics. He honed his methods of learning the lay of the land by observation, and found out the importance of supply sources. Approachable, the militias saw him as an oddity, but trustworthy, and so they shared information with him, in exchange for his help with tactics.

He learned that many Mexicans were on the side of the invaders, having grown discontent with the ever-increasing directives of the central government. They too, wanted more say in how their lives would be managed. Karmo reasoned that their concerns were legitimate, but the observation of many skirmishes convinced him they would be betrayed after battle. The invaders from the east were fighting two wars; one secret, one not; one for land, power and money, the other for rights to their own way of life, and for their own people. They were relentless and, once entrenched, the land would become theirs forever.

Word of this strange black man eventually reached the nearby Mexican army outpost. Again, the Shadow showed itself. Karmo was subsequently found, and dragged in for questioning. The Mexican captain was intrigued by Karmo's understanding of the terrain and kept him as a consultant, albeit while under "house arrest." Word of his value came to the ears of General Santa Anna, who sent for him.

～

In his lifetime, General Antonio López de Santa Anna would be President of Mexico eleven times, and would be banished from the country four times.[38] He was a brilliant military man, but a ruthless leader, as arrogant as any American invader. Repeatedly, he was brought back from exile to lead either the government or the military into battle. His modus operandi was extermination and subjugation of anyone who dared threaten the King of Spain. Once Mexico gained its independence, he continued in the service of this new country. He remained a successful slash-and-burn commander for his entire military career, brutal and seemingly invincible.

～

The new year had come; the weather was cool, with a lingering edge of crispness. A new crop of volunteers from Louisiana arrived, ready to fight and protect fellow invaders from the tyranny of the Mexican government. Sons, given up by the farms, left behind families who would struggle all the more because of their absence to get crops planted, butcher pigs, grind corn for meal and the hundred other chores that are necessary for subsistence. The hardship of those staying behind is a different type of sacrifice and survival.

Four young men came from the same farming community. Karmo regarded them through field glasses.

"My God, some of them are so young!" he said out loud to no one in particular.

The General said matter-of-factly, "Yes, they are young; nevertheless, they carry rifles and will join the others over that hill," he pointed. "Do not forget that. Our job is simple. Kill them. We have shut down all but one of our cannons, so they will think that is all we have. In the meantime, we will move other cannons to better positions. When they charge, with only their rifles, we will fire all the cannons. Their scouts have either been eliminated or bribed. Karmo, when you know your enemy's needs and desires, his fears and faults, you can leverage those factors to make deception complete," General Santa Anna added.

Karmo recognized this strategy. "Yes sir, you are correct, of course," replied Karmo quietly, as he turned back to observe more and grimaced. He was so sick of all this war-mongering.

～

16-year-old Bobby pushed his glasses up to the bridge of his nose with his index finger and looked around. Rail-thin and sandy-haired, he had never been considered strong or powerful, like some other boys his age. Nevertheless, he volunteered, he thought, to become a man like the others. Over the hill, he heard gunfire and an occasional cannon blast. He flinched, then eased back upright, not wanting anyone to see his fear. Even from this distance, though, he could feel the energy and electricity around him.

"They have cannon?!" he asked tentatively.

"Sounds like it," answered 30-year-old Amos, also from the same farm community. The "old man," they called him. Bearded, and with longer hair than most, he looked more like a man of the mountains than the farmer he was. Amos had only heard cannon used for ceremonial purposes, and knew nothing of their actual force.

Brothers Paul and Luke were just ten months apart in age, both now 17. They looked at each other and blinked. It had all been so exciting, to think about their adventure to become men, until they looked at Amos. Reality quickly turned their excitement to vapor. "Our side has cannon too, don'we?" asked Paul.

"I dunno know, Paul. I dunno know nuthin'. Let's go see where we're s'posed ta be," answered Amos.

The men reported in and received their assignments for the next morning. They brought their own rifles with them, as instructed. No training was offered. After taking down their names and hometowns, the commander's aide looked them up and down and said, "You boys just follow what the Sergeant here orders you."

"Yes, sir," they answered in unison.

They were taken to a make-shift kitchen to get their supper, and met up with others just as green and confused as they were. A late-season rain shower came up suddenly and they took cover under the trees, squatting, eating their beans and a chunk of fat as the drizzle dripped from their hat brims into their metal plates. The fat started to float. Paul speared it with his fork, looked at it thoughtfully and popped it into his mouth. The two boys stared vacantly into the hills in front of them. The silence was palpable. The young men thought there would be many more soldiers than volunteers.

"We're goin' ta fight tomorraw?" asked Paul quietly.

One of the earlier arrivals, Jim Hawkins, nodded, then added, "They jist started fightin' two days ago, so our guys are pretty rested still. Besides, them Mexicans have only been taking pot shots at us. They ain't even kilt anybody yet. But they keep on firing that dad-gum cannon. I'm so tired of it! Cain't rightly think straight!"

The boys slept fitfully that night. One is never so alone as when everyone around you is asleep, and you have only your own thoughts to keep you company. *I can't go back now*, thought Bobby to himself. *They'll call me lily-livered, a coward.*

The Mexicans' intentional barrage of noise all through the night made sleep elusive. In the early dawn, Bobby was almost lulled to sleep by the distant blasts when Luke jabbed him in the side with the end of his rifle.

"Get up. They said it's time ta move," Luke whispered quietly. He and Paul already had their boots and jackets on, rifles gripped tightly.

"Huh? Yep! I'm up. I'm up," said Bobby, slipping on his glasses before pulling at his boots.

Amos, Paul and Luke were already in formation with 27 others, two Sergeants and a young Lieutenant. Bobby ran up to them and looked around, thinking there would be more of them.

"Listen up! The Mexicans are right on the other side of that small rise. One of our scouts determined it's jist a small contingent," barked the Sergeant. "We'll divide up into three squads of 10 each; two on each flank. The third'll go straight over the top with the Lieutenant here. Follow your squad leader. We'll take them off-guard. Should be easy. Got that?! Now get in line!"

"Yes, sir!" answered the group. No one dared to ask questions. They stole sideways glances at one another. Someone whispered, "Are we really goin'in?" but there was no response.

They marched to their positions, throats tightening, mind alert, eyes open. "Sergeant says there ain't that many of 'em. How many is that exactly?" came a voice from the back. Such thoughts abounded. They tried to reassure themselves, this group of strangers.

Luke wondered to himself; *What do I do if I come face to face with 'em? What should I do if they see me? Can I shoot them? Will they kill me???* Thoughts flew through his mind as his body moved with the others.

Once in position, the men awaited for their command. This made no sense. One wondered, *"Why would we charge blindly, even if there was only a small group to attack?"*

"Charge!" came the order, and the squad of men ran over the hill as directed, screaming their lungs out, rifles at the ready, into the maw of devastation no one expected.

The Mexican Army added reinforcements through the night and placed their cannons on three sides. As the invaders from the east showed themselves at the top of the rise, cannon fire roared around them. Under the barrage, the hillside exploded, smoke and dust filled the air, a burning smell of black powder and sounds of booms, rumbling earth and screams assaulted the senses.

The Sergeant next to Paul was hit, his right arm blown off. The man picked it up and ran screaming back towards camp. Movement assured him he was still alive. He got back to the camp, breathing hard, terrified, looking up at the smoky sky, he closed his eyes and bled out.

The noise was deafening, as huge chunks of earth exploded like volcanoes. Bullets whizzed by, kicking up dust and stones all around. Soon, they were under heavy fire from three directions. All they could do was keep down and return the gunfire. The noise was horrendous. The earth quaked with each landing ball, and more yells and screams reverberated through the dense air. The constant roar was disorienting; some of the men shook uncontrollably. Hawkins, his clothes shredded, limped to the back lines on a splintered stump, having lost his lower leg. He could no longer scream, but rather tried to suck air into his fragmented lungs. There was no sound from his lips, just twisted anguish. He collapsed, writhed grotesquely and, mercifully, died moments later.

Amos was helping a comrade fumbling with a tourniquet, when he saw Bobby get hit with shrapnel and go down. Mad with pain, drenched in sweat, Bobby's hair matted tightly to his head, he tried to crawl into the relative safety of a ditch. As he lay there trembling, clouds of smoke and bloody red mist drizzled from above. He shut his eyes tightly, choked and allowed the tears to flow, but he stood up, wobbly and updazed, no longer understanding his surroundings.

Amos ran to Bobby to help, pulled him back down on the ground, his own face now lined with strain under a foundation of dirt and ashes. A blast from a cannon ball exploded a mass of rocks into their faces. Amos was killed instantly, but Bobby's glasses shattered into his eyes, bits of glass reflecting moving smoke and the dissipation of hope. He forced himself up again and ran blindly, disoriented, scared beyond belief. No one had time to help him. Another blast relieved him of all worry forever, as a rising darkness enveloped him.

"Fire! Fire! Fire your damned weapons!" came the panicked order from somewhere out of the din of blasts. The men had a combination of arms, muzzle loaders, rifles, handguns and grit. But with the ceaseless barrage ringing in their ears, they could only watch and imitate what others did. A searing brightness of lightning and the rumble of dry thunder mimicked the cannons. They had entered Hell and there was no way out.

First, the Sergeant, then Hawkins, then Amos and Bobby; they were all lost, one by one, some witnessed and others not, some together and some alone. They died the way soldiers have always died, quietly, loudly, brutally.

Just as it had started, the cannon fire stopped suddenly. Eight volunteers, including Paul and Luke, returned to camp, exhausted, mute and shattered. Hearts destroyed, they collected themselves around a fire and shivered. No one would look at each other. Even their Lieutenant was gone.

The cook stared at the motley crew, dumb with disbelief. Presently, he said to them, "Let's go." And they followed him.

19

San Antonio 1836

Every man must do two things alone; he must do his own believing and his own dying. –Martin Luther

Eusebio Ramirez, a Mexican citizen born in the coastal town of Matagorda near the Guadalupe River, lived a relatively peaceful life—despite the uneasiness around the small farm inherited by his wife Maria. Their three daughters, Louisa, Angelica, and little Maria, and their ten-year-old son Gilberto adored their parents. The Ramirez home was built of adobe, with a small courtyard, located not far from the town square. The house was situated amongst a stand of shade trees and provided a simple, pleasant domicile.

Eusebio had planted coastal morning glories around the east side of the house, a remembrance from his hometown. The vining flowers skirted the home in waves of ground-hugging white blossoms. Those flowers, together with his wife's red rock roses, presented a welcoming and comfortable place.

Eusebio was every bit the family man. He cherished his children, but made sure they worked on the farm according to their abilities and the family's needs. Even the youngest, Maria, had her chores. They were not wealthy, but had enough, which they appreciated as a blessing. Although they were tired from the day's hard work, the family gathered around their Papa after supper each night to hear his stories of fantasy and adventure.

"And then the Maestro," as Eusebio referred to himself, tongue-in-cheek, "using only one hand, struck down the beast with a quick chop at the neck—saving the poor grandmother so she could go back to her family!"

"Bravo, bravo for Maestro Papa!!!!" the children sang out.

"Tell us another story, Papa!" begged little Maria.

"Ah, my beautiful princess, now is the time to sleep—for it is dark and the crickets are singing a lullaby in your honor," answered Eusebio lovingly.

It was the time of year when the Big Dipper turned upside down, draining its contents of dreams upon a hopeful land. Before daybreak, dark but for the stars, the air was clear and crisp when two men loudly pounded on the adobe's thick wooden door. Eusebio got up quickly to answer, lest the whole household awaken. *Perhaps they are travelers,* he thought to himself.

Two uniformed soldiers were standing on his doorstep, one stating, "Señor, by order of General Martín Perfecto de Cos, you are ordered to accompany us to the city center for muster."

Eusebio's blood turned to ice. He did not know what to say, and was taken off-guard. Just then, his wife came up behind him. "What do you mean by this?! He is no soldier! You are mistaken, Señores," she said excitedly, but trying not to be too loud.

Eusebio turned to her, "Do not worry, Maria, there are not many separatists in this area and hundreds, maybe thousands of soldiers here. They may need me only to show them routes out of the city, or where there could be hiding places. I will not be gone long," he said trying to convince her as well as himself.

"Where are you taking my Papa?" mumbled Gilberto, who had wandered into the front room on stiff legs, rubbing his eyes, waking slowly from a hazy sleep.

"Do not worry, my little man," said Eusebio calmly to his son. "I will be away for just a little while. You are the man of the house now. Take good care of your mama and sisters, eh?"

One of the soldiers looked away and took a deep breath.

"We need to move now!" said the other in an urgent tone.

~

General Martín Perfecto de Cos returned to San Antonio to take back the town and garrison.[39] The battle had been going on for 12 days. About 200 separatists barricaded themselves in a small church called the Alamo, shooting their single cannon and taking potshots at the Mexican Army, which numbered in the thousands and had surrounded the church. It was unknown how many of the soldiers were left inside. Instead of biding his time and letting the separatists run out of food and water and become weak, the General stubbornly ordered his men to storm the building repeatedly. The surrounded men did indeed become weak and sleep-deprived, but they had lasted this long—out of pure defiance and a defensible position.

Day 13, March 16[40]

"It is time to finish this," thought de Cos. His Mexican Army had sustained heavy losses that were disproportionate to how the battle should have run out. He ordered a small contingent of twenty men to storm the breach in the north courtyard wall in order to distract the inhabitants, followed by expert marksmen and swordsmen. Eusebio was shoved into this contingent for the pre-dawn assault.

"You men! Get in there good. You'd better not come back until those jackasses are ready to give up!" yelled one of the commanders. "We will be right behind you!"

Eusebio looked at the man next to him; a shiver of icy understanding went down his spine. Recognizing his neighbor Jesse, he whispered, "Tell me there is a heaven, amigo, for surely we are about to enter Hell."

"I thank the Virgin Mary I sent my son, Juan Pablo, to Alta California," cried Jesse.

The two men readied their rifles, knowing they had no choice but to shoot in order to protect themselves.

"I will see you on the other side, mi amigo," whispered Jesse as he jumped forward.

They ran through a broken wall at one corner of the church, screaming for their own encouragement. Inside the church, they were immediately faced by at least 70 men with rifles trained directly on them.

"Madre!" said the man next to Eusebio. "We have been sent to slaughter!"

The first bullet ripped through Eusebio's knee, but he continued to fire as he went down. The second and third bullets hit him in the belly and chest. Falling on his side, he tried to hang onto his rifle, but his hand quivered uncontrollably. Blood spewed from his mouth as he looked up at the yellow, smoky sky. A shadow hovered over him for an instant as a large knife sliced into his face just under his eye, and then all went dark.

The marksmen followed as promised and made short work of the holdouts, butchering them all.

Word came from Santa Anna to execute all existing the prisoners and burn their bodies. "Give no quarter! Make them ready for hell!" it was rumored he said of the action.

~

There is no greater power than to kill someone. It needs neither strength, nor even much intelligence. If a man is angry and feels his dominance slipping away, he can always grab a gun.

She saw them coming, shadowy figures approaching her house. Maria pulled the rifle bolt back and heard the lugs move into place. Locked and loaded, she aimed, waiting for them to get closer. The men approached Eusebio's adobe home slowly but deliberately.

As has happened since the beginning of time, men who are angry, lonely, enraged, take out their vengeance on the innocent.

~

The Mexican Army was victorious, yet General Santa Anna was enraged by the squandering of his men due to incompetent commanders.

"What the hell!" he stormed at de Cos. "You wasted over 700 of my men, most of them soldiers! What were you thinking, you bastard!?"

"Sir, the separatists and the invaders were all dispatched, after all!"

"At what cost, de Cos?! At what cost?! Even Pyrrhus would not have engaged so!" fumed Santa Anna.[41] Volatile as ever, he took a deep breath and thought for a moment before continuing. "This is just the beginning, General! We will exterminate any foreigner who takes up arms against us. Anyone! Summary executions! Annihilate! Exterminate! Eradicate! Our survival depends on winning and on preventing such uprisings again. What matters in the beginning of waging war is not righteousness, but victory! Close your heart to pity. Proceed brutally!" he exploded, pounding his fist on the table. "This message will be shared with only a few of the commanders for now!"

"Summary executions?! Why are you telling *me*, General? Am I the only sane person you know anymore?" asked de Cos.

Santa Anna turned his head sharply, lowered his voice, and grimaced condescendingly. "You?! You are like a helpless rabbit, like a lost kitten." Then he stormed, "*You* are a complete idiot! Three-quarters of you is insecurity. The rest is giblets! I *have* to tell someone or I will explode! I tell *you*, because you can keep a secret! We need to fight smarter. And as for Houston, that coward who never fights his own battles, the strings he pulls today will become his noose tomorrow!"

～

East Tejas

The cook on his ox-drawn supply wagon, and the eight remaining volunteers dragged themselves wearily for four days towards the tiny village of Alba when they met up with a group of Texican soldiers and volunteers. There were about 500 of them. Some 300 were engaged with small enemy groups around their perimeter, just enough to give neither side rest. Once again, they were vastly outnumbered by the enemy.

The contingent was loud and raucous. They had one cannon and a goodly supply of bullets, balls and powder. All the men were well-armed, though with mixed weaponry. Luke and Paul tried to settle in, but again, the noise of guns in the background and the tension of the men around them was disconcerting. They soon became jumpy, their bodies vibrating from the constant barrage of noise assaulting their senses. Their minds could not forget who and what they had left behind.

The next day, they and a few others were set to work digging latrine ditches, and to divert some of the nearby stream to help dissipate the waste. Another group was sent to dig wide holes, six feet deep by twelve feet wide.

"I could be doing this at home," muttered a man with a perpetual grimace. Barrel-chested, with spindly arms and legs, he looked like a bloated tick. He stood up to spit tobacco juice.

"Yeah, but would you be doing it in this paradise?" taunted another sarcastically.

"Shut your pie hole," the tick man hollered at the crew. "At least, uh, wait, uhhhh," he made a long, sustained grunt, a deep breath witness to his excrescence, and finally exhaled a long constipated groan, "Unnnh!!" Breathing heavily, he muttered, "That boil on my ass just popped! Damn, it hurts!" Dirty, sweaty, breathing hard and shallow, he tried to reorient himself. He cursed again, pulled down his trousers, twisting his torso to get a look at his left buttock and groaned. The skin on a fist-size pustule hung in shreds. He poured dirty water on it to loosen the fabric that was stuck to the center filled with blood and pus.

"Get away from us!" yelled another.

Luke and Paul just looked at each other, sweat pouring down their shirts in rivulets of dirt. Their faces looked like raccoon masks, and they breathed hard, like the others. Only shoveling broke the silence abiding within them.

The evening breezes did nothing to muffle the ceaseless roar of cannon fire. They were joined by five more volunteers. One of them, Billy Bean, was a Louisiana neighbor from the next farm over. He was two years older than the brothers, sent by the community to check on their boys. Luke and Paul were at the same time excited and sad to see him in this hostile world of death and misery.

"How'd you find us, Billy?"

"I traveled hard, boys. On my journey through the wilderness, rivers and valleys, I started hearing battle noises, guns and cannons from miles away. So I just followed the roar to here. I had no way of knowing I was on the road to hell. Are you kickin' their asses, at least?"

"No," whispered Paul to Billy. "We *ain't* kickin' their asses. One by one they're killin' us. We're hungry, we're dirty and tired, and I ain't afraid to admit it. I'm scared to death, Billy. Scared to death."

"Please don't let on to Ma and Pa when you go back, Billy," whispered Luke. "We don't want to worry them none."

Billy Bean looked at the two brothers before answering. "Too late for that. Your Pa is silent as ever, but you can read his face true enough. He misses you, and he looks so worried, sometimes I think he might just keel over. And your Ma just breaks my heart. Her eyes are always red and wet. I came to help you or fetch you back, but now that I'm here, reckon I gotta stay too."

Intermittent shots rang out. "Damn! Is this how it is every day? Shots for no reason, cannon fire all night?" asked Billy.

The brothers just nodded.

Over time, the men of the force developed a bond, a brotherhood, devoid of sentimentality but abounding in loyalty. They would always be one and the same for each other. No distance or time would ever change this alliance.

"Bobby, Bobby got hisself killed," said Paul, without giving details.

Billy made a horrified look; he had not actually seen fighting yet. He stayed quiet.

Later that evening, the brothers spoke to each other. "I have a bad feeling .... Did you see what happened to Bobby? I don't wanna die, Luke," whispered Paul. "I'm young yet. Whadda I care about these people wantin' to live in this hell-hole? I just wanna get back home and be normal ag'in. I don't mind working hard, workin' with Pa and Ma. I miss them. I miss hunting for rabbits, the smell of corn silks, curing pork, all that stuff." He got louder. "I ain't never even kissed a girl! I ain't never been to, you know, been to New Or-leans!"

"Neither have I, Paul," responded Luke quietly, looking up into the sky. "I hear tell the women there are right purty, and friendly as all get-out. I'd been aimin' to get myself there one day, at least once."

Under a nearby tree, one of the battered survivors laughed at the boys. "You know, you have to pay for those women in Naw'lins." There was no privacy in this group!

Another laughed back and said, "Pay! Well, you betcha I'd pay, at least once! They say the women there are mighty sassy, have powder on their faces, red, red lips and smell like flowers. They wear shiny dresses that rustle like dried cornhusks and are bounded up so tight, their body parts stick out in front and in back. I sure would like to pass some time with one of them!"

"Yeah, me too! Just lookin' at them would be grand," joined in another.

"Uh uh, not me. I want some real time!" says the first.

"You fellas just hush up now!" It was tick man who turned towards Luke and Paul, the curling lip under his moustache forming a taunting sneer, "Peach fuzz here don't know what the hell he's talkin' about. Ain't neither of you skinny-ass boys got the gumption to even get close to that kind of woman. Ya cain't even smell your own piss yet!" he yelled. "Now, here!" he thumped his chest, "is some prime aged beef! *This here's* what them women want. Not some prissy veal! Heh, heh, heh, heh!"

"We need a dream to hold onto! We can dream, damn it! We can dream! And after we're done here, we're headin' straight to New Orleans! Right, Lukey? Yeah! Let's promise we're gonna get outta this mess and head for New Or-leans! Promise!!" yelled Paul.

"Sounds good, Pauley, we should do that. I reckon they won't miss just the two of us. We came and we fought, and now it's time to go back," said Luke, with little resolve. "But you're right, Pauley." Barely audibly, he repeated, "You're right."

Paul looked at him solemnly. "We ain't goin' back, are we, Lukey?" cried Paul.

Luke looked long and hard at Paul before answering, "I reckon we have no choice but to stay a bit longer. If we try to hightail it outta here, our own kind will shoot us as deserters, even if we *are* volunteers. And if they don't shoot us, you know word will follow us home."

"T'was a good dream, though, weren't it?" murmured Paul.

"'Twas indeed," answered Luke resignedly.

~

Karmo saw the boys and remarked to Santa Anna that they're the same ones seen earlier. "They survived. A miracle!"

"Ah, so you have started to like these boys who are your enemy, Karmo? That is allowable, but be careful. If a man starts to love a chicken he is meant to strangle, he will end up starving."

~

The Mexican Army fired indiscriminately into the enemy camp all night. There was no time for the Texicans to rest—and that was the intention. Karmo, taking his cues from Santa Anna, became inch by inch harder, edgier. He focused on victory. Kill or be killed. The new plan was elegant, but its execution was ugly and vicious.

The dawn of a new day can be hopeful, beautiful or ominous. Today, it was all three. Luke and Paul were assembled with their assigned squad, one of many in this larger army. There was a good deal of grumbling among the ranks about carrying out an ambush, but no one knew for sure when or if it would happen.

A Sergeant yelled out, "Even though you are volunteers, you all swore an oath to follow orders, and this is an order!"

He shouted to them which direction to charge, with the goal of killing as many of the enemy as possible, and capturing their flag on a distant hill. They looked at one another, trying to gain strength from each other.

Waiting for the order to attack, the muscles in Luke's neck and shoulders clenched, breath held, head ached; sweat poured. Tried to focus but could not, intermittent exhaling between holding his breath again, unaware of the holding breath, struggling for control. Those around him were doing the same—silent, waiting, hearts pounding so that one could almost hear it.

"Let's get 'em!" said someone in the front. And with that, a loud roar of encouragement from both men and boys was sent up into the sky.

"At the ready! CHARGE!" came the order. They engaged their enemy, shooting whomever was behind the imaginary line ahead of them.

Excitedly, one of the volunteers yelled, "I think I got one of 'em!" "But he was white?!"

"Not one of us, I hope," answered a brother-in-arms.

A veteran looked out across the field and spat out a juicy bit of tobacco. "Yeah, he was white, but he was fightin' for them. A lot of 'mericans came here to farm. They married locals, too."

The boys looked at each other bewildered. "Who we fightin', then?"

The Texicans fired off their cannon, but got no response. As the men ran closer towards the enemy, they were met with cannon fire from three sides. The trap had worked again! Half of their men were killed in the first thirty minutes, and the rest retreated to safer ground. Luke watched in horror and helplessness as a veteran who was hit in the chest grabbed at the shrubs, rocks and finally the hot, smoky air above him. Then the major cannon fire stopped.

Ceaseless rifle fire rang out from the enemy's side. Smoke and dust emanated around the soldiers like tornadoes. One could hear the wounded, screaming in the battlefield, but few of them could be retrieved. The stretcher-bearers would immediately be picked off themselves. The screams continued throughout the long night, the screamers begging to die or be killed. Towards dawn it became quiet.

It seems that once you give up hope, it becomes surprisingly easy to die.

The fighting raged on eight more days, and food became scarce. The latrine ditch turned into a putrid, oozy haven for green flies and other flying insects. Stench; foul and assaultive, pinched nostrils shut, but persisted into the senses nevertheless. Ticks, fleas, and mosquitoes plagued the men as much as any bullet. Horses died and became bloated in the river above their water supply; the river no longer flowed, blocked by the roiling poison of offal. The men became profoundly thirsty. They sickened and became weak from vomiting and diarrhea, their skin dry and sallow, tenting to the pinch. Then came muscle cramps, dehydration, and their heart pumping too fast to sustain the pace. Breathing became ever more labored. Death embraced men slowly in a suffocating cloud of indifference.[42]

Karmo continued to observe. At times, he suggested another tactic for success. There were losses on each side, but clearly, the Mexican Army was the superior force. *This is no way to live, digging each others' graves.* He tried to put these thoughts aside and focused on actions. After two more days, the ox was killed for food. And the constant noise continued. Stretcher-bearers carried the wounded they could reach to a makeshift tent set up for treatment and surgery. This abattoir had the smell of sulfurous, metallic putrefaction and rot; the dirt floor was sticky and sloppy with blood and tissue. In one corner was a pile of dead men's boots; in another, a pile of severed limbs, proof of the attempt to save lives. The sole surgeon looked up with a face that no longer showed affect, betraying the horror in his mind; his movements became slower, words eluded him. The incessant buzzing of flies droned into his ears as he let drop his instruments to the floor. Finally, he turned and ran. One shot downed him, and he was quiet forever. He had gone mad. The dead were piled up in the back, waiting for burial in the prepared pit. The small army ran out of lye.

Food was gone, destroyed. Men pulled up grass to chew. Some ate dirt. Out in the field, the remaining men were trapped and pinned down, for days. The older men had their pasts to think about. The younger men had no past and, now, no future. Their souls were dead, but their bodies didn't yet know it. They got no rest, ever.[43] The din of battle had been too long and intense for thinking sensibly.

"They should at least give the hope they took from us to someone in need," whispered one of the men to himself.

A committee of buzzards, the memento mori, took their positions in the trees around the camp, waiting, waiting.

First, one cannon boomed, followed by successive blasts. He heard the whistling sound. Paul tried to see where the ball would land, but it was followed by so many cannonballs coming now; smoke and dirt were flying everywhere, quaking earth, watching, waiting, tense, on-edge, no relief. A nearby explosion forced him to lurch forward. He grabbed onto the earth and took hold as if he could somehow dig himself to safety. His pants filled with what little was left in his bowels; he put his hands to his ears to shut out the penetrating sound of the blasts. Another cannon ball exploded two feet away as a tremor went through his whole being. Seemingly out of nowhere, Luke crawled over to him.

With an involuntary tremor of overexcited and confused nerves coursing through their pathways, Paul lifted a handful of soil and let it flow down and across his palm. "It's good dirt, Lukey," he said with a weak and fading smile. "Lukey, promise me you'll get to New Or-leans."

Luke held Paul's hand and whispered hoarsely, "I promise, Paul. I promise." *It's dishonest dirt*, Luke thought to himself.

There was no apparent trauma on his person as Paul's breath went from shallow gasps to his final exhalation, his innards liquefied by stress waves, that concussive force of the explosion.

Blast-wind smoke and debris sucked the air from around him. The burning grasses caused more heat and choking smoke. Luke, crying huge tears, roared his oath of anger and vengeance, got up from his brother's body and ran toward the enemy, his ears deaf to calls to retreat, awareness having been shut down. Not even a moment went by, not even a sound, before the blackness overcame him. Shot in the neck, he dropped instantly into the dishonest dirt.

There was no time, none, before the final offensive took place. It was exquisite in its brutality; close quarters, Mexican bayonets to Texican knives. Men were disemboweled, sliced under the breastbone, ripping upwards into the chest along the cartilage, or into the jugular; groans and gurgles. Only an hour long, this eternity of the damned dissipated into an eerie quiet.

A handful of men staggered back towards camp, covered with dirt, trembling, their eyes wild, their lips moving without sound. Torments of war would long persist as demons in the survivors as they returned from that desolate wasteland of glory. They took refuge in the forest; some curled up and died. Their actions were perhaps noble and just, but back home, in towns and villages, nothing could fill the silence of the missing.

20

Karmo in Tejas

Sometimes the hardest thing in life is to know which bridge to cross and which to burn. –Bertrand Russell

Although his primary role was advisor, Karmo took part in several battles in which the Mexican Army was victorious—whether through his expertise or not, no one can know for sure. He fingered the grey voodoo pouch given to him by Old Okeke. "Foresight?" he said to himself.

It was night. The chilly sky was so dark, the shine of the stars made them appear almost touchable.

"Ah, Karmo," said Santa Anna, pointing to the northwest. "The Bull's Eye. That is good for us."

Karmo's eyes tracked the direction of the General's arm, pointing northeast of Orion's belt; there it was! The red, fiery bull's eye of the constellation Taurus, a fixed star often hidden by the moon. It was known also as Aldebaran, the follower; hunting prey, as Ansa used to tell him.

"It portends riches and honor," said Santa Anna.

It also presages restlessness, dissent and revolution, thought Karmo to himself. *Yes, Ansa would have a story to tell—if only he were here.*

❧

MARCH 14, 1836

Fighting continued in Refugio, then just days later, March 19 and 20, in Coleto. The victorious Mexican Army moved quickly from town to town.

March 27, General Jose Urrea had never lost a battle, and the one at the town of Goliad was to be no different.[44] About 350 Texicans surrendered, convinced by the General to lay down their weapons; in exchange, they were promised freedom. Urrea obtained their agreement to leave Tejas and go back home. However, his order for release was countermanded by General Santa Anna, who sent a contingent of men to escort prisoners out of town in three different groups. After some few miles, they were all slaughtered at sunrise. Their bodies were piled up and burned, left for the vultures and coyotes. Some very few escaped that fate after persuasion by a brave woman to spare medics and doctors, among others.[45]

Goliad was troubling to Karmo. While the Mexican Army could not feed and care for so many prisoners, promises of release had been made.

Santa Anna stated philosophically, "Karmo, the greater a person's need to perceive truth, generally the less willing they are to perceive undesired truth regardless of their ability to do so. This is war."

Just eight years prior, Santa Anna repulsed an army sent by Spain's King Ferdinand VII to retake Mexico. In this young independent country, with a federal system of self-governing states, people had not yet developed the theory of responsible government and anyway, no one had the experience to initiate one. Uprisings had persisted ever since, and chaos abounded. The military was too engaged in quelling dissent to offer stability. The danger, then, was putting trust in generals who had no keen sense of national destiny and /or were only after their own gains.

~

Spring was upon them. Karmo would enter yet another close-quarters skirmish alongside a small contingent of Mexican specialists; men who fought hand-to-hand. The enemy was camped along a creek as his small band approached quietly. Almost in position, an owl hooted and someone stepped on a dry branch, alerting others. They had to move quickly and charge in. The enemy had no time to grab their guns, which were stacked upright near their campfire. As they grabbed knives and rocks, the fighting persisted, and sounds of punches and exhaled oaths emanated about the firelight.

As he was finishing off one man, another jumped Karmo from behind. He turned and whirled the man around like a cape; the man finally loosened his grip. The sweat on Karmos fist put his aim off as he swung and sliced the enemy under the eye, opening up a gaping laceration. He stomped his boot into the man's face before clubbing him to oblivion.

The fighting was finally over. Breathing hard, Karmo looked about at the ruined men on both sides. In the haze of dust and flame, he imagined spirits rising from the dead. His soul torn asunder, he mumbled, "There must be another way!"

Two days later, Karmo was back with Santa Anna. The soldiers were exhausted, and supplies were dangerously low. The General had heard of a small band of invaders not far away, and wanted to wipe them out before returning to Mexico.

Karmo felt strongly that enough was enough. The Mexican army was vulnerable to runaways. Although their numbers were large still, they were starving, spread thin, injured and exhausted. "Sir," said Karmo, "I advise you to let your people rest, and not go forward to San Jacinto for such a small prize.[46] My spies tell me that all but one bridge had been blown up such that, once crossed, neither retreat nor reinforcement was possible."

The two men argued back and forth for some time, Santa Anna, although weary, was adamant. "We need to finish this, Karmo! They are just over the bridge. We rage against our foes! We roll like thunder and strike like lightning! Hear our cannons roar!" bellowed Santa Anna, his arms outstretched above his head for effect.

"You are very eloquent, General, but remember about the need to perceive truth. I do not think these people deserve such attention," replied Karmo. "They know they have lost."

Santa Anna glared at this black man who dared parrot back his own words to him.

"If you please, sir," continued Karmo, "You are intelligent, strong and articulate, but if you do not know when or where to use these gifts, you will be swept away with the morning winds. Your rage and desire will unite and defeat your mind. Therefore, you must learn patience and perseverance, and be in control of your decisions. Your lands are dangerously exposed, too vast to be governable. Avoid war among your own peoples. Listen to them. Give them more freedoms so they will be stronger together. Do not allow outsiders to hover over and take advantage of a disorganized, mistrustful people."

"What you say is true, Karmo," answered Santa Anna, highly annoyed, "but we have them on the run. If your enemy cannot find you or understand your ways, you become a mystery to him. He cannot kill what he cannot find or know. He is biased in his ideas of you, his fears and needs. We have stealth on our side."

"Sir," implored Karmo, "They know us now. The species that most readily adapts to the environment survives, not the strongest, or most intelligent. Your men are exhausted, and thus, disadvantaged. Send emissaries to Houston and negotiate peace from a position of strength. Pretend you are strong when you negotiate."

"Houston!" screamed Santa Anna in a knee-jerk reaction, "He thinks wherever his foot treads is law! Well, I am telling you, wherever I step, the law is what I say it is!"

"You are correct, sir," said Karmo as he tried to bring the General back to calmness, "Now is the time to wrap things up, as you say. Both of you win. Mexico has been fighting for decades. She needs peace."

Santa Anna looked at Karmo with narrowed eyes and curled lips as he exploded, "Who do you think you are to talk to me this way? Yes! I have been fighting for decades! I will *not* give in to that cur! I would give my left leg to just once kick so far up his ass that he spits out cobblers' nails!"

Karmo, losing patience, said loudly, "You have learned a line of success, but a book of failure, General! Look at the long view! Mexico's holdings are too large and the government is not strong, not ready to assert its influence. You will be fighting until you fall over a cliff of defeat! Stop now, while you and your people can do so honorably! Those lands you absolutely must have, tax them! Tax, in return for your promise not to annihilate them! This tactic has been successful for centuries. But use some of the money to build roads and to improve trade. With improved trade comes wealth, and the locals will then be appeased."

～

Santa Anna uncharacteristically sent emissaries to San Jacinto to talk with the leaders of small bands, and subsequently to Houston, and even to the U.S. government. Both troops and national treasure were exhausted. The U.S. , too, was fighting on too many fronts to help the Texicans. Houston was cornered and desperate. They were losing, but Santa Anna was damned if he was going to give up. When word of the peace offer came, it was his chance to cut his losses and still claim victory. A power-sharing agreement was negotiated whereby a border line was created along the Guadalupe River. Both the peace and the line were accepted by the General and Houston.

～

One of the most coveted announcements every day for soldiers away from home is Mail Call; letters, even just a scribble, a piece of home, proof of not being forgotten, memories to cling to, and more to look forward to. Rarely in these parts, nevertheless, does an occasional letter from home reach its intended recipient. One such letter was from a land across the ocean. Alas, the troops had already moved out, and letter went dead, unanswered.

～

ONE MONTH LATER

While the foot soldiers, however brave, were clothed in tatters, the Mexican cavalry, who were more elegantly uniformed, including waist-coats and tails, rode on sturdy and beautiful mounts. In these foreign lands, Karmo had seen only a few of the small horses called Tackies in the northern part of Florida, but did not know how to ride horses. In truth, he had some fear of the Tackies, for even these animals were still quite large.

Mid-day was warm and serene. Santa Anna and Karmo sat under the leader's canopy, the General in a large, comfortable armchair that

was brought by wagon to every destination he went, Karmo perched on a simple stool. An array of mouth-watering delicacies was on the table before them, including a refreshing beverage of fruit-laden wine. Alcohol was new to Karmo, and he liked this beverage, even though it made him feel a bit dizzy and silly. Two officers on horseback rode up to the tent to salute their greeting to the General. Karmo reared back in apprehension from the hulking animals.

"Look at them, Karmo," said the General, pointing to the horses. "They move like poetry, do they not? But if you really want a show, watch the Comanche. They are masters with the beasts my people brought to this part of the world."

"They are something, indeed," said Karmo politely, but unconvinced.

The General smiled wryly, then laughed, "Well, Karmo, let us get you up on a horse, my friend!"

"Oh no, no, sir!" protested Karmo, "I would not want to impose."

"What is a little imposition?" the General said, smiling, and motioned to a lieutenant with a flick of his hand. "Bring me Safiya!"

"Si, mi General!" the lieutenant answered, clicking his heels and bowing his head. He returned quickly with a steed not so tall as the western horses, grayish-white with a dark mane and tail, a prize Arabian specimen shipped by way of Europe.

Karmo was not a man of faint heart, but this animal was so close, he had to struggle to maintain his composure and not show fear ....

"Ah, my Safiya! That is her name, Karmo. She is my jewel!" said Santa Anna, rubbing the horse's jawline. "These are war horses. Horses of courage and stamina, yet they are kind and of gentle temperament. Look at these large feet, this short back! And agile! They are quite swift, and turn easier than a wheel on a wagon!" he expounded as he moved his hand lovingly along her flank. His hand moved slowly against the hair growth, letting it flicker to expose the horse's black skin. "Hey, heh, *negro*!" shouted Santa Anna, smiling at Karmo gamely.[47]

Karmo looked at the General, puzzled.

The horse was saddled. The lieutenant tightened the girth, then handed the reins to Karmo, who just stood there next to the beast, not knowing what he was supposed to do.

"Get on the near side," explained the General.

Karmo looked at him, "The near side, sir?" he questioned, puzzled.

"The left side, the horse's left side," directed the General.

Karmo walked to the horse's left. The young officer motioned Karmo to put his foot into the stirrup, told him to grab the pommel and to swing his other leg over the horse's back. As Karmo did so, the lieutenant boosted him from behind. Karmo swung his leg with such force that he fell over the other side of the horse, while his left foot still hung in the stirrup.

"Hey, hey, hey, help me!" yelled Karmo, struggling to right himself from an upside-down position. The lieutenant and a sergeant pulled and pushed Karmo upright, while Santa Anna sat in his chair, rocking back and forth, roaring with laughter at the spectacle.

"Now what? How?" stuttered Karmo. He was becoming nauseated from both the change in orientation and the fruity drink.

"Now, we will show you how to stop and go, and how to ride!" boomed Santa Anna.

Karmo rose late the next morning, while the sky was grayish-blue, before the sun fully lit up the day to become a bright and balmy oasis of peace. He and the General met for breakfast.

"Karmo," said Santa Anna. "You know I could just as easily have run you through with a sword as accept your counsel about San Jacinto."

"Yes, General," Karmo replied, "I considered that, but both sides were weary. I am weary. There is a time to put down our weapons and reconcile. We needed to catch our breath and take care of our wounded, and our families."

"Perhaps. But you told me you have no family, Karmo. Is there no one who cries for you?" asked the General.

"I am so far from home and my love, sir. I know not if I will ever get to see her again."

"Ah, love! Yes! Karmo, love is about dedication, not pursuit. Have faith and do not give up. If it was meant to be, you will have your love."

Karmo looked at the General, somewhat confused by the gentleness of his voice, and thanked him for his encouragement.

"So, where will you go now?" asked Santa Anna, changing the subject.

"Perhaps west, perhaps to see the other great ocean, perhaps just to die," sighed Karmo.

Santa Anna laughed. "Karmo, you need not die! A river will find its path, Karmo, and so will you. Listen, you served me well. I will give you papers to present to Alvarado, the governor of Alta California.[48] [49] You will have all the space you need to live in eventual peace. But do not think this world is ever without conflict. Mexico still fights with some local Natives in the region, and the American invaders will not stop until they march us all into the Pacific! They are relentless! The British and Russians make incursions into our trapping lands, both with and without permission. There are conflicts at every corner. Remember, Karmo, rifles and women can withstand anything but being forgotten. There will always be fighting."

Karmo reflected aloud, "Is there no peace anywhere? Is there any way back from this road? It is a mortal world, General. I have to get used to losing people. I have to move forward."

"This world will eat you up, Karmo. The evil will find you anywhere."

"Perhaps," replied Karmo, "but you cannot see the good things if your heart is blind. I myself am struggling to see. I struggle to grasp any slice of happiness, to accept the life dealt me."

Santa Anna took all this in before answering in a quiet voice, "There is peace at times, sometimes even for many years. But we are human beings. We are always on the prowl. Try Alta California."

Karmo became pensive, shrugged, "Perhaps with two horses, I can use both to get across the expanse of land to the Pacific."

"You cannot travel alone across the desert, my friend. If the heat and thirst does not get you, snakes or gila monsters will. And while you seem to get along with the Natives, they will have you eating or smoking star weed, and seeing giant white rabbits!" said the General, smiling. "No, no. That medicine is not for you! You go south along the coast to Tampico, and take a freighter through Panama. Go north, up the coast to Monterey, then present your papers to Alvarado. He will treat you well."

"Thank you, General. I may just do that. May I ask, where do you go from here, sir?"

"Ah yes, where to go," answered Santa Anna thoughtfully, glancing upward into the clear sky. He looked at Karmo and took a deep breath. "There is always a place for me, Karmo, always an insurrection somewhere to put down. If it is not in the territories, then back home." The General looked wistful; then he smiled as he spied an exquisitely designed Feuillet porcelain plate on the table. He picked up the plate and offered it to Karmo, asking, "Pastry?"

OREGON TERRITORY

ALTA CALIFORNIA

COLORADO

SAN FRANCISCO

TEJAS

PACIFIC OCEAN

MEXICO

GULF OF MEXICO

TAMPICO

MEXICO CITY

MEXICO & TERRITORY

21

Christian Mullen in San Francisco 1837

At once he became an enigma. One side or the other of his nature was
perfectly comprehensible; but both sides together were bewildering.
–The Sea Wolf, Jack London

Christian Kyle Mullen, one of a handful of native-born white San
Franciscans, was an outlaw who maintained a set of beliefs into
which he merged his code. He reasoned that, given the chance, all men
will steal one way or another. And so, what is theirs could be his, be it
land, horses or women. About women, though, he had a soft spot: they
had to be willing accomplices, period.

Despite his outward persona as a legitimate businessman, Christian
was the leader of a large criminal ring composed of diverse, renegade
men of dubious repute; Californios, whites and Natives.[50] Their main
source of business was horse thievery, or "trading", he would sometimes
call it. His turf ranged mainly from the northern San Francisco Bay
Area to the foothills of the Sierra Nevada Mountains near the Truckee
River Notch. Through intermediaries, the illegal trade of horses sometimes reached as far as Colorado and Missouri. The ring also ran secret
gambling halls, at which recalcitrant debtors could meet an untimely
end. Tall and dark, his hair and beard meticulously trimmed, with his
low-pitched vocal "fry voice," Mullen was as articulate in speech as he
was definitive in action. He sported long leather duster coats and broad-
brimmed hats that were popular with men exposed to the outdoors.
His vests, however, were of the best silk or damask. At first glance, one

would think him a gambler, but he was a designer and a planner. To him, details mattered.

He had "lieutenants" in different sectors, including Lt. Dan, his right-hand man, whom he kept at his side as much for amusement as for his conduit to others in his circle. Dan's greatest skill was that of a fixer. His appearance belied his gift for reading people and situations. Corpulent, hirsute, he was of crude demeanor, sloth-like in his movements, with an unfailingly irritable disposition. His wiry sideburns grew into his mustache; nevertheless he fancied himself a ladies' man. He could surprisingly, switch on a wit and charm that accounted for many a dalliance within the feminine populace. This trait, despite his otherwise lumbering mode, was cause for many a fast exit (as quickly as he could manage) from various boudoir windows and then a hasty exit out of town.

~

At dawn just outside the Presidio, the marine layer was thick and the damp fog was the kind that settled into one's bones regardless of warm clothing. Three men were gathered in the small basement of the Mullen Building. One was sitting, tied to a chair. He was a gun smuggler, hiding the booty amongst the wares in legitimate shipments, in a business run by two others. When one businessman learned of the scheme, he threatened to turn the guilty parties over to the authorities, and in turn, lost his life for that threat. This gun smuggler, who wreaked havoc everywhere, ordered the murder. In due time, he, too, was caught in yet another fraud that forced the suicide of a head of household and left a family destitute.

"You're nothing but a common horse thief! Who are you to take me on!" yelled the smuggler as he struggled against his bindings. "You'll pay for this! I'll see you both hung *and* shot!"

"Oh, the sincerity!" said Mullen sarcastically, his gun hand across his heart.

The smuggler paled. He pleaded desperately and struggled all the more frantically. "Look here! I can make you rich! I can give you the deal of your life! Just let me go, *PLEASE!*"

"Perhaps, in another life," muttered Mullen, who was fixated on using his hand gun.

The smuggler became stone quiet, with enlarged eyes and sweat pouring over his brow.

"Look, boss!" exclaimed Lt. Dan. "He threatened to write the saga of our death if we turned our guns on him, but now he can't even put two words together."

"Mr. *Christian*!!!" yelled the gambler, working his whole torso against the chair.

Turning around, he said calmly, with assured emphasis, "That's Mister Mullen. Mister Christian Kyle Mullen, Sir." Mullen looked at the man and wondered about his callousness as he took aim and shot the smuggler square in the forehead with a new Colt . 45 pistol.[51] Amid the smoke of discharge, Mullen looked at the weapon appreciatively, turned it over in his hands, and spun the revolving cylinder. "Hmmm, not a bad pistol, Lt. Dan. And from where did these come?"

"They're new, Boss. We just brought in a batch from the east," reported Lt. Dan.

The two men walked through the main doors out into the sunlight and onto a plank landing, taking in the morning's fresh, still damp air. A great rustling from above got their attention, followed by a hail of feathers gliding down upon their upturned faces. The ruckus of wings flapping and screeching voices pierced the quiet as a horned owl evicted a red-tailed hawk from its nest.

"Housing must be getting tough to find," mused Mullen aloud.

"Err, Boss, what about …," queried Lt. Dan, ticking his head toward the body indoors.

"Oh, Joe?! Dump him somewhere near Henson's. He'll at least get buried, and won't stink up the place," answered Mullen, holstering his pistol as he walked toward the steps to leave.

~

One of Mullen's small crews, scouting the area for "vagrant horses," rode up to the adobe house of Don Cayetano Juarez outside of Napa City. Juarez's wife was tending a small garden, musing that one of the small delights of a well-tended garden were the late blooms on second-growth flowers. These determined little blooms stood proud in the late summer heat. She first heard, then saw the scouts approaching. Grabbing her bullwhip, she cracked it and quickly ran them off.

The riders, Jorge and Casio, reined up, turned and ran off a distance before turning to eye her up and down as she stood there, hands on hips, fiercely eyeing them back.

"Tough woman," laughed Casio.

Unexpectedly, Mullen rode up to them, his face flushed and steaming. "What the hell!" he roared.

"Boss?! Boss! We thought you were up north visiting with the Wanderers or Gatherers, or whatever you call 'em! We meant no harm, just foolin' around, honest!" offered Jorge.

Mullen would have none of it, "I bust my ass trying to get in Cayetano's good graces, and here you are harassing his wife?! I should shoot you right off your horses for harassing any woman! What the hell! What the hell! God almighty!"

"We weren't here to bother her anyways," said Casio, smiling, trying to soothe Mullen.

"Don't you give me that bull! Don't even try!" yelled Mullen.

The riders hung their heads, staying silent lest they set him off in all earnestness.

"Damn ignoramuses! Get your asses out of here! Move out!" growled Mullen. He rode slowly towards the adobe with both hands in the air intending to apologize, hoping to stay in the family's good graces.

Casio looked back slyly at the adobe as he rode off.

~

The lands north of the San Francisco Bay were replete with outcroppings of live oak, bay laurels and wax myrtle, all providing welcome relief from the summer heat. The grasslands and hills, which were glorious with golden poppies and wild blue lupine in the spring, were now a golden-brown and would remain so until the rains returned again. Mullen's place was near the mouth of the Napa River, where it enters the bay proper. Not far are the straits where the San Joaquin and Sacramento rivers converged with a network of smaller rivers before entering the bay.

This part of Alta California was better controlled by the Central Government in Mexico than parts farther north. And, while the government had secularized the Missions and abolished slavery, the action left a number of Native bands bereft of family ties and customs. Some became assimilated, some found bands farther north and east with whom to ally, some learned to become outlaws like the white man. Others joined Mullen.

Competing horse thieves were at times not only bold, but malicious. They cared not that the horse owners would be injured, or even killed, in a round-up.

"Some of the thieves are blackmailing the owners for the horses, Boss. They either hold the family ransom or demand money to be left alone. And Kreisler's ring is on the prowl again."

"You know we draw the line at using families for extortion, Lieutenant. We solve our problems among men. These guys need to be eliminated," said Mullen. "They give us *honest* horse traders a bad name."

Trying to deal with a reticent horse thief who is unwilling to give up extorting protection money for his horses, Lt. Dan whispered into Mullen's ear with a suggestion to make an offer that couldn't be refused.

Mullen jerked his head away, and with both hands on his desk, fists clenched, he bellowed, "We may be outlaws, but we are *not* barbarians!! And we don't abuse our stock! Don't you ever suggest such a thing again!"

He looked at the other men. "We need to get Kreisler out of our hair, boys," stated Mullen flatly. "He's not just competition and a thorn in my side, he's a thug with no honor at all."

"That's for sure, Boss," replied Lt. Dan. "He stampeded horses right over a family last week! Didn't even have the decency to bury them!"

Mullen looked over at Lt. Dan with a frown, saying, "You think anyone who would have a family trampled to death would care if they got buried? Kreisler wouldn't give a rat's ass about them!"

"Yeah, that's right, of course, Boss. You know, one of our guys reported back last week that Kreisler goes to the Pink Palace Tuesday and Thursday nights when he's in the area. Maybe we can get him there?"

Mullen winced as he looked thoughtfully at Lt. Dan. Momentarily lost in the murkiness of distant thoughts and memories, he answered, "That broke-down palace? Perhaps. It's a bit risky. His crew is likely to be watching his back, and you know who *else* will be there. But maybe we can get the drop on him in a room. Let's check it out next Thursday. Talk to our guy following him, and get the lowdown on how many of his gang are following him and where they make their lookout points. Oh, and don't tip off my ex."

"Sure Boss, will do. We'll get things set up for you," answered Lt. Dan.

There were a number of wide places in the road along the river. Dance halls, boat docks and pleasure palaces gave way to dry goods shops, blacksmiths and small residences, with dusty roads farther away. Farms were even further out. One could see the lights and hear the music upon approach to the river. These communities all looked alike.

The following Thursday night, the front of the Pink Palace was hopping. A piano man and a fiddler were beating out tunes, while a Native woman, poorly dressed and seemingly out of place in these surroundings, sang her songs amid the raucous crowd, who was paying her no attention at all. That did not really matter to her, as she was paid for her singing and expected no appreciation from this crowd. But she changed her tune when Kreisler walked in.

"You think you are so clever,
trying to make me be …
What you think I should be,
but still, I will never be free …."

Her voice warbled the lyrics with a personal despair.

A stranger made his way to the Madam, Miz Maura, standing at the bar, painted and obviously up for it. She had a bored and vulgar countenance that somewhat covered up the melancholy of a youth squandered on petty endeavors and favors, and peppered with double-crosses. She looked him up and down before telling him to get lost.

"But Schwartzy sent me," he said.

"Schwartzy, huh? And what exactly did this Schwartzy tell you?" she answered, without looking at him, but at the same time thinking of her Schwartzy. "Well, he said you had an assortment of packages—young'uns," whispered the stranger.

Miz Maura looked at him casually, and in a low voice stated, "Red, white, tied-up or untied?"

"Now you're talkin'," answered the stranger as she led him to a back room to conduct her business.

Getting quickly back to the front part of the Palace, she saw that Kreisler had arrived and was sitting at a small table near the singer, gazing at her with a certain understanding. Miz Maura took it upon herself to ingratiate herself with Kreisler. He had money, and she knew it. With her hands on her hips, her bosom thrust forward, leaning with her back on the bar, her aspect was only just manufactured as he looked her way.

Kreisler had a genuine affection for the Palace singer. Theirs was a quieter and more complicated relationship. He glanced at her and nodded, as she continued singing, looking straight into his eyes. Miz Maura saw the glance and moved in. Fickle, greedy, and dissolute, Miz Maura promoted her own self-esteem by tearing down that of others'. Her intent was clear. Kreisler, for his part, had no illusions, and despised Maura even as he used her. Their characters melded in perfect synchronicity.

Not bothering to tip his hat to the Madam as he got up from the table and walked towards the staircase, Kreisler took the Madam by the arm and commenced escorting her up the stairs to the room that was always at the ready for him.

"Ouch! Dear Sir! Careful there, I'm very sensitive and bruise ever so easily!" whined Miz Maura as she gamely allowed him to lead her, yet tugging back lightly. "Bitch!" mumbled a sneering Kreisler. "Move your big ass!"

Waiting a few minutes, Mullen got the all-clear signal and made his way to Kreisler's room with two of his crew. With a kick of the door, he entered and pointed his revolver at Kreisler's head. Miz Maura sat up, screamed, then laughed as two of Kreisler's men came out from behind the curtains and pointed their pistols at Mullen. One of the men moved slowly to the door, blocking any exit and checking for Mullen's men, who were already racing up the stairs. They stopped when they saw the situation.

"What the …?!" screamed Kreisler, clearly shaken. He looked angrily at Miz Maura, then pushed her off the bed onto the floor. "What the hell is going on here!"

Miz Maura got up and straightened her skirts before she spoke, "My friends here like to watch, and besides, this time it was to your benefit as well, my love," she said mockingly.

The air in the small room was still, and heavy with tension. It was a standoff. Even though Kreisler felt betrayed by his men, they had also saved him. He looked at Mullen, then smiled as he stated calmly, "Well, well, well, my friend. Looks like your little plan didn't play out quite the way you expected, thanks to your ex-lady here."

"You exaggerate, Kreisler," replied Mullen. "She's no lady, but you and I, we *will* meet again. In the meantime, enjoy what time you have, and cherish every breath." He looked over at Miz Maura and just shook his head. "Are you my punishment on this earth? Are you happy being bad? You're next, you know! You may think you can escape this place, but you will drown in your own poison and take your own fire to hell!"

The man at the curtain cocked his gun and put it up to Mullen's face. Lightning could not have struck faster, as Mullen grabbed the man's wrist and twisted his body to use as a shield just as the man at the door turned and fired at him. The bullets struck his partner, and with another twist of his body, Mullen fired the man's gun, which was still in the standing dead man's hand. He shot and killed the partner at the door. Like clouds and rolling thunder descending onto his face, Mullen pulled the gun from the dead man's hand and pistol-whipped Kreisler before leaving the room. Kreisler's remaining men backed off as the Mullen crew quickly backed out of the Pink Palace and got onto their horses to ride off amid gunfire. Getting Kreisler would have to wait.

~

The next day, Mullen rode up to Bockarie and spotted Karmo. "Nice outfit you have here, Bockarie. You did good," he said as he looked around.

"Someone has to, Mullen. We need to protect ourselves against outlaws, you see," replied Karmo, always suspicious of this man.

"Hahahaha! I rather fancy myself the Robin Hood of the West ... going about doing good for the poor and downtrodden," He smiled wryly.

"Your methods are not to be admired, Mullen." The two were not enemies, but just had different goals and methods.

Mullen pulled a cigar slowly from inside his coat pocket, bit the end off and spit it out before lighting up. He made vigorous puffs to get the cigar going. Eyeing Karmo closely, he allowed, "That's the difference between you and me, Karmo. You teach your people to kill. I teach my guys to die."

Karmo just stared before wordlessly turning around to walk back to his work. Mullen rode off in a different direction.

22

Benoîts to Alta California 1837

Recognize yourself in he and she who are not like you and me.
–Carlos Fuentes

Passage was booked. The Benoîts, Mrs. Marshall and Ansa Kabbah were on their way to San Francisco. They would be on a hybrid ship; powered by both steam and sail.

∼

A sailor on-board reported the events in his log:

"In Mattapoisett harbor. We made loading preparations for sea; reeding, studding sail gear, putting on chafing gear, taking on powder and provisions, and lastly, passengers. Once we were out of the harbor, the pilot directed the ship; we hauled into the bay, settled in, and waited throughout the night. The next morning, a breeze sprang up out of the northeast. The pilot gave the order to hove up anchor as he departed the ship by bark and the captain took over. We began beating down the bay. At length, the crew heaved at the windlass. Sheets of water crashed from the bow as the ship leaned aft, rolling with each new groundswell. It will be a long trip.

"The sailor's life is one of constant labor, all dedicated to keeping the ship in order. The watches were set in the mornings, very prescriptive; three watches of four hours each throughout the 12 hours of night, unless there be dog-watches of two hours thrown in to alternate start times. Rigging was constantly inspected, overhauled, repaired, replaced; tarring, greasing, piling, varnishing, painting, scrubbing, deck-swabbing. It never ends. Absent storms, Sundays are usually free from duty hours, other than necessary to sail, feed and monitor.

This is the one time the crew can get together to talk, smoke, read, and mend their clothes."

◌

The trip was arduous and longer than expected. The ship stopped in Panama City, and forced nearly twenty persons off to be quarantined and treated for typhoid.[52] Marie-Therese was beside herself, trying to minister to these unfortunates by herself, as no one, whether crew or other passengers, wanted to get near them. They were kept separated in the hold of the ship, which was steamy, dark and had few comforts. She pressed the more able patients into helping her feed and try to keep the others clean. Only Marie-Therese was allowed to leave the hold to get fresh air and, occasionally, rest.

◌

The ship continued on, uneventfully cutting through Panama and sailing north along the Mexico-California coast. The temperate climate of the Pacific soothed the heat and left a gauzy haze along the coastline. They sailed well to the westward, taking advantage of northeast trade winds during the night. One morning, they turned due east towards the coast. This stop was Monterey, seat of the government, and site of the only custom-house on the Alta California coast. Obliged to report its cargo before trading could commence, they waited two days for the ship's company agent to inspect and document the goods and condition of the ship. The sailors were allowed ashore for one night. They made a beeline for the cantinas or gambling dens, where they could play Monte or other games.

It was such a relief to set foot on land! The sick and their belongings were taken away to an infirmary of sorts. Neither the crew nor remaining passengers would ever learn what became of them. The two days were bustling, as boats ferried local people, men, women and children to and fro, to purchase wares on the ship itself. Anything imaginable could be found among the sundries; sewing needles, fabrics of all kinds, glassware, shoes, hats, raisins, molasses, teas, coffee, nails and tools.

Madeleine watched and reflected on all this. She hoped Henri was able to fill her order for fabrics from France, and that they would either be waiting for her in San Francisco or arrive shortly after the ship arrived. It was all so exciting to see and hear the activities of civilization again, and she was anxious to bring her family to the city and start life anew.

Suzanne took the opportunity to speak to the local merchants, some of whom were retrieving their bulk orders. She happened upon a disconcerting discovery, namely, that most dry goods were imported, and many eastern merchants were using raw materials from Alta California, as there were few goods that Californians manufactured themselves. Suzanne was shocked as she pondered upon this; she reckoned that, with the numerous duties and tariffs involved in commerce, the Californians were paying much too much for goods they could likely produce right here for less money. She wondered what products her family business might introduce, and what machines and skilled labor would be required to make products. She started writing down notes, ideas and plans to discuss later with her mother.

Of note, too, was lack of credit. Everything was paid for either in silver coins or in cow hides, since raising cattle was a major endeavor in this land. Her family had managed to convert their holdings to gold, so they felt assured of their security. Banking arrangements would be needed very soon, however.

Monterey was a beautiful town, with sunsets and sunrises laced in exquisite colors over pristine beaches and a calm ocean. The Benoîts, Mrs. Marshall and Ansa took it all in, silent in thought, each remembering another place far away.

They were intrigued by the Californians, who were Mexican citizens, now that independence had been won from Spain. Nevertheless, here too was a clear system of class and rank, mostly depending on how much Spanish blood each person had. The more "pure" Spanish, the higher the class; and with that came more rights and privileges. Suzanne thought this odd, as had not the Mexicans, mixed blood from many sources, defeated the Spanish? By conventional reckoning, ought not the mixed-blood peoples, the victors, be the higher class—if, indeed, class was a necessity? She would mull this over for years to come.

By and by, the ship dropped her fore-topsail, signaling her departure. She unmoored and warped down into the bight to get underway. The steam engine revved to life and the vessel cut through the beachy waters out of the bay towards open sea. The crew worked relentlessly at heaving the windlass, for now they would go the sail as long as the winds were favorable.

~

After some hours, "Sail ho!" cried out one of the crew. Headsails appeared around the point, moving towards a coastal inlet. The ship drew around and showed the broadside of a full-rigged brig. She rounded to, as a crewman called out the name and city of the ship, which was out of Oahu, American passengers mostly, with a goodly number of dark islanders as crew. As neither crew had current word from their homes on the east coast, both ships simply continued on their way.

They reached Yerba Buena, sometimes called San Francisco, in late October 1837. It boasted a population of 700 persons: Natives, Mexican citizens and others. This number grew considerably larger during trading months. At length, the Benoît party and their belongings were all dockside. The air was cool, fresh and inviting. Perhaps the impression was enhanced by having completed such a long trip.

"Madame Benoît?" a man called out as he approached the family.

"*Oui?* I am Madame Benoît," said Madeleine, turning toward the dapper mustachioed man questioningly.

"Allow me to introduce myself. I am Mr. Wilson, Thomas Wilson, Esquire, your agent."

"*Eh, bien sûr*, of course, Mr. Wilson!" exclaimed Madeleine. "So good of you to meet us here. These are my daughters, Suzanne and Marie-Therese, and our good friends, Mrs. Marshall and Monsieur Ansa Kabbah."

The small group exchanged greetings and Mr. Wilson arranged that their trunks would be transported to the hotel, where he had secured rooms for them.

"Please take some time to rest. You must be exhausted from the trip. Shall we meet together at the hotel for supper to discuss business?" suggested Mr. Wilson.

"That would be just fine, sir," responded Madeleine, grateful for a bit of reprieve from the ship's continuous rocking and confinement.

Marie-Therese remained in her room during supper, still recovering from her long ordeal of trying to help the ill passengers on the voyage. She was greatly troubled. Although weak, she fumed to herself, "That illness should never have occurred! Totally preventable!" She pulled out her trunk and dug about until she found her medical books. It was a long and restless night as she read, considered and made notes.

Madeleine, Suzanne and Mr. Wilson met for evening supper, as agreed. *The dining hall is opulent for such a frontier city*, thought Madeleine. Velvet drapes, damask tablecloths, chandeliers, carved ceiling panels and highly polished mahoganies surrounded them. The environment was neither raucous nor subdued. Sounds of cutlery on china plates and tinkling glass formed the backdrop, as well as the low voices, with an occasional outburst of polite laughter. All in all, it was quite an elegant and pleasant place amongst the potted foliage, a far cry from the weeks aboard the ship with its coarseness of food, bed linens, and company; all in all, a stark contrast to the dust and chaos on the docks.

"I am quite impressed with the fittings in this establishment, Mr. Wilson," said Madeleine approvingly.

"Ha! Wait until you taste the food!" said Mr. Wilson, amused. "Don't let this frontier façade fool you, Madame! San Francisco was founded by the Spanish more than 70 years ago. This bay was discovered by accident while looking for Monterey Bay, south of here, heh, heh, heh. Their padres established a mission close by and a whole string of missions, mostly along the coastal region, to civilize this land.[53] Yessiree, this has been a bustling, growing town ever since then. Someday it might reach three or four thousand people, I would reckon!"

"I am ignorant of this land, sir, but I do wish to learn more. My late husband Jean always spoke of coming here to continue our ship-building business," replied Madeleine.

"Hmmm, yes. That can be a profitable business, indeed, but that's not what you outlined in your letter," stated the puzzled Mr. Wilson. "Was it not mercantile in which you were interested?"

"You are correct, sir," answered Madeleine. "I only spoke of my husband's dreams, but he was also a practical man. Alas, I have neither the time nor the inclination to set up such a new endeavor as ship-building. The mercantile business is indeed what I had in mind. Were you successful in finding a suitable establishment?"

"Oh, yes, yes, absolutely, Madame!" Mr. Wilson responded with enthusiasm. "As a matter of fact, I have several sites with favorable conditions that should meet your needs. Let me outline them to you, and we can visit each one at your leisure."

Madeleine felt Mr. Wilson to be a kindred spirit; newly acquainted, they found themselves in effortless conversation. He was neither forceful nor reticent. He was just as he appeared.

That evening in their room, *"Ma mère?"* asked Suzanne. "What are we going to do about all the trades and manufacturing in this land? Could we not perhaps initiate a small enterprise, so that others may consider doing the same?"

"What do you have in mind, *ma chérie*? Besides a plan, we need skilled tradespeople and machinery."

"There is bound to be someone around who can give us information. Perhaps we can ask Mr. Wilson tomorrow," answered Suzanne thoughtfully.

"D'accord, we will inquire of him."

～

Large tracts of land, sometimes thousands of acres, were granted to individuals by the Mexican government. Some grants invalidated the Spanish land grants after the war of independence in 1821. As Mexican citizens, the Benoîts could petition for land, but had little need, nor desire, for being large landholders. They were mystified at how land could be taken from one person and given to another with just the stroke of a pen. And if they were granted land, how certain could they be that it would remain theirs? They were even more perplexed about the Native peoples, as the Mexican constitution had granted them citizenship. What happened to *their* lands, they wondered?

~

The intervening years had a few ups and downs, but gradually the business started growing stronger every day. The Benoîts did the best they could, keeping apprised of the growing unrest with the central government in the southlands. Their Mercantile Shop was one of the first to offer credit, and a liberal return policy of up to six months. Madeleine determined that if the return time is liberal, customers were less likely to return the items. The policy would encourage them to return to a business that engendered their trust, to buy more. Wherever there is credit, there is trust. Naturally, there would be a handful who would cheat or default, but that was just part of the cost of doing business.

Madeleine pulled out a bolt of *tissu de Nîmes*. "Suzanne, please take this to Madame Blenheim. Her seamstresses do wonders in making work trousers with secure pockets. I predict she will be known throughout this city for sewing sturdy apparel."

Suzanne fingered the close-woven dark-blue cotton fabric, then pulled with both hands across its width with a snap. "I believe you are correct, Maman. We need to send a letter to Henri and order more fabric as well."

"Yes, of course. Henri can get us some beautiful fabrics, but I have discovered spinners and weavers here. We need only to get the more luxury-quality items from him," Madeleine replied with an air of satisfaction. "The industry is growing. Is it not exciting?!"

23

Jonny Henson in San Francisco 1837

Every morning in San Francisco was like waking up on the edge of the earth: beautiful and damp and wild, full of the strange music people make, open-armed, into the wind.
—*All Stories are Love Stories*, Elizabeth Percer

While at most it was a bustling trading town, the unofficial mayor of San Francisco was active in making the city as modern and habitable as his home back in Boston. With the support of the Yerba Buena Alcalde, Francisco de Haro, Jonny Henson determined to walk the unnamed streets and lagoon areas in order to assess their fitness for accommodating a growing population.[54] This area was mostly isolated settlements and homes, terrorized at times by the many panthers and bears that still roamed the hills, along with red deer, elk and antelope.

Henson was a big, bearded man, himself a bear. At first glance, his aristocratic bearing gave way to an aura of aloofness, save for his glittering light eyes. He was a confirmed bachelor who nevertheless enjoyed the company of intelligent women, as well as men of his own proclivities. His dress was impeccable, but not ostentatious for this frontier town. He was a deeply caring man of good taste, deeds and enthusiasms. His only detrimental practice was a tendency for over-analysis in self-contemplation. He was quite a thinker. As he made his daily walks, he took notes, looking for areas where life could be improved. He believed that the safer and more comfortable the townspeople were, the more the town would flourish and the more people would come here to grow this town into a vibrant city.

The town had seven hills, each with their own charm and habitat. Though even summer days could be laden with a chilly fog that pooled in the town's valleys, when the sun broke through the thick marine layer San Francisco became a paradise, at least in most areas. Henson ventured east to the sketchy tracts. In this part of town, the estuary pondings and sandy, alluvial land outcroppings were littered with construction debris castoffs, most gathered up quickly by the local inhabitants for their own makeshift shelters. Shanties sprung up from whatever materials were around. Taverns, dim with fug, boasted mostly rotgut whiskey, filled with horrid-smelling "strings of unknown matter" and laced with anything from benzene to camphor, served on a bar that was nothing more than an old wooden board held up with discarded freight crates. A tinny horn emanated from the bar, amidst the thunk of heavy glasses set down noisily. Scrubby shrubs and sand plants dotted the area. The distinct odor of human waste from the estuary, with its top notes of dead fish, wafted pungently to the senses; it took all of one's control not to retch. And yet there was accordion music among the campfires at night. And small whiffs of smoke emanated from the shanties.

A woman, a mother, appealed to Jonny to seek out someone in particular, her man, called Red Cap. Street kids pointed the way to a secret fighting barn run by the enterprising Fat Cat Malloy. But it was a crooked place, drawing in the discontented and hopeless to pass the whiskey around and pin their honor and bets on a competition not their own. As Jonny opened the door, a cool, swift flow of air whooshed in, but in no time this most squalid of habitats almost overcame him with smoke, steam and the stench of sweat. He saw Red Cap, waving and shouting at the combatants who were fighting bare-fisted, their blood flying all about, their eyes swollen shut from too many punches.

Suddenly, Red Cap's man goes down, but surreptitiously eyes the hissing crowd as he does. Incensed that he had been cheated, he looks at Fat Cat Malloy, who is grinning broadly at him. Red Cap lost mightily ... and was derided.

"Ha, ha, ha, Red Cap," guffawed Fat Cat, "You no more have any sense in you than yer fella on the floor there! Ha, ha, ha, ha!"

Red Cap sneered back at Fat Cat, "Yeah? Well, you just wait. Your business will come to me soon enough. If I had me a shotgun, I'd blow you straight to hell, and I'm sure I'm not alone in those thoughts."

"Ha, ha, ha! Listen to you, big man Red Cap! I'm shivering in my boots! Ha, ha, ha!"

"Why you … whaaa?!," Red Cap lunged towards Fat Cat, just as Henson grabbed him by the collar.

"Do you think you can make easy money by risking your hard-earned pay like this in such low-down places? Did you become a rattle-brain? Your children are hungry, and here you are. This place is crooked, and you don't even care! And *that* man, Fat Cat, you don't fool with!" lectured Henson.

"Do you know my life!? Do you know what I hafta do every day for a pittance?!" scowled Red Cap, grabbing at his neck and rubbing it to erase the burn. Me and Sam over there are grave-diggers!" he said in his gruff, gravelly voice.

One would expect that voice from a grave-digger. His was not the most advantageous of professions, but at least he could make a living, nevertheless. Henson dragged him out of the fighting barn. Outside, he said, "Look, you can't go home like this, all liquored up and ready for a fight. You're coming with me."

Henson took Red Cap a ways up stream, where they sat on the bank of the dark, muddy river and listened to its groans. "What's with you? What's your story, that you should be so sour?" Henson asked Red Cap.

Red Cap turned to Henson in confusion. No one had ever asked him about his background. He was brought west as a child only eight years old, by parents who promptly disappeared, leaving him to run wild with other abandoned and orphaned street children. His first paying job was to bury a body for a murderer—and keep his mouth shut about it. This gnawed on him, but at least it was a living. He sat there with Henson, thinking about this. For once, he was not angry. What was his emotion? Something was overwhelming him, as if stones were flowing from his eyes instead of tears, a release within him; regrets of the past, present and future unfolded and came to the forefront of his conscious-ness. *I am in misery*, he thought to himself. *What else can I do?*

Henson looked at him kindly, then put his arm protectively around Red Cap's shoulders. "You have a home. You have a family," he said quietly.

Red Cap nodded. "Yeah, I do."

"And you provide for them as you can," added Henson.

Red Cap stayed silent for a few moments before exhaling deeply. "I reckon I should get back to them. They do need me, after all."

"Yes, they do, Red Cap. Yes, they do. Let them enjoy your coming home to them. You will feel better."

～

There was this life, this existence, but there was no law in Red Cap's part of town. Men who passed for police or sheriff's deputies did not venture to this area. For who but the refuse of humankind would be here? The poor, the deserted, the homeless, who may as well have taken part in their own fall from existence and subsequent demise. *There's no helping these repulsive types. They chose this squalor*, believed the more "cul-tured" people in any town, even as they disregarded their own complic-ity in commending these wretches to this fate, knowing that their labor was cheap and their motives desperate.

Several days later, Red Cap waited under an awning, looking out at the thick drizzle, wishing it would let up a bit so he could get home for what he hoped was a hot meal of rabbit stew. Giving up, he am-bled down the street towards Benoît's Mercantile, from where he saw a limping man turn around the corner and duck into an alley. He thought nothing of it until he spied a worn leather money purse in front of the shop. He picked up the purse and bounced it in his hand. The contents clinked; it was heavy. Looking up and down the street first, he paused, then entered the shop.

Mrs. Marshall gave him a sideways glance before stating rather slowly, "Yesss?"

Red Cap nodded to her, "Ma'am?"

"Yes?" she answered again.

He held out the purse, which she recognized right away. "What are *you* doing with that?!"

"I found this in front, Ma'am. I thought p'raps you would know ...."

Mrs. Marshall grabbed it from his hand. "You thief! You get out of here. Get!"

Red Cap's face darkened with rage. He had tried to do the right thing, and this was his reward! "Sure, I can use the money. I found it, but I ain't no thief! Take it. It belongs to that limping man what just left here!" With that, he turned and started for the door behind him.

"Hmmpf," snorted Mrs. Marshall. "Right, then. What's your name!?" she demanded.

The would-be Samaritan huffed and said in a loud voice, "I'm too poor to have a name! They call me by this here red cap," he said, pointing to the ragged cap on his head. He turned suddenly and left, muttering to himself, disappearing down the street into the wet fog.

~

At times, Henson slept outdoors on the Pacific side, gathering in the sensuality of the waves and breezes. It was his way of clearing his head, so he could later focus on the work at hand. No one assigned this work to him. He had the means and desire to help make lives better in this wild place.

He made the acquaintance, too, of Natives, many of whom paddled down creeks and rivers into the bay camps, in boats from missions or ranchos in the vicinity. A few Natives even had small steam engines, gleaned from abandoned Russians settlements in the north. This handful of Natives parlayed their boats into a ferry business that enjoyed a small but steady trade. He admired them for their entrepreneurship and their adaptability.

One night, he felt the need for time and a place to just think. A knot of memories jockeyed for dominance in his consciousness. He planted himself at the opening of a shallow cave on the beach, protected from the winds, and casually watched a flock of brown pelicans fly back to the wetlands near the Bolinas campgrounds. With his knees under his chin, sitting next to small tufts of shore plants, he gazed into the fading sunset. Then he turned around to watch how the breezes swayed the flowers by his feet.

The more Henson watched, the more he noticed; the dry, bent grass offering what shade it could to the nearby mound of pink sea thrift blossoming early, and in all its glory. Next to it was some little sprout upon which he had stepped unwittingly, spreading its root system, which was now struggling for the foothold of its survival. "Life," mused Henson. Contemplating the impermanence of life, indeed of all things and all constructs, he spoke aloud. "Whatever we build will disappear at some point. But for now, build the best way we know how. We will all be replaced. We will all return to our place." He smiled, and again turned his face up to watch the skies, as night fell and the stars reintroduced themselves. The constellations played out their dramas as his thoughts became liquid. He lay down on the sand and went to sleep.

Gently aroused awake by a stunning brightness dancing on his eyelids, Jonny blinked. Through the slits in his lids, he first saw the three parallel stars of Orion's belt in the western sky. There was Sirius, the Dog Star. Breathing deeply, he struggled to open his eyes more completely. It was the time when the sun, the moon and earth aligned; the time when the moon's orbit was the closest to the earth, making it appear bigger and brighter than ever.[55] The ocean roared as it released its waves to crash upon the rocky shore. Windy, brisk, smelling somewhat of seaweed—life took on another dimension that was vital and enduring. The small rivulet next to his cave just the evening before was now a flooding stream, with a fierce indifference to his proximity.

The tides were named King this time of year. It was close to sunrise. He shivered in the damp coolness, a bit regretful about his decision to sleep outdoors during this season. What had he been thinking? He turned up his collar against the chill and started back. Gaining the dunes' crest, he gazed upon the rough-and-tumble town, his town, his home … now. As he shivered his way home, he could not help but think of water movement. How to use it, how to keep it moving? "Ah, hah!"

〜

At length, he made the acquaintance of the Benoîts, taking particular notice of Ansa and Marie-Therese. Upon his first meeting, he looked at Ansa curiously, with a cocked head. "I believe I know you, sir. Perhaps we are of the same church?" he said with a broad, friendly smile.

"Perhaps, kind Sir," replied the agreeable Ansa with a bow of camaraderie. "Let us sit and talk a bit."

Marie-Therese intrigued Henson as well; she was a physician interested in the health of the public, as was he. *A wealth of knowledge she has,* he thought to himself.

Henson met frequently with the two and was also enthusiastic to meet Ansa's new acquaintance, Allen Light, a black man under contract to the Governor to work with trappers in curtailing the killing of sea otters and beaver to extinction.[56] Light knew the coastal areas and its inhabitants particularly well, and was both a valuable and an eager participant in the undertaking, which was discussed and outlined in the backrooms of Benoît's mercantile store; a new nation, independent, yet bonded together by equal rights and freedoms.

"It seems we all have been thinking separately about this for some time. I was only amusing myself with the thought until I met you, though," stated Henson enthusiastically.

"We are not likely to be alone in our thinking, Jonny," added Ansa. With that, he nodded towards Allen Light, who had been listening with a pensive expression.

"Yes, you're right," answered Light. "You are not alone in your thinking. I've traveled up and down the coast for several years now. I hear the dissatisfactions: that the central government is so far away in Mexico City; that this land is still a territory and not a state. There is even talk of separating from Mexico. As more invaders from the east come to the land, and no longer try to assimilate here or follow our laws, the Natives and Mexican citizens become more concerned. The invaders may soon outnumber the rest of us!"

Ansa mused about this for a while and studied the small group around him, smiling. "I understand you clearly, my friend. But is it not a little bit amusing that none of us here is native to this land? You, Allen, jumped ship in Santa Barbara and owe your position to Mexico; Jonny here, came from Boston. And I came here from Freetown, by way of Mattapoisett, with the Benoîts. I wonder what the Natives think of all of this."

"They think we're here to kill them! That's what they think, Ansa!" answered Light.

Ansa interrupted, "But I have met many of them casually, and they do not seem to be afraid of me."

"Humpf! Well, I exaggerated, Ansa, but only a little," continued Light. "For the most part, the Natives of Alta California are peaceful and accommodating, but that accommodation is what has cut their numbers unmercifully. Traders, settlers, and missionaries simply took over their lands; enslaved some of the Natives, others died of diseases unknown, until the invaders made their way here. I can tell you, they may not be so accommodating much longer. Their patience is not unlimited."

Ansa appeared deep in thought. "I believe I understand what it might be like," he said. "We absolutely need to get them on our side if we are to start a new nation. We need to meet with them and perhaps ask them to join our team of travelers."

Henson agreed, and arranged a series of travels throughout the north land. "First, we need to agree on our message and our basic tenets. Then we must request that they send representatives to help us determine governing guidance, including leadership and our boundaries. Of many things I firmly believe, one is that there can only be one nation. If one group decides not to join us, they may serve as their own sovereign nation, independent from us, even if within our boundaries. We will set up a system of friendly and mutual trade with that group; the same goes for travel. They have been here for many generations, and will have valuable ideas. I want to be optimistic, but realistic."

The others nodded in agreement.

CAMP BOCKARIE
LAKE TAHOE
SACRAMENTO

SAN
FRANCISCO

PACIFIC
OCEAN

ALTA CALIFORNIA

24

Karmo and Allen Light in Alta California 1837-1839

How did I escape? With difficulty. How did I plan this moment?
With pleasure.
—The Count of Monte Christo, Alexander Dumas

The Pacific bay city of Monterey was the capital of Alta California, a territory of Mexico. Juan Bautista Alvarado was governor. Alta California residents were agitated at its territory status, and wanted it to become a state of the Mexican nation with the same rights and privileges of a state.

Karmo left Tampico on the Mexican gulf to sail to Monterey by sea, hoping once again it was his last ever ocean voyage. More pleasant than his first was a massive understatement. Once crossing through Panama and reaching the Pacific, he felt more at ease. Catching the sounds of the waves shooting along the ship, he peered into the green Pacific waves, lost in thought as he imagined reflected faces of those who perished on his first voyage. Shaking his head to rid himself of these thoughts, he walked on the starboard side for a view of the new land. Though not able to secure a cabin, he was content to hang his hammock on deck like many others. Again he wrote letters, planning to post them in Monterey. *No, they will never get home, but I must pour my heart out. I must give tidings and submit my hopes to the written word.* Later, he was sleeping, gently rocking in the cool night breeze until he was shocked awake, his slumber suddenly and mercilessly came to an indignant end. With a crashing boom, he was flung out of his hammock. He scampered back, grasped the hammock ropes and wrapped himself in tightly. *No! Not this again!* he told himself. The ship lurched and tipped so much, he found himself dangling, suspended weightlessly for a moment before the next crash of waves flipped him in the opposite direction. Trunks, carpet bags, rifles and other goods which had been inadequately or neglectfully secured, slid back and forth on deck, knocking passengers and crew alike off their feet, sending them spinning on the boards. Giant dark waves looking as if they would engulf the ship hovered, disappeared and then surfaced again, over and over as if alive, spraying everyone with their salty breath. His balance wavering, Karmo covered his ears to steady himself and dampen the roars of this so-called peaceful ocean. *This is no game,* he said to himself. *We all could die! And I for one, am not ready! Never again will I get on another ship, that is, of course, if I live to get on land this time!* Hours of heart stopping tension went by, but with the rising sun, light melted the darkness and revealed spits of land peaking on the horizon. The once errant waves started to subside. The ship leveled out as it cut through a wide stretch of calmer water. Karmo was drenched, but there was nothing to do but wring out his clothes and let the sun do its best.

"There! There is Monterey!" someone hollered. "We're saved from the storms!"

The sailors smiled with a strange satisfaction. Their rendezvous with their wild, untamed beauty was over for now. "No, no," they chuckle at the passengers. "That was not a storm, just a lover's rough patch!"

Once in Monterey, he found his way to secure a meeting with Governor Alvarado and presented his papers. Karmo Bockarie, a black man, was recommended by General Santa Anna. There was no question. While Bockarie requested only a small parcel for a training camp, he was nevertheless, granted huge swaths of land in the northern half of Alta California.

"How can you just give me all this land?" he asked highly perplexed, "I have been told it is inhabited by people who have built villages, tend their farms and fields."

Alvarado, looked at the papers from the General, then up at Karmo and smiled. "Señor Bockarie, did you not realize that the General was Presidente of Mexico when he penned these documents? And he probably will resume the post in the future."

"No Governor, I had no idea," offered a surprised Karmo. "I am grateful for the generosity, nevertheless, I also am most confused."

"It is how we do things here, Señor Bockarie. There is much for you to learn. We grant land, we register the owners who become citizens of Mexico. You grantees have the right to leave people on the land, levy rent or to require them to move," explained Alvarado. "And do not be surprised if you find that some grantees are women. Our constitution allows them to own land and property, bank and even to divorce, many things, other than to vote. Oh no! That would be ridiculous! Ha!" replied Alvarado with a loud cackle. "Also, there is no slavery. The missions have been secularized and the Natives set free to go back to their homes or stay where they are for wages," he added. "Many of them stay as they have lost their families and community to disease or unfortunate incursions by others."

The two men reviewed maps of the region and his granted land in particular, before Karmo departed with his documents.

～

He purchased a small buckboard and traveled around the land granted him in the Sacramento region near Culloma Valley. He met the occasional settler and a number of Native camps. After speaking to them about water and hunting sources, he settled on a small parcel to set up his own defense training camp and contracted with the Native peoples for employment and governance. At length, he developed a working relationship with Cayetano Juarez, a large landholder to the east side of Napa and some of the former Americans who also had received land grants. He met up with another black man, Allen Light.

Light had been granted sailor's papers in New York City in 1827 and jumped ship in Santa Barbara to hunt sea otters. In 1839 he became a Mexican citizen and got his commission from Governor Alvarado to engage trappers to curb illegal otter trapping in the Santa Barbara area and points north. Light worked closely with Native peoples who also were concerned about the over-trapping by invaders, mostly Russian, British and Americans, without regard for the requisite licenses. He was rewarded with a large land grant along the northern coast which he later turned over to the Natives as he believed was right and just and preferred to live a more simple life.

The two men shared their histories; similarities, yes, but vastly different experiences before they reached Alta California. Nevertheless, they were of similar dispositions and frame of mind. For although they had suffered greatly, they both came through their travails relatively intact, and in fact, felt well rewarded.

"Karmo," said Light one evening. "There's a man in San Francisco, goes by the name of Henson, Jonny Henson. You would find him quite an interesting man. He's talking to folks about separating from Mexico and making at least the northern part of California its own country."

Karmo looked at Light incredulously, "An American? Would this be another American state?"

"No, no!" offered up Light quickly. "He was born in Boston, now a Mexican citizen, but is gathering information about making a separate, independent country with its own government. There is a crowd of them all talking about it, me too."

Karmo blinked. "A separate country …," he murmured.

LINWANE LOWA

SAN
FRANCISCO

ALTA
CALIFORNIA

PACIFIC OCEAN

25

Marie-Therese and Lokni in San Francisco 1839-1842

You cannot think yourself into right living. You live yourself into right thinking. –Native American Elders

Marie-Therese found her niche within the fledgling city of San Francisco regarding its drinking and wastewater plans. Two freshwater sources converged at the east side of town. During the rainy season, fresh water flowed east, down from the Twin Peaks area. Those streams met at what once was a salty tidal estuary. Cows and people drank fresh water from upstream; their waste was deposited and carried away in the estuary's flush of outgoing tides.

She was able to influence city planners, two men, one being Jonny Henson, who had already made plans for moving and securing fresh water. The two men had arranged for a crew of laborers to trench out a stream area and build freshwater holding tanks. Marie-Therese and other women went door-to-door to convince people not to dump waste into the drinking water and to practice basic hygiene with food preparation. Wash your hands! Wash your produce! became their calling card.[57] Naturally, some people were resentful or dismissive, but others appeared thoughtful and thankful.

∼

Marie-Therese wanted to assess citizens' habits across the bay and get her message through to families there. To cross the bay, one often rode on a water taxi, ferried across mostly by Natives. Mr. Henson introduced Marie-Therese to one of these ferrymen, whom he thought was reliable and spoke English as well as Spanish, but she had forgotten his unusual name. She was to cross the bay north-west to where the Spanish had named a camp "Sausalito." This was the ferryman's home and that of his people, at the nearby Linwanelowa settlement. Marie-Therese was determined to travel alone, as she believed she would have more credibility with the women she wanted to address if she arrived standing on her own two feet.

A rare day, the morning sunlight glistened on dancing waves like so many jewels. A vivid blue sky peered through the small, scudding clouds. During the crossing, she watched the ferryman as he stood at the wheel of the small steam-powered vessel, managing both the engine and the rudder, which was attached to a strong rope, paying careful attention to the currents and his route. The little boat pounced along the waves, sending up a fine ocean spray, a mist both familiar and reassuring to Marie-Therese. He was as tall as she. He wore a broad-brimmed hat, but his shirt was sleeveless and she could not help gazing at his muscular arms. *What strength!* she marveled to herself. Unconsciously, she moistened her lips and blinked.

As if reading her mind, he turned his head and gazed directly at her, causing her to blush and turn quickly away.

He smiled and spoke to her, "We do not often have the pleasure of seeing white women willing to cross the bay unaccompanied, Mademoiselle. Do you have someone expecting you?"

Still somewhat flustered at nearly being caught in her musing, Marie-Therese swallowed hard and screwed up enough courage to put on a placid face. She turned towards him.

"I do not, sir. I am going to speak to the women of the camp, but perhaps it was unwise for me to travel alone. I do not even know if I can communicate with them." At that point, her eyes started to tear up and she laughed in nervous embarrassment.

"Oh, just look at me!" she said. "I have not the slightest notion of what awaits me. I think because I have certain knowledge, people will welcome me with open arms! How naïve!"

"I thought as much, Mademoiselle," he said bemused. "My family lives nearby, and you can start by talking with my mother and sisters. Mr. Henson asked that I take you there. My name is Lokni."

"Oh, Mister Lokni, you are most kind!" laughed Marie-Therese nervously, still flustered by his presence and by being caught when she was so vulnerable.

"It is just Lokni, Mademoiselle. Not Mister," he told her.

"And I am just Marie-Therese, no Mademoiselle, Mr. Lokni," she murmured with uncontrollable coyness.

"Of course, just-Marie-Therese," he responded with a wry smile, as he turned back to look towards the approaching bay shore. Lokni, well-traveled in the north lands, was friendly with other Native tribes. He could be non-threatening but firm, in trade negotiations. From the Russians, he had learned to operate steam engines and carpentry. He had mastered the mallet, and made elegant shakes for roofs—with which he transformed his own parents' house. His principal tool was a long, straight blade with an equally long, perpendicular handle. With this and his mauls and wedges, he learned to listen to the sounds in the wood as the movements acquired a particular rhythm.

He also worked at small boat-building and repair, including water taxis and ferries for the bay. It was a steady business. When steamships arrived in the bay on their way east to Sacramento, or north as far as Napa, to take supplies, he volunteered to work with master builders on the those ships as well. He was flexible and open-minded, believing that learning could come from anyone, at any time.

∼

Once they docked in Sausalito, Lokni escorted Marie-Therese to a small camp of rough-hewn houses near a creek. Large oaks protected the simple homes from the coastal winds; the deeper woods nearby were plentiful with game of all types. Wildflowers had burst open everywhere, with a riot of colors that gave the camp an overall look of enchantment.

"Oh, my," exclaimed Marie-Therese "This is indeed like a fairy tale."

Lokni laughed out loud, "Yes. It is quite beautiful, but do not let that make you think life is easy here. Still, it is honest, without malice, greed or coveting. One, however, certainly lacks the amenities of a fancy city, to which you are accustomed, Mademoiselle."

"Amenities to which I am accustomed?" she asked him, surprised. "Are you not the fancy talker? Oh my, but I did not intend to sound condescending. No, not at all. Naturally, I am surprised at your vocabulary. Where did you learn this phrase, may I ask?"

Lokni looked her up and down and just nodded. "Naturally, through exposure, Mademoiselle. Exposure to others, people of all kinds."

They made their way to Lokni's parents' home and determined that Marie-Therese should settle in for the night to rest. His sisters would help organize a meeting for her to speak the next day. Lokni then sat with her for a while to tell her more about the area and propose a well-thought-out plan for the next few days.

~

Over the next weeks and months the two of them made numerous crossings together—to Sausalito and to other camps, Native and otherwise. They became comfortable with each other. She watched him closely as he started to tell her about the coastal villages. Astonished by the quickening within her and the shudder of excitement, she reined in her impulse to jump into his arms. Lokni turned around, facing her, to answer her. When he saw the eager look in her eyes, he turned his back suddenly, lest his tumescence embarrass both of them. He then took a deep breath and adjusted his footing.

Desperate to shift their stance, Marie-Therese asked, "Lokni, what can you tell me about lands farther north of here?"

"There is a place up north about 90 miles from the city; it is called Fort Ross," he explained, relieved to change the topic. "But only a few people are left there after the epidemic."

"Epidemic? What epidemic? Tell me about this Fort Ross place, Lokni. You were saying the Russians built it? Russians are around here?"

Lokni looked at Marie-Therese somewhat bemused. "Russians, British, Canadians, Americans, Mexicans, of course ... they all are invaders, to my way of thinking. But this is their nature. They see us Natives, some roaming from our winter to our summer quarters, and, because we do not build homes just like theirs or live like them, they call us savages. *That*, they believe, gives them the right to destroy our homes, our people, take our land and build settlements."

Marie-Therese looked at him pensively, but remained silent.

"Sorry. Sometimes I come across as bitter. Many of us have adapted to white ways, and some of us have even welcomed the settlers. It is the memory of the epidemics that effectively killed so many of us that tends to leave one suspicious. I do not know if it was done with malice or not, for a good number of whites died as well," he said quietly. "Anyway, yes, Fort Ross was Russian, the southernmost outpost of their Empire. It started out as a trading post for the sea otter and beaver trade, but after only about eight years, the animals were nearly extinct; so the trappers and traders needed another form of commerce.

"Because the climate was mild, the traders thought they could grow crops and raise livestock to ship to their settlements in Alaska. So they built harbors, houses entirely of wood, brought in glass for windows, stoves, steam engines, bathhouses and kitchens. There still stands a windmill that is used for grinding wheat and barley. Fort Ross was quite a vibrant little community. Some of the Natives attended schools, and were taught in Russian. A few were even sent to St. Petersburg to study medicine. Russians also met with Mexican officials in San Francisco to discuss provisioning for the settlers.

"The Kashaya Pomo Natives tried to help the Russians farm at first before the sickness came. But the summers up there are too cool and foggy, so the venture was not very successful. It became clear to the Russians that the colony, being so far north in California, was too expensive to maintain. Their homeland was using up their men and treasure to fight wars on various fronts, civil revolts throughout the country, gathering unrest in the Crimea, participating in battles with Persia.

"The colonial administrator was named Alexander Rotchev.[58] He was directed to sell the fort and return to Russia, but the Pomo said he had no right to sell the land, as it was theirs in the first place. Finally,

Jonny Henson convinced Rotchev to sell it to the Pomo for a nominal price."

"Wait, wait! Jonny Henson? *Our* Jonny Henson from San Francisco?" asked a perplexed Marie-Therese.

Lokni smiled and replied, "Yes, *our* Jonny Henson. Actually, he managed to get a few people from the city to donate funds to buy the land and let the Pomo use it. The Pomo wanted their land back outright. Nevertheless, this was preferable to invaders buying and keeping the land. The final sale was just last spring, in fact. The Russians have until 1842 to move out."

"Jonny Henson?" said a still-perplexed Marie-Therese. "He went all the way up there?"

"Oh, yes. He and a few others traveled up and down the coast to talk to the peoples about creating a new nation. I went with them on occasion. There is some support for the idea. The group is still traveling about. As for the Russians, it was they who taught me carpentry, and how to repair and run this boat engine. Sometimes it is good that foreigners come to our land," he said as he smiled at her playfully.

Marie-Therese blushed as she added, "Yes, indeed. We learn so much from coming here as well." She blushed again. "Lokni, what do you know about the epidemic?"

"I know what some cousins told me, and in truth, mostly what Mr. Henson told me when he returned from the travels," replied Lokni. "There were different diseases, all of them deadly. Mr. Henson said that at first, the diseases were mostly in the north and inland, but then spread south and west. Every time the fur trappers came, they brought diseases with them. People would die with shaking fits, vile fluids coming out of their bodies."

"Oh, Lokni, I had no idea! How horrible!" she exclaimed. "Something must be done to prevent this from ever happening again!"

"Yes," he replied simply and solemnly.

"But there is now a vaccine for smallpox. And cholera is a matter of sanitation. Malaria? Well, I do not know, but I believe clean water and air serves all of us," she said. "I feel so guilty, Lokni. I am healthy, but to think that others brought in diseases that didn't exist in these lands before their coming is unbearably sad."

"Mr. Henson told me the Russians brought smallpox vaccine to Monterey before the great epidemics here. Perhaps it was not available for the Natives. Also, it is one thing to bring medicine, but quite another thing to get people to accept it," mused Lokni.

"I must talk with Mr. Henson. It seems he has a good rapport with Native peoples. Perhaps we can help everyone understand," said Marie-Therese, urgency in her voice.

~

A beautiful man, she was drawn also to Lokni's open-mindedness and contemplative manner. She looked at him admiringly. She appreciated his mind, his physique and his dark hair that had a shock of white hair on one side. That white hair!

"Ha! My family told me that was when the rain first fell on my head as a baby," he smiled sardonically.

After several more months of crossing the bay together and spending time with Lokni, Marie-Therese became conscious of feeling a lightness and an anticipation at seeing his boat chug through the fog towards her. She put both her hands to her face and felt the warmth of her blush, despite the biting cold at the wharf. *Oh, could it be ...?* she thought to herself. In a panic, she tried to stop these thoughts, but it was as if the recognition and acknowledgment of love gave even more strength to the roiling inside her mind and body. Alas, she had allowed herself to succumb to her heart's desire.

Lokni saw her waiting on the wharf. He saw the expression in her eyes, and he was glad. "Marie-Therese, you lit a fire in me. One for which I am willing to burn. Let it be our destiny."

"If we must burn, we will face it together," answered Marie-Therese.

~

"Marie-Therese, you haven't told your mother this, have you?" questioned Leah Marshall.

221

"No, Ma'am, not yet. I have been thinking about how to bring it up. It's not at all what any of us expected," answered Marie-Therese thoughtfully.

"I should say not!" answered Mrs. Marshall. "You will give her a fright of the heart! No, no, he's not for our kind, dear, whatever good qualities you believe he has!"

"But how can you say that, Mrs. Marshall? You have never met him! If only you would, you and my mother would understand and see him for the good man he is!" responded Marie-Therese.

"Look here, missy! If you were so sure of his reception, you wouldn't be hesitating to talk to your mother and wouldn't be asking me these questions!" answered Mrs. Marshall, who was getting irritated. "There are plenty of good, white Christian men around here to take up with! You don't need to bring home a heathen!"

"Mrs. Marshall! You, of all people, should know better than to judge men by such superficial criteria! And who are we to call people heathens!? *We* came to *their* land!" cried Marie-Therese, "*They* didn't invade *us!*"

Mrs. Marshall muttered something to herself.

"What was that, Mrs. Marshall? Did I hear you clearly?" questioned Marie-Therese.

"I said, and I repeat, there are plenty of white men here to choose from! Take Mr. Roberts or Mr. Ainsworth, for example. Both of them are sweet on you, missy!" answered Mrs. Marshall, getting more and more annoyed.

"Oh, yes, of course, those two!" replied Marie-Therese. "I know them; ne'er-do-wells! They are opportunists, and are forever feigning unavailability when there is hard work to be done. No, no, Mrs. Marshall, I'll not tolerate a lay-about waste of skin as a husband! My man must be at least half the *man* I am!" exploded Marie-Therese.

Mrs. Marshall looked at Marie-Therese with surprise; she had never heard the young woman raise her voice as she did just then.

"Marie-Therese," she said, modulating her voice and cadence, "Dear, I didn't mean to offend. You just pricked a scab on my heart, and I took

222

out my pain on you. You know, I was the one who always said the quickest way to a man's heart ... is with a knife!" Her face was blazing red. She closed her eyes and took a deep breath. "I'm not the best person to confide such matters in."

"Oh, Mrs. Marshall! I am so sorry! I wasn't thinking! That was so long ago. Please forgive me," pleaded Marie-Therese.

Mrs. Marshall took a deep breath and answered. "Come sit with me, dear. Let me make us a cup of tea. It will do us both good." Mrs. Marshall believed that a cup of tea could cure all ills.

Marie-Therese sat down at the kitchen table dejectedly as Mrs. Marshall put out the tea and some fresh baked scones. "I cannot imagine a life without him."

Sitting down, Mrs. Marshall looked calmly at Marie-Therese, whose face was still red after their interactions, and said quietly, "There, there now. Decisions aren't hard. You always have two choices; live or die!"

Marie-Therese's head jerked upwards suddenly as she looked towards Mrs. Marshall, who only cocked her head, her eyes glittering mockingly as she sipped her tea.

～

SIX MONTHS LATER

"Stop! Just stop a minute and listen to yourself!" he told her in that low, steady way that sometimes infuriated her—because he was usually right.

Marie-Therese was passionate about a community being responsible for one another's well-being, regardless of individual resources. Some things are just a given, she believed. But her husband, Lokni, was always there to support her with his moderating, philosophical voice.

"I know, I know, we cannot just kick people out because they do not believe like us, but ...," her voice trailed off.

"But ... we need to find a way that makes it palatable and fair," he said. "It's called compromise, my love." This was the pattern for any number of proposals, be they about vaccinations, people's health in general, or learning the ways of residents of the region.

ROAR!

She looked at him and took a deep breath, "Right. You know how I get. This is why I run my thoughts by you, to pull me back to reality."

26

Jack to Alta California 1844

Per aspera ad astra

No one knew him. He had no family, no home about which he would speak. He was young, maybe 23 or so. A rangy-looking young man, he had sandy hair and eyes the color of topaz, but with a nearly vacant expression. He was already hardened, matter-of-fact, and spoke sparingly. Jack Marshall had come recommended as a sharpshooter, and in return for food and a horse, would provide his services to hunt game and act as safe passage escort for the Stephens-Townsend-Murphy covered wagon party, out of Missouri.[59]

The immigrants purchased heavy wagons filled with provisions and possessions to serve as their temporary homes. At least two yokes of oxen were needed to pull each wagon. Young beef cattle and milk cows were brought along for sustenance. Most immigrant families had a pair of saddle horses as well, and a guard dog or two. The families hired teamsters to drive the wagons and bushwhackers—sturdy single men who walked alongside the caravan—to help steer the beasts, keeping them on the trail, as well as to urge along the livestock, and attend to various chores in setting up and breaking down camp.

The trip through the Great Plains was grueling. Most of the Natives encountered along the way were helpful, giving directions and even trading or purchasing food and other supplies. In other areas, the Natives stole livestock as the train traversed their hunting grounds. A quarter of the immigrants perished due to disease or attack. That was a considered, and expected loss. Once, the Missouri covered wagon caravan came across the grisly remains of a former caravan burial site that had been dug up and ravaged by wild animals. The animals were still gnawing on the bones as they were approached. Birds were pulling out the beards and hair of the deceased to line their nests. The group paused, looked at the dead travelers in despair, reburied them, said their prayers and journeyed onward.

Travels across the plains were slow and tedious. Time was monotonous, save for the few messages from previous caravans that were wedged into trees or rocks along the way. These were both exciting and comforting. Mirages became more frequent as the caravan progressed through the plains, and more than once a group of men rode off in pursuit of imaginary herds of antelope.

Jack looked up at the sky. The sun was so bright, the sky seemed nearly white. He took a swallow of water, swirling it over his dusty tongue and gums before spitting it out. Now he could relish a sweeter taste as he drank again. The weather was hot, dry and noiseless, save for churning wagon wheels and the snuffling and snorting of livestock. Momentarily, Jack's head nodded and he dozed off in the saddle. His head jerked up suddenly as he blinked sweat from his eyes, wisely deciding to gallop farther ahead, to better attend to his duty.

As the wagon train finally reached the Platte River, brilliant and fearsome lightning roared and crashed about. At times, electrical sparks rolled down the sides of wagons, shocking both man and beast. The caravan continued onward. Nature seemed to be playing tricks on him, as for hours there had been nothing but flatness; but now, clearly, mountain peaks rose in the distance.

Headed west through yet another demanding and miserable leg of the journey, they were in Colorado Territory. The Rockies were just ahead. The day had been uneventful, until there came a sudden chill. Flocks of birds scattered in flight, screeching into the distant thunder. Hearing the loud whoosh and rattling of quaking leaves, Jack looked towards the disappearing birds just as the first big drops of rain splattered his upturned face. He watched strange, dark, mammatus clouds in the far distance, which disappeared in the darkness, followed by the din of a most ferocious rain, the likes of which few in the train had ever experienced. He felt a tangible presence of malevolence. A momentary break to blue, and then the skies carved open to reveal the anvil of the storm, bright and scary before it morphed into a dark, ominous funnel. The dazzling flashes of lightning came again. The rains came back in pounding torrents, and the wild dark wind eventually turned away from their direction. The fierceness of the wind's edge, however, cut into the grove in which they had taken cover.

Trees about them huddled above before commencing to wave furiously, buckle and snap, flying upwards into the maw of what had been their sky. The sound was thunderous and physically assaulted their ears, their quivering skin and nerves. Roars of wind and crashing debris struck fear into their hearts, as they believed it surely was the end of days. The teamsters and bushwhackers struggled to move the livestock towards the trees. In their terror and disorientation, some of the beasts balked and stampeded into the open plains. Some were literally swept up into the sky and later found dead in trees; others were never seen again. All of a sudden, it all stopped. Snow flurries brushed the sky for a time until they too dissipated into a quiet grayness.

～

Ever on the alert for signs of troubling weather, for food and for bandits, the caravan persisted, plunging into the limitless and unknown world, through the great salt flats and eventually on through the Sierras. Exhausted emotionally and physically, the traumas and heartache they all endured had many questioning their initial decision to embark on the journey, but they had traveled too far and could not risk the dangers of going back. Their encounters with Nature laid bare the futility of human pride in daring to stand up to her.

Jack watched the evening sky and wondered to himself, *Why are these people leaving their own comfortable homes for Mexican Territory? Why would they leave their home country, with their families, for a foreign one, one with a people primarily of a different culture, who speak a different language? A better life, said some. while others said adventure.* He remained puzzled.

He shrugged, concluding that he was on his own and was looking for a home too. This caravan was merely his path.

As they came to the Sierra Mountains, they looked for the passage used by Jedediah Smith in 1828, but instead found themselves heading upstream along the Truckee River, which was named for the Paiute Chief who befriended previous travelers.[60] Here they had found a notch in the mountains this late spring. The timing was good, but they were on a tight schedule and needed to get through the Sierras while there would be grass enough for the horses and pack animals to eat. The air was clear but thin at this elevation, as in the Rockies. The travelers were constantly plagued with headaches, dizziness, and labored breathing. Many faltered, so the pace became slow, by necessity.

At the summit, the ceaseless roar of the wind at first stunned Jack's senses, but at least one could see for miles in this clear, thin air. They proceeded around Truckee Lake. Carved by glaciers, it was fed from springs and snow melt. Small willow trees and short, needle-like grasses dominated, but he could see the progression of tree types as the elevation decreased; some were similar to trees he knew from the East Coast. There were stands of lodgepole pines, aspens and hemlock, followed at a lower elevation by cedars, white fir and some type of giant, needled trees that he had never seen in his life. *It was a beautiful sight*, he thought, *a paradise of natural riches. Nothing bad or evil could ever happen here.* That was not true. The plotted trail was new and filled with boulders as high as a man's waist. In this thin air, they cut logs to leverage the wagon wheels over the stony out-crops. Some wagons made it, some overturned and slid off the winding road in a scree of loose gravel, then fell apart, irreparable. Oxen pitched and slipped in their struggle under the whip, to pull the wagons forward. Those on foot hiked through the shifting gravel and the streams of water spraying down from the sides of the pass. The rivers were a riot of white water, rushing from their origins, swollen with snow melt. Some days it took hours to find a safe place to ford, but again, the group persevered until they managed to get to the lower elevation.

Through the foothills' abundant oaks, willows and buckeyes, they spotted foxes, cougars and bobcats. Jack went ahead of the party, scouting for passage. Along a hillside he saw four-to-five-inch plugs of desiccated scat and paused, standing high in his stirrups to look around. Two small bear cubs appeared ahead of him on the path just as he passed the fork. His horse at first snorted, then froze and became quiet. Jack made himself alert and looked around, as he suspected the mother was close by. Momentarily, she came lumbering out of the woods, sniffing, saw him, and stood on her hind legs, reaching a height of nearly seven feet. Her front legs outstretched as if she would embrace him, she tilted her head upwards and roared with all her might, advancing menacingly several steps before stopping. Jack backed up his horse slowly. She was an impressive, amazing beast in her determination to protect her own. He did not need to interfere with her, and so he chose the path less traveled. The sight would, however, remain forever indelible in his mind.

At last, the party entered a large valley, where rivers and streams were abundant. They camped next to a lake, across from which Natives had built their village. Ever on the alert, they posted men to watch through the night.

They need not have bothered, for the next morning, a small Native group galloped over to them, their rifles holstered, no weapons in their hands. Through a mix of English, Spanish and hand signals, they learned of the friendly inclination of these Native peoples. Just as important, they learned the direction of two outposts in the area. One was the trading post they sought, called Sutter's Mill. The other, about a day's travel slightly to the northeast, was a small village and military-like training camp, called simply Bockarie, at the foot of Histum Yani, Spirit Mountain.[61]

Jack Marshall, two families and various single men headed out for Bockarie. The majority of the travelers went on to Sutter, to rest and decide their next steps. They were foreigners in this land and, while welcomed, were required to register their presence.

~

John Sutter had requested a rather large land grant from the governor of Mexico, but received only a fraction of the request when the administrators learned of his background.[62] His experience as a trader among the Natives was helpful in keeping the peace and establishing an economy, and recommended him. However, he had abandoned his family in Switzerland to avoid an arrest warrant, and had at one time passed himself off as a captain in the French military. He was a fraud, and therefore, an incomplete and unknown entity. Having learned the lessons of Tejas, the administrators were unsure how he would honor this land, or their government.

~

It was getting on to evening. Jack and his small party decided to camp out before riding into Bockarie. As dusk faded, he watched the constellation Scorpius disappear in the southwest sky. He remembered the story Mr. Ansa told him back home about how Gaia sent Scorpius to battle Orion because she felt the great hunter was killing too many animals. When the two fighters killed each other, Zeus maintained peace in the sky by placing Orion in the winter and Scorpius in the summer, so they would never see each other. *And there is Antares, the red heart of the scorpion,* thought Jack to himself. *How can the skies look so peaceful, give us comfort and hope? How do they give refuge to the dead, and yet pay homage to battle?*

The next morning, Jack and the others found Camp Bockarie, a bustling community of Natives, Californios, Americans, Russians, and a few black men, all working at their trade, all mingling and conducting business. He was perplexed at the diversity, for while he had seen a mix of peoples on the docks back home in Mattapoisett, they had not mingled so much in town. Some of his companions found the scene quite disconcerting. After asking around, he was pointed in the direction of the head man, an African named Karmo Bockarie.

Jack harbored no animosity towards Karmo, rather he was curious about this black man with perfect English diction. The meeting was cordial, and after a few inquiries, Karmo looked at Jack hard and said questioningly, "So you fought in Florida?"

"Yes sir, I was there almost two years before I left for Missouri by way of Tennessee," answered Jack.

"You must have been very young. It could not have been easy," reflected Karmo, watching Jack's reaction.

Jack turned pale and hung his head a moment before looking Karmo directly in the eyes, "It was not easy. It was hell, and I will carry what I did and saw with me for the rest of my life. But in the end, I feel justified."

Karmo was silent, stared at him for a moment, then nodded. "So you can shoot and ride. What do you know about defense?" asked Karmo.

"I hired myself out as a gunfighter and a scout. Sometimes I made mistakes. I'm a sharpshooter, and very good with a handgun. I would not use either now, when there are other means of protection or negotiation. I understand many other tactics of protection now," explained Jack.

The two men discussed such tactics, and Jack's potential role as a gunsmith and sharp-shooter trainer at the camp. "You need not work here exclusively, Jack," explained Karmo, "but be careful to whom you contract your services. It is not always clear how clean they are."

"I understand, sir," agreed Jack, looking around at the passersby.

Karmo took notice and said to him, "You are wondering how all these peoples can live together peaceably. Am I correct, Jack?"

Jack looked at Karmo and shook his head slightly before saying thoughtfully, "Yes and no, sir. I saw all this growing up on the docks of my hometown, perhaps not Russians or as many Natives, but white men from different countries and black men. Mostly they worked as laborers; few had their own enterprises. And if you will pardon me, sir, never have I seen a black man head up such a large venture."

"I see," said Karmo with a smile. "Look over there, son," Karmo said as he pointed to a large oval dirt track where people were learning to shoot guns as they rode horses. Who do you see?"

Jack had not noticed this until it was pointed out. His face blanched, then reddened. " Wo ..., women?!"

"Women, yes. They are people. Not curiosities," Karmo shook his head, somewhat amused. "Yes, Jack, women. Every bit as capable in the skills we choose to train them, and perhaps even more skilled than men in the art of subterfuge. Never underestimate them. Though our enemies surely will."

"But why are they here, sir?" asked Jack. "Why do they want men's jobs?"

"Men often must leave their homes and families for days, even weeks, at a time, herding cattle, horses, trading, hunting or other business. Should not women know how to protect themselves? Should a 10-year-old boy left at home be given the burden of taking care of his mother and siblings on these occasions? No. Women must take up the burden as well, a shared burden. True, in normal times, the sexes have their assigned roles, but the philosophy here is that all persons must be trained in and capable of defense when needed. These women come here for training voluntarily."

"And their fathers and husbands allow this?" asked Jack, still perplexed.

"Hmmm, well …," said Karmo slowly. "It remains a work in progress. The more women who enroll, the more emboldened others become, and request, demand, finagle, plead their way here. But come, they do. Do not be so naïve as to discount *otherness*, people who are different from you. Note that in some places in this land, that is all they talk about. And sometimes otherness is maligned. That is a big mistake."

"Natives too, I see," said Jack as his eyes followed one such young woman skillfully hitting her mark from a galloping pony.

"You will be surprised, as I was when I first arrived, that a number of tribes are matrilineal. Native women often determine the ways of their Band, and inform their men, who then go to council to present the ideas and decisions as their own. These things are not always openly spoken about," said Karmo with a wink.

"Hmpf," grunted Jack, taking this all in. He then pointed towards the massif. "Are these Natives all from that Spirit Mountain area?"

"Yes, mostly. There are fewer Natives than just ten years ago. In this area, easily two-thirds of the Natives perished from smallpox, cholera and other diseases unknown until white men—mostly fur traders—

brought the diseases here. Farther north from here, some Native bands will kill a white man on sight without mercy because of the death his kind brought," said Karmo his face taking on a serious demeanor. Karmo then asked Jack, "You are about 23 or 24 now, correct?"

"Yes, sir," replied Jack, "about that. I've lost track of time."

"Hmmm, right. Yes. Jack, you should see more of this land. Meet its peoples. Learn about them, live with them, and listen to them. It will serve you well. But also, remember, you have a place here if you want it."

"I'd like to stay here a while, sir. It seems the right place for me," said Jack.

"Then come into my office and I will get you registered right now. It is mostly a formality, because the Mexican government has its hands so full with insurgencies throughout the territory. They mostly control only the coastal lands. But if you plan to stay here, even for a while, I must tell you about this land and its practices," said Karmo. "You can even apply for land grants if you have good intentions and become a citizen."

Jack nodded yes, but his eyes kept being drawn to the strange mountains.

"Yes, they are mesmerizing," said Karmo patiently before shifting his gaze there too. He realized that Jack was not ready for administrative formalities. "That big one to the left, Spirit Mountain, is sacred to the Maidu and Wintun Natives. They believe the buttes rose up in the plains after a great flood, and that the first man and woman were created there."

"A great flood?" questioned Jack.

"Yes, this is their belief, as valid as anyone's; do you not think so?" asked Karmo.

Jack was deep in thought, reflecting and remembering.

"Jack?" asked Karmo.

"What? Oh yes, sir. Why not?" responded Jack.

"Why not, indeed?" said Karmo, smiling. "The Natives believe that after death, their spirits rise to live in these buttes. Therefore, it is sacred land. Down here is excellent land for grazing, stony brown loam up there," Karmo pointed at the base of the buttes, "and sandy dark loam and more grasslands just below us. It is a good place to set up a living, Jack. The river, El Río de las Plumas, flows close by, and so do other powerful, wide rivers. They converge in Sacramento and flow westerly. The San Joaquin River joins them and they meld into a large delta at Rio Vista in the land of the Natives Suisunes, then towards Yerba Buena cove on the bay, before flowing into the Pacific."

"I would like very much to travel to that other ocean someday, sir," said Jack quietly.

"Of course, Jack," replied Karmo softly. "It is not so far away, and is like magic to behold." Karmo liked this young man, which was unsettling, as he had only just met him that day. But Jack's balance between questioning and accepting was appealing. "I am telling you this because at times I must travel to Yerba Buena on the coast for supplies that do not always reach Sacramento. Perhaps you might want to accompany me," Karmo continued.

"Yes, sir. I'm taking it all in," replied Jack. "Yerba Buena? Is that the same as San Francisco?

"Yes, it is, Jack," answered Karmo. "It's all a matter of to whom you are speaking. Someday, one name will become the standard, and the other will fade away."

27

Jack and Pompo, Mullen 1844

It's life that matters, nothing but life—the process of discovery, the everlasting and perpetual process, not the discovery itself, at all.
—The Idiot, Fyodor Dostoevsky

Jack's life at Bockarie was busy with hard work, but he experienced a peace that soothed his soul as he tried to forget his past. It gave him time to contemplate a future, even if at times he doubted that much of a future was even possible. He was grateful to Karmo for the opportunity given him, and diligently attended to his tasks of teaching gun-handling, specifically long-range sniper training. Jack spent his off time hunting and exploring the lands Karmo had described to him, listening to the conversation of men coming in and out of camps from the coastal areas of the west and the mountains of the north.

He spent time also watching horseback riders go through their paces. He watched one rider in particular until he got up the nerve to walk up to her when she stopped to rest under a tree to fix something on her left hand. As he approached her, he turned quickly towards a screaming blur of mahogany that was racing towards his head and that of the rider.

"Do *not* move!" she shouted at him. "He has already tracked his course!" It was a red-tailed hawk, her own hawk, who alighted with wild flapping onto her outstretched hand. He appeared quite at ease on her leather glove as she fed him raw quail scraps from a pouch strapped to her waist. Sated and otherwise fed up, the hawk eyed Jack closely. She tied the bird's feet with the gloves' leather jesses to contain him. "His name is Hawk," she said smiling. The bird of prey spread his nearly four-foot wing span before resettling, and looked at Jack with fierce eyes.

The young woman's name was Pompokum, which was Maidu for Moon. She explained that she was Nisenan, one of the few Natives from that tribe who had survived disease epidemics because her parents sent her away when the Hudson Bay Company workers came to her community, bringing malaria. The people she knew as her parents and more than three-quarters of the Nisenan perished. She had no other family now, other than Bockarie and Hawk.

Jack had not heard of such a disease, nor of the full extent of the deaths by malaria. It was incomprehensible to him, yet he understood being alone and that brought him closer to her. He called her Pompo for short. She had dark, wavy hair and dark eyes that reminded him of looking into a deep well. She wore men's clothing as a practicality, but added a flowing green scarf to honor her femininity. She hunted both with a rifle and with Hawk. He was totally enthralled.

～

Months went by, and it was already August. After hunting in the morning with Hawk, Pompo sent him home to the mews. She and Jack rode out alone towards the buttes to wait for the night sky, when the meteor showers commenced. First one, then more, until there were dozens at a time, followed by more than could be counted, lighting up the darkness.[63] The meteors shot through the black sky, leaving faint traces behind, in fact and in memory.

The two made a small fire to cook dinner and to keep warm. Pompo took a deep breath. "I never get tired of watching these showers," she said quietly.

Jack turned to her and nodded, reflecting, before saying, "I remember watching meteor showers at home when I was young. A friend of the family told me star stories and said to always look at the sky as if it was my first time, and that we are all made of star stuff. Because of that, we are mighty. I remember that, for sure, I remember."

Pompo said thoughtfully, "He sounds like a wise and spiritual man, Jack."

"He is, or was. I left home when I was 14, and don't know what happened to my family," he answered, his eyes started to glisten. "Sometimes I think we don't get old through age, but because of what we go through," mumbled Jack, feeling regret for betraying his family.

"I am sorry," murmured Pompo.

He looked at her, swallowed hard and said, "I don't know where I belong. I don't even really know where I am in the world, Pompo."

"The only way to know where you are is to make yourself a home, Jack, and stay there a while, not always be hitting the road," she said, with both concern and a touch of annoyance.

He turned away and pulled the mess of quail off the fire spit, then threw some greens into the shallow pan, which had been catching the drippings and stirred them quickly. Pompo had brought fresh bread and juicy August peaches. Together, they ate heartily, if silently, for the first few moments.

Sitting by their small fire, Jack took a stick and aimlessly flipped over random rocks and dead leaves, sending insects scattering in all directions. He leaned in on them, observing their world, watching the black beetles and roly polys.

"Roly polys," he said quietly. "The clean-up crew."

"What did you say, Jack?"

"Oh, just thinking out loud, nothing important." He wanted to change the subject.

The moon loomed bright in the sky as Jack said quietly. "I remember when there was no full moon one month. I think it was February of the year before I came out here." It was just filler talk, but he needed time to get his thoughts together, as a chorus of tree frogs croaked their songs of love in the darkness.

The two of them remained there, watching the sky, for hours, until the sun showed its nose at the peak of dawn over the eastern rise and the glowing star Venus became more visible.

"Look!" said Jack, "just east, low in the sky."

"Yes, said Pompo, "the morning star," she smiled at him.

The cool air turned to a gentle warm as the earth revolved yet another notch. After a long silence, Jack turned to Pompo and said, "I'll be leaving soon to join up with Christian Mullen for a while. But I'll be back, Pompo. I'll be back for you."

Pompo turned her head to face him suddenly and exclaimed, "No! You are going to do what?! Off you go, again! Are you that foolish, to join the likes of an outlaw gang!" Pompo's demeanor was the complete reversal of the previous idyllic moments. "Even *I* know about Mullen! He may not be as unmerciful as others, but he is still a killer, Jack! You have no business taking up with the likes of him and his gang! None at all! You will screw up your whole future! Our tomorrows!" she screamed at him, breathing hard.

Jack remained quiet but thought to himself, *She is my breath, my whole life.* If only he could say it out loud to her! His gaze became fixed on her, and then he suddenly snapped to and understood what she meant to him. Hesitantly he slid towards Pompo, who did not move away.

But a darkness welled up inside him. Jack had had misgivings about joining up with Mullen; nevertheless, but his stubborn pride would not allow him to be told what to do by anyone—not even Pompo. Quietly at first, but working towards a crescendo of feelings, he chided her. "I've been making my own decisions for a long time now, Pompo. I'm old enough to decide who I'll hang out with! And I don't need anyone, not *any one*, to tell me different! All I have is what I am. No name, no family, no wealth. Just me and my honor, what's left of it. I had hoped that would be enough!"

He hadn't meant to become harsh and reactive with her, but he could not help himself. And now there was no way he could tell Pompo that he was only doing it to get seed money to start his own gun repair shop at Bockarie. Dirty money, she would say. So would anyone, but he hoped perhaps he could sign on for jobs where no one got hurt. Now, he needed to save face with her.

"Look at me!" he said with a raised voice at first, then calmly, "There is no yesterday or tomorrow. The only thing real is here, this moment.

The rest is just air! You need to accept that" He was attempting to justify his own words to himself.

"Dumb ass!" she hollered at him, biting her lower lip involuntarily.

"Did you just call me dumb head?!" he asked, startled, with a flicker of something remembered.

"No! I called you a dumb *ASS*! Dumb *ASS*! You are a dumb ass, Jack Marshall!" she screamed back at him as she got up, took her rifle and stomped off to her horse.

~

Freedom! Taking pleasure in being one's own master; to go wherever and do whatever, and attend only to oneself, thought Jack as he traveled west to meet up with Christian Mullen. There was no urgency, so he took a day for himself—to just be. He breathed deeply the herbaceous air and listened, actually listened, to the birds. Presently, he stopped to rest atop a small hill, later made a campfire, cooked and ate the fish he had caught in the nearby creek, before taking a nap. He woke to the sunset, an optical explosion of magical colors such that he thought his heart would burst in awe and appreciation. It would only have been better if someone special was with him to share the experience. Ah yes, freedom also could be lonely.

~

The sound of a low growl woke him the next morning, followed by a wet, warm tongue licking his ear, and hot, labored panting. He jumped up with a start to see the spongy soft muzzle of a big yellow dog facing him, eyeball to eyeball.

"Where in tarnation did you come from, hound?!!!" Jack sat up and looked around, seeing no one except a small pack of coyotes staring down at him from a rock outcrop about 50 yards away. The yellow dog was gaunt, but amiable, as he laid down on his belly a few feet from Jack.

"You been running with the pack, fella? Looky here, I got something for you." Jack carefully pulled out some leftover fried fish from his saddlebag and gently tossed it to the dog, who pounced on it immediately and swallowed it whole.

"Careful now, don't choke, fella," Jack said with a laugh to the dog as he looked at the coyotes. They were eyeing him closely, but presently turned around and trotted off.

"Alright, I guess you're with me now," he addressed the yellow dog, as once again Jack took in his surroundings. Droning bees working the wildflowers, a luxuriating somnolence of warmth radiated from his rocky perch. The sun cast a light so soft he could almost sense its texture. The air was so clean and sparkling, his nose twitched. He squinted his eyes in the brightness, then shook his head to clear the dark images one sees after having stared into the sun's aura.

"Let's get going, fella. I got a meet-up to take care of."

His first assignment was a delivery; easy, and paid well. He simply picked up a wagonload of boxes and drove them to an assigned spot. The second assignment required his skills as a sharpshooter. No one would get hurt, he was assured. Mullen had been caught by the law and taken to a nearby village known as Swingtown to dance from the gallows. Breezy and clear, there was a carnival-like atmosphere—every Thursday was hanging day. The day's entertainment was plentiful; picnics, horse shows, Indian dances, and more. When the main event was about to begin, the sheriff led Mullen up the creaky steps to the top of the scaffold and placed the noose around the condemned man's neck. The crowd cheered boisterously. How quickly they adapted to the spectacle in this isolated village!

Jack, behind the false front atop the saloon, checked the winds, looked into his rifle scope and paused to exhale. It was only about 450 yards away, but a rope is a small target. He saw the sign given and squeezed the trigger. As the bullet cut through the rope just as the trap door opened, it ripped through the sheriff's hat, blowing it off his head. What a risk! Mullen dropped through the trap door, his hands still tied. His men were there below to whisk him away on horseback, followed in hot pursuit by the townspeople. Suddenly, they stopped, terrorized, as dynamite blasts went off, first at one end and then at the other end of town. Explosions and smoke were everywhere as the unguarded armory also went up in flames, Lt. Dan's handiwork. Mullen's laugh traveled through the canyon, "Hah ha ha ha, hah ha ha hah!!! See ya, suckers!!!!"

Jack felt that uncanny pull to a former life, the stalking and the violence. He climbed down from the roof, jumped onto his horse and galloped off in the opposite direction from Mullen and his crew. They would meet up later. *This I can do*, he thought to himself. Fella ran after him.

~

The gang met up at an agreed site near Oak Hill. Jack and Fella came along soon after. Warily, the young man and beast approached.

Mullen walked up to the two and looked at the dog before bending down to scratch its neck. Fella rolled over, exposing his belly, the ultimate sign of surrender and trust. Mullen then uttered a bizarre animal sound, smiling with closed lips. Fella guffawed a strange broken belly laugh in return.

"Ha!" hollered one of the men. "The Boss can make a dog laugh!" The others joined in, laughing as well.

Fella jumped up on all fours to nuzzle Mullen's hand.

"Well, boys, pay attention!" said Mullen. "Let this be a lesson for you. Never trust anyone a dog doesn't like. They have a keen sense of good and bad." Looking over at Jack, he added, "You did damn good today, son. Damn good!"

Jack was so relieved.

28

Karmo, Jack, Ansa in San Francisco
1844-1845

No distance of place or lapse of time can lessen the friendship of those who are thoroughly persuaded of each other's worth. –Robert Southey

His contracts with Mullen fulfilled for the present, Jack went back to Camp Bockarie.

There he met up with Karmo, who was just coming back from a corral, tired and thirsty. They sat outdoors on a large flat rock, sharing a canteen of water. The sun was setting and a gentle swirl of wind blew bits of grass and dust around their feet. Karmo looked at Jack patiently, for it was clear that the young man had something on his mind. It was the first time in his adulthood that Jack felt he could share thoughts and feelings with another man.

"At home, I never saw fighting like in Florida." There was a long pause while he struggled for words before continuing, "I saw arguments, double-crosses and even murder on my own side, but what was that? Not real war? I fought the enemy, but it wasn't the same as the fights among ourselves."

"They are all related, Jack, remember that," answered Karmo. "Peace is relative and temporary. There are always those who want more, even if they have to take what is yours. It does not matter what side you, or they, are on."

"I saw good people do horrible things, Mr. Karmo. And I did horrible things. We never would have thought to behave as we did in that fighting. I saw men who became thieves to steal bread for their families to survive! Are they not just desperate and trapped?" asked Jack.

Karmo considered this before speaking. "Yes, there are such people, of course. Always have been. But tell me. What are the conditions that would lead someone to resort to these depths?

Jack became silent. "Yeah, I see what you mean. But the government was doing the same. I thought I understood until I engaged the enemy. They were not the savages we were told. They were people with families who were protecting their land and farms."

"Looking back, you can see how the American government and the businessmen first sent in their citizens to settle the land and do their fighting. Many people were sacrificed to stave off counter-attacks on American towns. Then they sent in their army, because the Natives no longer had the strength of numbers or arms. The soldiers and volunteers attacked without mercy. Only when the Natives banded their tribes together, did they even have a chance to keep some of their lands. I saw this happen with the Cherokee, Choctaw and others," explained Karmo.

"And I saw that later with the Osage," added Jack.

Karmo nodded. "The Apaches, Comanches and others are still fighting fiercely, but independently, and lack the weapons they need. They will be annihilated, unfortunately. It is a recurring pattern of history."

"It was horrible, Karmo. Just horrible. And I did horrible things," mumbled Jack. A shakiness came over him, and he wanted to change the topic.

"The hell of war makes it hard enough to contend with the violence around us; it is even harder sometimes to deal with the violence we did or with what we did not do in battle, but should have. We humans are meaning-making beings. We endeavor to see a story or seek an explanation for things around us. Win or lose, sometimes life after war becomes a second hell. Do not let that happen to you if you can help it, Jack! Do not let the hell of war follow you around."

"It's a struggle, Karmo," answered Jack before pausing. "Do you think that what happened in Florida will happen here? Will the Americans come to Alta California?"

Karmo took a deep breath and shrugged, "I do not know for sure, Jack. But I think they certainly will try."

∽

Every other month, Karmo led a small group of tradesmen and their wagons west towards San Francisco for supplies. They loaded the wagons onto ferries to cross the water to the city proper, some stopping on one or two of the several islands in the bay to rest or mend their reins or wagons.

Once in the city, there were few places to spend the night, other than to camp outdoors, but Karmo and Jack found a boarding house where they could get a bath with real soap and hot water.

"Ahhhh!" exhaled Jack, coming out of the bath, with his skin rosy. "That was so good! I hadn't had a good bath in weeks!"

Karmo laughed at the young man and said, "Simple pleasures, son. Simple pleasures!" He then eyed the lanyard with a familiar talisman on Jack's neck. He asked curtly, "Where did you get that?" pointing at the well-worn wooden disc with the sun and moon carved into it.

"This?" asked Jack as he held it up. "I'm surprised I was able to hang onto it after all these years. It's very precious to me. It reminds me of the worst and best of times."

"But where did you get it?" asked Karmo, becoming ever more anxious and serious.

Jack looked at Karmo's changing demeanor, seeing something he had not seen before, an almost uncontrollable cloud of anxiety developing before Karmo's eyes.

"Well, well …. ," Jack said with hesitation.

"Jack! Where. Did. You. Get. *That*?!" said Karmo forcefully.

"A friend made it for me, Mr. Karmo! A kind, wise black man made it for me when I was a kid in Massachusetts!" exclaimed Jack, somewhat puzzled but now getting anxious himself.

Karmo felt his chest get tight and his heart pound. He tried to control his voice to a well-modulated tenor.

"Jack, do you remember the man's name?" asked Karmo with a soft quiver in his voice.

"Of course! It was Mister Ansa, sir. Ansa Kabbah," said Jack, still bewildered.

My brother! whispered Karmo hoarsely to himself. "Tell me! Tell me everything, Jack!"

∾

Karmo and Jack were back with a crew just two months later, in late winter. They awoke to a milky dawn, shivering, but anxious to get on with the day. Here they were in San Francisco, which in the course of only eight years had expanded from a busy trading town to a small city for shipping goods in and out of Alta California, with shops for the trades, and even a couple of hotels with restaurants. The Bockarie party headed for the trading posts in the marina area. Rested, Karmo and Jack turned their eyes to the mercantile shops in the city center, not far from their hotel.

"Benoît's Mercantile," said Karmo out loud to Jack.

Jack, who was watching pretty girls walking in pairs down the dusty street, turned suddenly and exclaimed, "Benoîts!?"

"That's what it says on the window," answered Karmo, nonplussed. "You spoke of family with that name not long ago."

Jack blinked hard as he stared at the sign, and said quietly, "Yes, I lived with a family of Benoîts back in Massachusetts when I was a kid. Maybe they know the family. Let's go in, sir."

Karmo was amused, as common surnames did not mean acquaintanceship. But he was game. "Why not? Of course," answered Karmo.

The shop was a well-organized and well-appointed set of rooms. Bright and clean, the mixed fragrances of perfumes, candles, provisions and leather permeated the air. The first person they saw was a woman of about late-40s, stout, her hair pinned in a severe bun, facing away from the counter. She was busily polishing glassware and placing pieces on shelves backed by mirrors. She paused, and looked at a reflection she knew as well as her own.

Karmo cleared his throat, "Good morning, ma'am."

The woman quickly turned around, blinking, but seeing only Karmo across the counter, looked him up and down with great interest, seeming to regain her composure before answering rather curtly, "Good morning. How can I help you?" She peered at the tall black man, perplexed, when they both heard a whack, thud, whack, thud. Jack had bent down to pet Fella whose tail wagged against the wall of the counter. Standing back up, Jack turned to face the woman, who dropped the glass she was polishing.

The crash of glassware sounded the alarm for the rest of the shopkeepers who ran in from other parts of the store and from behind office curtains. Confused, they all stopped and stared at the two strangers incredulously.

"Mother?" inquired Jack, as he ran to keep her from falling over in a faint. "Mother, how ...? What are you doing here? Oh, Mother!" he cried.

Mrs. Marshall had fainted momentarily. Awaking, her eyelashes fluttered, her eyes blurred before focusing. She couldn't speak. Tears welled up and began to pour from her eyes as she choked out a greeting, "Jack? My son? My son!" She started gently patting his face, his hair, his chest, trying to ascertain if he was real.

Just then, from behind the curtain, Ansa appeared and took in the scene. He saw Jack and exclaimed, "Jack, Jack! Is that you, my boy?" as he ran over to him and grasped the young man by the shoulders. When he looked up at Jack's companion, he was momentarily stunned, his chest and throat tightening as he released a barely audible whisper, "My brother!"

Karmo struggled for composure before he stepped forward to grab Ansa by the shoulders, then he kissed him on the head frantically. Staring into his face, his eyes drilled into Ansa's thoughts. Beyond all their wildest hopes and dreams ... imagine finding each other safe and sound!

Madelcine and Suzanne helped the overwrought visitors and shopkeepers to chairs, and brought them water. They were excited and mystified at seeing Jack again in this place, so far from Mattapoisett. And who was this man with whom Ansa was hugging and crying? They had never seen Ansa, their rock and counsel, so shaken, and in such a state.

Suzanne, herself was stunned. Panic and anxiety nearly overtook her, for she truly did not realize that men had the capacity for tears.

That evening, they all had a wonderful dinner at the Benoît's home, filled with laughter and healing. Everyone had so much to talk about and explain!

The normally stoic Mrs. Marshall stated, "My heart was burned to ashes, Jack! Oh, how I missed you!"

"I know, Mother. I missed you, too, and I'm so sorry for leaving as I did. So very sorry. Can you ever forgive me?"

Karmo tried not to stare at Suzanne. He felt disoriented, struggling as he imagined Brima was across the table from him. Something about Suzanne's voice beckoned to him.

Ansa whispered to Madeleine, who was regarding Karmo, "He lives in the shadow of his beloved's love, long dead."

Madeleine's eyes started to glisten as she looked downward. "I understand. We are so … ," she murmured, but stopped short.

～

Some months later, a Cape Cod man from a ship out of Boston dropped off mail to the dock-master. A mail packet arrived for Madeleine. It was from Patrice in Mattapoisett! She reported that none of the normal goings-on had changed, other than that Alwyn Baker died in the asylum. The biggest prize was another letter! It was from Peter Kroupa, who had sold the shipping business and was soon to depart for San Francisco with his wife and children. *How exciting and how fortuitous!* thought Madeleine. "He has such a facility for all things mechanical, and is a good fabricator. Perhaps he could help with some factory machines. Oh, it will be so good to see him again!"

But what took her breath away was a bundle of newspapers from Boston! Nothing feels like being home as much as reading the hometown newspaper—simple, prosaic things; what's for sale, rooms to let, shops opening or closing, foreign happenings, social happenings, ships coming and going; just so much to know, and to think about.

"Oh, look here! New York has a Philharmonic Orchestra! Looks as if their first performance was already held, in 1842! And the British are fighting in China over opium sales and ports?! I do not understand this. Oh, and the American president is sending troops to raid Mexico for gold to pay war debts? Patrice must have gathered papers for several years for us. What's this? Massachusetts passed child labor laws! Children under 12 years old may not work more than 10 hours a day?! Why would they not be in school instead?!"

Suzanne entered the room with a huge grin when she saw her mother smiling and sitting at her favorite spot at the table reading a pile of Boston newspapers.

"Oh Maman! News! And letters too! Who has written?!"

"Patrice, ma Chèrie! Such news, Peter will come soon to California and … "

Before she could go on, Suzanne sucked in a deep breath, her hands to her face as she felt flutters in her chest, followed by an intense, radiating sensation low in her pelvis.

"Oh, oh, Peter is coming?" she croaked to her mother.

Madeleine had again picked up the letter and was looking down, still reading it. She didn't notice her daughter's flushed face. "Yes, indeed! He is coming with his family; his wife and two children. Is it not just wonderful?!"

Regret had caught her unawares. A sudden dizziness struck Suzanne, as did the crushing pain in her chest that had supplanted the fluttering. She put her hand down on the side of a chair to steady herself, before turning around to leave the room, her face tense with a pain she did not expect or even understand.

"Suzanne? Suzanne?" called Madeleine looking up from the table. "Where did she go so quickly?"

～

A month later, Karmo and Jack were back in the City. They sought out the Benoîts to catch up and share news. Karmo and Ansa talked about the haphazard land grant situation, the incoming settlers and the Native peoples, as well as the California expeditions of John Frémont sent by Missouri Senator Thomas Hart Benson and U.S. President Polk.[64] Frémont's party included surveyors to map the country. Both were suspicious of these invaders from the east. "They are relentless, Ansa," said Karmo. "They are not just exploring for map-making. They are expansionists! They want all the land as far as they can see, from ocean to ocean. They believe if they say it, it will come true."

"You know them better than I, Karmo. My experiences are with many peoples, but not so much in depth," answered Ansa.

Karmo nodded distractedly, followed by a period of silence.

Ansa looked at Karmo before stating, "We knew each other when we were young. I see who you once were, Karmo. That part of you is still here, but has there been a shift, a hole made in your soul?"

Karmo continued to stare ahead, then let out a deep breath. "Life has surprised me, my brother. I did not expect it to be easy, but neither did I really believe it could be so cruel. Nevertheless, I see dedication and bravery from the young people in my camp; I have no doubts about the training quality there. I only hope our motivations to defend are honest. For anyone else, I cannot yet speak."

~

The next evening, Ansa and Jack went out to the back garden. Fella dozed at their feet. A neighbor dropped by to say hello, when Fella jumped up and growled.

"No, Fella!" called Jack. "Sorry, sir. Fella is just defending me. He's really a friendly dog."

"No worries, boy," said the neighbor. "I was just coming to visit some. I best go on inside."

"Please do," answered Ansa.

Before another minute passed, another neighbor dropped by, and Fella again jumped up, bristling and growling. "Fella!" shouted Jack, "No! What's gotten into you! So sorry, sir."

The man just frowned and nodded, and passed beside the men, then entered the back door, muttering a bit.

Jack took a deep breath, looked up at the stars, then at Ansa, and smiled before saying, "The night sky always reminded me of you and your stories, Mr. Ansa. They say a man is not a man until his father dies.

That's when he is no longer there for advice, but you were like a father to me back then, you and Mr. Benoît. And then I left secretly."

Ansa smiled kindly at Jack, and patted him on the arm. "Tell me what is on your mind, Jack. You are clearly burdened."

Jack told him of his actions in Florida, the people he killed and saw killed. While he had no remorse for killing some of the men on his own side, he wondered at his willingness to do so.

"Sometimes you feel so much pain, you forget who you once were. Rage strained my heart, Mr. Ansa. A fire in me burned my mind. It was all inside me, and I was secure in my belief about their guilt. They deserved to die; truly, they did."

Ansa studied Jack's face for a few moments. He had listened carefully to his words and voice. "The good in you does not die when you do evil, son. And yet, this possibility weighs heavily on your heart and mind, Jack, does it not?"

"It does. It does. I must have evil in me to have done such killings, however justified they were."

Ansa looked at him closely. "Would you kill today, if you felt it was justified?"

Jack looked at him somewhat surprised, but then answered, "Yes, I would, but perhaps more humanely."

"Then you have grown up, son. It is not so hard to become a man, Jack. It is staying a man that is the challenge. Do the right thing."

"How do I know what the right thing is, Mr. Ansa?" asked Jack.

"You know it in your heart. You know with all the information you have at the time of your decision making —*at the time*—and you maintain your calm. Sometimes we must make hard decisions in life. But these decisions mature us and define who we are."

"Sometimes I wonder what does this all mean, this life?"

Ansa patted the young man's hand, "Oh, Jack, my boy. The meaning of life?" He looked into the darkness and drew a long breath. "Meaning is not something you can find behind a tree or under a rock. You have the power to create your own meaning, son. Make your own meaning, your own life."

Jack nodded quietly, then said, "There's something else then—or rather, someone else. Her name is Pompo. I left her back at Bockarie." Jack continued to relate his interest in Pompo, and his decision to take another path, if only for a short time. "I'll go back. I hope I didn't make a mistake in leaving. I only hope she waited for me," said Jack, concerned.

"Breaking someone's heart is easy. Mending it is harder. We human beings only seem to learn things the hard way, Jack. Happiness is earned with difficulty, but lost easily. You must protect and cherish your love. *Love* is not *won* by regret. *Love* is *lost* by regret. You have to fight for it! Fight for her love. A simple question will help you decide if she is right for you. Can you imagine your life without her?"

"No! I never knew being with her was that important—until I thought I might never have the chance to be with her again," answered Jack quickly, his breath quickening, surprising himself. He stared at Ansa, and smiled quietly, questioningly.

The fog had come in from the bay and a chill settled in. The two men stood up and stretched their legs before going back into the house. Ansa held back and said to Jack thoughtfully,

"Life is short, Jack. Take time to remember those you have lost. Mend any hearts you have broken. Forgive those who hurt you. You will find your way back to her."

"Thanks, Mr. Ansa."

Nearby, a cat yowled and slinked her way across the garden. Again, Fella jumped up from his light dozing and growled. Shushed again for the third time, Fella finally realized he would get in no decent growling that night. So he belly-flopped back to the ground, and let out a defiant snort and a low whine instead.

"You see? He's a good watchdog." Scratching the dog's head, Jack said to Ansa, "I have a request, sir."

"Certainly," said Ansa.

"Can I leave Fella with you for a while? If you don't mind, that is. I'm afraid he'll get hurt trying to keep up with me."

"He may stay here with me and the Benoîts for as long as you need, Jack. Someone is always around to care for him, rest assured. I will speak with Madame Madeleine."

As Jack stepped into the house, his mother passed him at the doorway. She could only gaze into his face and smile, holding back the tears in her eyes, barely able to croak out "son." He smiled at her and kissed her forehead before going inside. Mrs. Marshall took up a seat next to Ansa. "How is he, Ansa? How's my boy?"

"No matter how much time passes, no matter how much you grow up, the pain of not having a father never goes away, but he's fine, Leah. He's fine."

~

Suzanne rose before daybreak the next morning. She gazed at the mist in the meadow beyond the ceanothus hedges next to the house and smiled at its ethereal entreaty. Stepping through the hedge opening onto a dewy pathway, she inhaled the moist and sweet air. This was a realm of its own, albeit temporarily, until the morning sun rises in the sky, dissipating the mist and presenting yet another transformation.

Lost in thought, reality intruded once again on her with a sense of loss and longing. The painful stab in her heart was renewed with every beat. She had not been unkind, only ungrateful. No, that was not true. She *had* been unkind, and for the naïve reason that she thought it better for Peter to hate her, in order to forget her. Yes, it was foolishness! It's how she hid her fear, her sense of inadequacy, her expected heartache. *Did I think it would be that easy?* she asked herself.

We do not choose whom we love, only whom we leave. She was ill-prepared for affairs of the heart, for Peter had indeed moved on with his life, even if she had not.

For all her despair, Suzanne took an interest in Karmo, this strong, quiet man, the confidante of their rock, Ansa. She watched him at breakfast and determined to approach him.

"I noticed something, Mr. Karmo," she said.

Karmo was silent, startled at the suddenness of her appearance, and curious about what this woman would tell him. "I beg your pardon, Mademoiselle Suzanne," he replied, trying to maintain his equilibrium.

"Please excuse my intrusion, but I had been speaking with Mr. Ansa. He is family to us, you see."

"Yes??"

"I understand what you have been through; that is, who you left behind," she continued.

Karmo's internal voice roiled, *How dare she think she can understand. As if I left Brima!* Nevertheless, her voice and sensibility lit up his imagination, again with a recollection of, and a familiarity to, Brima. He stilled his emotions and turned to look Suzanne directly in the eyes. "And just what do you believe you understand about me, Mademoiselle?"

"I understand about *her,* Bri ...," she started.

Karmo held his hand up to her. "Do not say it."

"Mr. Karmo, please let me speak. The fire in your heart will burn out, and you will be able to breathe again. It takes a long time ...," she trailed off, not believing her own words, but trying her best to be convincing and to help him.

Karmo stood there mute, looking at her, yet hearing that voice from another place and time. "Thank you for your concern," he said, bowed his head slightly, turned and walked away.

NATIVE TRIBAL LANDS

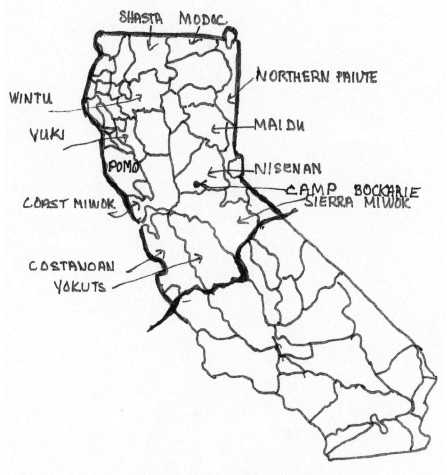

SHASTA MODOC

NORTHERN PAIUTE

WINTU

YUKI

MAIDU

POMO

NISENAN

CAMP BOCKARIE

SIERRA MIWOK

COAST MIWOK

COSTANOAN

YOKUTS

ALTA CALIFORNIA

29

Camp Bockarie 1845

Invictus

They came from diverse backgrounds, some even from the northern lands, but all had the same goal; learn to fight, go back home and train the others. Word spread, and tribes, villages, ranchos and small cities sent their men *and* their women. All would learn about the use and maintenance of weaponry. The women would gain additional insights as to their fighting abilities and true capacity for fighting. It was unusual to send women to such training, but the words of the traveler's group, of Ansa and Henson, rang true to leaders' ears and their consciousness.

"It can be easy to fight the invader with weapons. But there are other ways to take down a nation. They rape, kidnap, kill our women. We boast about the bravery and power of our men. That is all true, but when the enemy takes away our women and their womanhood, it is like a knife stabbed into the heart of the nation. If a nation loses the ability to be a family, it loses everything. We must prepare our women to fight as mightily as ourselves, for all our sakes!"

～

At camp in the late fall afternoon, Karmo instructed the women on using shadows and the sun to advantage. "You there, Nell!" he called out to one of the women. "Run down to that bank of trees to the west and wait for me to call." The woman, lithe and swift, found her mark.

"Now, step in amongst the tree shadows. You others, do you see her?" There was a brief murmuring before someone said, "It's hard to see, because the sun in our eyes. She's just another shadow."

Karmo nodded and smiled. "Yes, that is my point exactly. At certain times of the day, particularly close to dawn and dusk, it can be very difficult to see someone so hidden, perhaps the enemy, or perhaps it is you hiding. Make your observations over the next few days and you will get faster at identifying the time and the placement. You may need this knowledge to evade, capture or kill your enemy."

One of the women, about 24 years of age, watched the demonstration carefully.

"I do not think I could ever kill a person, even to defend myself," she said softly.

Karmo regarded her thoughtfully for a moment before he spoke. "There is no halfway in fighting! Everyone has the capacity to kill when the circumstances are right. Have you children?"

"I have a six-year-old daughter and a younger son."

Karmo nodded, "Women!" he bellowed to the crowd. "Imagine the enemy attempting to mount your child! Would you just stand there?!"

The young woman paled, then her face flushed. She screamed, "I would rip out his heart with my bare hands! I would cut off his manhood and shove it down his throat! I would … "

"Exactly!" interrupted Karmo. "You have the capacity. Trust in that capacity and in the training you will receive here when you are dealing with danger. You must learn to rely on yourself, for there will be times when that is all you have."

The women nodded and murmured affirmatively. The young woman stood taller and said, "Well, let's get on with it!"

The women were strong and hard-working—most, having grown up on farms, had had their share of butchering hogs and cattle. Karmo trained their focus on transferring those skills to human combat. But blinding the enemy through eye gouges were among the more challenging of endeavors. The training commenced, and lasted for several weeks. They also learned to care for and handle knives and firearms, and even mastered some wrestling moves. They learned to read the tracking signs of animals and humans, and how to be alert, how to be patient. "Impatience is your enemy," extolled Karmo repeatedly.

"Men will expect at most that you bite, scream and kick," announced Karmo. "Do all of these when you must. But remember, men will more often overpower you by approaching you from behind and pinning your arms behind you. This is how you get out of the hold." He demonstrated, and they practiced. The women learned those corners of the anatomy where the most desired effects could be achieved efficiently. They learned to conserve movement, handling weapons with accuracy, to offset their smaller frames. And above all, to be ready for, and learn how to neutralize, rapid counter-maneuvers by the enemy.

"Excellent! Keep up your strength and agility! So now you broke the hold. What will you do next?"

"Run!" said a breathless woman.

"How far do you think you can run before he catches up with you?" bellowed Karmo.

The women looked at each other. "Not very far, I am tired even now," offered one of them.

Karmo nodded. "Listen carefully. He will not expect you to fight valiantly. This is the time to take him down, and I mean absolutely and completely! Hit him in the head or on the back with a rock, or anything at hand. Hit him repeatedly until he is down and *out!*"

"And then we run!"

"No! *Never, ever* turn your back to a live enemy!" said Karmo with a fierce steadiness that was almost frightening. "If you expect help imminently and can bind him securely, do so. Otherwise, you must kill him!"

There was a huge sucking of air as the women again looked at each other in recognition of what Karmo had just said.

"Yes, I said *kill* him! Take your weapon and kill him. Be sure he is dead! Cut his throat, bash his brains out, shoot him in the heart! However you can do it, *do* it! If you merely knock him out, he will come to, perhaps quickly, and he will be more angry than ever. He will seethe with malice and great strength. He will have no mercy on you! No, you must not leave him breathing. Finish the job first! And do not waste time crying! Just get up and fight!"

The women looked at Karmo, awed by what they heard, but agreed that he was right. They saw exactly such things happening in raids on their villages. After all, an injured bear's wrath grows to twice its original size and strength when he is challenged.

~

The water was cold, but with a clearness and sweetness like no other. The small ponding off the river was just the place for a soaking relief of his tired and sore body. Secluded and shaded, Karmo first looked into the pond's mirrored stillness at his own reflection. *What a toll this handful of years has taken*, he thought. *Already I look like my father, at twice the age when I last saw him.* He waded into the pond, found the familiar flat rock upon which to sit and leaned back, taking in his surroundings. Letting his mind wander, he breathed the fresh, piney air deeply, watching the river water, reflecting the sun's light, like Brima's eyes. His thoughts went back home, to her, to family, to college, then to Ansa.

Karmo thought about his Camp and wondered what Ansa would think of it. He had not yet shared the camp's mission with his best friend. *When we are dead, if we are remembered at all, I imagine we will be remembered not for what we had to go through, but for what we put others through. I wish we were together like in the old days, my brother. I need your wisdom. I need you to help me determine what is right and what is wrong. I have doubts. I have longings. Big, strong me has tender feelings too.* Mesmerized by undulating tree branches in the gentle breeze, he sensed an invisible presence caressing him, enveloping him, providing a comfort that had been missing for so long.

As his mind drifted again, he dropped his gaze upon a pair of towhee birds hopping on slender, springy legs amongst the leaves and grasses, in search of sustaining morsels. A bright chirping accompanied their search. When one found a mounding of seeds, the other came hopping over. He let himself be distracted for several minutes when, inexplicably to him, they flew away into the tree branches above him. *What it must be like, their world, their short life?*

Hot tears of recollection trailed slowly down his cheeks, reflecting flashes of his past life. He let himself sink under the water to cool off, and to remember more quietly. The Caribbean Natives, Dosar, Haco, the Cajuns, Jesse, Santa Anna; all had helped get him here. *Could any man achieve victory alone?* Karmo watched as a large river turtle made its way slowly to a nearby fallen log, there to bask in the sun. A tiny smile formed on the big man's lips. Life ... it only moves forward.

There is a time when a man must take a stand, but in doing so, he must also account for his actions. We are often expected to make major life decisions with the least amount of information, the least preparation, the least maturity.

30

Aunty Mullen in San Francisco 1845

He who is not content with what he has, will not be content with what he wants. –Turkish proverb

He was not always a cad, a cheat, a scoundrel. Indeed, he was raised by a solid and supportive family, and had the benefit of financial stability and a good education. Having wrought havoc throughout the coastal cities of the American states, this Easterner, like so many others, escaped to the West to start his life anew. In addition to some long standing deviant proclivities, he became enticed by the excitement of confidence games and gambling. Over time, he succumbed to the habit's ever-tightening grasp, becoming indebted to a more-than-rough group who initially backed him, then pulled him into their web of dishonesty and betrayals.

The Mullen crew, as well as others, was looking for him. Outlaws themselves, they nevertheless abided by their own code of justice. Schemers, confidence men and debt defaulters were often their targets. Sometimes vicious, always merciless, the crew handled these scoundrels in one of two ways. The first was to ruin only the physical body of anyone who neglected debts owed them, but not his reputation. This minor gesture regarding a man's name, the crew reasoned, was to allow the debtor's family to forgo humiliation and scandal, as the crew had a few morals to commend them. They would not harm women or children. The second way was more permanent; sending the culprit to his maker. It all came down to the fraudster's history and intent.

～

ROAR!

At a well-appointed hotel in San Francisco, the Easterner seated himself at the corner table, where he could survey the dining room and entryway. Well-dressed in the fashion of the day, he wore a waistcoat with an edging of brocade, and a broad cravat, elegant but not so ostentatious as to draw attention to himself. Clearly, he was not one of the roughnecks, sailing officers or plain, honest family men who frequented the establishment. His briefcase with its deeds, bonds and documents was kept close to his side. *I need to close these deals before the Mullen crew catches up with me,* he thought to himself. *A couple of months should do it.*

Not far away, the Aunt finished her preparations to leave her house. She continued to dress in black, having been widowed some years before. Her dark, greying hair was pinned up in a loose bun, with wisps trailing girlishly here and there. Still of winsome aspect, she was alone, but not lonely. She came to the hotel at least twice a week, treating herself to a nice mid-day dinner, and delighted in watching the younger crowd, perchance to engage them in conversation about the goings-on of the day—at any rate, to be out amongst the living.

She was not well-versed in her late husband's business affairs, but was doing her best to acquire some mastery. Her business demeanor required a stony façade, she thought, but that was not reflective of her true heart. The softness hidden within would be revealed as she progressed further into the autumn of her life. She wanted to make a grand gesture before she died, something good, useful and helpful to others.

The Easterner studied her for almost three weeks. He watched as she would give a coin to a street urchin or other child of misfortune, in exchange for some nominal task she didn't really need, her shoes shined, a newspaper fetched, a flower purchased; all minor efforts, which nevertheless supported a small economy. These street children fetched and carried groceries or parcels, while others shined shoes. There was a boy, about twelve years old, with a ridiculous top hat, no doubt salvaged from some rubbish heap. His mind meandered. *Who were these children?* he wondered before dismissing them and refocusing on the widow.

Her schedule was regular. She walked the several blocks from her home, a large, rambling, intact affair, then crossed the rutted, dusty boulevard, and walked another block to the hotel restaurant. Today was no different.

Paid in advance, the coachman slapped the reins upon the twin horses' backsides and the wagon raged down the street, seemingly out of control, just as she was midway in her crossing. The hero of the moment appeared out of nowhere, quickly grasping her around the waist and pulling her to safety. The horses and wagon disappeared in clouds of dust and straw.

She was grateful. Breathing hard and brushing debris from her dress with shaking hands, she allowed him to take her by the elbow and escort her into the hotel dining room for a heart-settling cup of tea. She believed him to be a gentleman of high regard by his dress, countenance and demeanor. He did, after all, just save her life. And would she have thought the same of a man dressed in rags?

She sat at the table, catching her breath, then was thoughtfully silent before speaking. "I am in your debt, kind sir. Please tell me your name so that I may remember you in my prayers."

"Taylor, Madam. Matthew Taylor at your service," he answered, as he boldly took her hand and kissed it. "My presence was fortuitous, as I had only at the last minute determined to take myself to dinner at these premises. It is a pleasure to make your acquaintance."

A bit startled by the boldness, she nevertheless allowed, "Oh please, sir, won't you join me for dinner? It's the least I can do, and I so much want to be better acquainted with you."

"It would be my honor, Madam. I'm much obliged," he responded.

She nodded to the server, who placed menus on their table, and inquired if they would like more tea. Taylor gave the widow an almost imperceptible head shake.

"Not right now, Max. We need a few moments, please," she said in a low voice, so as not to embarrass her guest. She was acutely aware of men's delicate sensibilities, and their need to take the lead in such transactions.

At first, their conversations were of a superficial nature, but nevertheless revealing. How long have you lived in the city? What do you do with your time? Do you come here often?

"I've only a nephew in the region, but he does stay near the city. He calls me Aunty," she said with a smile of satisfaction. That Taylor was a banker piqued the good lady's interest, but she kept herself wary.

During the next two weeks, they met regularly. By and by, conversations turned to one's thoughts and concerns in life. "The street children … What kind of people are we that we would allow them, some orphans on their own, others used for profit, to surrender their meager earnings to vicious, black-hearted overseers!" she said with dismay. "Something must be done for them!"

"Indeed, it is a disgrace. This city remains devoid of basic human needs for all but the well-to-do, but do you think it is our responsibility to care for everyone?" he inquired thoughtfully.

"Who might you think provided the labor for our enterprise and success, sir? For surely your hands are soft and your person has never been sullied by sweat or labor," she admonished lightly.

Taylor nodded mildly in feigned agreement, then placed his hands on his lap. "You have a fair point."

"I've been thinking, Mr. Taylor. I do want to establish a Home for them and a Trust to secure its future," she announced quietly. "We owe it to our children to set an example of hope. *They* are born innocent and pure. It is *we* who teach bigotry, fear, greed and violence. We owe them better … so that they can stand tall and fashion a better future for all of us."

Taylor gave the woman an experienced, soulful gaze into her eyes, took her hand and spoke in a well-practiced, heartfelt manner, "By whose design was it that we two should meet, my dear Lady? As I stated earlier, I am a banker, here in this very city. I am Taylor of Wilson, Taylor and Franks Bank and Trust. Might you consider my assistance in securing a stock-backed Trust for your orphans? I have information here in my satchel."

"Oh, oh my!" she said hesitantly, "Yes, you may, but give me some days to read about it and get my thoughts together, Mr. Taylor."

"Of course! Perhaps it is your destiny to establish such a place as you described, ... for the orphans," he responded. "Absolutely do take some time to plan. The children need you. If I may be of assistance, please do not hesitate to ask. Shall we meet back here in three days?"

"That should be adequate for me to get started," she told him thankfully. She was excited just thinking about the endeavor, her grand gesture.

Three days later, the two met at the hotel restaurant to discuss an overview of the project. This was followed by a short walk over to Mr. Taylor's office in the bank's second story. The office was substantial, floor-to-ceiling windows, heavy velvet drapes and a large oak desk. She settled in one of the comfortable, tufted armchairs in front of his desk, with her back to his safe.

After an hour of review, she asked, "So when shall the project proceed, Mr. Taylor?" "Madam, you've outlined basic staffing needs, and you already have your building. With your permission, I will advertise the positions and hire qualified personnel for administration and education. They will, in turn, be tasked with hiring adequate staff to care for the children, and all the usual avenues and supplies for running such an establishment. You need only to sign the Trust documents to initiate the financial transfers. If you allow me to assist you, I will start on this today," he said confidently.

"Oh, yes, that would be quite helpful. I ran my husband's business after he passed, but was not involved with establishing it. This will be such a grand enterprise. Thank you so much, Mr. Taylor!" she said enthusiastically as she signed the contracts he put before her.

"At your service, Madam. Just one more signature, right here," he said as he pointed at the signature line.

～

Departing the hotel, her mind at ease, she cast her eyes at a small band of street children about to turn around towards the back of a vacant building. She wondered about them. Nameless and often invisible, some managed to become independent; while others, often younger and smaller, were bonded to adult miscreants who used them to beg, steal or serve in various capacities, including the flesh market. The independents slept in groups of six or more for safety, never alone. It was too dangerous. Cut, bruised, ragged and often barefoot, the street children often developed a pack-like mentality.

Jonny Henson, making his daily rounds, came around the same corner, stopping abruptly as the pack of children ran in front of and around him, stirring up dust in their wake. He saw the widow and proceeded to greet her. "Good day, Ma'am. And how are you this fine day?"

"Oh, Mr. Henson, what a nice surprise. I'm quite fine, thank you. And you? How are you?'

"Fine, absolutely! May I escort you home?"

"Yes, thank you. How kind you are. Tell me, those children, just who are they?"

"It isn't a pretty story, Ma'am. They are unfortunate, indeed. That older boy is called Top Hat. He was old enough to escape former masters and form his own posse. His 'Wolf Pack' make their home in one abandoned building after another, moving every few days to avoid being discovered and raided or evicted by adult gangs. It was he who trained the children to watch for where they might get food and other provisions, to spy, both for their survival and that of their neighborhood, however poor. They rummage through the landfill, side-street garbage, anywhere they can scavenge for clothes and food, occasionally for matches to build a warming fire. Always on the move, always unsafe, they are wary, hardened and often appear older than their age."

"Oh my, Mr. Henson, why do they not have homes? Where are their parents?"

"Their parents died or abandoned them. Adventure for a handful, but mostly due to poverty, abuse at home, some ran away. Knowing little else, they accepted this life. Like Top Hat, some still see their dead parents in their dreams, and call out to them. It's heartbreaking, and while they may approach you, it's hard to approach them. They won't trust just anyone. *They're almost feral.* For some, we managed to get jobs; shining shoes, and such. One must take time and be patient with them."

The widow thought to herself, *We'll see.*

ANSA & JONNY'S TRAVELS

NISENAN LANDS
CAMP BOCKARIE
SACRAMENTO

SIERRA MIWOK LANDS

SAN
FRANCISCO

PACIFIC OCEAN

ALTA CALIFORNIA

31

The Companions 1843-1845, Part I

If you talk to a man in a language he understands, that goes to his head. If you talk to a man in his own language, that goes to his heart.
–Nelson Mandela

Karmo fingered the grey bag around his neck, the gris gris from Old Okeke, and became thoughtful watching more and more invaders and settlers enter Alta California. Upshots of trouble turned up here and there as the invaders, from the east in particular, claimed land as their own, ignoring the settled law. Karmo thought to himself, *I was trying to solve troubles, but the troubles were the solution. Should this not be its own nation? And how will we speak to the people who have long been here before us? What would they want?*

～

Some few years before, Karmo and his neighbor, Allen Light, traveled together in their land-grant regions and met with many Natives, Californios and American settlers, inviting them to gather to discuss a regional government where they would all have a say in governing. At that time they met up with Christian Mullen and a cadre of businessmen of his ilk, who were gathering information and mapping clusters of people; who they were, what they did and what property they possessed. Mullen was studying the lands for business opportunities.

Karmo and Mullen had different goals; the government made no difference to Mullen. The two men shared their findings, however. "Hmmm, well yeah," allowed Mullen. "The Natives have inhabited these lands for so long, you can benefit from their ideas and experiences,"

Light raised his eyebrows, but stayed quiet. Karmo nodded pensively. Neither trusted Mullen completely, but this was a rather good bit of observation, coming from an unlikely source.

"Hey, don't get me wrong, added Mullen. "I'm here to make a buck, like anyone else. We all have to make a living, right?" Karmo looked at Light and smiled. "Talk to the Natives. Talk to them, but listen well. They'll tell you just what's on their minds and how they get by."

~

Karmo and Allen Light figured that a government system would need to be set up before they pulled away from Mexico. It was clear, in speaking with the Natives, that women, too, would be involved equally. Sometimes there was much resistance to this by some non-Natives; at these times the two men were hooted out of town. Nevertheless, the two were somewhat protected, as they had Mexican citizenship and as grant holders, had the government on their side. They were landowners, and needed to be taken seriously for now. Some of the First Peoples insisted on sovereignty of their own lands rather than a confederation, but in light of the relentless influx of foreigners, many Natives began to see unity as an opportunity for better protection and a larger say in their own governance.[65]

"Human rights and equality for our citizens must be foremost, our lodestar, because that is where we derive our legitimacy, our security, our economic well-being and prosperity," extolled Light.

Karmo arched his eyebrows. "You can be quite eloquent when you want to be, Al."

"Life, Karmo, life," answered Light wistfully.

Karmo nodded and said solemnly, "Yes, life." He took a deep breath, "But for all that to happen, a nation must take care of its people. We have to show good faith, lest they succumb to the empty promises of the invaders. An empty belly has no ears, after all."

~

Months later, Karmo went back to Bockarie, and Allen Light joined Ansa, Lokni and Jonny Henson. The travelers teams had already made several trips south of San Francisco, as far as Monterey Bay, to get an idea if peoples there would be amenable to the idea of a new nation of their own. By and by, they named themselves the Companions.

Between them, they could speak many of the languages of the Natives and settlers alike. They visited the Costanoan and other Natives who, rightly, were wary of this group. Lokni's presence was only somewhat reassuring. Land grantees, Mexican citizens and former American citizens were also wary, as they did not want to lose their property.

In 1828, the Alta California territorial governor, upon direction of the central government in Mexico City, had converted missions to secular parishes, granted lands to some Natives and made them citizens. This, however, did little to protect them against unfair treatment in a country that did not have a meaningful judiciary but that did have flagrant racism. Ansa's group, however, presented the Natives with a concept of a different undertaking; an altogether different nation.

One of the white citizens eyed Ansa and then spoke to Henson, "I dunno about everyone bein' the same, ya know. Your boy there may need to wait his turn."

Although this was not said in a malicious manner, a cold chill ran down Ansa's back. He felt dread and a sense of choking in his throat. Worse, none of the Companions took issue with the man's comment … not even Jonny. Ansa stared at the man, again feeling betrayed, and thought to himself, *so, here I am again. No! I should not have to wait for my time. I fight, work, love in real time. I will not wait!*

It was not left out of the discussion that a national border would depend on existing borders of tribal or grant lands, for it would not do to separate Mexican Alta California from the new nation arbitrarily. In the absence of these considerations, natural boundaries such as rivers or mountain ranges served as geography's revenge. The Companions learned and used the various arguments for consideration; protection, equality, maintaining control of open land, and, last but not least, a responsive central government. But everyone had to give up something to share in the vision. Ideas were solicited.

One Native group told the Companions, "Sometimes joining outsiders was an advantage for trading goods, ideas and language. At other times, they stole our lands and killed us with better weapons and disease. The missionaries wanted to *make us* white through their religion as if that was better. Even so, they did not want to *treat us* as white. We must consider carefully and hope we make the best choice."

Henson nodded in all seriousness, "Yes, of course. That happened, and it was wrong. But this is life today. We need to do better than to live between fear and hope," he said thoughtfully.

After three more weeks of seeking information to take back to San Francisco, the Companions made camp along a river bank. A soft, cool breeze came up and they breathed it in deeply. Tired, but generally of good disposition, they settled in to cook supper, when a loud commotion of grunts and slapping of flesh broke the peace from behind the trees. Two of their members were slugging each other with an unexpected animosity and viciousness. Red froth poured from their mouths while snot, blood and saliva striped both men's faces. The remaining Companions ran up to them two, separated and restrained them.

"You blasphemer! God will rain fire upon you if you do not repent! You will burn in Hell!" screamed one of the fighters, breathing heavily.

"Don't talk to me about your pre-mortal life! You and your kind should all be exterminated!" screamed the other man, glowering with contempt.[66]

"I pity your post-mortal life! Your plan of salvation is sorely lacking!" spat out the other.

Henson stepped in between the men. He was both angry and frustrated, "Stop it! Stop it, you two! God Almighty! Both of you are in the wrong, for fighting and for disrespect. Beliefs are personal, and to be shared only when you are invited to do so, not foisted upon another against their will. You disrespect each other's personal freedom. This is not right by our mission. You," he pointed at each in succession, "you profess values of humanity and caring, yet you fight for your own way and against others. Such hypocrisy!"

The two men were not convinced. Too angry for reasoning, they mounted their saddle horses and galloped off in different directions.

Henson looked at the others and took a deep breath, "Even amongst ourselves! I'm afraid there will always be an undercurrent of bias. We have to learn to at least reign it in peacefully, lest we all fail as one nation."

Ansa walked up and gently put his arm around Jonny's shoulders before quietly saying, "Indeed you are right, my brother. We only can try to be good examples." He gazed after the flying dust of one of the fighter's horses, his lips tight.

A latecomer, Murphy Fitzgerald, was the oldest of the group. He was a short, wiry man with still vivid blue eyes. His health was failing and his breathing was labored at times, but he wanted one more adventure—to see the country and do something useful with others. No wallflower, he vented his frustration to the group, " … and they fight! These 'holier-than-thou' people resort to physical altercation to make their point? No bunch of writing will put an end to our innate savagery! We will only evolve when we can be honest and forthright, without the fear of torment in Hell!"

Henson looked at the man, surprised. This otherwise quiet person spoke with such passion and insight. He nodded to Fitzgerald deferentially, "It's our humanness, Murph. We cannot deny it. We all have our limits and our failures."

Ansa became pensive before stating quietly, "Such a piece of work is mankind."

Fitzgerald stared at Ansa before stating, "I see that."

~

Back at camp, Allen Light suggested that the group turn eastward the next morning to visit a cluster of Native and white traders who lived together, particularly to speak with a Native woman named Carlota Zimi. He had heard about her, and subsequently met her several times as he deviated from his coastal assignments for the Governor.

"Miz Carlota, as they call her, is an organizer for many camps in the region. She knows how to bring people together, determines what works for each group, a unifier. She is kind, shrewd, speaks a number of

Native languages, English and French; and is well-respected, although she holds no official title or authority. Just taming and marrying that French trapper, Wild Deniz from the Hudson Bay Company, was a huge feat. But then she was alone and obliged to raise their three sons, albeit into fine young men!" He laughed so hard he snorted. "Alas, the trapper suffered from *"La Grand Maladie,"* a horror of a fixed location to call home.[67] On Carlota's account, he stayed with her for three years until he was knocked dead in a logging accident," he noted more soberly.

"Fascinating! So, tell us, Mr. Light," said Ansa. "How might she be of service to the Nation?"

"That woman can get people to do most anything," answered Light, nodding his head up and down. "She appeals to their vanity, greed, intelligence, or whatever is useful to do things for the greater good. She organized men from multiple Bands to become a bargaining unit with other tribes. They obtained shared winter quarters in the south through collaborating, through sharing chores like hunting, making tools, blankets, and defense. She uses caucuses—talking circles, where anyone can speak and everyone listens, just like the Iroquois Natives back east have done for generations.[68] She understands the tactic well. It fits her strategy,"

They all mumbled approval. Ansa thought about this discussion more and more, but wondered what was her overall strategy.

~

Light educated the group the best he could about the local inhabitants, stating, "The Natives listen to their elders, those wise and experienced in the ways of the land and peoples. Their young bring new ideas and ambitions, and so together, they forge order into their communities. They are not afraid to listen to one another. Tolerance can only thrive in a self-assured and confident nation. We might consider such a model to meld together our people and beliefs."

Oaks of many kinds, live oak, white, blue and black sycamore trees and various pines surrounded the small community. Rivers were icy-cold with fish aplenty. It always struck the men as to how serene and wild the northern regions were, with small outcroppings of humanity nestled quietly in the mist.

They managed to meet with the ephemeral Miz Carlota. Decidedly of Native heritage, with more than a pinch of something else, she was tall for a woman of her generation. Her long hair, plaited and circled upon her head like a crown of authority, was the color of roasted acorn, and matched her eyes.

"We have been expecting you," she said matter-of-factly. "Come inside and tell me about this new Nation of yours."

The Companions were puzzled. "How did you hear about that, Miz Carlota?" quizzed Light.

"It is not a secret. A newsman makes the circuit up these ways about every two months. He was here just last week, bringing old newspapers from the east, announcements from San Francisco and Sacramento, and bits of gossip he picked up along the way. It is quite an event when he gets to town. Everyone comes by to hear him read and talk. We even pay him a bit," she reported. "I am surprised you have not run into him."

"So are we," Light answered. "What a gift. Can you believe what he says?"

"Most of us take the gossip as gossip, and try not to put much stock in it. But some are more likely to believe a lie when we can't make them believe the truth. It's hard, and depends how often we hear similar talk from traders or travelers like you," she answered.

Ansa stuck out his chin a bit, "So, what do you think? About a new nation, that is?"

"Well, first, tell me more. A new nation, as I understand it? And what is the place for women and Natives in this nation, sirs?" asked Miz Carlota.

"All will be equal in rights and opinions, Madam," remarked Ansa.

"And just how will this happen? Heh? How do you think white men will accept this?" she queried, somewhat sarcastically.

"There will be some from both sexes and peoples who will question it. Some even will be vehemently against the proposition. This is why we are stating it forthright. We cannot waste half the nation's resources for tired and shortsighted practices," said Henson.

Miz Carlota scrutinized them carefully, and determined they were sincere, even if she was not sure any success would result from their proposition. They all continued to speak throughout the evening. *Perhaps this is the time to make my move.* Carlota thought to herself. *I have had enough of these petty negotiations.*

The next morning, as they were loading their wagons and horses to depart, Miz Carlota walked up to the group. "Send a messenger to inform me of your next large meeting. I am curious to hear about the plans and thinking."

"Absolutely! We will!" answered Light. "I'm glad to have had the pleasure to meet with you again, and introduce you to my fellow Companions."

The men all bowed and nodded. "Well then," said Light," let's roll away."

"Adieu," said Carlota, with a knowing smile.

～

Small forays of Companions continued to make their way to large and small enclaves of peoples throughout the northern region of Alta California. At times, they were attacked suddenly and deliberately, particularly along the route of the Oregon Trail, the route of the "Great Migration," Some Natives had had enough of these white invaders who commandeered their lands, trapped beaver to near extinction and brought deadly diseases with them. Turning to the northeast corner of the Alta California territory, the group came upon a large, placid, pluvial lake; deep blue, and teeming with all manner of bird life. Ducks with green wings, blue-gray cranes and white geese abounded. The myriad of earth tone ducks were a delight to behold; mallards, goldeneye and more. Above, eagles, songbirds and coots, attended to their commutes. It was like an Edward Hicks painting of peaceful fowl, a paradise fiercely guarded by the Modoc Natives.[69]

There was a good distance to go before reaching the Native camp. The men, all of whom were weary and dirty, took advantage of the

278

tranquil setting, deciding to throw themselves in the lake for a good cleansing and to refresh themselves.

Stripping to their drawers and tossing their clothes into the bushes, they jumped off a small cliff together into the deep, frigid lake.

"Eeeeyow! It's freezing!" screamed Ansa.

Henson and Light laughed as they treaded water and splashed the others. "Don't worry, you'll warm up as long as you keep moving," guffawed Light. He knew this lake well.

The men crawled onto the stony beach and scrambled quickly up the cliff to get dressed.

"Ahh, but this feels good! Are we alive again?" gurgled Fitzgerald.

"No!" exclaimed Light. "We are all dead and gone to heaven!" he sputtered good-naturedly.

They camped for the night, grateful for their small fire, and they watched the crescent moon make its way through time and dark skies, the earthshine beaming. At sun-up, they set out again. "This may be another of our losses, boys," stated Light flatly. "These Bands will just as soon shoot you as to talk to you. So, heads up!"

"Above all, we will not interfere with their ways. We'll present options, listen and leave," added Henson.

The Companions managed to meet with a few Modoc Bands, gave their message, listened in return, but left without even a tentative commitment. Nevertheless, they felt fortunate to leave with intact bodies.

"Perhaps the hardest thing to do is to reject one's tribalism for its own sake, and become open to the greater good," offered Fitzgerald. The greater good was the prevailing message of the Companions, but it was a message requiring a great leap of faith by the receivers. At length, members of the Shasta, Wintu, Yana, Yuki, Maidu, Nomalki and Konkio Bands came together on their own, and determined that there might be safety in numbers. The Bands selected representatives to attend meetings with these strange foreign travelers so that they might consider ways to show definitive reconciliation as needed and unite to better survive the onslaught of invaders. They were concerned too, as to how to maintain their Native identity while melding with these outsiders. As it turned out, they had reason to be wary.

～

From the northernmost part of the region, the Companions made their way a bit to the south. They had heard of a community midway between the proposed northern border and Sacramento. Trade routes helped determine a crossroad of culture, ideas and language. A large snow-capped mountain named after the Shasta Natives reigned supreme over the town, which took its name. To get there, they had to travel through a narrow canyon where the footpaths would only let them hike in single-file. Henson looked up into the hills. He thought he saw movement on the mountain crests. A feeling of vulnerability was at the forefront of his thoughts. "We're being watched," he said in a low voice. The others whispered agreement or only nodded. "All stayed alert."

As the Companions entered town, they were met by about a dozen men. It was a small city or a rather big town, but booming with prosperity, this riverside community. Surprised, Ansa stepped forward to greet them.

The mayor spoke first, "Hello and welcome!"

Ansa replied, "Thank you and hello. We come from Sacramento and the coast to visit the peoples of the land, speak with them and get to know them. We come in peace, by all means."

"Yes, we know. We've heard of your group and watched you enter the canyon."

Henson was relieved. He appraised the welcome party. They were armed, but relaxed in their bearing.

"So, this new nation you talk about, will independence give everyone freedom?" asked the mayor.

"That is the intent, but it may not happen immediately," answered Jonny bluntly. "But it's a start. Those who are pushed down have two choices; stay down or poke up their heads and holler. We hope they won't have to."

"I like it," pronounced the mayor, turning his head to his men, who nodded in unison.

The town boasted a library, rare in these parts, also, a budding science and medical center. Ansa was impressed and made mention of it. And Henson mused silently, *no wonder Mullen visited up here so often.* This community developed roads, and pioneered irrigation to improve crop yield, which in turn supported the growing city. Farmers no longer had to travel as far or with so much difficulty for goods they did not or could not make themselves.

"Of course we're armed," stated the mayor. "But we have been favored with peace and have put most of our money into learning. In the last few years, we have drawn both the educated and those thirsty for education here to take advantage of our learning centers. Scholars as well as exquisite artisans, tradesmen, builders and poets, they all come here. In turn, they enhance our lives and teach us ways to improve. I myself am a teacher most of the time. So are most of the community leaders."

How did we not know of this place? thought Ansa.

"Quite impressive, but are you not concerned about attack, Sir?" asked Henson.

"Do not misunderstand," replied the mayor. "Yes, we are concerned and always on the alert, but we have gained enough size to be a deterrent, for the most part. The farmers and ranchers on the outskirts, however, are more at risk from invaders who want to take their livestock and land for their own. We are defended. And we do have a voluntary militia, some trained in Camp Bockarie in the south."

"Camp Bockarie, you say? Did you ever meet Mr. Karmo Bockarie?" asked Ansa.

The mayor looked surprised before answering. "Oh yes, my wife and I both trained there and met Mr. Karmo," he said proudly. "Quite a personage, I must say, and quite an enterprise. The training is excellent. Do you know him?"

"Yes, of course! He is like a brother to me! This is so exciting!" exclaimed Ansa.

"That look of his, though ...," chuckled the mayor.

"What look?" asked a confused Jonny.

"His eyes; they bore right into you. Fierce, right?" asked the mayor smiling.

"Ha, yeah. That they do. But he's just thinking too many thoughts at one time. Nothing personal about it," explained Jonny.

"Mr. Henson's right. Karmo Bockarie is a serious and passionate man, a good man who feels strongly that learning to defend oneself is beneficial to both the individual and community at large," added Ansa.

"Yes, Yes. Well, then, sir, you will understand *our* outlook on defense." The mayor continued, "We are gifted by geography, an opportunistic location that allowed this community to settle and thrive. The narrow canyon is the most direct route in, and so the most likely route for invasion from the north. And, as you saw for yourself, it is easily defended. Our land to the south is vast and much more flat. But we can see for miles, should strangers come our way. Expansion without defense is useless."

Henson mulled over the mayor's words, *Expansion without defense is useless.* He looked at Fitzgerald, who was studying the interchange, then tapped him on the shoulder expectantly. Fitzgerald just nodded and the two moved towards the pack mules to talk.

"You've got something on your mind, Murph?" asked Henson.

Fitzgerald steadied his eyes on Henson and answered, "Not about this place, about your friend, Ansa, there. He's just a little too much," he paused, "too much … something. I just don't know what, but I don't trust him. I get an uneasy feeling about him, that's all."

Henson's head jerked back and his eyes popped wide open. "Oh, no, Murph. You need not worry about Ansa. He's as true as can be. Yes, his speech can be somewhat formal, but that is his education speaking. He is a kind and thoughtful person. No worries there. No worries there," replied Henson.

Fitzgerald huffed. He wasn't convinced, and in fact felt rather dismissed.

On the other hand, Ansa was impressed that such a city could develop in what others would think was a backwater. *What inspired them? Was it only the exposure to others because of trade routes, or was there something in their being that inclined them to work these endeavors? Which came first, and how can I use this information?*

The Companions stayed for several days as guests of the town. Open meetings were held in the great hall, and spirited discussions were had. They left the region with many ideas and lots of inspiration.

A few miles south, in another riverside community, the Companions observed employees of a large delivery business; Natives, a handful of Africans, some whites and Californios. Their jobs were just as divided. "I hire all kinds of folks, makes no difference to me as long as they can do the job," said the boss man.

"That is most remarkable of you, sir. How well are they paid?" asked Henson.

"What do you mean? I pay fair, according to who they are!"

"Who they are? Oh, you mean, their job?"

"I said, who they are, of course! You can see for yourself from here; *who* they *are!*"

"Yes, I do see," replied Henson, finally understanding what that phrase means.

The Companions sat around the fire that night, silent in their thoughts below translucent clouds gripping a full moon, when one of them asked, "Why have we not noticed this before? We have all experienced it, yet ignored it until it was presented so blatantly."

"We ignored it, for the same reason the boss man ignored it. Conscious or unconscious, I do not know. The man seems decent enough. He believes he has a monopoly on truth, and wanted the illusion of equality, so he hired everyone who could do the work, but he pays them according to his biases," observed another.

"But we see it now," answered Henson, "Knowledge makes things messy, but being silent is a choice."

The others all nodded in thoughtful agreement.

～

1845

Jack joined the group to see the northlands and help with the Companions travels. He was happy to be looking at familiar faces.

"Hey! The kid is back!" whooped one of the men. Jack grinned, shaking hands with each of the Companions as they thumped him on the back good-naturedly. They asked him about Camp Bockarie, about Karmo.

"The Camp is always busy. What a place! And Mr. Karmo, I can't say enough. He trains people to lead the way, to intercept, to defend. He's about planning and taking action; no speeches. He may not have the gift of pretty words, but he showed me how to be a man; dedicated, accountable and loving to country and family and more."

The Companions stared at the young man, blinking, when Fitzgerald broke the awkward silence, "Well, of course he did! That's Karmo for you, son!"

They traveled for three days and made camp somewhat inland from the north coast. The following morning Ansa took a walk to gather his thoughts. Shafts of sun rays, fuzzy with floating plant particles and insects, filtered wondrously through the mist. Each bit reflected life of a time long ago, as their glints of light drifted upon his upturned face and embraced him.

Presently, he felt a hand gently patting his shoulder as Henson lightly called his name, "Ansa? Are you all right?" Jack was there as well, but remained silent, looking upwards, his mouth open.

Ansa blinked back the tears, for emotion had overwhelmed him. "I was lost in my thoughts," Jonny. What a place this is! Is it even real? Look at these trees! I am in awe of their size; enormous, and as wide as three wagon lengths!" He looked at the wood, ruddy red in color, the tops hidden in the mists. He had seen smaller versions in the Sierras and at the lower coast; enormous, themselves, but these! He looked around at magnificent ferns as tall as a man, rhododendrons, and the small three-petaled white or burgundy flowers that mingled within. Even the small animals took on a more regal air here. Birds magically became flying gods. Here was a world of symbiotic confluence.

Henson smiled and added, "They are really something, indeed. The Natives call them Sequoias. They're also in the Sierra Mountains and some other parts of Alta California."

Jack turned his head towards the two older men. "I met a man called Sequoya when I was traveling through Tennessee. His real name was George Gist, I think; a silversmith, a blacksmith or such."[70]

"And?" asked Henson

"Oh … well. He made up some writing system for the Cherokee language. There was a big stir about it. Some whites didn't like it at all, and thought it a huge waste of time. Anyway, that's about all I know. Sorry for interrupting. It was just a coincidence, hearing the name Sequoya. But I heard a lot more about the Cherokee as I traveled. Oklahoma was formed, they explained, by a buzzard who flew for seven days and nights. When the bird became tired, its wings fell into the mud and formed valleys. And when the buzzard lifted its wings, the mountains and ridges were formed. It has ever been thus, they say."

"Marvelous, just marvelous!" answered Ansa. "Both this place and those stories. Thank you, my son." He smiled at Jack. "Sequoia!" he said, "as good an explanation as any other. Jonny, we should pay more attention to the youngsters!"

Henson smiled at Jack. "Let's get back to camp."

∽

Again, with Henson as lead, Ansa, Lokni and a small group of others made their way along the northern coast. They didn't know how far they would travel, as the population became more and more sparse the farther north they ventured. By and by, they came upon a remote village described as "*where the waters flow down.*" The village consisted of both Natives and whites from different countries. The closest person to a leader was their sage and spirit guide, Alif.

"Come, come, whoever you are!" Alif called out as he waved to the travelers.

The Companions looked around the village and an aura of calm descended upon them. Henson inquired as to the serenity of the residents.

Alif took them to nearby cliffs, there to gaze upon the enchanting light on the sea with satisfaction. "What more do we need?" The shimmery waters were roiling and undulating, roaring and crashing over the rocks below. "It is both limitless and promising. It gives sustenance. It gives beauty and joy to the soul. Breathe deeply, take it all in," he said as if in prayer. "Do not get us wrong. Some of us venture out for trade with others, and news. There is no place where winds do not reach. We are not ignorant, but we are content here with the way things are." The men looked at the dancing light upon the waves. "Yes, it is peaceful. Look at that light," murmured Ansa.

Alif looked at Ansa and nodded, "Light comes to you each morning, to greet you, to warm you and enter your heart. Light is life, my friend. Life is energy, and energy can never be destroyed. It is enduring. Living on the land lends a sense of sovereignty. Time moves differently than in towns. It moves from dark to light, then dark again. Time to slumber, time to toil."

Ansa found a kindred spirit in Alif, who was somewhat of an animist, but above all, spiritual. *Perhaps too much so, for the realism of the new nation which is to be*, he thought. Ansa was a master in the art of the dialectic regarding mythologies, yet felt no lessening of his own spirituality.

The small village was at peace in its isolation —for some, their own oblivion—and did not need outsiders stirring up anxiety and disruption. They were kind and hospitable, but determined, as they fed the travelers and then showed them the way out of their village.

"Feel free to call on us when you change your minds!" offered Ansa. "We are a patient people."

"They are defenseless," a worried Henson mused to Fitzgerald.

The men turned in for the night. A shadow approached them. That night, Murphy Fitzgerald appeared to have died in his sleep. Small red blood vessels had burst in his eyes, and his expression was one of surprise. Henson closed Murphy's eyelids. They buried him under a large coastal Sequoia. "Your adventure is over, my friend. Rest in peace," intoned Henson.

Ansa was particularly quiet when he approached Henson. "Jonny, between the Sequoias, Alif's village and Fitzgerald's death, I feel quite afloat, overwhelmed, like the earth is shifting under my feet. I think it best I go ahead alone, to get rebalanced and scout the territory south of here."

Henson nodded, but said in a concerned voice, "Ansa, you'll be fine with a little time. This has shaken us all, but yes, I know you and your sensibilities. I'm sure the others will be agreeable." A short discussion determined when and where they would meet up later.

～

Some days later, together once again, the Companions traveled into the interior, the northern tip of a long central valley. Rolling hills of grass and outcroppings of native trees dominated. Cattle grazed upon the open grasslands, and small farmhouses dotted the land. They watched a dust-up in the distance and as it approached, the Companions recognized approaching horses carrying a party of armed settlers.

"What's your business here?" barked one of the men, seemingly the leader.

Henson spoke, "We mean no harm. We've come to gather your counsel towards developing a new nation in these parts, and to share what we have learned from others during our travels."

The men looked at the travelers suspiciously, but escorted them into the settlement, where they became more at ease. "You can't blame us for being jumpy. Just this morning we are making ready to bury one of our own. Slaughtered out on his land, for heaven-only-knows-why."

The community suspected a neighbor. But no one knew for sure. The victim was a rancher, tied to a fencepost, beaten, shot and left to be eaten by foraging animals. The Companions would stay to pay their respects.

It was a gray, somber day, fitting for a funeral. People walked slowly, still in shock. How could one's neighbor, one who had lived side by side with them for years, helped each other out, worked together to raise barns, to harvest …. How could one turn so vicious? There was no proof, but the suspect had left his ranch suddenly on horseback early the morning of the killing. That was convincing enough.

The pastor preached his words, "God decided to take him home," he told the family. "It was His will, and he is in a better place." The casket was lowered.

The rancher's six-year-old son was crying silently, his shoulders heaving until he heard those last words. In the time of a breath, a blink, he jumped into the grave upon his father's casket and turned his tears streaked face to the pastor. "No! You don't say that! I want him back!" The child grabbed and pounded at the plain pine box with all his might. "You give me back my Pa! His place is with me and Ma! You, you, you!" The little boy, his face contorted with rage and sorrow, held his balled fist up at the pastor as two of the mourners jumped down into the grave, to pull him out. He ran to his mother, her own swollen eyes on the verge of overflowing, and who quickly pulled him to her and covered his mouth with her hand.

~

The Companions did manage to sit down with a few of the settlement leaders to hear them out. "They might support us for defense and let us die for the new country, but I'm not so sure they will share the land or honor the sacrifices others made who are not like them," Henson told the group. "Let's go home."

32

Suzanne in San Francisco 1845

There is no greater wealth than wisdom, no greater poverty than ignorance; no greater heritage than culture and no greater support than consultation. –Ali ibn Abu-Taib

News of the returning Companions and their mission spread slowly through the city. Benoîts Mercantile had set aside a room where they could meet and strategize. Madame Benoît, Suzanne and Mrs. Marshall frequently sat in on these meetings—sometimes asking questions or offering their perspective. This was to be a land where all persons, men and women, Native or otherwise, would have a say in the formation of a new government.

Suzanne was particularly interested in these meetings. She was now in sole control of the business; her mother was available for consultation from time to time. Suzanne maintained a working knowledge of American economics, and referred to the latest information about the shipping trades for the mercantile negotiations. Then, of course, there were always the taxes and laws of the Mexican government, under whose auspices they were required to work. In short, Suzanne understood the fundamentals of economics and working in a system with others to get things done.

Over time, public visitors dropped in on these meetings to ask questions or voice either their support or protest, whatever their inclination. San Francisco was growing, and people were getting impatient with the Mexican government's decisions and overlong response time.

～

A public meeting was scheduled. Jonny Henson returned from his traveling early to moderate and catch people up on what was happening in the outlands, the opinions and philosophy regarding the establishment of a new nation. These regions needed to be heard, and their concerns mattered, for they worked in the natural resources, the grist for the mill from which the new nation would be built. This evening's meeting was especially packed with a wide diversity of residents.

Madeleine was the opening speaker. There was murmuring as she took her place at the lectern, but it subsided once she looked out at the audience, nodded her head and welcomed them.

"My fellow citizens," she started. "We need to be a society whose government values and encourages intellectual pursuit to look for humanity's place in the universe. For this, we need to be at peace and above all, be living a life beyond mere subsistence. We must normalize the 'otherness' amongst us. Do not hide or be ashamed of the diversity of our peoples. Show them in all the variations in which they exist; farmers, hunters, traders, merchants, scholars, whatever. This avoids stereotyping those who are otherwise seen only as subservient. We need them all to have a healthy, thoughtful nation!"

There was a general nodding and murmuring.

She continued, "There is so much more to us than how we look and what we do for a living. We struggle to balance our many facets and impulses, and to center our internal compass. Let us endeavor to also show our compassion and helpfulness outright, and take action accordingly. It behooves us to encourage all our brothers and sisters to think, to be educated, for we never know from where a great discovery or thought will come. Mindfulness and discovery. Inspiration might come through contemplating the rings made from a droplet of water into a pond, or the wind thrust of a butterfly's wings, or the sight of a tiny piece of sand being pushed along by an insect. Anything can change our understanding of the world profoundly. Ideas blossom, and better ways or better tools develop, whether from a ploughman, an academic, a seamstress or a hunter.

"All this …."

"All this?" … boomed a man in the audience who regarded the speaker carefully.

Madeleine drew in a deep breath and looked into the sky through the large window to the east. "All this, and we barely understand each other, let alone that which we cannot see; ideas, beliefs, cultures. We must try harder. Remember that!"

"What she says is right!" said another man from the audience. Jonny Henson nodded to him to continue.

"We are many peoples in this land, and we have many beliefs and practices. But we can be more than a Native, a Mexican, an American, a Russian, a farmer, a woodcutter, and so forth. For example, I am a citizen of this land. The melding of our 'otherness' is part of what brings us together regarding trade, ideas and living in general. When I am hunting or sawing wood, or sitting on a tree trunk in the forest, my mind often wanders. I am not particularly thinking about *my* ways as opposed to *others'* ways. I wonder about the sky, the beasts, the neighbors. What the land will be like when my children are grown, my grandchildren. I am using my imagination."

Again, there was a generalized nodding and murmuring of agreement in the audience. Some struggled to take in all the ideas being floated about.

At length, one large, well-dressed man, cigar in hand, perhaps forty years of age, stood up. He had been granted the floor by Mr. Henson. "Sirs," he said, surveying the crowd. "I am not opposed to the formation of a new government. Indeed, I applaud it! It is a great opportunity for us."

The crowd applauded politely.

He cleared his throat and continued, "However, I do take exception to women being allowed to vote or serve in office. They may serve me dinner, but not serve in government administration!" He smiled broadly at his own attempted joke.

Henson leaned forward, thinking, *And so it begins. Here we go.*

There were a few mumblings before Suzanne stood up, stiffly. She looked for permission from the dais to speak. Henson nodded an acknowledgement, "Yes, Mademoiselle Suzanne."

"Sir," she paused and looked around, "We no longer live in the times of ignorance. The women in this room would like you to tell us specifically what you fear about us having the same rights as you? Why would you demean us by relegating us only to the kitchen? Please enlighten us, sir, as well as these good men who are listening."

"Fear?! Fear?!" answered the man, clearly annoyed. "No, it is not fear, madam. It is a plain fact that women only have half the brainpower of men. They merely are not fit to determine the fate of a town, a state, let alone a nation!"

Small gasps here and there could be heard through the room. Suzanne realized this was now a debate. She sized him up and took her shot.

"Upon what scientific studies or historical reference do you preface such a statement, sir?"

The man looked at her with great animus and arrogance. "I need no damn scientific study! It's in the Bible everywhere! Women are always subjugated to men. Look at history! Look at the rulers of the world!" he mocked.

"Oh, you mean leaders such as Queen Nzinga of Angola, the diplomat and military leader who resisted the Portuguese invasion? Or perhaps Queen Elizabeth of England and Ireland, who governed with relative stability and prosperity for 44 years? Or perhaps you should consider Catherine the Great, Empress of Russia, who ruled for 34 years and who revitalized the military—making Russia one of the great world powers of the time![71] As for the Bible, who wrote that? A bunch of old men who could not agree on the rules for doctrine, and expressed more about their own culture and politics of the time than the facts!"

There was a huge sucking of air and grumbling from the audience. Suzanne reddened as she realized she had gone too far. So she continued, calmly, "I realize the Bible is sacred to many people, maybe to most people here, and I mean no disrespect. However, you have rendered only an opinion and no proof of your statement, sir! We need to be a fact-based nation, not one of prejudice and baseless accusation."

The man became livid, his face contorted. He screamed, "You have no idea! You just don't! Women lack capacity, plain and simple, and shouldn't be allowed anywhere near decision-making beyond running a household and cooking my dinner!"

Suzanne let his words float across the room and drop from the air like black smoke before she answered quietly.

"So that's it? Do you really think we can hear you better when you scream? Does volume make you right? You moving your lips and making utterances about something does not make it so. You have much to learn, Sir! Listen, consider and ask intelligent questions. We need to ascertain answers for ourselves, not chase after dogma. We must discuss with others, including those who are not like-minded, lest we perpetuate ignorance. We are on the threshold of a new adventure, a nation with the goal of harmony among its peoples … united. And you? What do you offer that is constructive and new?"

With that there was brief, but sparse, applause. For although it was clear the man was ignorant, many people felt as he did and had not thought to include others in their thinking. *Somehow we need to include people like him. This will not be an easy transition,* Suzanne thought to herself.

The meeting continued with much less contention until it was time to disperse for the evening.

At the last moment, another man stood up, looking for recognition and permission to speak. Henson nodded to him.

"Good people! I am new to this land, and am ignorant of its ways and history. But I do know something of government, having been involved in it for many years in the U.S.," the former state senator commenced, "I read from his own memoirs, and none other than George Washington himself warned of hyper-partisanship, excessive debt, and foreign governments influencing elections. Here, you enjoy a balanced economy, but there is much divisiveness and mistrust.

"Please indulge me to say this: I believe that you are wise to convene these meetings to air out questions, grievances and fears, lest they go underground to fester. I must add that the first American President put forward guidance for leadership; belief in peace through strength, belief in moderate compromise, and just as importantly, chosen leaders must have certain personal, moral attributes; humility, honesty, integrity, and a lifetime of service to the people. Find people like that to lead your nation."

Suzanne was the first to stand and applaud, followed closely by the rest of those in attendance.

The man added, "America is an aspirational country, and an idealistic country ... a *determined* country. Your leaders need to be at least as aspirational, idealistic, and determined. Your speakers are correct about including everyone—as only equality creates respect for the law. I am not in consideration for office, but I am willing to add my experienced consult any time. Thank you all."

Standing in the back of the room, quietly observing, listening to the speakers, and taking notes about all that transpired, was a small, dark woman. Born in the American state of Virginia, Mary Ellen Pleasant was hopeful.[72] She had traveled by buckboard and ferry from Napa City in the north bay to attend this meeting. *Here is a land where there truly may be opportunities for all peoples,* she thought to herself. *Perhaps this land will be the land of the free. It is certainly a home for the brave.* She had given much thought to the nation she left behind. *Such a land of hope and beauty and yet plenty of despair and brutality, both ideas to embrace and ideas to quash. America stays at war with itself. It is an ever-changing, wonderful land that stands for freedom ... for those who are chosen, not people like her.*

～

Immediately after the meeting, a frustrated Suzanne made herself a cup of tea back in the kitchen. "How ironic, here I am in the kitchen, after all!" She laughed out loud at herself. "Ha! No matter how many times I tell myself not to speak, *'Just shush, Suzanne!'* I cannot help myself when these oafs start in on their rants. The ignoramuses! At least not all of them are that way!"

Mrs. Marshall stepped into the kitchen and started banging around. Suzanne took one look at her. "If you have something to say, say it, Mrs. Marshall. Don't make the pots and pans do it!"

"Hmmph! That was quite a speech, Missy. How do you think we women are truly going to have a say in this new nation? It's just not the normal way of things, you know."

Suzanne looked up and answered in a tired voice. "I'm so sorry for snapping at you, Mrs. Marshall, I can always rely on you to state out loud what others might think. And yes, you are correct. Women's voices will not be readily accepted in government, or business. But what is also true is that times are changing. Some women are ready to be part of the labor market, business owners, legislators and equal partners with their husbands—or even without a husband. And they are not all man-haters for wanting to do what a man normally has done. What is particularly manly about book-keeping, shop-keeping, law-making? And you, Mrs. Marshall! I have seen you roll up your sleeves and swing an axe to chop wood as well as any man could! It is a fallacy that women should be relegated to limited functions."

Mrs. Marshall flushed and then laughed heartily, "Ha! Well, when you put it that way, Miss. I only think it'll just be hard to win people over to this new way of thinking."

"Well, you are correct there. Yes, you are absolutely correct, Mrs. Marshall. I heard of a distinguished woman from the United States who said that we women need to find the formula for accessing power and authority while still projecting a womanly persona. We cannot show rancor against men, rendering them obsolete, or we will be perpetually stuck with boys. No, without strong men as models to either embrace or resist, women will never attain a centered and profound sense of ourselves as women."

Mrs. Marshall was silent, bobbing her head as she considered this, when Madeleine entered the kitchen. "Ah, Madame Madeleine! You're here! Come, have a seat. I'll make you some tea as well."

"Thank you, Mrs. Marshall. That would be so lovely."

"Ah, *chérie*," sighed Madeleine, "This hill is a steep one. But, I sense more of an openness in this land, especially if women persist and we have men like Messrs. Henson and Ansa to support us. As for me, I fear that I have buried myself in a hole of despair. My public face is no longer easy to show. Talk of a new nation may promise a new start, but for me, I am just tired. I support you young people, so fresh and energetic; eager to make something great. I just no longer know how I can help."

"But oh, *ma mère*," cried Suzanne, "How can you say that?! Your perspective and wisdom are what tempers that energy. We need you, and others like you, to gently hold and guide our reins. We need your insights into business and governance, in general. You saw how I put my foot in my mouth tonight."

Madeleine smiled up at her daughter and patted her hands.

"You did well, little one. Let me tell you this, Yes, the times have changed since my day, and will continue to change, of course; be it by evolution, revolution or the tendency of mankind to make something new for their own purpose."

"Isn't it odd that people keep *talking* about making something new, but not *thinking* new?" Mrs. Marshall said aloud, as much to herself as to the others. "We often won't change in beliefs, but there must be better ways to get things done than grouse about."

Madeleine smiled and continued, "Yes, Mrs. Marshall, you hit the nail on the head, as the young people say. Those specially crafted items so handy or so dear, such as tinder boxes and muskets, are no longer needed, since today we have matches and rifles. And how many other countless items have replaced old ones? Ideas should follow that course to fulfill the same destiny. *We must adapt, or be left behind in a cloud of dust.* We must not isolate ourselves from our neighbors, lest we become numb in our own ignorance, rather than having a say about our own future."

Suzanne nodded as she took in these words. "Yes, yes," she answered. "The Companions have been talking about their meetings with peoples, and the ideas that were put forward. So many ideas, so many possibilities! There are whole networks of small economies that allow villages to survive, but we will need to scale up to grow, and we need coordination to support ourselves as a nation."

"If the citizens want a nation that will benefit us all, we need to encourage and support our crafts persons and our traders. Remember what you learned on the ship when we first got here? How Mexico was paying more than double, sometimes even triple, for imported goods made of its own raw materials? If a nation cannot raise its own traders and master craftspeople, they will always be second-rate. But just as important, if a government is to be successful, it will need an established set of moral principles; freedom, justice, truthfulness, democracy and, above all, equality. Without these, human life becomes worthless, and the government is just a continuous battle for power, greed and even religion. If we lose our principles, we have no future," expounded Madeleine.

"So, what you're both saying is that we all have to just get with the times, and do it together! Right?" said Mrs. Marshall.

The Benoît women looked at Mrs. Marshall, at first astonished. Smiling, Madeleine said, "To the point, as always, Mrs. Marshall!"

~

There was a knock on the front door. "Now who could that be, at this time of evening?" muttered Mrs. Marshall as she stood up to answer.

Madeleine followed her from the kitchen, while Suzanne sipped her tea. There were excited utterances and Suzanne turned her head to listen. It was Peter Kroupa and his family!

Mrs. Marshall ushered them in, delighted to see them. Madeleine rushed up to Peter, throwing her arms around him, exclaiming, "Oh Peter! You are here! You are here, and with your family!" She extended both hands to Peter's wife in a warm clasp. "Oh, and your children! Two sons, oh my! Come, come in and sit down! Suzanne, Suzanne, come here! It's Peter and his family!"

Suzanne walked cautiously into the front room. Peter stood up, followed by his wife. "Let me make the introductions," said Peter. "Mademoiselle Suzanne Benoît, this is my wife Summer, and my children Lisette and little Pete." He turned towards his wife, "Mademoiselle Suzanne is Jean and Madeleine's eldest daughter, dear." Mrs. Kroupa bowed her head to Suzanne before stating in a friendly, cheerful voice, "So nice to meet you, Ma'am. You are a physician, correct?"

Suzanne was caught off-guard, but quickly steadied herself and in a calm voice answered, "Oh, that honor belongs to my younger sister, Marie-Therese, who is not here this evening."

"Oh, my mistake!" Summer laughed. "I didn't realize Madam Benoît had two grown daughters! How absolutely delightful! Again, I'm so glad to meet you!" she said, extending her hand to Suzanne.

Suzanne made a perfunctory handshake before speaking further. Her face reddened and the back of her neck started to perspire. She was hurt, mortified and humbled. *I deserved this*, she thought to herself, *but did he have to be so cool and aloof, so cruel to me, as if I had never existed?* "Please enjoy your visit," she managed to say. "I must attend to something in the kitchen." She turned and left the front room as fast as she could.

33

Aunty Mullen in San Francisco

It was beautiful and simple, as are all truly great swindles.
–O. Henry

The San Francisco scam was to last only about six months, but in that period of time, four projects and trusts similar to Aunty's were running concurrently. All came to an abrupt halt within a week of each other. Staff had been hired and paid, but no supplies or children ever reached the safety of a domicile set up just for them. Taylor paid off the staff, his team of grifters, and assigned them to projects in another part of the city. The bulk of investments, naturally, he kept for himself. *Hmmm,* he thought, *I'm going to need to get out of town in a few weeks, at this rate!*

$\sim$

They met in Taylor's office, as planned. The project's update report was not good.

"But what happened, Mr. Taylor?! What do you mean, the money disappeared?" Aunty said, in a panic.

"My dear lady, you hired a number of ill-chosen people to run your establishment. I fear they have accepted your money and absconded with it. They are nowhere to be found!" replied Mr. Taylor. "I'm so sorry for your bad luck! I only wish I could help you!" he said with all the false empathy he could muster.

"But, Mr. Taylor! I thought you had vouched for them!?"

"I took them at their word, as I am wont to do, Ma'am," he replied. "And, then, of course, there is the issue of *your* signature on their contracts."

"But I trusted *you*, Mr. Taylor. I trusted *you!*"

"Again, I am so very sorry, Aunty. Ma'am. But there is nothing more I can do. I bid you good-day." He gestured to the door and tipped his head to the side, his eyes dull and unmoving.

She searched his face before turning to leave the room, dumbfounded, at a loss for words. *Oh dear, oh dear! Now what?! I don't know what to do!* she said to herself in dismay. When she reached the bottom of the stairs, she turned and looked back at the office once more, livid about the situation—and about Mr. Taylor. Just then, it dawned on her. *I've been had! We'll just see what my nephew can do about this. Oh, Christian, my boy, I wish you didn't live so far away!*

CAMP BOCKARIE
SACRAMENTO

SAN
FRANCISCO

PACIFIC
OCEAN

ALTA CALIFORNIA

34

Gold in Sacramento Valley 1845

That man is richest whose pleasures are cheapest.
–Henry David Thoreau

He told no one about how he got to Alta California. Most likely, he was a runaway seaman, like a number of black men. He arrived in 1828 and commenced prospecting for gold in the southlands, working his way north. There had been a drought for four years before the rains. But even with the drought-busting rains, this region's rivers and lakes were still not at capacity. Through a lattice of gullies, one could walk into dry or shallow river beds where that was not possible before.

This is exactly what William Warren, sometimes called Uncle Billy, was doing in 1845.[73] Uncle Billy was visiting Karmo at Bockarie, bunking out in a shack on the river bank, when he saw something shining in the water. Kicking clods of dirt off his boots as he neared the object, he picked it up and immediately knew what it was. He grubbed a bit amongst the cold, water-polished pebbles, finding much, much more of the shiny yellow metal. He stood up, scanned about for onlookers, and then stuffed the *gold* into his pocket before pounding wooden stakes onto a perimeter, staking out his claim.

"Glory be!" he exclaimed. Excitedly, he filled his saddlebags and headed for camp. He had searched for the colorful metal so long in the southlands and in the north, and here was his lucky strike—at last! As he approached the camp, his excitement abated and he started thinking. This is trouble, he mumbled to himself. "Best show Mr. Karmo," he said aloud, looking about again to see if he was being watched.

~

Karmo closed his eyes and tilted his head upwards. "This is both a gift and a curse, Uncle Billy," he said.

"That it is, Karmo. Down in the southern part of the territory, gold was discovered some years back. It drew in every breed of miscreant and fugitive from across the continent, and even from overseas. The land was lawless, almost as much as here. With gold, it became a malicious land; murder was rampant, and many prospectors were taken advantage of."

"No doubt, Uncle Billy," replied Karmo, taking a deep breath. "How do we mine this and keep it a secret?"

"We can't. At least, not for long. News will get out. This is too large a find to keep quiet, but at least we have a head start. Why don't we talk to the Natives, who put less value on the metal? They can help us. We can hide it in tunnels, at least for a while, until you can get that new nation of yours up and running. Of course, at least *I'll* be rich! Right?" he asked grinning.

Karmo considered this. "I suppose you *will* be rich, even though this is land granted to me. There will be plenty who will disregard whether lands are granted or not when news of this gets out. Yes, talking to the Native leaders is a good idea, but I am conflicted, Uncle Billy. I feel like I am withholding riches that could belong to them, whether found on my land or not. This weighs heavily on me. I need to think about this."

"Think rationally, without emotion, Karmo, like you do when you plan a fight. Only this is a different type of fight. You are avoiding a crush of lawlessness; reserving the gold for yourself will benefit more people who deserve it. Speak to the Natives. They will have good ideas. And don't you know people in San Francisco? They could help, too."

Karmo considered this advice as he stared into the sky. He was at odds with himself and only needed a nudge to make a decision. "Yes, you are correct, Uncle Billy. These words help chase away the clouds in my head. It brings me back to the light," replied Karmo reflectively. "This could go wrong so many ways—or it could be an incredible opportunity."

~

The Natives were not so naïve as Uncle Billy had thought. While they accepted Karmo's presence on what still they believed was their land, they tolerated him because he asked little of them, was friendly and hired many of their clans to work at the Camp.

Karmo met with local Native leaders and struck up an agreement. The Natives would mine the gold and hide it for him. In return, they would get a good portion of the gold to improve their lives and the lives of those in their lands. Yes, there would be more settlers in the area. They saw this happening—with or without the gold. At least this way, they would benefit, as long as they stayed healthy. After a number of months, Karmo took stock and set out for San Francisco. The only person he trusted to tell and who would know how to manage this wealth was Jonny Henson, who was back in San Francisco, conducting various meetings regarding the Companions' findings.

～

"You have got to be kidding me, Karmo!" said Henson, holding up bags of gold nuggets in awe. "Damnation! This is a mess! A beautiful mess!"

Karmo was having trouble reading Henson's reaction. "What do you mean? Should I not have told you?"

Henson looked up at Karmo, still holding bags of gold in both hands. Slowly putting them down on the table, he said in a low voice,

"No, no, you're right to show me. You know that, and I know that. I'm just thunderstruck. And you say you have wagon loads of this?"

Karmo nodded, his eyebrows knitted, "We do," he said simply.

"There's no way to use this for payment for anything, without the news getting out, and hiding it in caves won't do, either," said Henson thoughtfully. "We can put it in a bank. There are only two banks in the city, and both are well guarded.

"Can we trust them? The banks?" asked a concerned Karmo. "Will not word get out?"

"It's our best bet, Karmo. We need to get ahead of this whole situation, and secure as much of the gold as possible. Word will get out, still. The more people who know, the more likely someone won't be able to resist telling of such an incredible find. It's a mighty temptation, a mighty temptation! We can only hope to limit the reaction, but to do that, we need a plan for keeping the gold safe, and for using it. I have some ideas to talk to you about. You can share them with the Native leaders as well. Just ideas, Karmo, they're just ideas. Let's sit down and talk." Henson stoked the wood stove and put on a pot of coffee to boil as the two men sat down at the table in his small hotel suite. "Look," said Henson, "This is scaring me. This is big, serious stuff. You know that, right?"

"Of course I do! I have heard of gold fever, and even more, I understand the evil men will do to have wealth! Even a little wealth!" Karmo struggled to be calm as he remembered Sahr's betrayal years before.

"Alright, alright!" said Henson. "I meant no offense. I was talking as much to myself as to you, Karmo. Let me talk to Wilson and feel him out about a large deposit before I tell him exactly what is happening. This is actually not bad timing, because many regions are sending their representatives to our travelers' meetings, and there are even plans for a convention of sorts.

"If we can get our new land, and independence from Santa Anna, we can tell our new leaders about the gold. They're forming committees for all kinds of different needs; finance, defense, education, roads. You name it, they have it! But first things first, safety in the bank, get independence, talk to the leaders about how to use the gold for funding what we need. They will have already determined their needs. What a surprise when the funding just appears! This is like a miracle, Karmo! If we can pull it off!"

Karmo was excited, amused and thoughtful. "I think the gold is safest in the cave until we get independence. That way, fewer people will know about it. After independence, it will not be too difficult to transport it to the bank. People are used to seeing supply wagons setting out for the city, and I will use my most trusted people to load and escort the wagons. I will talk to Jack about contacting Mullen to escort. You need to be sure the bank is ready, and well-protected at all times."

"Mullen?! Well, yes, actually that's not out of the question," said Henson thoughtfully. His demeanor brightened. "I can't believe this is all happening, my friend. It boggles my mind, and how improbable! Did you hear what we said just now? We'll get independence?! Just like ordering up a beer!" laughed Henson.

"This can happen a couple ways, both of which mean taking advantage of circumstances and of a person who trusts me. Trust must be sacrificed to forestall the bigger threat from the east," responded Karmo, with a wan smile. "I should leave very soon."

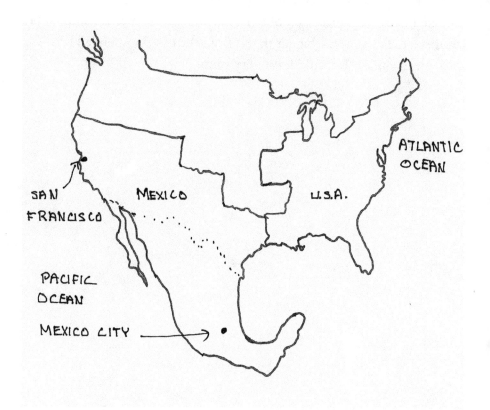

ATLANTIC
OCEAN

SAN
FRANCISCO

MEXICO

U.S.A.

PACIFIC
OCEAN

MEXICO CITY

35

Karmo in Mexico City 1845

"No" means ask another way. –Unknown

The clang of the metal door was cold and grating. Karmo looked through the door's cell bars and the confining walls of mold and spalling stucco. At first, a dreadful panic set into his chest, then he stopped holding his breath. "General," he thought. "So like him. Give us both the night to calm down." A few moments later, "I know what I want, but why do I really want it?" He lay down on the straw that had been tossed onto the damp, dank floor and let his mind wander before he smiled. "Yes, that is it!"

The next morning, he allowed himself to be dragged out and slammed unceremoniously into a chair across from a massive table. He sat there silently, looking about. The table was actually a large, imposing desk of carved mahogany, with charts and maps strewn about its surface. There were metal floor lamps and an elaborate metal chandelier. At length, he heard the door behind him open.

The General limped into the office and seated himself across from Karmo in a high-backed leather chair fashioned much like a throne. Again, Santa Anna was up to his elbows in fighting the French, the Americans, and his own people, who were fed up with an incompetent centralized government. Some territories were even left ungoverned, his troops were stretched so thin.

Karmo sat up straight and looked the General in the eye. He waited to be addressed.

"You have some nerve coming here with such a demand! I should have you taken out to be shot dead, you know that, do you not! Everywhere I turn, someone is demanding, revolting, undermining, double-crossing! Now the Americans are threatening war! At least you have the decency, if not foolishness, to ask outright! Do you really think you can walk in here, ask for half of Alta California, and depart alive?!!" The General slowly calmed down and stared at the table, letting out a long breath. He took a long sip of black coffee and made himself more peaceful. He even smiled. "Karmo? Do you have an answer?"

Karmo had already determined that he would neither mention that gold was discovered, nor that there were petitions for independence of the northern territory in Alta California. It was better to tell a partial truth than to tell a whole truth in a defensive manner.

"Sir, I ask for your consideration of possibilities. Consider the events since we parted ways in Tejas." Karmo eyed Santa Anna's left leg.

"Oh, this?" laughed Santa Anna as he hit his left leg with his cane, producing the hollow sound of ringing wood.[74] "Yes, well, this was a fluke, and yes it has been one thing after another, and yes again, the administration has been fickle."

Karmo, thought carefully before speaking, but persevered, "You can easily move the territory capital to Santa Barbara," explained Karmo. "There already is a Presidio there. It is a good-size bay, calm and beautiful as well. Besides, the settlers and citizens in the north are near revolt. And once again, Mexico has neither the capacity, strength nor treasure to keep these lands in line. Let the North have their independence; they can be a friendly nation, an ally on your border, for is that not the intent? We will fight invaders, including the Americans. We can establish productive trade and be supportive of one another."

Santa Anna thought this over, then shouted angrily, "Damn you, Karmo! Damn it, damn it, damn it! You are right, and I am tired! The government exiles me, then *drags* me back over and over. I am done with trying to hold on to so much with so little resources. I am surprised you do not ask for the gold fields in the south!"

Karmo held his breath steady before answering, "The northern territory in Alta California is relatively uninhabited, General. We want to avoid an influx of people who do not have our land's best interests at heart."

Santa Anna eyed Karmo, tilting his head a bit, "Come back in the morning. I have some considerations to look into. Also, I believe we can find some accommodations for you that are a bit nicer than last night," he said, winking.

The next day, the two men negotiated boundaries and bickered a bit over the bays. Karmo wanted both San Francisco, and particularly Monterey, the current capital of Alta California.

Santa Anna called in his secretary, "We will draw up the papers while I still have the authority to do so." But his pen broke while he was writing down Karmo's name. "Is this an omen?" he asked.

Karmo, anxious, almost frozen, maintained his calm. "Of what, Sir?"

Santa Anna laughed, tossed his pen aside and snapped his fingers at his adjutant for another to complete the documents. "This will ruffle a few feathers," he laughed. "I will almost enjoy it, though! Does the territory have a government in place? You need laws and a finance system ready to go, or else the land will fall into chaos and you will have a revolution of your own on your hands."

Karmo, paused, but stated openly, "We do, sir. Teams of people have ventured about the countryside for several years, gathering information and consensus. Congresses of companions have met all kinds of peoples; Natives, Californios, former Americans, African peoples and more have had their say, and will continue to do so. They are ready for elections. And they have been trained to defend the nation, their nation."

Santa Anna appeared stunned, but then allowed, "Impressive! But then, you were always prescient, Karmo. So be it!"

Karmo couldn't help but finger the gris gris bag around his neck before stating, "There were many people who had similar views at the same time, sir. I believe it was meant to be. At least, it was meant to be tried."

Karmo stayed another week to work on the details, including borders, how the ceding would be made and how potential fallout could
be handled. He pointed out borders as the northern committees had
determined. Other members of the administration were brought in and,
though there were protests—mostly concerns about regional landholders being relatives—the boundary matter was finally resolved.

"You know you will have to fight the invaders from the east for the
land, even though it becomes a sovereign nation," said Santa Anna as he
was inking the final documents.

"I am aware, sir, but that may best be left to others. I lost my innocence long ago, and I too am weary of the fights and battles," answered
Karmo thoughtfully.

Santa Anna stopped his writing to look up, "Trees die on their feet,
Karmo. And as for innocence, innocence is the old shed skin of a man.
One finds innocence no longer possible to recall," said the General, with
an air of loss, almost wistfulness, in his tired eyes. In a flash, his demeanor turned dark. "But if you do not rip that skin off, it will trip you
up and perhaps even cause your death. And *how* does one rip off the skin
of innocence?" he asked rhetorically. "Through violence, lying, secrets
and betrayal!"

Karmo stood there, saying nothing. *This man is so mercurial: charming and generous one moment, vicious and rigid the next*, he thought.

During the weeks of riding his horse back to Sacramento, Karmo's
hands would sometimes sweat, sometimes shake, as he struggled to keep
his composure while carrying the documents that could actually shape a
new world; a new life he could not imagine, even now. As he got closer
to the capital city, a deep breath slowly cleared his head. *There is so much
work to be done,* he thought.

36

San Francisco Bay Area 1845

There are two kinds of spurs, my friend. Those that come in by the door;
and those that come in by the window.
–Tuco, a character in the film, *The Good, The Bad, and the Ugly*

The nation's gold was disseminated slowly and quietly, and it would not be long before changes were to be seen in cities and villages alike. San Francisco was growing, and people from the South Bay and East Bay regions were moving in. The waste and water confluence throughout the city had to be dealt with. Because of the homes, shops, fish markets, and manufacturing operations, more and more waste was simply dumped onto the sides of the streets or into the bay, drawing unwanted flies and vermin.

Sooner or later, a pestilence will come to pass, thought Marie-Therese. She spoke with Jonny Henson, who in turn spoke with the Alcalde about a city project that would employ people and develop a great service to the city. Together, they read Edwin Chadwick's position notices.[75] That English social reformer was making quite a stir about the state of health for the public, particularly for the poor. Europe was reacting to epidemics with decrees to fumigate dwellings, burn bedding and whitewash floors, since the source of disease was unclear. In the inner cities, the normal infant mortality rate was greater than fifty percent; the annual adult mortality rate was over thirty percent per one thousand persons. A similar pattern was shaping up in San Francisco. Already Marie-Therese, now a full-fledged physician, made a standing order that on all foreign ships, cargo was to be inspected before unloading, and passengers were to be given health assessment examinations before disembarking.

The Alcalde consented that both Dr. Marie-Therese, and Jonny Henson should meet with engineers and craftsmen to design a system of water pipes that would be buried underground throughout the city, and end in a network of shallow drainage pools, which would evaporate over time.

As in Europe, the social elites, and therefore the leaders of government, pointed to the indigent as the cause of disease. Over time, enlightened researchers convinced them that instead of disease causing deprivation, the deprivation of the poor caused disease; social and biological diseases such as psychological degradation led to desperation, alcohol abuse or even revolution; that the poor were relegated to the least favorable parts of town with little to no access to clean water or sewage treatment and the poorest quality of food and air. However, just as big a question as to how to fix social ills was how to finance this infrastructure undertaking. The city already had a system of taxes; however, a handsome portion of the city's budget came from the Nation's gold reserve. Even so, the City's budget was not so robust as to be able to take on a project of this scope. So, as the great cities had done in the past, taxes in the form of bonds were levied for a limited period.

Henson and Marie-Therese worked with the city's new civil engineer, Ernesto Gonzalez.

Looking to the dimensions of the many shipping kegs in the area for inspiration, Gonzalez determined that, by tapering them at the ends, clay pipes could be formed, connected and buried. A huge factory kiln was built, and laborers were hired to dig deep trenches throughout the City. Waste collection areas were identified and built. The City appointed Gonzalez to manage and maintain the infrastructure. He could hire staff appropriate for the job within his allotted budget.

Marie-Therese was appointed the Medical Director of Health. Her staff would focus on educating the public in basic sanitary practices, such as washing their hands and proper food handling and storage, monitoring disease outbreaks and, above all, disease prevention. She was in her element! Her passion for being a medical professional was being satisfied, and also, she found a conscientious and intelligent partner in Señor Gonzalez. Jonny Henson was at ease as well. He saw the making of a model city for the future, and became hopeful.

The three made their rounds to the construction sites, each lending their expertise, asking questions and listening to the concerns of foremen and other workers. The heavy clay pipes were carefully lifted by cranes and placed into the trenches. The pipes were then walled with brick, rendered with waterproof cement and surrounded by 18-inch concrete casings. "Will they hold for a good, long time, Señor Gonzalez?" asked Marie-Therese.

"Señora Marie-Therese, these lines will last beyond your great-grandchildren's life-times," he assured her. "It would take a tremendous force to breach them."

She shivered as she watched, remembering the story of her father's tragic death long ago. She urged safety, as she prayed silently.

Jonny bent over the support railings to get a better look into the trench; suddenly the railing gave way. The fall launched a small mudslide and the fencing debris almost engulfed him.

"Hold up! Stop the cranes! Stop 'em!" hollered the foreman as he waved his men to get down into the trench to rescue Henson. All work was halted. Marie-Therese scanned the scene quickly and scrambled down into the trench as well. With the help of ropes and a makeshift stretcher, they all managed to hoist Jonny out. He was dirty, exhausted, and ill-tempered. There was blood low on his trousers, but at least he was alive.

"I'm ok! It's my ankle! It hurts like hell!" he yelled, as much embarrassed as he was in pain. Nevertheless, a possible fracture was not to be overlooked. Marie-Therese pulled herself out with the ropes, went to her healing bag and gave him laudanum, which he promptly spat out. "That's disgusting!" he cringed.

"Then bite on this!" ordered Marie-Therese, offering him a smooth stick. Her small, lithe body belied her secret strength. She moved both smoothly and confidently, barking orders to the men; lift that, get this, bring that! All the while, her hands worked nimbly to stop the bleeding, reduce and set the ankle fracture, and sew up the wound. She carried in her healing bag, magpie feathers, and a number of tinctures, distilled from local plants, mostly learned from Lokni's people—and some from her old mentor, Dr. Galen. Once treated, Jonny would likely be just fine.

"Yeow! Shhhh … Shibble, datter frat!" yelled Jonny. "Stupid, stupid, stupid!"

"Accidents are bound to happen at such dangerous sites, Señor Gonzalez," said Marie-Therese as things calmed down. "Perhaps my staff and I can train a few men in first care? Someone who always will be on-site."

Señor Gonzalez was at first silent, then spoke deliberately, "The idea has merit, but let me give it more consideration. An extra person to pay wages, whose only duty is to stand-by, will add to the bottom line, and the city may not be pleased. But perhaps that person can have other duties as well. I need to weigh the costs, mull it over, and get back to you, Madam Doctor."

～

While some were working out a system for city health, others found their well-being through undertaking other endeavors. On one of those warm, sultry nights in the more raucous part of town, the Sachmalik Tavern appeared at first glance a derelict affair; quirky yet exotic, it distinguished itself as having exceptionally fine whiskey, a gift of Lt. Dan's procurement abilities. It was an adobe structure that over time had added extra rooms by using scavenged timber and stones. Beloved by the locals, its windows were covered by drafty shutters, glass having been broken out long ago during brawls. Nevertheless, it was *the place to be* for entertainment and debauchery. Tinny sounds of improvised horns, a hopelessly out-of-tune piano, the rustle of skirts, and the shuffling of feet gave the place its own beat. When the tavern could no longer contain them all, the dancers spilled out into the street. People were swaying, whooping and hollering, and generally having a good time.

Already finished with his card games, Lt. Dan was in his own element, having found an emergency goddess; a raven haired beauty who towered over him and could help support him in his wobbly dance. But in due course, even she had trouble keeping him upright.

Mullen arrived, surveyed the scene, and gave a look to one of his crew, who then sprang to Lt. Dan and helped the woman sit him onto the edge of the wooden water trough. His head moved as if on a wheel axle, turning down and around as he commenced singing and laughing.

"Lieutenant," said Mullen quietly, "I think you've had just about enough for the night."

"Wadda, waddaya sayin', Boss? Enough?! Enough?!" asked Lt. Dan, looking up and trying to wink. He put his index finger to his bottom eyelid and pulled it down a bit, groggily. "Too much of ever-thing is jist enough for me, Boss!! Hahahahahah! Oh! Oh, Boss! Did da boys tell ya? Did dey? Did dey tell ya 'bout your Aunty t'day?" Just then Dan fell backwards into the trough. The gush of bubbles surrounded him, and nothing could be heard but the glub, glub of him swallowing water.

Mullen looked at one of his guys and said loudly, "My Aunt? What the hell? What's going on? You!" he pointed to one of his men, "Speak! And you there, get Lt. Dan out of that damn trough!" he ordered.

～

The next evening, across the street from the bank owned by Wilson, Taylor and Franks, four men watched as two of the three partners left their offices after closing time. The banking staff had already departed. Only Matthew Taylor was working late in his upstairs office. With its heavy drapes drawn and just one lantern to illuminate the room, the office was cast in shadows, save for the eerie light. On his desk lay a dozen or so documents, from which he had just completed tallying figures. One of the bank's four-foot tall safes was next to his desk, with the door open. It was a rectangular, double-walled, cast-iron affair—typical of the times and tight as a drum when shut. He carefully wrapped and thoughtfully stacked bills of higher denominations inside.

"Not bad at all, Matt-boy," he said out loud to himself. He leaned back in his overstuffed jacquard cloth chair and looked at the crystal tumbler in his hand which held a clear, amber liquid. He took a sip of his favorite Kentucky Whiskey, a spicy rye, then looked at the glass and smiled in appreciation. "Glorious! Yes, Matt-boy, life is good."

Mullen brought in Lt. Dan, Jack Marshall and another lieutenant for this mission. Lt. Dan stationed himself in the alley behind the bank. The others quietly scaled the carpeted staircase to the landing, casually opened the hardwood door, walked in and closed it behind them.

Taylor, startled, looked at them, but quickly regained his composure. "Sirs, it is quite late. We are closed to business for the day," he said courteously, but perplexed.

"Mr. Taylor, I presume?" said Mullen.

"You are correct, sir. To whom do I have the pleasure?" he said, standing up, his hand extended for a handshake, looking from left to right at the other men.

"Mullen, Christian Mullen," answered the first man, as he took the outstretched hand, quickly pulled forward and twisted the arm so much that Taylor went down on his knees.

"What the …!" screamed Taylor in pain, but before he could get another word out, a second man kicked him in the face, while Jack muzzled him with a kerchief and bound his hands and feet.

"Jack! Clean out the safe and kick out those wooden partitions; it's coming with us," directed Mullen. Jack nodded.

"What do you mean?" asked the lieutenant. "We're leavin' all that cash here?!!"

"We aren't here to rob banks, lieutenant. That money belongs to someone else!" muttered Mullen. "Now, boys, let's drag that safe and this badass banker to the back."

Lt. Dan was waiting for them on a buckboard, with a sturdy team of horses in the back alley, ready to accept the large, metal safe.

There was a shudder behind the curtain. Jack pulled it back swiftly and muffled a gasp.

She was a servant. Taylor's servant. Abandoned by her parents, her subsistence, if not her very life, depended upon Taylor's largesse and whim. About nine years of age, wraith-thin, she had long, dark braids and a pallor that defied life itself. Her light-colored eyes were vacant. Her simple dress was tolerable, though she was shoeless.

Mullen looked at Taylor with contempt.

"Jack," he said softly, "the boys and I can take it from here. You take the girl to my Aunt's place. Then come meet us at North Dock."

"Yes, sir," Jack said as he gently took the little girl's hand and led her away. She moved, soullessly and silently, with detached resignation.

"It'll be alright," Jack whispered to her.

"No!" Her voice was suddenly at once both low and anxious as she jerked her hand away. "Miz Maura will beat me!"

Mullen turned suddenly, rage filling his chest and face before he was able to calm himself. He walked slowly to the little girl, and put his hand gently on her head.

"Don't you worry, I'll talk to Miz Maura and make everything all right. Now you go on with Jack, and he will take you to Aunty, who will feed you and give you a real bed. Go on now, sweetie, go." Mullen turned to Jack and nodded.

Jack and the girl departed.

⁓

The safe was exceedingly heavy, but with wedges and planks for levers, they managed to get it down the stairs and onto the buckboard. They untied Taylor's hands and feet, but left him gagged. His eyes were wild and he screamed as much as he could, through the kerchief in his mouth. The panic in his eyes increased as the men shoved him into the safe.

"Humanity is the cheapest thing you can sell, fellas," Mullen said to his partners. "He sold his humanity for profit by taking advantage of vulnerable old ladies and the lives of young girls." Looking into the safe at Taylor, he shook his head slowly from side to side.

Taylor struggled all the more to get away, sliding his hand into the frame, but with a final shove from the lieutenant and then the safe door slamming shut, all was quiet. Only four amputated fingers were stuck on the door frame, the blood spatter slowly edding downward. Lt. Dan kicked the digits loose to the ground below, where a small, half-starved feral cat awaited. Out of nowhere, it was joined by a clowder of felines, who commenced to make short work of the severed fingers.

The smallest kitten stuck like a briar to his trouser leg. Mullen scooped it up and tucked it into his jacket pocket. "Let's roll." He looked around, and felt eyes upon him. The shadow of a top hat tipped towards him. In turn, he gave a bemused wink and tipped his chin into the darkness.

Quickly, the safe was covered with a tarp, the reins slapped lightly on the horses' backs to urge them on, their hot breath shooting streams of steam into the chilly night. A loaded buckboard was not an unusual sight in the city at any time of day or night; it was only 15 minutes to the end of the longest pier in the bay. Offices lining the North Dock were dark and empty. The whole process, accosting Taylor and dispensing with him, took only two hours into the dark of the night.

With a half-moon in the sky and one lantern, there was enough light to see by as they again wedged the safe off the buckboard and into the drink. It sank fast, the safe's bank validating logo blurring into the murky moonlit bay.

~

Twenty minutes later, Mullen approached his Aunt's darkened home, which she now used as a domiciliary for orphans. In the silvery moonlight, he could make out the makeshift scooters, pretend roadways for play wagons, and mounded dirt hills with twigs for trees that were molded by little hands. He smiled as he thought to himself, *the Wolf Pack*. The street children she took in made up their own gang. They were everywhere, watching, listening, reporting. Mullen tapped on the front door.

He made out the approach of candlelight through the curtained windows, and a smaller version of candle light that trailed quickly behind, as if fleeing the pursuing darkness.

"What on earth are you doing out at this time of night, son?! Get yourself in here and warm up, dear." A small boy stared out from behind Aunty's nightgown.

"I can't stay, Aunty, I just wanted to drop this off for the kid. She's going to need something to hang onto for a while," answered Mullen, pulling a tiny black and-white kitten from his jacket pocket.

"Oh, my goodness! How precious! Look how small! Oh Christian, she'll just love it! The poor child's sleeping now," she whispered to Mullen, "She's exhausted and frightened, but settled down quickly once I gave her some food and warm clothes." Aunty held the kitten gently, kissing the top of its head. "I reckon this little creature could use some food and a warm bed as well. Don't you worry none, I'll take good care of both of them."

"Help her be a child again, Aunty."

"I'll do my best. You get on home, son. This dampness will seep right into your bones."

"Yes, Ma'am." Mullen kissed his aunt's forehead, turned and departed into the cool, foggy night.

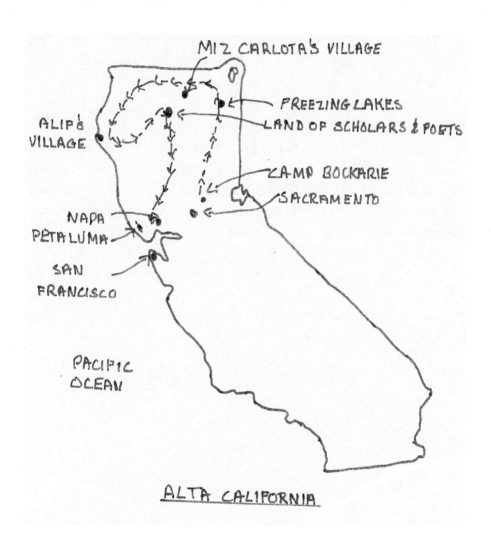

MIZ CARLOTA'S VILLAGE

FREEZING LAKES

LAND OF SCHOLARS & POETS

ALIPÁS VILLAGE

CAMP BOCKARIE

SACRAMENTO

NAPA
PETALUMA

SAN
FRANCISCO

PACIFIC
OCEAN

ALTA CALIFORNIA

37

The Companions 1845, Part 2

We derive our inspiration, not from heaven or from an unseen world, but directly from life. –Mustafa Kamâl Atatürk

The Companions separated from time to time, going home in smaller groups, in pairs, or alone. Future meet-up times and places were agreed upon. Ansa and Henson traveled inland to the Sacramento River region and met with the Nisenan and Miwok peoples. These Natives had been accommodating to white incursions in the past, and had even established strong trade relationships; however, the epidemic of 1833 decimated their population, making it difficult to induce them to participate in discussions. Nevertheless, some of the groups eventually sat down together.

"We cannot blame them for their reticence," said Ansa to Henson. "Even I would be hesitant to listen to such a proposition, about joining with other tribes and former invaders to form our own nation. Would I trust strangers with my freedom and believe they would allow me to participate in decisions? I do not know."

"It's a lot to ask, Ansa," replied Henson. "At least for now, we're only asking that they consider this, and come to meetings to discuss it. We need their ideas and decisions to make it work. It's like a congressional convention."

"Ha! Well, that it is, Jonny!" laughed Ansa. "Our trips are just the beginning of the inquiries. We have no authority whatsoever to make anything happen. I do not know how this will end, but what an adventure!"

Jonny smiled, but remained silent. Ansa stared a moment before moving closer. Forehead to forehead, eyes to eyes, they looked deeply into each other's souls and made a silent life pact.

Backing away, they both looked into the fire before Ansa spoke. "We are of like minds, I see."

Changing back to the original topic, Jonny nodded in agreement and added, "Ah, yes. We'll need to grow our authority. You know, Ansa, we might consider more traveling groups, somewhat as missionaries; missionaries for a new nation. Don't you think?!"

Ansa laughed again, and looked at Jonny thoughtfully. "That just might be a good idea!" he said as he clapped Henson on the back and with a long, wistful, breath said, "Indeed!"

~

They had been menaced before, but this menace seemingly worked alone. One by one, families awoke to find their livestock poisoned and dying, in the barns or on the range. One by one, a settler far in the pasture was shot dead outright. No message was left, nor was there a clue to be found. Who had this lethal ax to grind?

One evening, the Companions made camp, sat around a fire, continuing to discuss their planned speeches and strategies in sharing information with their audiences.

"Listen, listen, *listen!*" offered one of the Natives of the traveling group. "Yes, you have a message, but more importantly, you need to *listen* to *their* words; their concerns, responses, ideas. That is where you will get direction, and a sense of what is needed to make this all work. They are worried for their safety. Do you not hear it?"

Ansa looked at the Native and paused for a moment before he responded, "Those are wise words, my brother. The answers will be spoken to us by our audience. Already we heard from them that when one of us is threatened, we all are. When one is wrongly accused, we all are. We need to speak to the peoples to join together to form a strong nation, undivided by small differences, rather, united by our similarities. They can help us know these similarities."

"What if the differences are too much, like religion?" asked one of the Companions.

"Religion is threats and divisiveness, while spirituality is personal. The primary difference between the two is that religion has secrets in their decisions and intentions," answered Ansa.

The traveler gave a sideways glance. "I think I understand what you mean, but if you are not careful about how you say it, you might cause many to lose that reasoning and not really hear you, Ansa. Remember what happened within our own group a while back. Yes, again we must focus on the similarity of beliefs. Many will be surprised and perhaps more amenable to listening. No one ever wins an emotional argument simply by being right."

Ansa nodded, appearing deep in thought, "Yes, yes. You are absolutely correct, my friend."

Henson stared into the fire intently before speaking, "A religion for which one has suffered is all the more precious to him. Everyone has what they think is their own right way. We must tread carefully, and we must be tolerant."

The Native spoke up again, "*We* are the ones who must listen! I'll say it again! Yes, yes, you are correct about that religion thing, Ansa, but people cannot focus on philosophy or grand schemes if they do not feel safe. Fear is a tool used by enemies within and outside. We cannot ignore this."

The men stared at the Native. "He is right," said Lokni. We need clear steps to burnish our offer of protection. We cannot just say we will do something without having a plan. We need brass tacks, as you say. Perhaps we need to speak to Karmo some more?"

～

Henson and Ansa left the group for a series of meetings in San Francisco. Later, returning to the North Bay area, the two rejoined the Companions. They had plans to visit persons in particular. They met with the Tulkays and Ulucas, and native Napa Bands, as well as land grantees of substantial influence, such as Dr. Edward Bale, who became a Mexican citizen and had married the niece of Mariano Vallejo, Marie Soberanes. They stayed the night with Dr. Bale, who regaled them with his plans to build a grist mill and plant a vineyard in a most bucolic valley.[76] The evening was a pleasant respite from their otherwise arduous travels. The Bales' hospitality was not only generous, but also warm and elegant.

Departing the next morning, not far away they came upon a rancher from Illinois, William Brown Ide. He had been talking to other ranchers in the area about separation, a revolt against Mexico, he said. Listening to the Companions, he determined it wiser to hold off and see what developed.[77]

Farther south, they needed to meet with the formidable Cayetano Juarez, loyal soldier to General Vallejo, who was awarded an 8,865-acre land grant called Rancho Tulucay in 1841.[78] Approaching Juarez was especially precarious as he was a steadfast citizen of Mexico. Surprisingly, he later attended some of the consensus meetings, offering sound strategies and economic considerations for a new nation, thanks to his working relationship with Karmo and, to some degree, Christian Mullen.

At the urging of Karmo, Light and Ansa, Jonny Henson visited Señor Juarez at his Napa ranch to discuss finance. The group felt they needed both a long time, astute citizen to discuss further dissemination of the gold and its main security.

"Incredible! Incredible! Do not think I will not send some of my own men to search for this gold, my friend."

"Don Cayetano, please tread lightly for just a while longer. We already feel we're doing an injustice to the populace at large by only sharing this information with certain people. We select carefully to try to get the best consult, to handle this gift so it can do the most good and not have the deluge of fortune-seekers and all the malice and greed that brings," asserted Henson.

Juarez eyed Henson, became reflective, then laughed. "Yes, of course! Only certain people will know ... for the greater good. That is how it starts, my friend. That road is a slippery one; better to get on with it quickly. What do you have in mind to secure this fortune? Banks?"

"Well, yes. There are two in Sacramento now and two in San Francisco. We mean to use all of them," answered the chagrined Henson.

"Ah, yes, I heard about that one San Francisco bank. What was it? Wilson and so forth? One of the partners disappeared, eh?"

"Yes, but the banks are all the more defended since the disappearance of Taylor from the Wilson, Taylor and Franks bank. I suppose it's just the WF bank now. Wilson and Franks are two of the most honest men I know to take care of other people's money."

Don Cayetano looked at Henson a bit warily, "So what happened to Taylor? Did he run away with people's money?"

"Well, that's just a strange story. A while back, he just up and disappeared. Left all kinds of cash on his desk and vanished, never seen or heard from again. The funny thing was that his office bank safe was gone as well."

"That is strange, indeed, especially leaving cash behind," responded a suspicious Don Cayetano. "These two other bankers, though, can they be trusted?"

"Absolutely; it was Taylor who was questionable almost from the start, according to the partners," stated Henson.

"Well, yes. One must wonder about the judgment of the choosers, and the ethics of those they chose to do business with," answered the wary Don Cayetano Juarez. "Come closer, I have some ideas."

～

Near the village of Petaluma, north of San Francisco, a former American, now a grantee, was not so accommodating towards the Companions. He resisted, with the stubbornness of an old man who longed for days gone by, when men (white men, mind you), and only white men, had the status and prerogative to determine how others in his family and community would live, and even whom they would love. Although his land came from the Mexican government, he looked down upon her original citizens.

"*I* am here now!" yelled the man. "*I* am the owner and lord of this here land, as it was meant to be, and you, sirs, are but rabble rousers looking to provoke honest Christian folk to overtake a government?! You and your kind will take it away from *me*, I suppose?!"

"Sir," beseeched Henson, "we are here to gather information and share ideas. You are making so many assumptions. Is this how you frame your questions?"

"I'll not be directed as to the formation of my thoughts, sir!" said the man, as his face flushed and his hands gripped his rifle tightly. The landowner eyed Ansa. He was suspicious of black men, though he had never met one personally. He had his own ideas, and facts would not dissuade him.

Later that evening, "I tried to understand him, but his words seemed to unravel beyond the edge of logic. Perhaps I was unfocused, or is this how some people think and speak? Do they intentionally make you think they are wise and you are not? Do they aim to use these obscurities to advantage?" asked Johnny Henson of the group.

"Both!" answered Lokni and Ansa in unison.

"Yes, some people are born bamboozlers, and they know it. They get what they want by confounding people with fancy words or words juxtaposed to each other. People get confused and become too embarrassed to ask for clarification, setting them up for a swindle, betrayal or just to lose an argument. Such behavior is of no value to us, other than to be wary. For our part, we must be clear with our words, lest we undermine trust in the new government," explained Ansa.

"You are not going to change their minds, you know that," said Lokni.

"Perhaps not, Lokni," replied Ansa. However, these are the real people in our world. Because you and I do not agree or understand their thinking does not make their beliefs any less real and dear to them. But nothing can move forward until we lay all the cards on the table and expose our hand."

The group turned east at the bay, traded their wagon for pack mules, and ferried to some small trader camps. At one camp, the Natives were more amenable to settlers coming to their lands. The Companions listened intently and heard the recurring story, that of settlers and invaders.

"Yes, settlers who come to farm and care for the land, and respect those who were here before them should be welcomed. We are warning you about armed invaders. Those who want to take your land, subjugate or exterminate you. This is happening elsewhere, as the invaders expand their borders. They come from a land of rebels and visionaries who will carve their own destiny. They pursue their own happiness. Too bad it runs roughshod over yours," explained Lokni about the invaders.

Closer to the city, they came across a small white settlement with strong ties to their religious sect. As agreed earlier by the Companions. Henson would answer challenges from the whites when it seemed appropriate.

"What of the heathens?" asked one of them.

"Heathens? What is it about you that makes you better?" asked the weary Henson.

The man reddened, clearly perplexed by being called out, then angrily said, "Well, we just are! We dress better, we're Christian, we're white .... Alright, maybe your boys there are exceptions," his eyes were steady on Ansa and Lokni, "but most coloreds and Natives are just hapless beings who need the white man to live right."

"Is that so? Live right, you say? Clothes, religion, color? That's what makes you better than a man who believes in providing for his family, abiding by the laws of his tribe and honoring nature?" responded Henson.

"Oh! You know what I mean, Henson! They're, they're just not like us!" the man sputtered.

Ansa started seething and started to speak when Jonny interjected.

"You're right, sir, they may not be. As we are not like them. So let's get to know them," offered Henson as he thought to himself, *If one can't see that their own culture has its own emotions, interests and beliefs, then how can they begin to understand another?*

〜

It was time again for the Companions to take a break and go back to their lives and families for a few months. Several of them went to San Francisco or Bockarie. Lokni planned to go to his parents' summer home near the coast, across the Bay. If Marie-Therese got his message, she would be waiting for him there alone; the children would be with the Benoîts.

The skies were that clear cerulean blue Lokni loved to get lost in. "So many stories hidden in the passing clouds," he said aloud. Coming over the rise, he saw a small plume of white smoke emanating from the chimney, and smiled. *She is here*, he said to himself. Looking forward to embracing his wife and enjoying a home-cooked meal, he nudged his horse to gallop across the tall grasses, rhythmically moving to the wind's serenade, then along the narrow trail to their home. The first rains in a while had stopped, and the smell of damp earth pleased him. Home!

She must have a surprise for me, or she would be waiting outside when she saw me coming, he thought as he rode up to the hitching post. Entering, he saw her across the room, standing by the stove with a look of fear on her bruised face. Her eyes darted to a place behind him.

He turned, "You?!" he exclaimed, and almost the same instant was hit on the side of his head with a piece of firewood.

Coming to, he found himself tied to a chair, bleeding from a beating while he was unconscious. Groggy and in pain, Lokni looked at the intruder through swollen eyes. "But why?" he said. "What do you want?"

"What do I want?!" shouted the intruder. "What do I want?! You and your traveler buddies think you can take over *our* land? Our God-given manifest destiny?! Do you think I am going to just let you Injuns and foreigners decide you're going to keep this land for yourself? You all have another thing coming if you think *that* is ever going to happen. Ha!"

Lokni struggled frantically to overcome a concussed mind.

"I was never one of you. I only traveled with you to see what you were up to. Me and my friends will destroy your reach. You will be blamed for all the mayhem on your route. Did it not all occur about the time you came around? I have my own traveling group to undermine yours. Just wait and see!" The man turned towards Marie-Therese and flashed a big, gap-toothed smile. "Now, I think it's time for me to have a little dinner with the missus here," he said aloud before refocusing on Lokni. "Maybe even a little fun time, too," he winked, as Lokni blanched and struggled at his bindings.

"You touch her, and I will burn the world to make you pay!" screamed Lokni.

"Heh, heh, heh, you make me laugh, Injun!" The intruder sat down at the table, his gun trained on Marie-Therese, as she served him a bowl of stew. "Now go sit over there by your man, where I can watch the both of you."

Marie-Therese said nothing and walked quietly towards Lokni. Her back to the intruder, she puckered up her lips, and her cheeks gave the faintest hint of a smile forming, before she sat down. Lokni was puzzled, but knew his wife well enough not to let on that something was happening. His head pounding, his eyes remained steady.

The intruder ate heartily, licking his lips and wiping the excess off with his sleeve. "Mmmmm, that's mighty tasty. Too bad you're missin' out on this, Lokni boy."

In only a few more moments, the intruder bent over the table, cramping up. His stomach lurched and his bowels felt on fire. "You, you poisoned me?!" he sputtered at Marie-Therese. He dropped the gun as he grabbed his belly.

Marie-Therese got up, grabbed the gun and went to Lokni. Looking back at the intruder, she spoke quietly, "You will die in about six minutes."

Lokni looked at her in shock. "No, Tess, you are not a killer! You are a doctor! You help people! Untie me now and give me that gun!"

"I am sorry my love. Just wait a few more moments," she said apologetically.

The intruder pleaded, "You can't do this!"

Marie-Therese paused long and thoughtfully before answering in a breathy mock regret, "You are right. I cannot! She slowly dragged a chair across the wooden floor and sat across from the intruder. She folded her hands primly on her lap and leaned towards him. "Yes, you are dying. But I have the cure," she said, then holding up a small brown, glass bottle of pills between her thumb and index finger. She shook it up and down a couple times, allowing the pills to rattle.

He lurched forward trying to grab it from her, failing as she pulled it back from him. "Give it to me! Give it to me, woman!" Another wave of cramping overcame him, forcing him to double over. "You! You!" his grunt squeezed from low in the body.

She remained patient. "Yes, I will give them to you, I want you to do me a favor, though," answered Marie-Therese. "Tell me with which of the Companions you are working. Who are the leaders?"

The man was weakening; breathing hard, sweating profusely and looking pale. "Please!" he said.

"I am waiting, she whispered," again, slowly shaking a bottle of pills in front of him.

"Tess!" said Lokni urgently, struggling with his bindings. "Help him, Tess, help him! He is a vile human being, vile! But he is a human being!"

Marie-Therese, looked at her husband understandingly and nodded, "Patience, dear."

The man said in a quiet, croaky voice, "Alright, alright." He leaned over and mumbled to her.

Marie-Therese sat back, herself pale. "You are lying!"

"No, no. Think about it," the man gasped in pain.

"Here!" Marie-Therse said as she slammed the bottle of pills down upon the table. "The antidote is here! Take it now while you have a chance!"

Lokni looked at her in relief and amazement. "Help him, Tess! Untie me now!"

Marie-Therese untied her husband and he sprung to his feet.

The intruder grabbed the bottle, emptied the pills into his mouth and downed them with a ladle of water.

"More, and quickly!" hollered Marie-Therese.

The man took the rest of the pills and more water. He started choking, gasping for breath. Sweat poured off his face, his tongue swelled up as his eyes grew big and red. Looking at her, he could not speak. "Die!" screamed Marie-Therese.

Marie-Therese grabbed Lokni by the arm as he moved towards the intruder and looked at him. "You are right, my love, I could not kill him …. myself."

"What is happening, Tess? What have you done!" asked the astonished Lokni, as he rubbed his wrists, bending over to look at the intruder.

"There was only a strong purgative in his stew. He poisoned himself with the pills," she answered quietly.

The man fell out of his chair onto the floor with a loud thud. His wide and accusing eyes drilled into Marie-Therese' face.

Then, and only then, did the weight of the event hit her. A quick sucking of air, followed by a quick gasping, forced her back into the seat of the chair. "He was going to kill us both, Lokni, and we both know it," she stammered.

Lokni took her into his arms and held her close. "It is over now, it is over. It will be alright."

"It will *not* be all right," she whispered before looking into his face. "There are others. Didn't you hear him? Others! And we know some of them! Do you think he told the truth?"

"I do not know. I do not want to believe it. Who would?" he said, looking out the window at the waving grasses, then to the body on the floor. "Let me take you home. I will come back and deal with this mess somehow."

38

Mullen at the Presidio, late 1845

The answer, my friend, is blowin' in the wind. –Bob Dylan

Karl Schwartz nearly fell on his face leaving the Pink Palace late one evening. He spied Jack and the dog Fella and smiled fiendishly. "Well, well, well, look who's here! If it ain't that meddling Injun lover? Git over here, boy! I got somethin' for ya."

"I got nothin' to say to you, Schwartz. You're drunk, and you stink too!" answered Jack, just wanting to avoid the creature all together. Fella growled as Schwartz approached.

"Better stay back, Schwartz, or ... "

"Or what? Or what? Ya gonna sic your mangy hound on me? Such a man! Ha!"

"Stay, Fella, stay," ordered Jack.

Schwartz came closer and with his index finger poked Jack in the chest. "Jist what are you gonna do about *this*?" he said, trying to provoke him.

"I'm telling you, back off, Schwartz. Just back off!" yelled Jack. Fella was getting fidgety.

With that, Schwartz made a wild swing at Jack, but missed. Nearly falling to the ground, Jack reflexively reached out to grab his arm to stop the fall. Schwartz came back with another swing, pulling both men off-balance and onto the ground, where they wrestled, kicking up dust and letting the spit and snot fly, until bystanders—and Fella—pounced on the pair and broke them up.

"It ain't over, boy!" slurred Schwartz, pointing a shaking finger at Jack.

"Anytime, Schwartz, anytime ...." Jack picked up his hat from the ground and left, followed by Fella.

∼

The next evening, Schwartz met up with his boss, Adam Kreisler, at the Pink Palace. Kreisler was wanted for murder, bank robbery and horse thievery. He was expanding his territory and looked at Mullen's range with a hungry eye. Besides Mullen, he had a special dislike for this kid, Jack, who seemed to be everywhere, thwarting Kreisler's ambition. Shoot-outs occurred here and there, but nothing could budge the loyalty of Mullen's men, or the ferocity of their fighting. Another tactic had to be implemented. Kreisler finally found one.

Mumbling to himself, he slapped the table, knocking over a tumbler of whiskey. "What the ...?!" hollered Schwartz.

"Why didn't I think of this earlier? The easiest way! But it will take a bit of planning," mused Kreisler, ignoring Schwartz's oath of profanity. He crooked his finger, signaling Schwartz to come closer, put their heads together and commenced outlining a plan. "We'll get Mullen, and deal with the kid later."

Listening to Kreisler's plan, Schwartz grunted and whispered, "How is he going to get fingered for that murder? We took out that guy ourselves. No witnesses."

"No witnesses, you say?" snorted Kreisler. "There are indeed witnesses, Schwartzy ... I'd say we can find at least three, if not of stellar reputations, at least tolerable."

Schwartz shook his head in puzzlement. "How so, Boss?" he asked.

"The oldest trick in the book! You feed the birds, and they sing for you," laughed Kreisler as he pounded Schwartz on the back, twice.

∼

The Mullen crew rode up to the abandoned farmhouse, which was buried in an overgrowth of wild berry brambles. It was situated on a small knoll amongst native live oaks, hidden from the horse path below. To this hideout, they would never bring rivals, enemies for dispatch or even friends, for all crews needed one place that was absolutely sac-rosanct. The crew was used to traveling separately before heading to the hideout. Mullen got there early, but he had been followed. One of Kreisler's men had tipped off the local Deputy. A large posse of volunteers soon encircled the old house. In short, Mullen was trapped. Lies were told, witnesses bought, and there was to be no appeal. Captured in a military jurisdiction, Mullen would have the honor of being shot by a firing squad rather than face death by hanging.

～

San Francisco: The Presidio's garrison Captain and Mullen spent a number of evenings smoking cigars, playing chess and drinking—a clear departure from protocol; however, Mullen had the whiskey and cigars, and the Captain had the inclination. "I am going to miss you around here, Señor Mullen. I am stuck here, executing people, and I do not get the chance to enjoy a decent social life," he said, waving a cigar.

"Ha! Likewise, Captain," guffawed Mullen. "I guess we'll meet on the other side someday."

"It will be an honor," the Captain answered, with the slightest bow of his head. "Now, back to your cell. Oh, do you have family, anyone who will claim your body?"

"Compost, Captain! Compost!"

In the early evening before the condemned was to meet his Maker, he and another prisoner spoke about their families, their dreams, their fates. The cellmate was a giant of man. His form took up the whole door frame. Dead eyes, resigned to fate, yet angry, he told Mullen his story. Back east, a gang of robbers accosted his brother on the way to town. In short, they butchered him. "It was months before I found out. My brother's child died of starvation and his wife died of mortification in a brothel. The leader of the gang came out here. Big mistake. I found his hideout and watched until he was alone. I'd brought only an ax, and cornered him. He could offer no defense, save for raising his arm to hide his head. Little help that was, ha! I yelled at him, 'I've been dreaming of this day. You took away my only family!' I dragged that ax on the ground so he could see it coming. One swing was enough, but I couldn't stop myself. Hmmmph, his head exploded like a melon! But who do they get for murder? Me! Me!" He let out one big sigh, "Damn it all, anyway! I should be out there enjoying the sunshine."

Mullen stuck out his bottom lip and shook his head as he breathed out through his nose, "Sorry, buddy, you got a raw deal. But that's prison for you. Now you're in here, but your mind is out there," mused Mullen as he walked towards the barred window to watch large, puffy clouds pass by in the darkening sky. He turned and smiled at his hapless comrade. "We both knew this day would come, buddy," he added, "So let's make the most of it! How about a game of cards? Hey?"

His cellmate looked at Mullen warily and sneered, "Great! I get to spend my last hours with a philosopher! Ya just have to be an ass to the end, don'tcha? They'll bury us in a nothin' grave with no marker. Ya know that, right?!"

"Yeah, I know. Everyone lives to die, my friend. Which grave doesn't matter to the one in it."

As the hours went by, Mullen quieted down, his bravado morphing into contemplation. The last night was long, with intrusive thoughts. Several men were to be executed the next morning. He wondered if he was to be the first or the last. He wondered if he would face the rising sun, or if his back would be to it. Would he hear birds one last time? Instead of fear, he felt a strange curiosity as to whether he would be able to die as he foresaw.

The rosy dawn gave way to a golden sunrise before dissipating into the morning sky. The air was cool and fresh with the hope of a new day. The report of the firing squads broke the stony silence throughout the morning. No one in the cell block spoke; quiet, until the sound of jingling keys and thick boots shuffling on the compacted dirt floor came closer; followed by the scraping metal of the cell door revealed one last visitor.

Lt. Dan's skills in aiding his boss behind the scenes were unknown to many. Such was this last task for Mullen. Dressed as a monk, Lt. Dan had approached the garrison, looked back at the mule on which he had ridden, then down at his robe, and rolled his eyes, "The things I do!" he mused, then turned to knock on the heavy garrison door. He was there to offer comfort to the condemned.

In the cell, Mullen heard his visitor enter. His back to him, he stated his welcome, "Everything good in this life is a crime for me. A new life, a new love, a new land. Remembering your past is the biggest crime of all." He turned to his visitor and smiled broadly. "Come in, padre! Welcome to my humble abode!"

Lt. Dan looked at his friend, annoyed by the mocking words. He nodded and remained silent, looking around before whispering, "That bastard Kreisler framed you, Boss. It just ain't right!"

Looking out the small barred window into the morning sky again, Mullen mused, "Standing tall while knowing all my past wrongs has become unbearable, Brother Daniel. No, I didn't kill the guy they got me for, but I have enough others under my belt." Turning back to Lt. Dan, "We sure had *some* days and not a few drunken nights, huh? But it's alright. Let me go out my own way …. with a bang! Besides, you and the boys will take care of the two of them, right?"

"You bet we will, Boss!" spat out Lt. Dan. "Before the sun sets tomorrow!"

"Wish I could see their faces! So, somewhere under all those robes, you brought my cigars, hey?" asked Mullen with a smile.

"Yeah, Boss. The special order," replied Lt. Dan as he passed the package to Mullen, who simply tucked the cigars into his vest.

"Good job, buddy. I appreciate it! Ha! This will be quite a sendoff! You stand way back from the action, ya hear? Those lumpy legs of yours don't move as fast as they used to!" exclaimed Mullen as he laughed and clapped Lt. Dan on the back.

It was time. Guards took Mullen out of his cell and escorted him to his position before taking their places.

Mullen stood in front of the wall, facing the squad of soldiers who would execute him. Declining a blindfold, he spit out his cigar, "These damn things will kill me some day!" and motioned to the Captain to come close.

The Captain asked, "Do you have any last words?"

"I do have a request, if you would be so kind to oblige me, sir," replied Mullen.

Humoring him, the Captain bent his head forward as Mullen whispered.

"Ha! That's rich! And for you my friend, I will grant it!" cackled the Captain.

The Captain walked away, taking his place at the side of the firing squad, and nodded at them, with an ever-so-graceful outward wave of his arm towards Mullen.

Mullen squared his shoulders and shouted, "Men, at the ready!"

The squad looked towards their Captain questioningly. The Captain only smiled, and made the slightest nod to them again.

The squad snapped into the ready position.

"Center mass, boys! Aim!" ordered Mullen. He paused, then ordered;

"Fire! Ha, ha, ha …."

The crack of eight rifles sounded in synchrony, followed by an explosion, deafening to all in the surrounding area. The earth rumbled. A whirl of black smoke streamed straight upwards into the sky, followed by a cloud of dust fifteen feet wide, emanating from above. Lt. Dan's package was filled with black powder. The resulting blast shook the barracks. Little was left of Mullen, but his boots. A dusty, singed, broad-brimmed beaver hat wafted in the smoky gusts.

"Damn!" wailed Lt. Dan, as he took in the spectacle.

～

Still crapulous from the night before and on tilt, Lt. Dan entered the Pink Palace in the early morning, and shot two dead, without words or fanfare. By afternoon, a metallic odor of ooze prevailed. He looked at the corpses of Miz Maura and Kreisler with curiosity, asking himself what she ever saw in the guy. Placing his hand at Kreisler's crotch, he squeezed slightly. Looking up, poking out his lower lip, he grunted and turned his head to the side. "Meyh, not bad."

The bodies lay still and silent in the muck. Two men were huffing and puffing, breathing heavily as they dug separate graves, with Lt.

Dan on look-out. The acrid stench of the town's central waste depository wafted downwind to where they labored in the sticky earth.

One of the men, wearing a red cap, was muttering to himself.

"You there, Red Cap!" growled Lt. Dan, "What's got your goat?"

"Whaddya talkin about a goat? Nuthin's got my goat! My goat ain't got!" exclaimed Red Cap.

"Lieutenant, we wanna know why we don't jist dig one hole for the two of 'em, and cover 'em up? It'd be much easier," offered the other man.

Lt. Dan, highly annoyed, looked at the men and drew a deep sigh before answering, "Boss was married to her for eight years, and I'm sure he wouldn't want to give her the satisfaction of having another man atop her for eternity!"

"Hmmpf! She was prob'ly the one on top," muttered Red Cap.

"Show a little respect! They're dead now!" hollered Lt. Dan.

"Yeah, they're dead. Don'tcha think I know dead?"

The three men pulled off their hats for a moment, bent their heads. "Amen. Let's git!"

39

Madeleine and Mrs. Marshall 1846

She's taking her shot.
variation of lyric from the musical "Hamilton." –Lin Manuel Miranda

The representatives were coming in from the tribes, grantees and settlers within the proposed new nation. Madeleine was very anxious, as were others. *No one here has ever been faced with creating a government, and certainly not with the input of so many.* Word came in from as far away as the northern borders, and from the east, from the Sierra Nevada Mountains and foothills.

Afternoon at the Benoît home, Madeleine felt both excited and tired, and couldn't help but exclaim her wonderment and support for creating a new nation, for men and women alike!

"It's just unseemly, Madame Madeleine," scowled the prickly Mrs. Marshall. "Women in government, and taking up arms! It's just not the natural order of things! Women have their hands full taking care of their husbands and families!"

"No! Women need to be able to care for themselves first, in order to care for their husbands and families, and that includes employment and participation in the world in which they live," snapped Madeleine uncharacteristically. "What of us who have no husbands? Are we to sit around, waiting for someone to pity us and throw us crumbs, or exploit us for profit?" Madeleine paused and closed her eyes, then looked over at the stunned Mrs. Marshall to apologize.

"Leah, you look as if the earth underneath your feet has crumbled," said the remorseful Madeleine. "But oh, you would not understand what it is like to really lose your husband."

Mrs. Marshall, having had just about enough husband talk, turned livid. In a rage, she exclaimed, "At least you know where your husband spends his time, Madame! In a coffin, six feet under, the lid hammered tight with four dozen three-inch nails!"

But as soon as those words came out, Leah's eyes grew large, she covered her mouth with her hand, and both women crumpled into a jumble of fabric and tears onto the wooden floor.

"Oh, Madame! I'm so sorry. You know I didn't mean it! It's only that my heart hurts, as yours, but for different reasons. We were both abandoned, and we are both ashamed for it."

"Yes, yes, Leah, I know you did not mean that. And I did not mean to dismiss your pain. You are so correct. Only I never thought of it that way until I heard those words. Please accept my apology. We've been friends for too long to let anything splinter us apart like this. But we need to think about our children's future. What of Jack? What of my daughters, or that little one taken in by Aunty Mullen?"

Mrs. Marshall took a deep breath, "I'll make us a nice cup of tea, Madame. Come, you sit right here," urged Leah, helping the younger woman get up from the floor to the kitchen table.

"At least let me set the table, Leah. I am so very sorry."

～

It was still early in the evening and light out when Madeleine walked into her back garden to be alone. She postioned herself comfortably against the cushions on her garden bench and breathed deeply, holding her chest against the pounding within. She stared into the faces of the columbine flowers, their vivid petals and gently arching stamens barely moving in the breeze, yet mesmerizing the longer one pondered the kaleidoscope of shapes and translucent hues. The colors enveloped her in a soft, gently swirling vortex; a lightness of being, an embrace that had the sensation of pulling her body slowly downward into a supine position and cradling it benevolently. She could not be certain that she really heard it: so faint, so weak, the last tiny echo of a call made long ago.

Bijou? Where are you, ma petite? I wanted to see as you saw, observe the stars as you, believe as you, so that I will always be with you. But I did not take the chance. Her eyes moved heavily to the orb spider nearby, sitting amidst its elaborate web of gossamer silk. *Have I gone mad, little spider?* She looked at the spider in the shadow of the ferns, its tiny eyes like jewels, reflecting back with an intensity of understanding. A mocking-bird kept up its choral backdrop, running through the repertoire of bird songs; punishment for its ancestors' neglect.[79]

Madeleine was conscious of the sun's warmth on her cheek, of the subtle rustle of life under the decaying leaves, this sweet and pungent, musty and dank spot on earth. A whole little world was here, and she was falling deeper and deeper into it.

A fickle consciousness abandoned her for an interval. She came to, with tears in her eyes and such an ache in her heart that even breathing was an effort. Her head was pounding. As her consciousness moved in and out of various worlds, she sensed no fear, only wonderment. Scraps of memories flew out from the crevices in which they had been secluded. Jean was there, her parents …. She felt dissipation of spirit, a moment of splendid weightlessness and drifting. A few moments more, and she closed her eyes … forever.

Ansa stood there, frozen upon finding her. From his stupor, screams from somewhere deep in the universe drew his attention back to reality. "Oh, my dear Madame!" he cried.

40

Sacramento 1846-1847

Give me six hours to chop down a tree, and I will spend the first four sharpening the axe. –Abraham Lincoln

There were the philosophers, the business people, the traders, the farmers, the artists and the poets. They came from all reaches of the territory; representatives selected by townships, tribal councils and villages. Karmo released most of his land back to the people to develop their own local governments. He allowed himself his camp and his home, for that was all he needed. The new country stretched from the Monterey Bay east to the mid-Sierras, but included all sides of the great blue lake called Tahoe and tribal lands south of the lake. In the north, the boundary wove in and out of Oregon Territory. Meeting after meeting hammered out laws and practices.

~

A framework was ready, with executive, judiciary and administrative functions. The constitution was based on that of the Great Law of Peace of the Iroquois Confederacy.[80] Even the United States of America had adopted and incorporated parts of this into its own Constitution. But this nation would not be modeled as a poor cousin of the United States. Boundaries were set not by arbitrary lines, rather, they took into consideration existing settlements and historic hunting grounds, both Native and non-Native, so as not to divide peoples. Where geography was amenable, it was to be used as well. The new country was named, provisionally, The United Nations of Sequoia (UNS). Universal tenets were agreed upon. These would be the bedrock of the UNS society.

And, while amendments could be promulgated, amended, or rescinded to reflect the changing times, basic rights and responsibilities were held supreme. These were hard-won, and much more was debated, compromised and agreed-to with time.

~

But to replace the provisional committees running the government, it was now time for choosing leaders, not the least of whom as the Lead Executive of the United Nations of Sequoia. Seven representative regions were identified. Both men and women were deemed eligible for running, and had been selected representatives, a condition laid down by the Natives to reflect their beliefs and culture. Coalitions were formed, each side both gaining and giving up something to strengthen their alliances. These were the groups who voted for the first executive leaders.

~

"Regardless of race, religion, tribe or land of origin, if you live within our borders, speak our languages and share our ideals, then you are us: citizens of UNS," was the guiding principle. Some people moved out of the UNS. One group declared its own sovereignty, but later joined for better protection and economics. Representatives from all regions traveled about to express the will and beliefs of their residents.

The day was warming up quickly. A makeshift stage was built, and townspeople gathered around. Representatives from all regions traveled here to speak the will and belief of their constituent residents. Miz Carlota was one of these representatives.

"*All* of our people need a future to think about, to plan, to look forward to. While we must heed the lessons of the past, we must not be tethered by it. Inclusion is what protects us all! Interdependence is what is needed for the nation's independence. Those who seek to rise up to divide us are dangerous enemies of the nation!" She was an organizer, a compromiser, and passionate about the people.

"Who are you to put yourself up to be leader? We don't know you. Are you saying there is to be no dissent in this land?!" yelled a woman from the crowd.

Miz Carlota answered straightforwardly, "I am saying there always will be dissent. I am saying there often will be compromises. That is a far cry from attempting to destabilize the government by sedition! That is the difference, Madam."

The answer was ham fisted. There was a general grumbling, which died down quickly.

Another hollered, "You say we are all equal. Are there to be no heroes? What about Karmo Bockarie? He made this country. He is our hero! Why does he not speak?!"

Perplexed by the question, Carlota explained, "No one appoints heroes. They become heroes or they do not. And yes, their sacrifices are substantial, valiant and admirable. While our Mr. Bockarie prefers to leave governing to others, he surely is to be thanked and honored. But let us also recognize the thousands of small acts of decency by ordinary people who work hard and quietly go about their daily lives."

∽

The city of Sacramento was designated the nation's capital. Walking down the dusty street along the city's namesake river, Carlota Zimi recounted with restrained pride how her peers considered her a master negotiator. But to her mind, the experience and praise fell short, because she knew her goals ran deeper than this. Administration is so much more.

She was brought back from her thoughts, as the remains of the day blanketed the streets with darkening shadows. Laughter bade her to pause and watch a group of young boys run down the way, guiding old metal wagon rims with sticks. "Could the wheels of government move this way, as circles, linked together with guidance rather than blocks of hierarchy? How, oh how, can we administer rules and regulations without preaching to get at the order and framework that people really want? And who are we leading if we have no followers? I must speak with the Companions and executives to hear more of what they gleaned. There too, must be an overlapping of humanity; a way to keep people tied to, rather than severed from their beliefs, their culture. There must be a way to tie all beliefs to a common thread that weaves a stronger, more enduring fabric that can withstand and hold strong, where others have unraveled."

A strong wind whipped up from the river. Deep in thoughts of contradiction, she walked towards the water and peered downward. As her eyes focused on the slow, steady movement of the river below, her head cleared. The dénouement was that a strong self-declaration settled into her consciousness. *"I want this! This land will be mine!"*

The clouds parted. Carlota's gaze slowly rose from the water and upward towards the sky. The tense muscles in her face relaxed, and her lips slowly curved into a smile as she squinted into the light of the setting sun and said aloud, "Ah, there is my constant!"

Town halls and other meeting places were set up for the counting. Transporting the vote tallies to the Hall of Arbitration was allotted 21 days. The tallies were locked in a safe overnight each evening, and guarded, lest there be tampering. On the 23rd day, excitement grew as the cumulative totals were written and posted on the Hall's window. No one knew for sure how many persons would vote. The meeting attendees determined that a majority would do, but other formulas might be worked out in subsequent elections. Indeed, there were still many formulas and rules to be decided, but consensus and collaboration were the hallmark of these meetings and for the new government, even if it was not clear what that might look like in the future.

It was a surprise, yet it was not. Carlota Zimi became the first Lead Executive of the United Nations of Sequoia. Jonny Henson, the reluctant but duty bound politico, was selected Prime Minister, second only to the Lead Executive. Their terms would be six years, and they were required to live in the city of government. A young man originally from Tejas, Juan Pablo Martinez, was voted Chancellor of the Treasury. Ansa Kabbah was appointed Chief of Staff, as well as advisor on the nation's spiritual matters. Karmo Bockarie declined all appointed positions in the administration, but remained a key consultant and coordinator of defense strategy and training.

This cabinet of leaders worked with representatives from the seven regions, and none worked as closely as Juan Pablo, known simply as JP. He had the task of administering the all-important gold reserves, taxes and bills. The gold fields now belonged to the state, regardless of land grant or tribal boundaries. His staff would evaluate proposals from the state and local governments for financial disposition.

The gold reserves were burgeoning. News of the discovery spread like a rolling wave over the lands and seas, as outsiders made their way to the UNS. Many who came as usurpers were quickly identified and dealt with harshly. "We should hesitate to sell land or its mineral rights to foreigners without careful vetting, lest they run roughshod over us," encouraged JP. "If they are to be farmers or will establish useful businesses, we can consider carefully their requests."

Miz Carlota, now Madam Zimi, refocused on a clear set of objectives. She began a methodical planning, and streamlined her team of executives and consultants. The UNS would be the most powerful entity on the continent, and she would be its leader. She became less inclusive in a short period of time, and instead positioned loyal followers around her. As her power became stronger, so did her rule. The seduction of her own certainty made her less willing to listen to those who disagreed with her.

She mused to her confidant, "To control the most mighty of them, you first make them doubt themselves even just a little. Make it clear you are covering for them, then they start to appreciate you more and even feel obliged to you. It will not be long before you own them."

"Are they stupid, Madam?" asked the confidant.

"No. They are not stupid. It is their ambitions and desires that make them take a leap of faith in my favor. We will go forward with our plans."

Allegiance to her and to the nation was to be absolute. One by one, party leaders were brought to bear should their allegiance falter, as she would tolerate no ignorance, laziness or dis-loyalty. "*Graves are full of people who thought they were indispensable*," she thought to herself.

"She is straddling two worlds until it is time to make a final move," reported the confidant. "In the meantime, we can exploit the undercurrent of nationalism and cause division to manipulate one group against another. The gimp and old owl-eyes will give us the gold to seed agitators in the right places."

"Who will we blame, though?" asked another.

"It doesn't matter. She will let us know who to target. We'll probably wait for some small incident and fan the flames," answered the confidant, spitting tobacco juice onto the floor. "We'll pit one group against the other so that they're so busy fighting, we can do what we want. Yes, so *we* can do what we want, heh, heh, heh!"

"So, you're saying we might just make stuff up?"

The confidant smiled, "Exactly! We need to divide the targets from the rest of the people, so that she can impose tougher restrictions on them. Just wait and see. Others will join in against them, without even stopping to think why. We will do this from time to time, as she directs. Over time, it will become the default to blame that group for perceived sleights, maybe even insinuate that *they* are trying to take over. Ha!"

In her capital city office, Madam Zimi conferred with Mssrs. Henson, Kabbah, Martinez and a number of elected and appointed staff regarding national defense. Karmo Bockarie, wearing buckskins and his slouchy hat as the norm for his work at his Camp, entered after they settled in.

"Ah, you are here, Mr. Bockarie, please do join us. Take a seat."

Karmo looked about the room at the group, and tipped his head to them. "Madam, you wished me to speak to you and your cabinet?"

"Yes, Mr. Bockarie," she answered. Your knowledge and skills as a tactician are of great import to us. We would like your opinion as to how to handle invaders into our nation."

Karmo blinked and allowed a small smile as he gazed about the room. "Invaders, Madam," said Karmo holding back a chuckle. "We are most all invaders here. It has been the way of the world for all of history," he said more soberly. "What are your specific concerns?"

Madam Zimi took in a deep breath, annoyed by this perceived impertinence. "Mr. Bockarie, while the people of the UNS will support defensive actions to counter threats, they do not want to venture outside its borders to fight. Therefore, we must confront invading settlers, those who come not for a peaceful life, but for expansion of their own wealth and beliefs. If they are friendly and have no malicious intent, we allow them passage, and register them as citizens, so long as they agree to follow our laws. We need such people to grow our country."

The men shifted in their chairs as they took all this in. The words were not reconciling with their previous actions.

Karmo considered before he spoke, "That is all well and good, but we will not always know who has the potential for malice. We need, instead, to accept people for what they show us. When it is necessary to fight, we surely will do so. An ever-ready force of trained and armed citizenry is our best defense and, if necessary, yes, our best offense."

Mr. Henson interjected, "Ever-ready? Something in the spirit of all great nations catapults them to the forefront of others by their love of confrontation and profit. They purport peace, but must feed their lust. History is rife with the rise and fall of empires, rising like bubbles in a boiling pot, only to explode under their own excesses and then have to wait their turn to rise again. But are we not hypocrites ourselves? Are we becoming addicted to fighting in the guise of forever preparedness? Did we not just get land ceded to us to make a nation, whether some residents wanted it or not? Yes, we attempted to be fair about it. We tried mightily to get information, ideas and consensus, but in the end, we cannot pretend ... "

He stopped himself. There was a disquieting, but certain, lack of logic, and he needed more time to consider. After pausing, he then changed the direction of his discourse. "If we say we are neutral, we become their target, because the Americans in particular will not believe our neutrality, and will make up stories about us, that we threaten them and their way of life. Therefore, yes, we need to be ready to fight them, and so these invaders will be accommodated in like manner."

"Like manner, Mr. Henson? And neutral?" Madam Zimi was now sitting upright, a shadow cast over her face. She spoke slowly, her voice lowered, sounding intense and deliberate, resonating into the room. "Who said anything about being neutral? No! We must fight not just to win, but to win decisively, and send a strong message to anyone who dares attack us," she said in a more calm, measured tone. "There should be no mercy. None! We must do battle with all the ferocity of ancient times and spare no quarter. Stack bodies like cordwood for all to see. This is not the time to merely beat back intruders, rather, it is the time to stop them cold."

Karmo was growing impatient, but remained silent.

The men looked at their Lead Executive, this woman whom they once believed would lead with an altruistic and compassionate hand.

Madam Zimi took note and smiled warmly, "I can hold two seemingly contradictory beliefs at the same time, gentlemen, although emotion sometimes must be suspended. Ferocity in battle and compassion are not mutually exclusive. Because our nation is young, we have all the more reason to assure our standing and survival. Or do you not think so?"

A few moments of silence and reflection ensued before Mr. Henson spoke. "Yes, Madam. I understand completely. Believe me, I am only surprised that you as a woman, as a mother ..."

"Ah, because I am a mother, you thought I would not want to see anyone's sons and daughters brutalized. Well, you are correct there, Mr. Henson. I abhor violence. It is a repulsive waste of humanity and tears at my heart. That being said, war is a different matter, and when it is inevitable, then we must embrace it wholeheartedly. And as for neighboring lands, for now we enter into no agreements with other nations. We cannot afford this. We are not ready."

Karmo was a bit more relieved, but wondered at the mercurial nature of this woman.

Ansa turned to Madam Zimi, and nodded to JP. "Just to be clear, all being said and done, let us not divert the bulk of our wealth to war and its preparation. To do so is to invite economic collapse, as war cannot be sustained. The strength of our nation is not even our wealth, rather, it is the number of our friends, our brother nations. The intention is to use diplomacy to the highest extent possible, yes?"

"Yes, of course, Ansa, diplomacy must be ongoing, but we will not be naïve. Just as all citizens must be educated, all adults must be trained to fight and ready to mobilize," she answered.

JP mused aloud, "The gold gifted from these lands helped us overcome our past. How we use it will determine our future. What is that old saying from the Bible, Mr. Ansa? Give a man a fish and he will eat for the day, teach him to fish and he will eat for a lifetime? Something like that, no?"

Ansa looked first at Madam Zimi, smiled and nodded to JP in agreement, "something like that." The cabinet stood up to leave the room.

"Ansa, please stay a moment," Madam Zimi requested. She waved off the others so that they may continue on their way. Ansa limped behind her as they entered a smaller room of her main office.

41

Juan Pablo and Karmo 1848

Perimeter defense may not matter if the enemy is inside our gates.
–Robert Mueller

There were small battle skirmishes here and there about the country, but they were handily overcome. Karmo was relieved to work with others on strengthening the land in peaceful ways.

With JP, the U. N. S. Administration put into place meticulous checks to funnel trade towards the nation's port cities. JP was brilliant in his own way. He labored to design plans that considered obstacles, unintended consequences, and methods to reach goals efficiently. This was his habit. He set trade taxes to 3-to-5 percent of the total value of goods into Monterey—as opposed to the 15-to-20 percent imposed by Mexico, when it held sway. Yes, for now, they could afford to undercut their ally and competitor. Shipments began to be consistently traded in Monterey, rather than in the Mexican port city of Santa Barbara. Similar tactics were used in San Francisco for trade with the British and Americans coming from the north. Because of the rise of manufacturing centers, territories north and south shipped raw materials to Sequoia, instead of to the U. S. east coast, or South America, as Sequoia was now more cost-effective. But preserving the nation's resources was just as important to be self sustaining. The UNS ports and its surrounding cities flourished.

With Karmo's assistance, knowledge of the best travel routes and their defense, a series of relay stations were also put into place for quick and efficient communications. The two men visited each site and hired boys, 13-to-15 years old, to carry post and newspapers from station to station. The boys changed horses every 15 miles, and traveled up to 75 miles per trip.[81] They had to know how to ride well; plus, it was hard duty.

During this time, Karmo and JP became trusted colleagues and confidants. When their work was done for the day, they prepared dinner at a makeshift table under a spreading oak tree, taking in the breeze and fresh air. Karmo was feeling good with the break and the opportunity to do something else positive and tangible for the nation; this was clearly a departure from the ever-present fighting preparations. "There are so many working parts in government, JP. Sometimes I feel it is fortuitous that I can keep my life on one plane," observed Karmo aloud.

"Do you? I always thought your goals were all about this nation-building," answered JP.

"True. I had more philosophical ideas about nations and nation-building when I was younger. Then I heard a different plot amidst the roars of thunder, the oceans, the roars of cannon and the roars of humanity. And now I am finished with it all, and I have found my niche, and generally I am content with its limitations. I still have hopes, though," replied Karmo, sighing inside for losses far away in time and place. "I sometimes wonder about our actions—actions that are not measured in time we can see and feel, but where the results ripple into the future."

"Yes, Karmo. We may not know, and remembering the past can be terrifying if you cannot change the future. And oh, I have hopes, though! But content? Not me!" said JP emphatically. "I know there are so many irons to move, but when discussions about the *whens, whats, and hows* are discussed, I just have to be in the room when it happens! *This* is the country of my ancestors. It is my *duty* to help make it's offspring do well, and by that, do right by all of us. I want to see the country grow! Some of our leaders, though, I just do not know what to think of them. Sometimes they seem to be working counter to our best interests. Someone seems to be pulling invisible strings in attempts to unravel it all. I have heard rumors," sir, "and from trusted people."

Karmo was only mildly interested, but asked, "What do you mean? Who?"

"Well, perhaps I have said too much. I do not want to name names without good evidence, but both the plain and the eloquent speakers can hide their true thoughts. It is as if they are playing both sides against the middle. Just because something is not true does not stop some people from saying it. I hear them, Karmo. Those are the people I do not trust at all. Evil often has an ordinary face. Somehow there must be a way to penetrate their ruse. They meet secretly, you know."

Karmo perked up a bit and turned ideas around in his mind. "I think you are mistaken, my friend. Perhaps they are just testing out ideas in smaller groups. Some ideas are bound to be new, and perhaps uncomfortable because of that, but working counter to our interests? I do not believe so."

JP noted Karmo's pensiveness and was quick to make apology and entreaty. "Karmo, I have an understanding of your vision for the new nation, but if you are not involved or present to express your vision, the development will fall to others, and perhaps not in a way you would like. The people look to us for strength, courage and, above all, fairness. It would not be right to let them down. What would Madeleine and Suzanne say if they heard us now?"

Jack, and even that Mullen, too, thought Karmo to himself.

JP continued, "My own father fought for his land back in Tejas. We all have our duties. We will get the job done, if we stick together. Time and patience, my friend!"

"Your father was in Tejas?" questioned Karmo.

"Yes, he was born, lived and died there. Jesse Martinez, God rest his soul," intoned JP.

Karmo studied JP, his carriage, his eyes. "Did your father live near the mouth of the San Antonio River?"

"Yes, he did. Were you ever there?" ask a perplexed JP.

Dark clouds scudded across the sky as Karmo aimed his characteristic intense stare at JP, then at the hills surrounding them, before nodding silently.

Still curious, JP offered, "Supper is ready. Let us talk."

~

Well-defended, secure roads encouraged travel and trade, and the locals were hospitable. Foreign ground traders remarked that they felt safe, even traveling with large amounts of currency and goods. With the help of a committee of traders, farmers and citizens, JP published a handbook as to what goods could be found in the seven regions and their expected prices, taxes and even comfortable places to stay. The book was to be updated annually. The fledgling nation grew stronger, even as the drums of war started beating again.

42

Jonny and Ansa in Sacramento 1848

Do you know what love is? I'll tell you: it is whatever you can still betray. –The Looking Glass War, John LeCarré

Communication in the new nation was at times difficult, and prone to misunderstandings. The representatives used much of their time traveling to their home bases to hear out their people and share information from the capital. There were missteps, sometimes boisterous contention, but the fledgling nation would grow stronger over time. Dissension went underground, as a small but determined group planned disruption of the government. A network of UNS government guardians was assigned to spread into the larger cities, and some smaller towns, to gather intelligence, to ferret out talk of destabilization as opposed to dissatisfaction. Treason was not to be tolerated. As Chief of Staff, Ansa kept his pulse on such operations, reported to the Lead Executive, and granted field officers access to her when he deemed it appropriate.

～

As in San Francisco and other cities, large and small, Sacramento had its share of street children. Children of the disenfranchised, orphans and bastards roamed the streets, seeking a livelihood the best they could. These street children scampered about the fruit sellers and fish fryers, lingering at times near store entrances, saloons, cafés and anywhere the townspeople congregated. Some earned their living as buskers, playing music in hopes of small change. Most people ignored them, looked through them as if they were invisible—these wild, dirty creatures. Deputies on foot patrol befriended them and gave them food, for they knew these children owned the streets and provided eyes and ears for the city's goings-on. "Miscreants like to brag to one another, and do so in front of these grubbers without thinking," said one deputy. "Get the word out to the kids. Have them listen up at every dock, bar and rat hole around. We need to know what's going on."

Across town, a handful of settlers from the eastern lands who accepted the UNS land and nation, met secretly. It was rightly their land, they said to one another, their "manifest destiny." As in Tejas, they too formed their own teams of provocateurs, nurturing hate and bitterness with lies.

"Drumple, that old slave runner, is back in the game, and already has managed to place a few of his trusted people in government to weave discord, to confuse and weaken it. He gave us the all-clear for the raids. We will disrupt them, infiltrate, instill fear, chaos, distrust, whatever it takes. Start with eliminating the peacemakers to demoralize the populace," their leader announced. "We start now!"

"I don't think it's the right time. Don't you think we should wait until there is a dark moon?" answered one.

"Drumple said now, so it's now!" answered the leader. "If we don't do as he says, there will be hell to pay! Besides, it's gonna rain. Don't think so much about it; just do it!"

"I wasn't brought up in the woods to be scared of owls, you know!" answered back the man as he put his hand on his holster. *As for Drumple! Bah! Even his shadow's crooked.*

The leader nodded to two of the others, and the protester was led away. A gunshot was heard and one gunman returned, nodding his head to the leader. "Graves are full of people who thought they were indispensable, boys," muttered the leader, parroting words he heard many times before. The others in the group looked at each other, shrugged, then gathered around and passed a hat with folded pieces of paper. Some were blank, some were inscribed with an *x*. Those men who pulled *x*'s rode off on their horses into the night, towards the Prime Minister's home. Those with the blanks went to the Lead Executive's home.

Later that night, with still a crescent moon in the sky, street children pulled deputies towards the Lead Executive's mansion. "That owl-eyed man and his gang! They're gonna get her! They're after her! Come now! Now!" The deputies complied and surrounded the house quietly. They spied two men in dark clothing peeking into the windows, pistols in hand, as one nodded to the other. The deputies moved in quickly and placed their pistols to each of the would-be assassins' heads. Quickly, deputies took them away to their offices, but posted protective guards around the home of the Lead Executive. "Is this what it has come to?" asked a deputy. "Will we always need to provide such security?" The deputies did not realize the decoy assault.

"I don't see how we can avoid it," replied another. "We can't tell who it will be trying to beat up the government. Maybe the guardians will need to start talking to us more when they hear the crazy talk. We can't just rely on chance or the street children."

Just east of the mansion, the rain started pouring down with a vengeance. Prime Minister Henson was in his home, gazing contemplatively into the fire, mesmerized by its dancing blue-to-white flames. Men encircled the home as their lookout peered into the window. "He's in there," he whispered to the others.

"Go ahead to the door. You know what to do," whispered another.

Nodding, the man inched closer to the bushes near the entrance to the mansion. Mud and rain silenced his steps. His breath quickened as he scratched at the door.

Henson heard the noise and got up from his chair, looking towards the door. *Who would be out on this dark, forsaken night?* He took up a lighted candle holder and walked into the foyer, looking out the window into an inky void. He opened the door and stepped onto the threshold, but saw no one. Standing there a moment, he turned to go back inside, when he heard a weak voice.

"Help me, please."

A man, drenched and hunched low, was barely visible in the shadow of foliage. Jonny bent down to help him. "Come in, my friend, come in and get warm."

The man lifted himself up and, with that, his pistol was revealed. With unshakable sangfroid, he fired his shot directly into the chest of his would-be Samaritan. The bear man was blown hard back to the wall, knocking vases off a credenza, a look of abject surprise frozen on his face. Looking down at the wound, and then at his assailant, he was stunned speechless. The black powder residue on his vest at the bullet's entry point marked him, as his blood took the route of least resistance; it danced and dribbled from the wound with every heartbeat in his chest. A gurgle filled his throat as he looked at the shooter in disbelief; then came the second shot. But Henson did not hear it. First came the feeling of warmth, then bright lights and dizziness. In the far recesses of his mind, bright flashes slowly dissolved, and he was surrounded by his beloved ocean, as far as he could see, by turquoise water gently lapping around the small boat that contained him, so quiet. He looked upward to let the soft sun rays embrace his face. Silently, the sky slowly turned gray, ever-darkening. He saw the stars and felt at peace, freed of all his earthly burdens, his eyes wide-open; he was barely breathing.

The shots drew the neighbors, who in turn, summoned the authorities. The assassins faded into the gathering crowd of onlookers. Ansa pushed through them, rushed to his dear friend, and shakily crouched at Jonny's side, overwhelmed with a profoundly visceral shock. The unthinkable had occurred. *This was not supposed to happen! It was not part of the plan!* he said to himself, gritting his teeth.

"Do not leave me, my love." Ansa could not hear anything beyond the roar of blood rushing to his skull. Jonny's head slid slowly to the floor, where dust gently stirred with his last muffling breath. Then he was gone.

"Who silenced your big heart, Jonny? Who would dare?" Ansa whispered softly, "Lucky you. You will meet your friends amongst the stars, as the rest of us will. But did you have to leave so early? Watch over us poor mortals, my friend."

~

The next day, Lead Executive Zimi called her assembly to her office. Looking wan, with reddened eyes, it was clear that she suffered too. "Our hearts are broken, but now is not the time to collapse. We do not have the luxury of outrage. This is the time for action, and the time to be sad is later. We must do our jobs, our duty, and use our heartache to secure justice. We need to unite if we are to stand up to this insidious, vile wind. Rain starts with a single drop! We need to use patience, think wisely, but act decisively. Please send for Karmo Bockarie."

After all the years, the Shadow had changed, but did not disappear.

WAR IN THE UNS.

UNS.

BATTLE IN THE CANYON

SACRAMENTO

SAN FRANCISCO

MONTEREY

ALTA CALIFORNIA

SANTA BARBARA

43

War in the U.N.S. 1847-1849

*In war or battle, do not brag about the victories or how they were
achieved. Let the tormenter worry constantly so that their imagination
of more and worse attacks aid in their downfall.*
—The Art of War, Sun Tzu

They were few in number, but invaders and their internal compatriots marched and attacked where they could. "If we do not stop them now, they will descend upon us like a cold winter rain," said Karmo. There was no standing militia, but the young nation's defenders were organized and ready to harken to the call to action.

As requested by Karmo through Suzanne, Henri LeMurier managed to ship ten gun contraptions called the Macchina Infernale to the UNS. Finally, they arrived. Originally built in 1835 by the Corsican Guiseppe Fieschi, the machine was refined to correct design and fabrication errors.[82]

~

The Bay of Monterey was blockaded by American ships, part of Frémont's California Battalion who still used the Englishman Admiral Blake's "Fighting Instructions."[83] They did not yet acknowledge the separation of northern Alta California from Mexico.[84] The siege was threatening not just commerce, but the very existence of the nascent UNS. A fleet of five ships was anchored in the bay on this moonless night. Karmo observed the lanterns of the night-watch rounds for two nights. There were no dog watches, no overlap. Watch crews approached one another with boisterous laughing, exchanging gossip before separating. They were at ease, believing their siege was in the advantage. They were not particularly vigilant, but did their duty adequately.

"I need 20 of your best men, and they must be your strongest swimmers for this mission," Karmo ordered his second-in-command. "This will be a bloodbath!"

"Consider it done, Karmo! We will irrigate the beach with blood!"

"Just make sure it is theirs, and not ours. We kill when we need to. It is not about them. It is about us," added Karmo quietly. *Justice, not revenge*, he thought to himself.

While sailing, no lights are allowed sailors in the evenings, but these ships being anchored, and their arrogant captains feeling superior, allowed them to glow just enough to menace the townspeople. The ships' deadlights were opened, pouring out the brightness from within, and served as targets for Karmo's men. With their exposed faces and flesh covered with mud or boot-black, they paddled quietly in small canoes towards each of the ships, affixed explosive charges and held their collective breath, waiting for the sign from the shore.

The estimated time was nigh. There! Three torches, lighted one immediately after the other, the signal for which the drifting men waited. The charges, one on each broadside of each ship below the canon mounts, were all lit. The men paddled away furiously for all they were worth. The explosions were so great that huge, rippling waves overturned some of the small boats, tossing the men into the dark, chilling turbulence. Their flesh pierced with wooden shards, the men clawed their way by the light of the moon, holding their breath as long as they could. Bloodied and exhausted, they blinked their collective eyes towards the blazing ships, surveying the damage, then quickly swam towards the lanterns on the shore.

There had been horses on one ship and the explosives crazed them. The frenzied beasts stomped and escaped into the bay, rearing and lunging above the water, trying to see land. Several horses at once noticed a sailor, treading with his arms on the surface to stay afloat. The desperate animals determined him to be an object upon which they could rest. They snorted, gnashed their teeth and flailed viciously, their hooves beating the sailor to a pulp while whipping the water into a froth, only departing when his remains sank, disappearing into the sea.

The men on shore lit small lanterns to show the way for the swimmers. This was just as much a part of the mission as the first part. They paddled to a pre-designated shore, towards safety. Havoc broke out on the ships. The hulls breached and began taking on water at an extreme pace. Karmo watched the men on the ships. In time, they broke out into their emergency launches. Karmo nodded. The sun was coming up over the rolling hills east of the city. As the enemy launches neared the beach, they were met with volley after volley from the infernal French contraptions. The stench of blood filled the air, and the beach did indeed turn red. The remainder of sailors, wounded or otherwise, were met by armed citizens. This battle was done.

Such a cruel weapon, but effective, thought Karmo. *What will another 100 years bring?*[285]

He rode his horse over to see his men as they beached their boats or swam to shore. Miraculously, only one was injured, though his injuries were not clear. There was no sign of wounds on his body. He was unconscious and blood trickled from his ear. The doctor who had been assigned to wait for the men's return examined him and determined that he had been assaulted by the blast.

"I don't know when he'll come to," said the doctor, "or *if* he will. He may continue this way for days, weeks, or even years. I just don't know."

Karmo stared at the man, young, strong and helpless, his eyes open, but empty. "I have seen this before. His battle is done," Karmo said sadly as he turned and walked away.

Karmo and his men gathered back at the Monterey headquarters. "We will watch them for however many days it takes, to make sure the survivors are dealt with. You, Captain Gonzalez. You are to be in charge of debriefing them and determining who will be work prisoners and who to release."

"Release?" said one of the lieutenants. Jorge Gonzalez nodded to his lieutenant, then smiled at Karmo.

"Yes, release," answered a weary but patient Karmo. "We will put a handful of them on a ship headed for America, so they can spread the word that we are a force with which to be reckoned and not some poor outback refuge of savages and ignorant settlers. Release some others, if possible."

"Yes, sir. Ah, when is 'possible'?" asked the lieutenant.

Gonzales answered flatly, "Our people come first, Lieutenant. If we do not have enough food and supplies, we will execute the leftover prisoners."

Karmo nodded to Gonzalez, "I will meet back with you this evening." He was remembering Madam Zimy's directive, "*Stack them like cordwood!*" and let out a deep sigh, suspending his emotions and letting his mind dissociate from pity to better focus on the mission. Even so, he felt his own strings were being pulled. As he turned to walk into the next room, a familiar voice called to him.

"Mr. Karmo! Over here! I have someone I would like you to meet. This is Mr. Kroupa, Peter Kroupa, newly arrived from the Benoît's hometown in Mattapoisett."

It was Lokni. He was there with another man, both looking travel-weary, having come from San Francisco.

Karmo walked towards them, extending his hand to grasp Lokni's in a friendly handshake and gave him a clap on the back. He then nodded at and shook hands with the stranger.

"Nice to meet you. What brings you down here? This is an unstable place for the moment."

"I heard from Suzanne that you had the Infernale and I wanted Pete here to see it," answered Lokni.

"Madame Suzanne needs to be more discreet about operations. How exactly did this come about?" asked an irritated Karmo.

"Mr. Karmo, it was not her fault. I was there for the off-loading with her. She said she knew you would take them and I just figured out where," said Lokni, trying to assuage Karmo's annoyance.

"That tells me that anyone could have seen or overheard our business, Lokni. We will need to discuss better security with the committees."

Karmo was highly annoyed by this breach of security. The outcome could have been jeopardized by leaking secrets.

"Nevertheless, both of you are here now. How can I help you?" he asked.

"Sir," replied Kroupa, "Although I am a carpenter by trade, I have been blessed with mechanical abilities, and was intrigued when I heard about the Infernale." With that, he pulled out his Colt revolver and spun the barrel.

Karmo immediately pulled out his weapon, but stopped when he saw that the newcomer was only trying to demonstrate something.

Startled, Kroupa asked, "May I continue, sir?"

"Unload it," said Karmo. "Then you may continue."

As he did so, Kroupa explained how he thought the two concepts in weaponry might be combined into a third, useful, and unique weapon.

"With Lokni's help, I believe we can fabricate a more effective and more portable contraption than the Infernale, and one that is less dangerous to the operator, sir."

Karmo smiled and thought to himself, *Better weapons. Yes, that is good, but when will we ever put our energy into something for peaceful measures?*

"I see," he said. "Lokni, take Mr. Kroupa out in the morning to look at the Infernale. Let him measure, sketch and do whatever he needs to get information. This is another one for the committees. They were talking about setting up factories of different sorts and hiring people. Let them determine this situation and work things out. As for me, I have a particular need for portability." He turned to Kroupa. "Thank you for your interest. I hope something good can come out of this."

"Karmo, I need to talk to you about some important information I came upon, but find hard to believe," whispered Lokni.

A weary Karmo looked at him and asked, "Can it not wait?"

Lokni had mixed emotions. This could not wait, but he could see the exhaustion in Karmo's face. He thought to himself of the future conversation, *The most blind of men is the one who will not see.*

∾

Dark and after midnight, only the placement of the constellations told him so before they were clouded over. Safe and comfortable quarters had been secured. In his room, Karmo ruminated on the day's events for hours before he tried to sleep; the early morning hours were already approaching. He felt pulled into a black hole, into the core of distant worlds. Adequate sleep eluded him with recurring dreams of the corpse monster. At last, fatigue overtook him. Aware of his warm breath, the softness of bedclothes against his skin, his body finally yielded to tiredness, and he easily slipped into the glove of repose.

Tick, flickity, flick, tick, flickity flick. He turned the metal lever on the kerosene lamp and glanced at the mechanical clock on the side table. He had had 20 glorious minutes of sleep, when a moth commenced breaking its wings against the glass sides of his lamp. A few moments later, Karmo explored the patterns of jagged lines and the darkness of his closed lids, and took a long, deep breath, but could not let go the thoughts about the coming day. "Almost daybreak, may as well get up," he said aloud.

In the dark of the new morning, he walked along the beach, listening to the waves as they first crashed upon, then quietly embraced, the shore. He looked to the sky for comfort, but saw only complete darkness, like a black hole that could no longer reflect light. His head pounding and cloudy, he was perplexed and lost in thought as he walked around a large sand dune, where torchlights held by five or six men suddenly revealed them. They wore the uniforms of the enemy, drenched and shredded, apparent survivors of the blasts. But they bared their knives, and commenced to encircle him menacingly.

Surrounded, Karmo looked upward. The stars had reappeared. "So is this to be my time? Let it come!" He stepped to back up against the wind-sifted sand dune, and felt it shifting under his feet. He hunched down to make himself small, and got ready to finish out his last shots.

He didn't know what happened next. The stinging in his shoulder, then into his side, shocked him. Remembering the muzzle flash, he realized in the next moment that he had been hit, that one of the invaders must have had a pistol. Falling on one knee, he watched the enemy approach him and took a deep breath before lifting his own pistol.

An unearthly scream emanated from the dune behind him. He made a quick glance in that direction, to see a dozen citizens with clubs and axes begin attacking the invaders. They made quick work of them, before coming to Karmo. Still stunned and breathing hard, Karmo stood up, holding his oozing shoulder, and looked at them all in awe, as they smiled and nodded their heads.

One man stepped out among them. "We know who you are, Karmo Bockarie. When we saw those men, we followed to get them. Just knowing you are our leader, we feel safe. This is our country, and we will defend it. Let's get you fixed up, quick now!"

He was grateful for his life, but just as thankful, relieved and proud to realize he could have faith in these people, who would defend their homeland. "*Ultimately, our future is together. This is the only country I have now,*" thought Karmo. "*This is my home now.*" The Shadow had passed over him once more.

❧

Karmo again found himself gazing into the Pacific. The nutshell of history came to his mind's eye; the heroics and cowardice, compassion and cruelty, greed and kindness, intelligence and ignorance. More and more, the stuff of life burned into his experiences and into his very essence. He slowly became cognizant of his quick breathing, and slowed himself with a deep exhalation. It was time to journey north, to assess the coordination of another operation. Jack would be there as well. With Mullen gone, Jack had returned to Camp Bockarie, where he joined a defense company heading towards the northeast passage of the Oregon Trail to engage the invaders in the mountains. Some of the enemy, sadly, were local volunteers, formerly from the American states. It was disheartening, but it was reality. The plan was unusual, and Karmo didn't like that women would be intentionally put into the line of fire. But the Bockarie women were adamant and fierce that they would do their part to protect their families. "*They can do this,*" he acknowledged.

～

Before sunrise, Karmo was pensive, and held his hand up to a startlingly bright early-morning sky. The light from the stars was so brilliant, he needed no torch. This radiance was the living essence, and he was nothing but fleeting space. He shook his head to gain his consciousness. Among the scrubby shrubs, and along narrow pathways of shifting mountain goat trails, Karmo and the men stationed themselves, hiding in the rocky hillsides above the canyon walls.

The women were decoys who had a double mission. The first was to bring sorely needed supplies to their men, and the other was to lure the enemy towards them. They had been well-trained. For some, this was their first operation. This was real life.

Days before, the women worked furiously to make clothes and boots, weave blankets, and prepare food, then placed everything in a series of three wagons, along with ammunition and gunpowder.

"Wear your most colorful clothes, ladies!" shouted the leader. "And let down your hair! We want those men to know we're women!"

Karmo's men were situated both at ground level and above in the canyon walls. High on their rocky perch, they watched a large detachment of invaders ride through the forest, heading for the mouth of the canyon. His contingent would initiate the attack.

On the opposite side of the canyon, one of Jack's Native comrades slipped and fell from the precipice. As the man silently hurtled down the stony mountain face into the abyss, he had swallowed his fear and anguish in a selfless act for his brothers. Jack watched in both horror and wonder. The lead Native read his face.

"He didn't scream ..." whispered Jack, astonished. Never had he witnessed such control or such bravery.

"He knew he was going to die, and that his screaming would betray our presence to the enemy. His silence served the greater good," came the answer. "The hard part of our life is not to *die* a hero, the hard part is to *live* as a hero. He did both. For a warrior, death is *our* homeland."

Karmo saw none of this. He and his group were on the opposite side of the canyon. The men felt the tension, curling their fingers and stretching them out again. It was quiet, save for a slight flutter of leaves, when he heard a strange chattering. He turned towards his men. There he was, no more than 15 years old. How did he get here? Who brought him? The kid was shaking in his boots, scared beyond belief, deep in the shadows of scrub. Then Karmo recognized him: a sharpshooter, but still, he should not have been assigned yet. This was an error to be investigated later.

"You!" Karmo said as loud as he dared, "Come here!"

The young man inched his way to Karmo, and squatted low behind a boulder.

"Yes, sir, Mr. Karmo?"

"Look! You see Jack way up there, across the canyon? I want you to stay on this side and climb up as high as he is. You will help the sharpshooters with crossfire. You *are* a good shot, right?"

"Yes, sir!" answered the youngster, relieved that his first skirmish would be from a relatively safe position, yet would be something he could do well.

"Then go now!" Karmo furrowed his brow and shook his head. In the canyon, the intruders will be shooting up into the hills and toward the rising sun. They will be shooting blind, a big disadvantage. He nodded to himself, *The placement is good for us.*

Slowly, the little caravan made its way to the canyon's mouth, and traveled almost midway. "Be alert, ladies, and get ready to take cover," said their leader, a young woman with an even voice.

Only moments later, the enemy made their presence known. On galloping horses, they eased up towards the wagons. The head man smiled menacingly, "Well, hello, ladies. What brings you lovelies out here? Come to entertain us?" he added.

"Absolutely!" responded one of the women.

With that, shots rang out from above, hitting their mark. Amid clouds of dust and gunsmoke, arose the screams of men and horses. The enemy grimaced with looks of need and regret. Over half of the invading detachment was vanquished immediately. The rest drew their weapons, turning their heads towards the canyon walls before attempting to take cover amongst the wagons; but the women were suddenly armed as well, and they used their weapons effectively, holding off the men until their warriors could climb out of hiding and surround them to swarm and assist. One man was left, and he grabbed a woman who managed to get out of his grip with a swift twist, and a kick to his instep. She forced him down on the ground, quickly grabbed a fist-sized stone, and bashed the side of his skull. Breathing deeply, she turned to the others, "Got him!"

It only took a moment for the injured man to overcome his shock and hold up his gun with a trembling hand. As his last gesture for revenge, he fired, hitting her in the shoulder. The leader nearby, already in mid-jump upon him, took her knife and slit his throat. Frenzied, she continued to stab the corpse repeatedly. The other women grabbed her arms to stop her.

"Enough!" they hollered, pulling her away.

"Let go of me! Get away!" she screamed at them before stepping back. Now, he was done. Blood spattered on her bosom and face, she stood up, breathing hard, and looked up at the women who had rushed up to the injured, caring for her and brushing dirt and blood off themselves. "*Never, ever* turn your back on the enemy!" she yelled victoriously.

44

Pompo, Jack and Mullen 1848

"Good night, sweet prince ..."
–Romeo and Juliet, William Shakespeare

Lt. Dan and what was left of the Mullen crew were still looking out for Kreisler's man Schwartz, who was bent on revenge of his own, this time marking Jack as his target. The Lieutenant had always been Mullen's second, his fixer, who would organize and clear the way to get the job done, even though his persona suggested otherwise. Now, it was his time to step up. He had work to do, responsibilities.

∽

"The kid's tough," said one of Schwartz's men.

"There is always a way, though. Everyone has a weakness," mumbled Schwartz.

One of the men offered, "What about that Injun girl of his? I bet he'd come fer her!"

Schwartz looked at him and nodded, "I've been thinking on this. Listen up. Kreisler always called her his pumpkin, but wouldn't talk to her, just stare."

"Hey!" spouted off one of the men, "You don't suppose he and that Palace singer ...."

"Shuddup!" yelled Schwartz, "He's gone, and I'm the Boss now! Yeah, now that I think about it, that might just work. You!" He pointed to one of his men. Take two men, catch and take her to the meadow south of Oat Hill, *alive*! You know the place."

ROAR!

"Yeah, I know where you're talking about, but I can bring her my-self, Boss," answered the man.

Schwartz regarded him with hostile eyes. "She's a Bockarie woman. Don't underestimate them. You need eyes on them at all times. Make sure she's tied up tight as a drum before you move her."

"Sure, Boss, will do. But what if she *is* Kreisler's ...."

Schwartz threw a menacing glance at him before directing, "I'll meet you there day after tomorrow. Enough said!"

~

The foothills were dotted with live and black oak. Fields of wild grasses and mullet pushed up to rocky outcrops, and the air was a cacophony of chattering, cawing, and singing birds as Pompo and Hawk hunted on this crisp, sunny morning, bagging quail and doves. She was heading towards camp when three men came up on her from different directions. She had no idea who they were, but they were clearly trouble.

Pulling out her weapon, she attempted a diversion, but too late, and was hit so hard by a rifle butt, she fell to the ground, disoriented. From above, Hawk flew directly at one of the men's heads with such speed as to knock him off-balance from his horse and shred his face with his razor-like talons. Up back into the sky flew the bird, as one of the other men took aim, fired and missed. In full attack mode, the small predator bird dived again, the stripes on its face deflecting glare from the sun so it could focus on its quarry. It took two more tries before the bullet hit its mark. Hawk landed at Pompo's feet before she passed out.

"Damn bird!" said one of the men as he spat on it from his horse. The injured man, holding a wet kerchief to his bleeding face, walked to the still-fluttering bird and kicked it into the bushes.

Once she was unconscious and tied securely, one of the men pulled off Pompo's gun belt and scarf, then took off towards Camp Bockarie. "I'll drop this off and be back, quick like a jack-rabbit," he said.

"Don't forget to leave tracks!" yelled one of the men after him.

He held up his arm in acknowledgement as he continued to head out.

At camp, Lt. Dan and a few of his men were meeting with Jack. Fighting with the invaders was slowing down, and Jack returned to work on his gun-smithing for a while. They walked back from their morning meal in the mess tent towards Jack's open-air shop when he froze. "What's Pompo's gun belt doing here? And here's her scarf!" yelled Jack as he held the scarf to his face in panic. "They have her!"

"Who has who, Jack?!" asked Lt. Dan. "Are you thinking Kreisler's men, that Schwartz guy and crew? They've got Pompo?!"

"Damn straight!" muttered Jack. "He's been dogging me ever since we got Kreisler. I'm going after her!" he said, running towards his horse.

"Wait for us Jack!" yelled Lt. Dan after him. "You know it's a trap! We need to figure out where they are, so's we can sneak up on him!"

"I can't wait for that! Lord only knows what they're doing to her!" Jack hollered back at them, still running.

"Come on, boys! We're not gonna let him go alone!"

Jack was way ahead of them, following a single set of tracks that were obviously meant for him. "Probably Schwartz himself," Jack thought to himself. "I'll kill the bastard with my bare hands if I need to." He found bits of Pompo's clothing on twigs and shoulder-height broken branches. *Oat Hill*, he thought. *That's where he took her*, as he spurred his horse hard and flew into the forest towards the meadow.

∽

Her head throbbing, Pompo came to, tied to a tree. The men who had captured her were sitting around a small fire, cleaning their guns and drinking whiskey.

"Hey! Hey, there! I have to go! You know, *go!*" she called out to them. *If I can get them to untie me, I will at least have a fighting chance.*

"So go!" yelled one of the men, as the others laughed.

"Wait!" said another, "Not a problem. I can help her get her britches off," he said, with a prurient snarl.

"Ha!" said another man. "We can all help with that!" he said as he grinned menacingly at the third man, who yelped "I'm in!"

They pulled her flat on the ground. "Oh, such a big, brave man!" she screamed. "You can beat a woman who is tied, but you are afraid of a fair fight! Let me go, and I will show you *real* fighting."

"Shut her up!" one man yelled and shoved a glove in her mouth. Another kept her arms above her head, and re-tied her to the tree. One man held each of her legs as the other man cut her clothing, slicing her skin. Struggling with all her might, she could not overcome what followed, as they took their turns.

The next morning, Schwartz arrived alone on horseback. He looked at Pompo, then at his men. "What the hell, guys! Damn it all! What?! Is she even alive?!!"

"She's alive, Boss. No worries. We just had a little fun with her last night," came the answer.

Schwartz got off his horse and walked towards her still body. He bent down low, only to be kicked in the neck with a sudden burst of energy as Pompo came to life.

His head jerked upwards, "Damn bitch!" he swore. "I'll show you! Guys! Get over here and tie her legs back together. What a bunch of assholes! I told you not to leave her untied," he growled. An ominous darkness came over his face as he took his knife and cut the tendons behind each of her ankles.

Garbled screams came from her gagged mouth, and her whole body twisted and turned as she suffered incredible pain and indignity.

"You men take cover in the bushes down the path. Give me a whistle when you see Jack. Me and the little lady here are gonna keep each other company for a bit."

Another hour went by before Schwartz heard the whistle. "Time to get up on your feet! Lover boy is coming for you. I'm gonna do you a favor and ungag you, so you can say your sweet good-byes. Hehehehehe!" He hoisted her to her feet, letting her lean against him, since she could no longer stand on her own. His knife to her throat, he prepared to release the gag. Just as Jack came riding in like a bat out of hell, reigned up and jumped off his horse, running towards Pompo and Schwartz. He stopped short when he saw the knife at Pompo's throat.

"Schwartz!" he screamed. *"I'm* here. Your beef is with *me!* Let her go!"

Pompo screamed back, "Jack! It's a trap; get out! Get out now!"

Schwartz smiled at Jack and snarled. "Boy! I've been waiting a long time for you. Now you're going to suffer for all the wrong you've done in your life. You will see your lady love die in front of your eyes, and you won't be able to do a damned thing about it."

Jack became enraged, "Don't do it, you bastard! Don't you dare!" His rage dissipated quickly into panic, his heart rate accelerated to an unsustainable level. Words could barely escape his mouth. Suddenly, his eyes started to glisten, "No! No! Don't!" he choked. He could tell by the obsessed look on Schwartz's face, by his twisted, grinning mouth and snake-like eyes, that words no longer mattered.

Pompo looked directly into Jack's eyes, "Jack, Jack! Look into my eyes, just *my* eyes, Jack! Do not feel sorrow, Jack. My path is your path. We will dance among the stars!"

Jack's eyes grew large as he shook his head, "Take *me!* Don't do this to *her!*" His words vaporized in despair, as hot tears of terror and inevitability filled his eyes and went down into his throat.

Schwartz grunted. In the length of time it takes to take a deep breath, he slit the delicate flesh of Pompo's throat deep into the windpipe, allowing a gurgle of blood to emerge. She maintained a serene countenance. Schwartz threw both Pompo and the knife down onto the ground, pulled out his revolver, and fired two shots directly into Jack's belly. Shots to the gut are intentionally inflicted for maximum suffering. Another shot went into his right shoulder, followed by a shot to his leg, nicking his femoral artery, which pulsed and sprayed out with every heartbeat. Jack went down to his knees and fell over, his breaths heaving into the dust.

Schwartz's men came out of the bushes, a knife at the ready to plunge into Jack. "Let's finish him off, Boss!" one yelled. Schwartz grabbed the guy by the shirt. "Shut yer yap before I punch yer ugly face! Let him die a slow death, bellowing like a dying bull over his lost love. Ha! He'll be dead soon enough.

"Jinx! You stay back and hide. I want to know if anyone followed the kid. Don't fight 'em, just watch. OK, guys, let's get out of here! We're done with our business."

Jack, breathing hard, crawled to Pompo with every bit of strength left in his body. He stared into her now-vacant eyes and touched her still-warm face. "I won't leave you, Pompo. I love you. I've always loved you," he whispered with a weak smile before his eyes closed.

Jack was a quivering mass, barely breathing, just three minutes later, as Lt. Dan and his men rode in, dusting up the trail when they came to a sudden stop. Jumping off their horses, they ran to the couple. One man at Pompo's side saw her cut throat, checked her pulse anyway, and shook his head. "She's gone."

Lt. Dan put his head to Jack's heart, to listen. "He's still alive! Let's get him back to Camp quick!" They wrapped the wounds hastily to stop the bleeding, and started to move out. As they did so, Jinx stepped out of the bushes and leveled his pistol at Lt. Dan. A sudden whoosh passed by the Lieutenant's ear as a knife twirled and found its mark in the would-be shooter's chest. "Ahhhgghh!" Jinx cried out as he clutched the knife with both hands.

Lt. Dan, somewhat stunned, looked at Jinx and mumbled, "Nice catch!" He turned to his partner who had just saved his life, and nodded his head in thanks before jumping back on his horse and signaled the others to follow.

The men got the couple back to camp as soon as they could, and summoned a doctor. He quickly examined Jack, but the expression on his face told the story and the men hung their heads.

Jack remained unconscious until he breathed his last, next to Pompo in a make-shift litter. They were buried, side by side, the next morning at the foot of Histum Yani.

After the burial, Lt. Dan rode out of Bockarie alone, stopped his horse and looked back. "Where in tarnation do I go now? Being Boss is no fun. I wasn't cut out to be responsible for a bunch of ya-hoos."

He looked up into the sky, which was clotted with clouds. "Buttermilk sky, my mother used to call it. Hmmm, I can't go east or west, because I'll get hung for sure. North is just too crazy." A beam of light sliced through the clouds to the south of him. He turned to look at it, a big toothy smile spreading across his beardy face. "*Lucia*! Lucy!" he said out loud, and rode off towards Mexican Territory.

～

Months later, Karmo met Ansa in the Benoîts' garden late one evening. Ansa looked about before saying, "She died over there," pointing to the garden bench that was filled with vases of flowers. "Madame Madeleine was a good woman, Karmo, such a good woman. The Benoîts saved my life, you know."

"Yes, my brother. She was a strong model for her whole family, despite of her personal tragedies," answered Karmo.

They remained in silent thought for a few minutes. The beloved, tragic Jack was not to be forgotten, ever. Nor was Christian Mullen, with all his faults; he was Jack's mentor, perhaps another father figure.

"Mullen was an enigma, Ansa," Karmo said in a low voice. "He could kill without blinking an eye, yet could be considerate of another's well-being. He helped us transport the gold, and then he and his crew rustled horses on the way home."

Ansa nodded thoughtfully. "He kept Jack out of most of the ugly business, too, Karmo."

"True. I never quite understood what Kreisler and Schwartz had against Jack, though."

"Indeed, I do not understand it, either. Kreisler disappeared, and his crew went for Jack. Do you suppose Jack had something to do with Kreisler's disappearance?" asked Ansa.

"I cannot imagine that, my brother. No, it must have been something else. We may never understand it," replied Karmo.

Ansa let out a long sigh before reflecting, "Jack and Mullen would have appreciated all this nation-building. It would have been part of that great dream for which they searched."

"All Jack wanted was a peaceful life. He wanted to have a family with Pompo and live quietly," said Karmo, as he shook his head slowly. Looking up into the sky, his chest tightened.

"Is that not what most of us want?" he said quietly, "Time. Perhaps with time. But time is no more fixed than the stars at whose reflected light we stare." He became lost in his own private thoughts.

SAN FRANCISCO BAY AREA

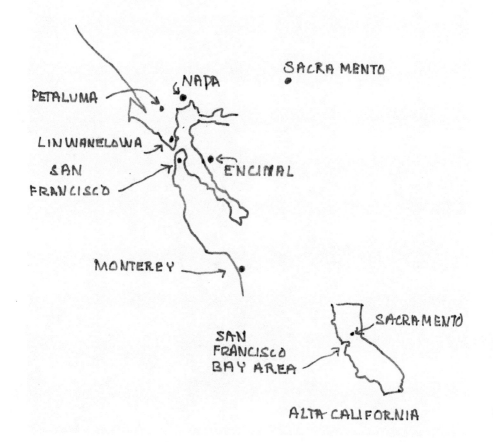

SACRA MENTO

PETALUMA

NAPA

LIN WANELOWA

SAN
FRANCISCO

ENCINAL

MONTEREY

SAN
FRANCISCO
BAY AREA

SACRA MENTO

ALTA CALIFORNIA

45

Peter and Lokni early 1849

A talent for following the ways of yesterday is not sufficient to improve the world of today. –King Wuling of Zhao

The autumn flowed languorously along for weeks, then crept insidiously up to the iron gates of winter. Warmed by the rising sun, a white, diaphanous mist rose from the damp earth. Puffs of breathy clouds escaped from Peter and Lokni's mouths as they spoke. Their arms wrapped tightly around themselves to keep warm, they explored the unnamed island, one in the east bay with a low-lying marshy lagoon to the west separating it from the rest of Encinal.[86] Not a true island, a narrow strip of earth formed a land bridge to the coast proper. The lagoon was sizable, however, and navigable to small boats. They found it by sighting the marker of bright orange-gold flowers covering shell mounds.[87] Abundant herons on stilt-like legs, stalked hapless frogs and small fish along the perimeter of the lagoon. Black birds with epaulettes of crimson called to one another as they danced in the wind, their claw feet clenched on sea grasses.

Encinal was covered in coast oaks, dense and evergreen, and the region enjoyed warm, rarely hot, dry summers. The land had been granted to the Peralta family, who mostly lived pleasantly and peacefully with the Ohlone Natives. Many Ohlone had been granted land of their own by Governor Micheltorena and, later, Governor Pico, in the South Bay along the coast, but here only a few random Bands made their livelihood.[88]

"We won't be bothering anyone here, Lokni," said Peter, looking up into the trees and around the area. "It's a good place for shipping out the goods—both across the bay and east towards Sacramento, if need be, even at this time of year."

"Did Karmo say he still really wanted our machines? Sometimes he seems like such a reluctant soldier," said Lokni quietly. "I do not know Karmo much at all. Ansa says he maintains a sense of duty to his craft, but has lost the passion." Lokni had questions about Ansa that he still could not discuss with Karmo.

"He has seen a lot of devastation, a lot of evil, according to Ansa," answered Peter. "Karmo always looks at me strangely, like he's trying to figure me out. I don't know, I don't know. Karmo said to develop the machine, and that the future will determine the need. He believes someone else will see the potential eventually, so we had better be first to have it."

"Ah, I see," said Lokni, taking a big breath. "Well, I can certainly help with setting up the work benches and the business. We can get workers together, but you'll have the best ability to study the workings of such a machine, Pete. I brought a couple steam motors to adapt our tools. Our work will go much faster this way. I like this place. It's close enough and yet secluded enough to get the project going. We will need to make friends with the Ohlone quickly, to get their help building a warehouse. We can cut enough trees right here for materials."

Pete nodded and responded, "Yes, but it's a shame. They're beautiful, aren't they? Look how some of their lower branches rise almost horizontally to the earth. It's as if they're inviting you to have a seat in their shade."

Lokni looked at Peter quizzically and shook his head. "There are plenty of them, Pete. It's not like we're going to clear the island of all its trees. No, we want plenty of trees to surround the enterprise, and for wind blocking …, and for shade, as you say. Come on, let's get going and tell the Peraltas we're accepting the lease on the area."

〜

It took three months to cut the trees, ferry them back and forth to a saw mill, to frame and build the warehouse. The hired Ohlone men were strong and efficient, and just as important, they were reliable and discreet. Five of the ten Macchina Infernales had been shipped from Monterey to San Francisco, then ferried to the island. Peter tinkered with metal cylinders, checking his drawings over and over.

"This should work," he said out loud to himself. "Let's see what happens if I put a crank handle here."

Over another two months, a first, then a second and a third model was completed and readied for trial. Peter called Lokni to come downstairs from the office and help him maneuver the machine. It had a chassis and wheels like a cannon, but also a rotating base, so it could easily be turned in any direction to fire. Using a steam-powered drill press, he had drilled along the circumference of the base. Wooden manual stops could be taken in and out of the base, as needed, to prevent the firing apparatus from spinning out of control and causing a great misfortune.[89]

"Turn it this way," directed Peter, "and face it towards those hay bales at the other end of the warehouse." Pete gave another look around the building to make sure no one was around.

"Pete, this thing is huge! How will it be transported, by wagon, by horse?" asked Lokni, looking over the machine from side to side.

"Either way. Also, it can be assembled and disassembled easily, so that it could be hidden in a wagon and no one would know it was there. Karmo was very specific about his needs. It's no good if it can't be portable, he said."

"Oh! It does move easily. Look! I can almost spin it!"

Peter, smiled and nodded. "That's how it needs to be. Come on! Let's fire it!"

The two men set the sight and the stops. Peter took the crank and looked over at his partner. "Here goes!" With that, he commenced turning the crank, which clicked into the rotating teeth of the spinner. One after another, the barrels clicked into place and fired their rounds. The machine roared to life and juddered with fury. The faster Peter cranked, the faster the shots fired.[90]

"Wow, wow, wow! Look at it go!" The two could not contain themselves, and were jumping up and down with delight. "Waaaahoooo!!!"

She came to surprise them with a basket supper. Peter's wife, Summer, entered the workshop with their hound dog, Bounder, just as the two had finished their test. Amused by the men's excited dance, she turned towards the contraption they developed and froze. Summer looked at her husband and took a step towards him, then looked back at the machine, the destroyed hay bales, the straw scattered upon the hardpan dirt floor. The birds had stopped chattering and only the rustle of leaves gave evidence of life as the wind's mild breath fell upon the building.

"You've developed a machine for mass killing," she murmured.

Surprised at seeing her, the two looked at one another. Peter paled, stepping away from the invention, and repeated his wife's words.

"This is a killing machine, Lokni. We've only developed a better killing machine."

Lokni looked at his friend, then at the machine, letting out a deep breath of resignation.

"You certainly did, gentlemen!" A voice from behind the barn door called out to them just before two strangers with drawn pistols entered.

"What?! Who are you! What do you want?" screamed Peter as Summer moved quietly behind the machinery. Peter eyed her and gave the faintest nod to her. Bounder growled and bared his teeth at the intruders, lowering his hind legs, readying to lunge at them.

Lokni took a step forward and one of the men shot into the ground in front of him, stopping him abruptly. Bounder froze, but every muscle in his body quivered as he warily eyed the strangers.

"Stop right there! No one will get hurt if you do as we say. You!" he pointed to Peter, "help my partner here roll that contraption out to our wagon!"

"The hell you say!" screamed Peter as he lunged towards the gunman.

The man fired a shot, hitting Peter in his right thigh. Peter went down, but managed to grab hold of the shooter's legs, causing him to fall to the ground as well. A burnished disc fell from the intruder's pocket. Struggling, the shooter hit Peter on the head repeatedly. Bounder bit into the gunman's side and clamped tight, refusing to let go of him. "Damn you all to hell! I'll kill you, your whole family, *and* your dog!" he said through gritted teeth.

The second man ran over to help his partner, though his eyes and gun were trained on Lokni. Suddenly, the intruder was hit in the back of the head with a piece of lumber. It was all Summer's doing. Disoriented, he lunged after her, then tripped and fell, hitting his face on the drill press faceplate. Summer lost her balance and fell against the drill switch. As she regained her balance, her heartbeat drumming loudly in her skull, she pulled down the guide handle without thinking and cursed the intruder loudly. "*Nobody* threatens my family *or* my dog!"

The drill bit made its rapid, downward, twisted journey into the man's skull. His screams, however, were barely audible over the sound of the machinery.

Everyone was stunned for a moment. Lokni helped Peter who was still struggling to subdue the first man. They managed to get him completely down and tied his hands to his feet.

Summer, extremely shaken, sat down and just looked at her husband as he limped towards her. Bounder followed, his tail wagging furiously. Breathing hard, her husband put his arm tenderly around Summer's shoulders, looked up and said, "Lokni, I'd like you to meet my wife."

46

Karmo and Suzanne 1849

When the heart speaks, the mind finds it indecent to object.
–Unbearable Lightness of Being, Milan Kundera

Suzanne was readying herself for a day with her nephews. Although she was looking forward to being with them, she felt distracted and off-balance as she entered the kitchen and sat down at the table with Mrs. Marshall to have a cup of tea.

"What is the matter, love? Your eyes are glassy this morning," the older woman thoughtfully.

"I am just tired, Mrs. Marshall. Nothing of real concern."

"Tired? Ah yes, the universal excuse one makes to mask that something is amiss, and yet one does not want to speak of it," observed Mrs. Marshal as she searched Suzanne's face for a trace of acknowledgement. "It is like you are walking around in a cloud of mist."

"No, really. No worries. I have to go now. I will be back this afternoon." With that, she stood up from the table, patted the long time housekeeper's hand in thanks and smiled as best she could.

≈

It was one of those days that comforted his soul, a bright, blue sky, both the sun and half-moon visible in the late afternoon. The valence of impact this minor phenomenon had on his well-being was disproportionate to the event itself. It made him smile broadly.

He had ordinary business to attend at the North Dock shipping office. But even business was appreciated, compared to the darkness of war. The smell of sea grasses and the screeching of gulls filled the air as he neared his destination. Today, like many other days, he posted a letter to Brima—more as a gesture of hope than laden with expectation. He exited the post office, remembering her voice—soft, like a summer rain, Suddenly, he stopped short as the voice became real. As he turned around, seeing Suzanne Benoît, eldest daughter of Madame Madeleine, he regained his composure, thinking, "Both Brima and Suzanne are delightful and intelligent people."

Suzanne was taking Marie-Therese's two sons, her young nephews, for an excursion along the beach, then onto the docks. She recognized Karmo about the same time he saw her. They both smiled in acknowledgment as they walked towards one another to offer greetings.

"Mr. Karmo, what a pleasant surprise. Such a delight to see you," said Suzanne as she offered her hand.

Accepting her hand and bowing his head, Karmo returned, "The pleasure and delight is mine, Mademoiselle Suzanne. I see you are being escorted by two sturdy young men." He smiled at the boys, gently and wistfully.

"Yes, indeed. These are Lokni and Marie-Therese's sons, Degan and Soren, my nephews. We were out for some fresh air and to watch the ships. Boys, this is Mr. Karmo. It's alright and proper to say hello."

"Hello, sir," said Degan, age seven, the oldest, as he held out his hand. He was echoed by five year old Soren, who too, offered his little hand to the large, tall man, to shake. "Nice to meet you," they said in unison. "We saw sea lions!" added Soren excitedly.

Karmo was struck by a simultaneous pang of appreciation and melancholy as he shook each little hand in turn, adding, "And very nice to meet you as well, gentlemen, and my, what an adventurous day!"

"Boys, you can walk about a bit, but stay where I can see you, while Mr. Karmo and I talk a moment."

"Yes, Aunty!" the boys answered in unison. "Yaaaay!"

"Race you to the edge, Degan!" yelled Soren, as he ran towards the end of the dock.

"No, Soren!" screamed Degan, as both Karmo and Suzanne turned to look their way.

Soren turned his head while running and started to slow down. Slipping on the wharf boards, he tripped and skidded over the edge, falling into the cold bay water below. Splashing and flailing his limbs he screamed as water filled his throat. He quickly disappearing into the bay.

Suzanne, pale and petrified, became speechless. She could only stare, mute and horrified. Karmo jumped into the drink, diving deeper, as the child had now gone under. The water was murky and only the top level was penetrated by scattered rays of sunlight. As he reached out his arms, they became entangled with seaweed. Debris thrown into the bay bumped into his body. His foot hit on something large, hard and metallic, but he ignored it and continued to search for the little boy. At last! He found an arm and pulled it towards him. Soren's body moved involuntarily, fighting to get loose, but Karmo held him close and propelled the two of them upward towards the direction of the light and the bubbles they emitted.

Topside, Karmo pushed the boy upward towards the outstretched hands of dockworkers. The child choked out inhaled water. Pulling him up and laying him sideways on the wharf boards, they slapped his back until water was spit and he was breathing more normally. He was quickly taken inside the dock office to recover.

Two men helped Karmo up out of the water. Breathing hard, standing on the dock, dripping-wet and trying to catch his breath, he looked for Soren. Suzanne and the boys were already inside one of the offices. Soren, whom they had wrapped in a blanket, was alert, crying and shivering, a cup of warm tea in his shaking hands

"Mr. Karmo, in here!" said one of the office men, waving to him. "Come here, sit!"

Karmo walked towards the office, but stopped at the door, dripping wet. He scanned about the room for the boys, when someone handed him a blanket and a cup of hot tea. Gratefully, he took both.

Suzanne's eyes were glazed as she sat next to the boys, not wanting to take her eyes off of them. Looking up at Karmo, she could only move her lips in thanks, before quickly looking back to the boys.

The next morning, Karmo set off to see Suzanne, inquire about little Soren, and assure himself as to the well-being of all. He had seen something in Suzanne that worried him.

The fog was lifting and rays of sun warmed his face as he made his way to the Benoît home. Closing his eyes for a moment, he felt a calming presence envelop him. Gone, at least for the moment, were the intruding thoughts of strategy and tactics, of war and battle.

Suzanne was both surprised and pleased by his arrival, and invited him into the back garden for tea and toast. "I cannot begin to thank you for your unselfishness yesterday, Mr. Karmo. We will *always* be in your debt."

"It was a natural reflex, Mademoiselle Suzanne. I am only glad I was there to assist," replied Karmo quietly, his eyes steady on her face, "But, tell me. How are *you* doing?"

"Me? Why, I am fine, quite fine," she answered haltingly.

Karmo stared at her intently, silently. He saw Brima's visage instead, and heard *her* voice, saw *her* gestures, *her* expressions ... he came back to the present conversation when Suzanne began to fidget. Her face was flushed, her nose felt pinched and the back of her throat loosened as her eyes began to well up with tears. She stood up and started to rearrange the china on the table in front of them before she sat down again, swallowing hard to regain her composure.

Again, Karmo remained silent.

"You know?" she asked.

"I do not," answered Karmo.

"But you *do* know?" she asked again.

"I know that you are deeply troubled, that something weighs heavily upon your heart, that you seem lost in conflict and emotion," answered Karmo, adding, "It is not my business, but nevertheless it is my concern."

Suzanne sat quietly. This man was a family friend, more of a pleasant acquaintance than family. Yet, he could see into her very being, as her own family had not. Or did she hide it better from them than from this relative outsider? Her emotions were slowly wending their way to the surface. The dull and persistent roar in her head was distracting. Her head was suddenly spinning. "Will you walk with me?" she said, her eyes darting to the house's back door.

"Of course," he answered.

They walked through the splintered sunlight of the scrubby ceanothus hedge to the meadow path beyond. Fella, the big yellow dog, started to follow them when Suzanne held her hand, palm-forward, the sign for him to stay. He sat down and waited as the pair continued into the meadow. At length, Karmo spoke, "You were quite distraught yesterday, for reasons other than the child's misfortune. Perhaps if you share your burdens, they can be lightened."

She hesitated and looked again at this dark man, who had experienced much of the world. This man she barely knew, but with whom she felt a closeness. "It is an affair of the heart," she stammered. "Everyone thinks I am so bright and accomplished, steadfast. But under this façade of competency hides a miserable person, Mr. Karmo; one with a thoughtless and regretful past, trying to make amends. I was a coward, behaved foolishly, and lost the best man I ever knew."

Karmo took a deep breath of relief ... or was it disappointment? "Ah, an affair of the heart. Yes, I understand, for I have suffered as well. I am not the best to undertake such counsel, but if you allow me, I will listen attentively and do my best to help put you at ease."

Karmo listened quietly as Suzanne unburdened her guilt and shame, long-preserved. At length, he said to her, "I understood as soon as I saw you, even the first time. We both have lives that slipped away from us. The pain remains like a vapor in our eyes. Even as life goes on, even as we laugh and enjoy the company of others, there is that part of our heart that secrets the pain and holds before us a dark mask. Every day, we live an unwanted destiny, we face our perils, we face life, striving to hide the defeat inside."

Suzanne looked at Karmo, and barely nodded before averting her glistening eyes. With their throats and chests tightening, their hands trembling at their sides, they stood across from one another, reflecting mutual understanding of those similarly afflicted. But they wished not to fool themselves with the moment's intimacy. So they both turned and walked away in different directions.

It was Suzanne who was in his crosshairs; the hired gun who was sitting on the rooftop of a vacant second-story home overlooking the meadow turned his head to watch as Karmo moved out of sight. He readied to squeeze the trigger, but stopped when he saw what happened next.

Suzanne had walked farther into the meadow before crumpling. She suddenly collapsed, silent and still.

Karmo continued on into the back garden, oblivious of the fading life behind him. He patted Fella's head as he passed by. The dog, who was gazing into the meadow, turned his eyes to Karmo, and then back to the meadow, whining. Only later that evening did Karmo get word from Marie-Therese that a vessel in Suzanne's head had burst and she had died right there, right where he had left her.

Top Hat and his crew saw the man with the rifle go into the home. He was a stranger, so they watched him enter and quickly leave the empty house. They followed him, then hailed a deputy, who gathered others and trapped the would-be assassin. The crew wanted answers, and would get them.

"He thought he could get by us," Top Hat told the deputy. "Nobody gets out of here without paying one way or another."

The kid sounds just like that outlaw Mullen, mused the deputy to himself. *Kinda looks like him, too.*

47

Reflections in San Francisco 1849

*Yesterday I was clever, so I wanted to change the world. Today I am
wise, so I am changing myself.* –Rumi

The damp ocean air squeezed the breath from his throat, and a fear-some pressure clutched at his pounding heart as he started running, running with all his might towards that silhouette.

~

Battles abated for the time being. The new nation was undefeated, but the government kept their people on alert, and training continued. *Know your enemy!* Karmo once again found himself at the Pacific Ocean, looking out beyond the breakers as the light of a new dawn behind him cast its rays onto the waters of the west. Incoming ships, their sails unfurled, gathered like clouds in the bay. The sparkling waves in the morning light are appreciated by those who look to them for peace, while those whose loved ones were taken by the waters see them much differently. Karmo fingered the grey pouch strung around his neck and wondered why he kept it. "Perspective," he whispered recalling the past.

He visited the city by the bay only when necessary to conduct business. But he lingered always at the ocean side, acknowledging that it was different than the one upon which Brima would gaze. Nevertheless, the timeless waves with their foamy reach beckoned him to remembrance, to the closeness, to feel the intimacy of proximity. *Something has passed since you have been gone from me,* said Karmo to himself. *Day followed by night, light followed by darkness, but alas, a new day was not born. My head is resigned to this destiny, but my heart still waits for you in the middle of an endless twilight. I pray for a new day for us both.*

He closed his eyes as the fog muffled all sounds except her voice. He could feel her breath and the flutter of her lashes on his cheek, hear her heartbeat.

A loud ship horn broke those sweet imaginings.

As agreed the night before, Ansa approached Karmo this early morning. The two friends, no longer naïve, idealistic young men, sat together at a dockside café and took their breakfast.

"So here we are, Karmo," said Ansa. "Can we still solve the problems of the world?"

Karmo smiled at his dear friend. "The times are certainly different, my brother. We are drinking coffee instead of tea, and you are a greybeard now."

"Ha! And you are nearly bald!" laughed Ansa, his eyes twinkling as ever.

Karmo rubbed his hand on his thinning pate, first slowly, then more vigorously, as if trying to erase memory. At length, reminiscing, he said, "I was thinking of the past, this fate of the people I met. I much admired General Santa Anna. It was only later I learned about his own atrocities, not just those of the invaders. I learned of the horrible treatment of Natives in the mission establishments, and later, by so many other peoples who looked down on them as lesser beings, such as we were looked down upon in America. You can look at any peoples and see both the good and the evil. They love their families, their land and their ways, yet they will not try to understand others who do not look like them, speak like them, pray like them; those are the least important differences among us. I want to think we believe in the inherent goodness and common good acts of all peoples. The reality is, unfortunately, we still must look at motivations."

"You cannot change the past, but the future is always in your hands, Karmo," answered Ansa with a well-worn saying.

Barely audible, Karmo murmured, "I am not so sure. Many of us are at a disadvantage from the start." Looking up at Ansa, he announced,

"Over there," he pointed, "the sailors aboard those incoming ships from China tell of great floods displacing inordinate numbers of people in their homeland. They are jumping ship here. Ever since the *Eagle* docked, there has been a continuous stream of new immigrants.[91] What is to become of them? Will more make their way here as well? Will we fight them, or embrace them? Another land, another fight? We have traveled so far, my brother. Where is the end to the fighting? Is this human nature, despite the chest-beating about loving your fellow man? And in the name of a god, no less?!!" Karmo recollected all the fights, the battles, the deaths, as he thought of the young men who were so eager for war. *Though they haunt me still, it is useless to fight with the people we have lost and killed.* It was just as Efendi said. "Maybe I was wrong," he murmured sadly.

"What's that?" asked Ansa.

Karmo was deep in thought and mused out loud, "There is an emptiness to war after a while, Ansa. I only started to perceive that after so many years. At first, it was the righteousness that drew me in. Then the strategies and tactics held me, but finally, I felt futility and emptiness, even in victory. For when we win, we also lose. We lose our humanity. We failed to work through our differences, and to consider the cost for present and future generations. And it never ends. Death is the only victor. Those who died, some were so young! My heart hurt for them. I feel so ashamed for my age, for how long *I* have been granted life, Ansa!"

"But do we not protect ourselves and our way of life, Karmo? Are we to just lie down and let others run us into the ground, perhaps enslave us?" asked Ansa gently.

Karmo looked at his friend with deep affection and weary eyes. "I wish I had the answer, my brother. Efendi once told me that, often, both fighting sides can be right. I just wonder, is there not another way in which to solve disagreements and find commonalities, other than resort to barbarity? Will our world stay in perpetual upheaval? The thunder roars, the ocean roars, cannon and all humanity continue to roar!"

Karmo let his words float and settle into Ansa's conscience.

Ansa could think of no good answer for human history. Presently, he allowed, "It is amazing that—despite our otherness—we, you and I, Karmo, have been accepted as well as we are. We were lucky."

Karmo looked up at Ansa quizzically, "Luck? You surprise me, Ansa. Luck is only what is left after we have calculated and planned everything else. That is why it can be neither good nor bad. But yes, my brother, not that there has not been suffering along the way. We are here together, free, unfettered and unmolested. It must have been ordained by the stars."

There was a long pause. Ansa looked at Karmo, "There is something else on your mind."

Karmo just shook his head slowly.

"Ah, of course—Brima," Ansa understood.

"I have given my life to this regret, losing her. When you look into someone's eyes it means you have taken a chance to enter that person's dreams. She is in *my* dreams still. There is a constant roar in my head and in my heart. Sometimes it is so hard to breathe. She is my destiny, Ansa, and destiny does not lose its way."

Ansa put his hand on Karmo's arm. The two men sat in silence, looking into their coffees. At length, Ansa asked,

"You are a hero to the people, Karmo. Would you not lead the nation in some capacity?"

Karmo smiled and snorted, "I am not so arrogant as to believe I have the skills or the talent for governing, Ansa. It is not my nature or inclination. Arrogance is like a rock tied around one's neck. One can ...."

"One can neither swim with it, nor fly with it," interrupted Ansa. "I know the saying well. "So what *will* you do now, Karmo?"

"I will go back to Bockarie. The new government wants me to run training camps for all citizens: men and women. It will be compulsory training for all."

"Indeed? Is the first order of this country to be an armed camp? Are we going to kill our way to freedom?"

"Inasmuch that all citizens will participate in a level of civil readiness," explained Karmo. "But I hope never to fight again."

"I understand, and it is a pity that we must resort to this. What was once your life's passion has become your burden."

Karmo just looked at him and made the smallest of nods.

Changing topics, Ansa continued, "Madam Zimi has her hands full. With both Jonny Henson and Mademoiselle Suzanne gone, new people were recruited. Fortunately, there are some bright young people out here. JP for one, but he is sometimes unsettling for me. *Too* eager, perhaps."

Karmo's eyes bored into Ansa, remembering JPs similar warnings about Ansa. "You need not worry about JP. I know him, and his father even saved my life! Yes, he is eager, bright and ambitious. But also, he is loyal to our Nation's tenets. If there are lies, they will reveal themselves with time. They always do."

Ansa cracked the merest of smiles before exhorting, "Ha! Do you hear us, Karmo?! Our Nation! Can you believe it? Perhaps this country can be a model for peace!"

Karmo's face clouded. "If it is to be our destiny, let us strive to make it so. Well, my friend," said Karmo, as he used his arms to push himself up from the chair. "I must get to the pier to look into my shipment. Shall we meet this evening at Benoîts'?"

"I look forward to it, my brother."

Another hour, his business concluded, Karmo wandered the docks, watching the waves and considering his ever-intrusive and random thoughts.

In war, there is more than one truth, thought Karmo to himself, then chiding himself. *Regret is the greatest form of suffering. One from which there is no return.* No one was around, and Karmo gave voice to his thoughts. "In the solitude of my mind, I thought and thought as to my actions and motivations. Finally, I have to admit; I am not innocent. I have made excuses for my actions; virtue, payback, justice; but these were not always true. Sometimes I gave in to rage and fear, and gave allowance to my own impulse to roar. And, so it might be for others as well, for how am I unique among human beings? I have come to this beach to mock the ocean's roar, but now I am humbled."

Thoughts of a time and place far away dissipated, like waking from a dream. He tried to grasp at the elusive memory, but it slipped away with the evaporating fog. "Will these waves bring you back to me?" he sighed deeply, remembering his own words to Suzanne. "Perhaps I must finally commit to leave my old life behind. It is gone, but will be secreted away in a special part of my heart."

Karmo looked out into the Pacific, casually turned toward the moored ships, squinted, and discerned with a recollection of astonishing fidelity, a familiar silhouette. Startled, his breath stilled.

The morning sun cast smoky shadows through the dispersing gauzy mantle of fog, as a woman in yellow stood on the deck of a ship that had just anchored. A halo of the sun's glare around her bonnet and an aura of lightness radiated about her as she gazed out at the city.

Presently, he heard her companion's voice, the voice of a young man, familiar and native, call out to her on the ship's deck: "Mother, this way!"

The damp ocean air squeezed the breath from his throat, and a fearsome pressure clutched at his pounding heart as he started running, running with all his might towards that silhouette.

END

Untitled

We will swallow the smoke, drag it down to our loins
Where the disquiet was born—peril and pain thereafter—
And let those children birthed to clamor go peacefully.
Atonement for the callousness coating our chest,
For our youth remembered as a bitter farewell,
And for the roar of death itself.

Lifetimes dedicated to the unraveling
To the reverting, the overturning,
Traced back into shadows in which we were wronged,
And the chambers and the plazas,
The mouths of our mothers and the hands of our fathers,
Long stretches of soil over which we did crawl,
And shallows in the faces that did not look away.
And refused to truly look at all.

We will make time to dream of the coast, and the immortal horizon,
And the promise she sends her sirens to sing.
Sweet melodies gliding over ruin and to the ears of soldiers—
Awaiting the blow that lulls them to perpetual rest—
And compelling them to resist once more.

Amy N. Wilson

ROAR! Endnotes

CHAPTER 1
1. College at Fourah Bay, Freetown, Sierra Leone was established in February 1827.

CHAPTER 2
2. Krio translates to Creole.
3. The Mane (or Manes) people were mostly traders and conquerors who attacked the west coast of Africa from the east, starting in the last half of the 1500's. Wadi translates to valley.
4. Sun Tzu, b. 544 BC, d. 496 BC. Chinese general, military strategist, writer, philosopher.
5. A) Recklessness, which leads to destruction.
B) Cowardice, which leads to capture.
C) Hasty temper, which can be provoked by insults.
D) Delicacy of honor, which is sensitive to shame.
E) Over solicitude for his men, which exposes him to worry and trouble.

CHAPTER 3
6. Louis Philippe I, b. 1773, d. 1850; Charles Philippe X, b. 1757, d. 1836.

CHAPTER 4
7. Sybil Ludington, b. 1761, d. 1839.
8. Roly-polys, also called sow bugs, pill bugs. Latin; Armadillidium vulgare.

CHAPTER 5

9. Sailor and pirate lore of the times; the story was that coming upon a sinking ship, only pigs and chickens were seen alive and floating in the water; hence, it was believed they were good luck, and subsequently, corresponding tattoos of pigs and chickens became protection from drowning.

10. Loose packing versus tight packing was an economic decision of the ship's captain, as to how many slaves could be crammed below deck. Loose packing allowed for more food, supplies and more room for individuals, resulting in more slaves to survive the trip. Tight packing packed in more slaves, but it was a greater risk as to how many would survive.

11. Job Terry, master whaler out of Boston, b. 1783, d. 1861.

CHAPTER 7

12. Spanish Captain Pedro Blanco, b. 1795, d. 1854, based off the coast of Sierra Leone, trafficked goods and captives to the Caribbean.

13. The Middle Passage was the triangular shaped shipping trade route over the Atlantic on which Western European businesses shipped their goods to trade for captive peoples from West Africa. The captives were then shipped to North and South America, and were sold in return for raw materials to ship back to Western Europe.

CHAPTER 8

14. Nat Turner, American slave who led a two-day rebellion of slaves and free blacks in Virginia, b. 1800, d. 1831.

CHAPTER 9

15. Frederick Douglass, American social reformer, abolitionist, orator, writer and statesman, b. 1818? in Maryland, d. 1895 in Washington D.C.

16. Thomas Dartmouth Rice (TD Rice), playwright, entertainer, b. 1808, d. 1860.

17. Andrew Jackson, b. 1767, d. 1845, military man, U.S. President. See also Bank War 1832-1836 and Panic of 1837. The cotton gin greatly decreased the labor required to pick seeds from cotton bolls, which lead to more cotton being planted for bigger profits. Farmers

went to banks for loans to buy more land to plant more cotton and other crops, using slaves as collateral. Banks bundled these debts as bonds and sold them to investors. When the market for cotton collapsed, so did the value of slaves. The investors called in their debts. There was a financial panic. The government found it necessary to bail out the cotton industry as it was too big to fail.

CHAPTER 10

18. First Seminole War, 1816-1819, first of three conflicts in Florida territory between Native Americans and the U.S. Army. General Andrew Jackson attacked Florida to do away with the slave refuge it provided and to gain land for white Americans.
19. Treaty fraud did occur during this period; however, Symes and Peacock are fictional characters here. Check historical reference for the actual secret Sykes-Picot Agreement of WWI.
20. John Horse, b. 1812, d.1882; Osceola, b. 1804, d. 1838; Sam Jones, b. 1760, d. 1860—significant leaders of the Seminoles. The Seminoles were an alliance of Native peoples, including the Creeks, Yuchis, Chickasaws, Choctaws, free blacks and runaway slaves. The Creeks and Cherokees had been Andrew Jacksons's initial main focus for removal.

CHAPTER 11

21. "Peculiar Institution" was a euphemism used mostly by white Southerners to describe slavery during this period.
22. The Leonids meteor showers occur each year, usually in November; however, the shower of 1833 was particularly spectacular.
23. An alternate mythology called Medusa, which meant Knowing Woman or Protectress, who was condemned by Athena, the daughter of Zeus.

CHAPTER 12

24. Half-models; wooden model of a ship without rigging in three dimensions, cut in half to show horizontally, the levels and design in an exact scale replica.
25. Penobscot, Native American people, primarily in Maine.

CHAPTER 13

26. Billy Bowlegs, b. 1810, d. 1854, significant leader during the Seminole wars.

CHAPTER 15

27. Worcester Asylum for Lunatics opened in January 1833 in Worcester, Massachusetts.
28. De Nîmes means of, or from, Nîmes, and is pronounced Nim. The blue cloth became known in California as denim.

CHAPTER 16

29. Greener balls, self-expanding bullets developed by William Greener, oval-shaped bullet with flat surface and small hole drilled through it, covered with conical plug. The design was improved by Claude-Etienne and Henri-Deloigne's "Minie balls" which became prominent in the American Civil War.

CHAPTER 17

30. Although the U.S. Supreme Court (Worcester v. Georgia, 1832) determined that the state of Georgia could not impose laws on Cherokees on Cherokee lands, President Jackson encouraged white residents to harass the Natives, set fire to Cherokee homes and plunder their fields. Subsequently, the state of Georgia mapped out Cherokee land and commenced a lottery, whereby whites were given the land without compensation to the Cherokee.
31. Marie Catherine Laveau, also known as the "Widow Paris," New Orleans Creole practitioner of voodoo, b. 1801, d. 1881.

CHAPTER 18

32. Tejas translate to Texas. The Mexican Law of 1830 (April 6) banned further American immigration into Tejas due to rapid acceleration of illegal immigration and concerns that the U.S. would annex the territory.
33. Sam Houston, b. 1793, d. 1863.
34. William B. Travis, b. 1809, d. 1836 at the Alamo.
35. David Crockett, b. 1786, d. 1836 at the Alamo.
36. James Bowie, b. 1796, d. 1836 at the Alamo.

37. Texicans; residents of Mexican Tejas who supported the Texas revolution. Sometimes called Texicans.
38. Antonio López de Santa Anna, General and President of Mexico multiple times, b. 1794/5?, d. 1876.

CHAPTER 19
39. General de Cos, b. 1800, d. 1854.
40. The Battle of the Alamo, Feb. 23, 1836 to March 6, 1836.
41. Pyrrhus, b.?, d. 272 B.C., Greek general and statesman, later King of Molossians. Although victorious, one battle in particular resulted in irreplaceable losses in both numbers and his best officers; also more of his men were killed than the enemy. It became known as a Pyrrhic victory.
42. Cholera.
43. For every 24 hours awake, one loses 25% mental capacity for useful work. Nita Lewis Miller, Lawrence G. Shattuck, Panagiotis Matsangas, "Sleep and Fatigue Issues in Continuous Operations; A Survey of U.S. Army Officers." Behavioral Sleep Medicine 9(2011); 53-65.

CHAPTER 20
44. José de Urrea, b. 1787, d. 1849.
45. Francita Alvarez, b. 1816, d. 1906? Also called the Angel of Goliad, was instrumental in saving a number of soldiers at various battles in Tejas.
46. Fiction. Santa Anna did not give up on attacking at San Jacinto; instead, it was an 18 minute battle lost by the Mexican Army and turned the tide to a Texican victory. There was no suing for peace. Events in the rest of the chapter are fiction.
47. Some white Arabian horses have black skin under their coat.
48. Juan B. Alvarado, b. 1800, d. 1882, Governor of Alta California, 1836-1842.
49. Alta California translates to upper California, Mexican territory later known as the U.S State of California.

CHAPTER 21

50. Californios originally applied to the Spanish-speaking residents of the Californias during both the Spanish California and Mexican California periods between 1683-1848.
51. Six-shot revolver invented by Samuel Colt. Patented in Europe in 1835, then in the U.S. in 1836.

CHAPTER 22

52. Fiction. The first ship to cross the Isthmus of Panama was a paddleboat steamship in 1861. The Panama Canal was not built until August 1914.
53. Mission Dolores was built in 1776. Catholic priests established 21 Missions in California, each approximately one day's ride by horseback or three days on foot. The first was built in San Diego, the last was in Sonoma.

CHAPTER 23

54. Don Francisco de Haro, b. 1792, d. 1849. Appointed first Alcalde (Mayor/Chief Magistrate) of Yerba Buena in 1834, the city later called San Francisco.
55. Super Moon.
56. Allen Light, b. 1805, d. unknown. Appointed by Alta California as Principal Arbiter.

CHAPTER 25

57. Ignatz Semmelweis, b.1818, d. 1865. In 1846, he is credited as being the first person to demonstrate that hand washing would drastically reduce postpartum maternal deaths. This was not due to germ theory, however (Pasteur 1860's), rather the deaths were due to organic matter left on the hands of physicians who had dissected corpses, then delivered newborns without first cleaning their hands.
58. Alexander Rotchev, b. 1806/7?, d. ?, was the Administrator. The Natives did not get Fort Ross land back. It was purchased by John Sutter in 1841; he then had most of it dismantled and the wood was shipped to build his own Sutter's Fort in the Sacramento Valley.

Chapter 26

59. Stephens-Townsend-Murphy party, departed from Council Bluffs, Iowa; first wagon train over the Sierra Nevada Mountains (before Donner Party). In reality, they made it over the summit in November 1844, not in the Spring.
60. Jedediah Smith, b. 1799, d. 1831. The Truckee Notch was later used by the Donner Party in 1846.
61. Histum Yani is a Maidu Native American name translating to Spirit Mountain, now known as Sutter Buttes, which rise above the flat plains of the Sacramento Valley, California.
62. John Sutter, b. 1803, d. 1880. John Marshall discovered gold on Sutter's Fort property in 1848. Sutter's Fort was the destination for many wagon trains, including the Donner-Reed Party.

Chapter 27

63. Perseid meteor showers occur in August.

Chapter 28

64. John C. Frèmont, b. 1813, d. 1890, American soldier, explorer, politician.

Chapter 31

65. First Peoples refers to the first humans to colonize America. Misnamed "Indians," many Natives identify by the Nation to which they belong, that is, First Nations, such as Mohawk, Inuit, etc.
66. Missouri Governor Liliburn Boggs (Gov. 1836-40) signed an Executive Order 44, known by the Mormons as the "Extermination Order," in response to ongoing sometimes armed conflicts between Missouri settlers and members of the Church of Latter-Day Saints. Mormons were allowed to be exterminated or otherwise driven out of the state at will. Born, 1797, d. 1860 in Rancho Napa, California. The Order was not repealed until June 25, 1976.
67. Coined by Charles Beaudelaire, b. 1821, d. 1867, French poet.
68. The Iroquois Confederacy is the oldest continuous democracy in the world.
69. Edward Hicks, b. 1780, d. 1849, American folk-art painter.

70. The Companions were mistaken. The trees were Coastal Redwoods, also red and gigantic. Sequoias are mainly on the western side of the Sierra Nevada Mountains. George Gist, aka George Guess, aka Sequoyah. Part Cherokee silversmith, b. 1770, b. 1843.

CHAPTER 32
71. Queen Nzinga of Angola, b. 1583, d. 1663; Catherine the Great of Russia, b. 1729, d. 1796; Queen Elizabeth I of England and Ireland, b. 1533, d. 1603.
72. Mary Pleasant, "Mother of Human Rights in California," b. 1814, d. 1904.

CHAPTER 34
73. William Warren, aka Uncle Billy, arrived in California in 1828. Born unknown, d. 1875. Northern California's gold was discovered in 1848 by John Marshall.

CHAPTER 35
74. Santa Anna was struck in his left leg by a cannon blast which resulted in amputation during the Pastry War, also known as the First French Intervention in Mexico. It included a French naval blockade initiated by an unpaid bakery debt November 27, 1838 to March 9, 1839.

CHAPTER 36
75. Sir Edwin Chadwick, English social reformer, was particularly outspoken about the Poor Laws and amendments. He put forth that poor sanitation and consequent disease was a primary result of poverty. Born 1800, d. 1890.

CHAPTER 37
76. Dr. Edward Bale, immigrant physician, b. 1807, d. 1849; Marie Soberanes Bale, b. 1816, d. 1901; Mariano Vallejo, military commander under the Republic of Mexico, politician, b. 1807, d. 1880.
77. William B. Ide was one of the leaders of the Bear Flag Revolt, an attempt to establish an unrecognized breakaway state that lasted 25 days in June 1846, in what is now Sonoma County, California.

78. Cayetano Juarez, soldier at the Presidio of San Francisco under the Republic of Mexico, politician, b. 1809, d. 1863. His adobe home still stands as a historical structure in Napa, California. However, as the Companion's meetings are all fiction, none of them met with him.

CHAPTER 39
79. The mockingbird's night song; old fable was that in ancient times, each bird family had been given the responsibility to take turns singing as they kept night sentry for the bird kingdom. The mockingbird fell asleep on duty instead of singing and as a result, much of the bird kingdom was annihilated. The Bird King cursed the mockingbird's descendants, so that they must sing the songs of all other birds for eternity.

CHAPTER 40
80. The Great Law of Peace is the constitution of the Iroquois Confederacy (six Native Nations). It was an oral constitution that was later written in symbols on wampum belts. It was conceived by the Great Peacemaker Dekanawidah (sometimes Deganawidah), b. around 1550, d. unknown, and his spokesman Hiawatha, b. 1525, d. 1595.

CHAPTER 41
81. The real Pony Express ran from April 3, 1860 to October 26, 1861. Maximum carry weight limit, including the rider, was 200 pounds; hence, young boys who were good riders were employed.

CHAPTER 43
82. Giuseppe Fieschi, b. 1790, d. 1836. Corsican conspirator who, with others, designed and built the "Macchina Infernale," a weapon with 25 barrels that could shoot all at one time, all pointing in different horizontal directions for maximum spread. First tested in Paris, aimed at the procession of King Louis-Philippe. 42 people were injured as were horses, 18 were killed, none of the deceased were of the royal family.
83. General at Sea, Robert Blake, b. September 27, 1598 in Bridgewater, England, d. August 17, 1657 at sea. He was one of England's

most talented military commanders. He wrote the "Fighting Instructions" training manual.

84. Fiction. The American war against Mexico, April 1846-February 1848, was fought to reclaim Tejas/Texas. President/General Santa Anna never recognized the Republic of Texas and attacked it. President Polk subsequently sent troops not only to Texas, but to other Mexican territories including Alta California, in his quest to obtain land across the entire continent.

85. 100 years later, the Atomic Bomb was first tested on July 16, 1945 near Alamogordo, New Mexico.

CHAPTER 45

86. Encinal translates to oak grove, former name of Alameda, California, across the bay from San Francisco.

87. The golden poppy was used for several purposes by the Ohlone Natives, including a decorative covering for shell mounds; some were burial mounds, others mounds were depositories for shells of edible mollusks, also for their oil. The golden poppy was later designated as the state flower for California in 1903.

88. Manuel Micheltorena, b. 1804, d. 1853. Pio Pico, b. 1801, d. 1894.

89. Drill presses of one kind or another have been in use for centuries. The steam drill, mainly powered by pulleys and line shafts, was in use a couple decades later than this incident.

90. The Gatling gun was invented in 1861 by American inventor, Dr. Richard J. Gatling, b. 1818, b. 1903. Patented in 1862.

CHAPTER 47

91. The first Chinese, one man and two women arrived in San Francisco on the brig, Eagle, in 1848. Two years later, 20,000 Chinese arrived in "Gold Mountain" as the California Gold Rush was in full swing.

Acknowledgements

A number of people were instrumental in various facets of the completion of this book from inspiration to cover. ROAR! Odyssey of Battle, Betrayals and Building a Nation was not a lone endeavor.

I would like to take this space to acknowledge Lisa Marquita Barker-Mullen for her unwavering support for this writing. Without her, I am not sure I would have continued to its conclusion. I want to thank and express appreciation to Amy Nicole Wilson for her thoughtful and beautiful poem at the end of this novel. I have enjoyed her thought provoking poetry over the years.

Many thanks to colleagues Linda Jay, copy editor and Val Sherer, publisher, layout designer. They were instrumental in the technical aspects required to prepare and publish. Their patience and understanding of a novice writer was meritorious. I want to give a big shout out to the beta readers; Rosemarie Vertullo, Steve Della Maggiora, Dick Maw and Karen Smith, M.D., for their help in pointing out areas needing clarity, suggesting alternative wording, further editing and support for this writing.

The outstanding cover art was rendered by my dear childhood friend, Steve A. Della Maggiora who always seems to know how to read my mind to put thoughts onto canvas. And who asked, "what about the sequel?"

Other influencers: There are too many to name or even to remember as they came from everywhere; a life time of reading books, watching films, listening to music lyrics, chance over-heard conversations or even a turn of phrase, not to mention observation of nature and steadfast stargazing. We all have stories to tell.

M. Marquis

About the Author

M. Marquis is native of northern California who has lived, worked and visited numerous foreign countries and the North American continent. A U.S. Army veteran, the author earned an M.S. degree in Rehabilitation Counseling and Psychology from the University of North Carolina at Chapel Hill and spent over 40 years in the medical field in various capacities including compliance investigation, regulation consultation, government medical programs management and emergency room direct care. Marquis returned to live in northern California and is an avid reader of history and culture who studies foreign languages.